DAUGHTER OF THE UNDERWORLD

JENN LYNN ADAMS

To the girls who chose to read over playing in the pool,
and the women they've become.

PROLOGUE

My hands tremble as I pull out each bottle, glancing at the label before returning it to its rightful spot.

No, no, no, I mutter as I come across the wrong ingredients.

Yes, finally!

No, no.

Aha!

Yes.

The basket at my side fills with the pots and potions I'll need. Most of the ingredients I have here in my small hut. The blood of a host. Candles. Some, I'll travel to the Land of the Living to obtain. Milk from Helios's cows. A dram of Dionysus's most flavorful wine.

One, in particular, will require extreme caution in collecting. Water from the Lethe, the river of unmindfulness, which flows through my home, the Underworld.

It'll be days before I'm able to fully prepare for the spell I seek to cast. The most challenging and dangerous incantation—a bloodline possession spell. I glance at the scroll in my hand, the enchantment written out in my scrawly handwriting. Having it on my person, reading it over and over, touching it, eases my fears.

*Agapití kardiá . . . énas ángelos pou koimátai. Sikotheíte apó ta vathiá sto fos,
xýpnioi apó ton vathýtero ýpno. Anadýetai apó to neró pou anavlýzei, eínai sto fos
tou matioú! Ela piso!*

I read the scroll, careful not to let the words pass my lips until the right time.

I can't mess this up. There will be no second chances.

This has to work.

> *"Now plain to the eye, now shadowy, now shining in the darkness."*
>
> -hymn to Melinoe

MELINOE

"Again, Princess," Hermes roars. My fingertips are blackened and my arms are shaking. Despite feeling drained, I squeeze my eyes closed, clench my fists, and contort my face into a grimace as I attempt to channel my magic toward the caged crow before me.

"*Tha se vasaníso. San stáchti mazí sou! Tíko!*" The crow cocks its head and caws, its shiny black beak mocking me. I grind my teeth. A headache begins forming along my temples, the pain sharp and stabbing.

Yet again, I have failed.

"You have neither tormented, disintegrated, nor liquefied the crow." Hermes sighs heavily, annoyance tinging his words. I've been at this for weeks, still unable to summon my magic for anything more sinister than putting birds to sleep with boredom. My blackened fingers are a stark reminder of my stilted abilities, as though the power within has tried to escape but remains stuck. I watch as Hermes languidly approaches the cage.

He flicks the lock and the crow hops out, moving up his arm to his shoulder. "I'm sure Pan is happy not to be violently destroyed, but you must work harder, Princess. Your mother returns from the Land of the Living tomorrow, and your life is bound to change with your coming birthday. Your magic must appear in order for you to succeed at your Underworld duties."

My body stiffens, but I nod tightly, holding back, and carefully control my tone. "Yes, sir," I say flatly.

Hermes holds up a hand filled with birdseed, and as Pan pecks happily, the cracked shells fall to the floor.

Moving away, I surrender to the worn leather chair in the corner of Hermes's hut, my limbs heavy. The fire crackles in the hearth, warming the cottage, while a book sits open on the side table. I pull it to my lap and begin mindlessly flipping the pages.

"If only magic were as easy as understanding the laws honoring the dead, Hermes." I can describe the three parts of a burial ritual, move seamlessly into the Land of the Living to collect offerings to the dead, and recite the "Codes of Justice for the Deceased," but I am still unable to magically summon the corpses who have been dishonored, my formal duty as heiress to the Underworld.

"I think that's enough for today, Princess." Hermes flaps his hand dismissively as he takes the book from my lap and begins to tidy the small cottage. I rise from the chair and head toward the door, knowing that my lesson was a complete failure.

"Please, Hermes. Please don't give up on me yet. We can try again tomorrow."

Distracted, he doesn't meet my pleading eyes. "Princess, you're almost out of tomorrows."

. . . .

The next morning, I blink sleepily, confusion knitting my brow as my dreams disappear before I can catch them. They're smoke and mist seeping through my blackened fingertips, refusing to be recalled. Frustration propels me out of bed, the rust-hued dawn peeking through my window. As I inhale and stretch my arms overhead, my mind finally sparks awake, and I remember what day it is. Foggy thoughts suddenly forgotten, a smile stretches wide across my face. Just then, my handmaiden enters the room.

"Good morning, Selene," I crow from the window seat.

"Good morning, Mistress," she replies, indicating I should take my place at the white marble vanity. "Is there a particular reason why you're so eager to get up this early? Normally you'd be in bed until midday." Her mouth quirks up at the corners as she winks. We both know I would never sleep past dawn. My rigorous training schedule does not allow me to lie abed and waste the day away, and even if I had the free time, I'd choose to put it to good use volunteering in the realm with my father, King Hades.

Selene begins unfurling my black curly hair from its plait. "Six months, Selene," I remind her, turning around. My handmaiden tuts, directing me forward with soft fingertips at my temples. "She's finally returning after six months away." I bounce my feet on the supple ivory carpet, squashing my hands under my thighs as anxious energy seeps from my skin, and wince as Selene rebraids my hair tighter for today's training, securing it with a leather cord.

"My lady Persephone sent a message that she is due to arrive by dinner, Mistress. She has formally requested your presence as she's brought a special gift for your upcoming birthday."

Releasing a breath I didn't know I was holding, I leap up from the seat, rushing toward the closet. It has been half a year since I've seen my mother. While my father and I have been busy running the Underworld in her absence, my mother's homecoming is celebrated each year on the autumnal equinox. I look forward to her return, mainly due to the festivities that will consume our lives for the next ten days, but her presence, the way she watches me, has always left me wary. Her lips pressing thinly as my magic fails to appear year after year. A heavy sigh as her shoulders droop. An uneasiness seems to settle over the Underworld, over our family, when she's in residence. And it's all because of me, her disappointment at my failure.

As I mindlessly flip through the outfits in my closet, I stop on my birthday gown and stare at it, a smile softening the tightness in my jaw. In just a few days' time, I'll be old enough to fulfill my heiress duties . . . if my magic appears. The smile falters and I sigh, hoping that today is the day I finally make progress.

"You've only got a few more days, and then it will be your twenty-third birthday, Mistress." Selene interrupts my thoughts. My mother's return culminates with my birthday celebration. I finger the delicate beading on the black gown. The seamstresses began working on the dress months ago, and I only had the final fitting yesterday. It truly is a beautiful work of art.

"Just a few more days, and I'll finally be able to fulfill my destiny," I whisper to myself as I stuff the beautiful frock back into my closet. I turn to Selene and hold out a pair of leather leggings, a matching belt, and a bloodred tunic. I'm expected on the training field upon waking, per my father's orders. "Can you help me get dressed? I have a lot to do before dinner."

• • • • ● • ● • • • ·

The sky has brightened to its penultimate bloodred coloring, and as I make the quick jaunt to the training arena, I ponder the day's tutelage schedule. After my morning sword and shield defense lessons, I break my fast with Father and we discuss the meetings I'm to attend. I may not be able to spark magic yet, but my diplomacy and battle skills are unrivaled. When my abilities failed to appear, and the years passed with nary a spark, Father ensured I was able to not only defend myself with a dagger and blade, but also with knowledge of our kingdom.

Athletically, I'm no match for Hades's Tartarusian soldiers, who have no life to lose and fight as such, but I have trained diligently with my father for years. Only within the last six months have I begun to outpace him. Because of this, he's assigned Trophonius, an upstart commander in the Tartarusian Guard, to assist in furthering my abilities. I approach the arena and notice my trainer leaning against the fence post. His tunic is open at the chest, a short sword hanging from his scabbard. He is utterly alone, waiting for me, and I sigh warily, my footsteps faltering as the hair lifts on the back of my neck.

"Good day, Princess," he calls, tossing a thick pomegranate from hand to hand. Taking a dagger and scoring the peel, he pulls out a section, handing it to me. I warily accept the fruit, pressing my lips into a fine line when Trophonius begins to rub seeds off the pith with his thumb in a circular motion. He winks at me and I cringe inwardly, forcing myself not to recoil from him. "Are you up for a little rendezvous after our drills? It's been a while since we had a little fun." Flicking his tongue suggestively, he lifts a bright red seed from his palm.

Instead, I offer him a wan smile and a shrug. "Today isn't good for me," I say, refusing to elaborate. Before becoming my trainer, Trophonius and I would spend the occasional evening together, mainly to ease the stress incurred by my relentless schedule. Since becoming my teacher, though, Trophonius has continued to pursue me, his attempts at flirting becoming tiresome, even after I've repeatedly rebuked him. I've been able to hold him off for the time being, but if my father knew, he would raise the Tartarusian Guard. Perhaps it's time I find a new instructor, one I haven't been intimate with, although I'll have a hard time explaining the reasoning to my father. I move to enter the training grounds, a smirk lifting my lips. "I think I've learned everything you have to teach me, Trophonius. It's past time I speak with Hades about assigning Rhadamanthus to train with me instead. He could also educate me on the administration of justice, something you know not."

He reddens, then chuckles brazenly, tosses the empty pomegranate peel on the ground, and grabs my arm roughly, squeezing the flesh until I gasp. "How about we spar for your release from me?" His eyes flash with malicious desire as he pulls my body flush against him. "If I win, not only will you remain under my instruction, but you'll put that pretty little mouth wherever I choose."

My stomach rolls, the stench of wine mixing with the sweet fruit on his breath. "And if I win?"

"You won't." His arrogance is disgusting.

I pull away. I don't have time for games. "Get your hands off me, filthy cave dweller," I sneer in his face.

He shoves me roughly into the shadows of the training barn, the cracked planks scraping against the back of my head. I stiffen, feeling his arousal against my belly. He grinds his hips against mine, and as I thrash against his clutch, my hair becomes entangled, my scalp tearing against the dilapidated wood. Grabbing my chin, he holds my face steady.

Lowering his lips to mine, he licks my lips and thrusts his tongue through my clenched teeth and into my mouth.

My body goes cold.

His hand snakes under my tunic and fondles my breast while his knee attempts to part my legs. I clench my thighs together, but this seems to excite him, and he drives into the barrier, my legs giving out. Finished violating my mouth, he brings his filthy palm up to cover my nose and lips, thwarting my ability to call for help. Trembling, I stare across to the arena, willing a soldier to glance into the shadows. As I struggle to draw breath, the scene before me becomes hazy. Red-and-white spots flash in my vision, and I realize I'm losing consciousness. My body slackens with lack of breath, and Trophonius unlaces my leathers and shoves his hand into their warmth. The cool air touches my exposed skin, and my mind jolts as though struck by lightning, my body springing into action.

Trophonius hesitates for only a moment as my muscles go rigid, but it's long enough that I'm able to clamp my teeth into his palm. His howl of pain alerts a soldier, who finally notices our entwined bodies in the shadows. The soldier starts making his way toward us, and hearing the approaching footsteps, Trophonius takes a slight step back, just enough to allow me to raise my sword to his throat. I press into the soft skin, drawing a bead of blood. My fingertips tingle, a heat spreading into my palms.

Slit his throat, a female voice in my head hisses. Trophonius swallows, pushing the skin of his throat further into the blade, but his eyes hold mine, challenging me.

Slit his throat, the woman repeats. *Make him suffer for his disrespect, his violation of our body. Flay him from ear to ear.*

I blink at the monologue, faltering in my defensive stance, and lower my blade slowly. Quickly flicking my gaze around the barn, I find no one else present. Whose voice did I hear?

Shaking my head, I narrow my eyes at Trophonius. "If you ever speak to or come near me again, I *will* flay you from ear to ear, you little prick." I echo the mysterious voice's threat before I sheathe the sword and shove past him into the arena, joining the other soldiers in their paces.

· · · ● · ● · ● · · ·

Later that night, I enter the banquet hall, my sore muscles massaged and oiled for the occasion, and immediately spy my mother and father sitting atop their thrones, the dark granite dais gleaming from across the room. I try not to appear overeager as I brush past the revelers, politely nodding and smiling on my way forward.

"Melinoe!" My mother spots me in the center of the room and beckons me to approach, her movements visibly stiff even from a distance. Climbing the steps carefully, I drop a perfunctory curtsy. "Enough of the court etiquette," she tuts. She stands and grips my arms, keeping us separated as her eyes assess me. I notice the hard, obvious swallow in her throat just as the skin around her eyes tightens. My own eyes sting, brimming with unshed tears as I inhale her familiar rose and almond scent.

"I missed you." My voice cracks as she releases me, pushing me away. She knows my magic has not appeared in her absence. I wipe a finger under my eye, careful not to smear the kohl Selene applied.

"I have brought you a gift," she says, her green eyes flashing with feigned merriment. While she's donned her queen of the Underworld crown, delicately made with black diamonds illuminating a halo around her flaming curls, her hand shakes as she gestures to my smaller seat on the other side of Father, who wears the matching king of the Underworld crown. I move toward the miniature throne, chiseled from white poplar wood, and sit gingerly, fanning out my dress as my father takes my hand. His palm is calloused but warm. I smile, but he casts me a serious look and my brows immediately furrow. Unfazed by my confusion, Mother nods to me, then addresses the guests.

"Family and friends, I am so glad to be back in the Underworld with my wonderful husband, Hades, and my beautiful daughter, Melinoe." The revelers clap politely as she continues. "My time away allowed me to visit a new Land of the Living, called Sparta. The Spartan people are warriors, beloved by the gods of Olympus, and they welcomed me with kindness. Their land is fortified, but beautiful. While there I was able to negotiate our princess's hand in marriage . . ."

I gasp as her words slowly sink in. My head whips toward my father, who is smiling widely at me and nodding toward a man I've just noticed behind the dais. My vision swims before I'm able to focus on this stranger, and I suddenly find myself unable to breathe. My fingernails dig into the wood of the chair, my chest heaving. I try to calm myself as my mother continues talking, but my body tingles, the panic setting in.

" . . . I hope you will welcome Prince Castor of Sparta with open arms, as you've welcomed me." My mother beckons to me to stand and join her, but my legs are suddenly useless. Father grasps my arm, practically hoisting me out of the chair, and pushes me toward this stranger, everyone around the room clapping heartily.

I am shoved into Prince Castor and the crowd cheers even louder. Feeling like a caged beast, unable to escape, I flick my gaze toward my father. Surely he hasn't condoned this nonsensical coup against his only child?

"The wedding will take place in ten days' time, on Princess Melinoe's twenty-third birthday!" he announces to the audience, the applause becoming deafening. My heart drops and I double over.

"No," I whisper before my stomach empties itself all over my newly betrothed's shoes.

MELINOE

I'm hustled into the antechamber like a petulant child, my mother and father turning to glare at me.

"You are a princess of the Underworld. What has come over you?" my mother hisses at me, baring her teeth. My father paces loudly behind her, rubbing his forehead.

"How could you act this way?" he roars, stopping midstride and facing me.

I'm taken aback by their reactions, looking between the two of them with my mouth agape. I finally find my voice. "How could *you* act this way?" I point to my father, eyes narrowed in accusation. "You had to know about this and you never said a *word* while she was gone? How could you betray my trust?" Turning toward my mother, I stab the air with my index finger. "And *you* . . ." The words leave me as I shake my head, unable to comprehend why they've sold their only daughter to some prince from the Land of the Living. I open and close my mouth, but no words come out. Drawing in air that does not fill my lungs, my chest heaves as I gasp for another breath. "Why did neither of you warn me?"

They glance at each other, and I notice a flush creep up my mother's chest and dot her cheeks. Why is she embarrassed? I struggle to understand, and then it dawns on me. "You want to get rid of me because I can't summon my magic." I speak the words softly but keep my chin raised in defiance, meeting their gazes.

I may be a failure, but I will hold my head high. "And now you don't think I'm strong enough to wear the crown of the Underworld . . . to be your heiress, to carry out my duties."

I reflect on the training I've completed during Persephone's annual absences over the years. With nothing else to occupy my time without a mother around, I learned to protect myself with a blade. I've had my ass kicked by every soldier in Hades's army, only to be told to "get up and go again." I've spent hours in the throne room hearing our people's concerns and learning how to run this kingdom. I've toured the Underworld and its domains with Hermes. I've volunteered in the worst areas of the realm, particularly the pit of Tartarus. But my magic . . . My magic has failed me. And I've failed my parents.

"Why didn't you tell me I wasn't good enough?" My palms burn, and I grit my teeth, nearly snarling the question.

Hades rushes to my side, but I back away. "My princess, you have been more than enough for *us* and the Underworld, but . . ." He breaks off as my mother gently takes his arm, pulling him back.

Persephone finishes for him. "This has nothing to do with what you're capable of." She hesitates. "It's time you knew the truth about your father, Melinoe, and what he has commanded I do to keep you safe." My gaze flicks to Hades just as Prince Castor walks into the room, clearing his throat.

I turn to the prince, my heart pounding in my chest. He stands awkwardly near the antechamber door. "Can't you see we're having a conversation?" I glare in his direction, but my gaze lowers to his shoes, which I see have been cleaned. I swallow dryly and tilt my chin, refusing to be embarrassed by my actions.

My mother, eyes gleaming with unshed tears, blinks and runs her hands down her bodice. "Melinoe, you will not address our guest with such rudeness. We must return to the banquet hall. We will continue this discussion later." She clears her throat and sniffs, transforming into queen of the realm instead of flustered mother. The mask descends, smoothing her features, and she forces a smile. As she turns toward the banquet hall, she grabs my father's arm and pulls him back toward the revelers. I watch their retreating forms, finding myself left alone with *the stranger*.

My hands fist at my side and I turn, taking stock of the man in front of me. His stature dwarfs me, and I feel—dare I say—dainty compared to his broad shoulders and thick thighs. I raise my chin and take in his features. His mouth quirks up and an eyebrow raises. He's caught me assessing his physique, and I tamp down the flush I feel crawling up my neck.

"I don't think we've been properly introduced, Princess. I'm Prince Castor." He bows from the waist, still with the smirk lingering on his lips, in what I can only presume is a mocking fashion. I roll my eyes and cross my arms over my chest. I squint, shooting daggers from my eyes. He may be good-looking, but I'm not in the market for a consort.

"I don't give a damn who you are. You can pack your bags and head right back to Sparta, *Prince*, because the marriage is off." I stalk past him and back into the ballroom.

· · • ● · ● · ● · · ·

Hours later I'm slumped in my seat, vision unfocused as my mother and father delight the crowd with yet another dance. I snort at the lovely couple and the admiration the entire Underworld has for them. I know what everyone thinks of them, and of me.

My father, the powerfully decisive and stately ruler of the Underworld. My perfect mother, the goddess of spring, bringing only life and strength to her people. And yet their only child remains useless, powerless. The people, the souls of the kingdom, pity me; I see the wary glances they exchange as I approach, how they watch what they say around me, afraid to insult their inept princess.

The wine glass in my grasp my only companion, I swirl the crimson liquid and gulp down the remaining nectar. Beckoning Selene forward, I tap the glass with my blackened fingertip for a refill.

"I think you've had enough, Princess." She eyes me warily, lips thinned and eyes cold. I know better than to challenge her, my stand-in mother figure. I huff indignantly and slam the glass onto a nearby table.

"You're no fun, Selene." I turn back to the dance floor and notice *the stranger* approaching. He meets my eyes and, before I can find a reason to flee, strides up to the dais with his hand extended.

"May I have this dance, Princess?" he asks gallantly. I huff and narrow my eyes.

"Have you finished packing your bags?" I retort, the wine making me bold. Regardless of the unwanted invitation, I find my own hand extending to his, as though it is possessed. I redden, hoping he doesn't notice my discolored fingers in his calloused palms, but the smile he gives me saps the air from my lungs. It's simply stuffy in this crowded hall, I assure myself. He pulls me from my seat and, as the effects of the wine hit me and my head spins, I stumble down the stairs. Luckily he's quick, catching me before anyone notices.

"I'm here." His words tickle my ear as his arm tightens around my waist. His muscular chest presses into my face, and I involuntarily inhale his scent. My insides warm at the closeness, and as I look up at him, I'm startled by how clear his blue eyes appear this close, the color of the Terranean Sea. I think about pressing my mouth to his. What would he taste like? I blink at the thought. Selene was right. I *definitely* have had enough wine.

Feeling a wave of embarrassment heat my cheeks, I right myself, pushing away from his grasp.

"Thank you, Prince. It seems my shoe caught on my gown." The lie clears my throat and I flick my dress out, purposefully swiping him with the hem, as I stalk toward the center of the dance floor. When I've found the right spot, I turn quickly, expecting Prince Castor a few steps behind, but instead find myself spinning elegantly back into the prince's embrace, catching another whiff of his heady scent. He holds my hand aloft and smoothly slides his other arm around my waist again. I cock an eyebrow, impressed. "So you know how to dance," I concede.

"Yes, Princess. I was trained at the Spartan court with my sisters and brother." We twirl effortlessly to the music, and I notice we've drawn many eyes as the other dancers have stopped to watch. From the edge of the room, Trophonius watches, his glare burning my skin. My stomach clenches at the memory from earlier today, but as the dutiful Underworld princess, I must compose my features. If there's anything positive from this night, it's that Trophonius will finally leave me alone.

I continue to smile prettily for the audience, even as my voice hardens, my gaze returning to my dance partner. "Listen, I know you think this marriage is going to happen, but it's not. My parents think I can't handle the crown of the Underworld on my own, but I can. I definitely don't need some pretty dancing prince by my side," I sneer.

Again, the corners of his mouth quirk up in a smirk. This must be his signature look, cocksure and handsome. My cheeks flame.

"So you think I'm pretty?" he teases, and I feel a flutter in my belly.

I roll my eyes and grind my teeth, managing to keep the smile plastered to my face. "Hear what you want, Prince, but you *will* be going home in ten days' time." Thankfully the song ends, and as we sweep each other a bow and curtsy, I spot my exit and take it, heading straight for my chambers.

CASTOR

I'm left abandoned in the middle of the vast dance floor, my bride-to-be having swept out of the room before I could offer her another dance. The music strikes up again, and as I start to make my way off the floor, I feel a tap on my shoulder. Turning around, I'm met with Queen Persephone.

"Care to dance, Prince Castor?"

A smile brightens her face, and I'm instantly reminded of my own mother, another queen who rose to greatness despite—

"Prince? A dance?"

I'm snapped out of my reverie as Persephone tilts her head, pursing her lips. Bowing low to hide my inflamed cheeks, I respond, "It would be my pleasure, Your Highness." I rise and reach for her hand, and we glide easily across the floor. The emerald-green and gold gown she wears accentuates her hair, red as a rose. As the goddess of spring, her dewy alabaster skin and deep emerald eyes make me miss the colors of Sparta. Everything in the Underworld is dark. Cold. Sharp edged and steely like my future bride. In Sparta we attend balls honoring spring's arrival, Persephone's arrival, and dance among the lush green hills, the aroma of rose and almond scenting our finest attire. Furrowing my brow, I refocus my attention on the task at hand.

"Your dress is beautiful, my lady." I've been told that flattery is necessary to win over the queen of the Underworld, which, luckily for me, is a strength of mine.

She tilts her head in acknowledgment. "You dance effortlessly, Prince Castor."

I nod in gratitude. "Your daughter said the same thing before she disappeared." I briefly scan the room but see no sign of my intended. While I am slightly shocked by Princess Melinoe's reaction to the engagement announcement, as well as her fiery personality, I am mostly intrigued by her. In the Land of the Living, princesses are schooled to control their emotions, which, when courting, makes for a rather boring experience. It's why my twin and I have maintained our bachelor statuses. For me, there must be more to a marriage than a brood mare who's willing to pop out a few heirs in exchange for the crown of Sparta.

"You'll have to accept my apologies for her behavior. Her father and I have spoiled her, for obvious reasons. I suppose we felt guilty about her lack of . . . skills." A flush of embarrassment tints her cheeks before fading back as her queenly facade returns.

My small smile probably looks more like a grimace in the dim candlelight, but from what I can tell, Melinoe is not lacking in anything. Her beauty surprised me, from her unruly dark curls to her piercing blue eyes. She certainly isn't what I expected from a daughter of the Underworld.

"From where I'm standing, your daughter seems exceptional." Her eyes are shrewd, assessing my motives.

"I hope you won't take her coldness and anger personally. We chose not to prepare her for this moment, against our better judgment. But ultimately, she must grow up and accept that this"—she gestures around us—"needs protecting, with the help of Sparta of course. Melinoe clearly cannot handle it on her own without the powers a goddess should have developed by now." Her gaze deepens.

"Of course. We just need to get to know one another and spend some time together," I reassure her. The lies flow easily from my tongue. If this were any other woman, I'd wonder if she would bring any of that passionate, hot-blooded personality into the bedroom once we were married. But Melinoe is not just any other woman—or goddess, for that matter.

"Spending time together is a wonderful idea, Castor. She does enjoy being out of doors, walking in the Elysian fields. You might try seeking her out tomorrow. She also loves traipsing down by the Lethe River."

"I'll do that," I reply as the song ends. I bow again to the queen, who curtsies in return. She is then swept up by a nearby courtier, dismissing me with nary a backward glance. Grateful to have a moment to ponder the evening, I make my way back to my seat, where I mindlessly swirl my wine glass.

"May I sit, Prince Castor?" I look up and find that I'm staring into the eyes of an old soul, the wrinkles and creases of her face a map. Her graying hair is pulled back and elegantly curled at the nape. She offers a friendly smile, and I pull out the chair next to me, gesturing for the lady to take it. "I'm Selene, Queen Persephone's longtime handmaiden."

I nod in greeting and fill her wine glass from the carafe.

She takes a sip. "I'm glad you're here, Prince." Her eyes glimmer in the flickering light.

I lean forward, sliding my chair closer. "Why is that, Selene?"

"My lady needs you, even though she'll try to push you away."

I laugh, surprised by this woman's eagerness to speak so confidently with a stranger to the Underworld realm, and take a gulp of wine. "It seems she wasn't expecting this. Me, I mean."

Selene is quiet, but her eyes never leave mine. "There is so much more to my lady. I hope you can help her discover that . . ." Her voice trails off.

I lower my eyes and frown into my glass. "It seems to me that she's lucky to have you, someone who cares so much about her."

She smiles conspiratorially and inclines her head. "Thank you for acknowledging that. We have been through a lot together, my princess and I, but I know her better than she knows herself, and she is not going to be easily won. She's steely nerved and strong-willed, skills she's developed and honed after years living in the Underworld. You've got your work cut out for you, Prince."

I chuckle and finish my wine, standing. "Thank you for the advice, Selene. I must say goodnight now, especially if I'm to win a princess in the morning."

"Good luck," she replies and gives me a wink. As I exit the ballroom, I can't help but wonder which room is the princess's, and if she's thinking of me.

MELINOE

A pounding headache greets me the next morning as a servant enters my room, placing the breakfast tray down rather loudly. As she flicks open the curtains, I squeeze my eyes closed, shutting out the bright red light.

"Where's Selene?" I croak sleepily, throwing an arm over my eyes.

"Queen Persephone and Selene await your presence in the queen's rooms," the servant replies brusquely. She moves about my chamber, picking up the discarded dress and shoes I heedlessly flung off after I fled the ballroom last night. "Chop, chop." She claps and whips the covers back, exposing me to the chill of the morning. I'm appalled at this maid's presumptuous behavior, but as I've got bigger problems, namely Prince Castor and a rumbling belly that's begging to be fed, I let her behavior go without admonishment.

As I grab a piece of bread and slather it in honey, the servant holds up a modest dress for my inspection. I crinkle my nose. I much prefer the leggings and tunic I wear when training. Noticing my disgust, the maid clucks in annoyance and thrusts the long-sleeved gray dress toward me. I hold in an eye roll and, instead, shove the bread into my mouth and lick the honey from my fingers loudly. I don the dress with her help and then, as an afterthought, strap a dagger to the underside of my forearm. After all, if I'm going into battle, I'd best be prepared.

· · · · ● · ● · · · ·

My mother's rooms are outfitted to match her personality. As the goddess of spring, one would presume her choice of decor would lean to pastels and florals. But the deep-emerald-green and cedarwood accents bring to mind a lush forest at the height of summer in the Land of the Living. It's a stark contrast to the rest of the castle's granite and stone coldness.

I approach and dip a customary curtsy. My mother gestures to a seat at her table. Selene, her expression stoic, stands just behind. "You left the celebration rather early, Melinoe," the queen scolds.

"I found the company not to my liking, Mother," I parry back as I drape a napkin in my lap.

She smirks and lifts a cup of tea to her lips.

I narrow my eyes and decide to wage war, disregarding my father's lengthy instructions on how the best rulers compromise and negotiate. "Why are you and Father doing this to me?" I demand, struggling to hold back the angry tears that threaten to spill onto my cheeks. I refuse to cry or show any weakness when my very life is on the line. My parents already think me too weak to run this kingdom in their absence; I cannot prove them correct by becoming overly emotional.

She lowers the cup. "Melinoe, this marriage is for your own good. There are things you do not know, and that's why I've summoned you here." She beckons over her shoulder to Selene, who steps around the table toward me.

"Princess." Selene kneels onto the ground and holds out her hands to me. I shoot my mother a confused look but place my hands in hers.

"As you are aware, Selene is gifted with the Sight. She has something to show you, which may help you understand the things I am unable to sufficiently explain." My mother nods at Selene, who inhales and closes her eyes. I follow suit.

The air is sucked from the room, and my ears roar loudly as though I'm underwater. My eyes snap open as panic sets in, but I'm no longer myself, nor am I sitting with my mother at her table. Instead, I'm gifted with Selene's Sight.

· • • ● • ● • ● • • ·

As I dress my lady Persephone, she hums lightly to herself. I clasp the bejeweled leather belt around her narrow waist and slide a set of gold bangles over her hand. My lady remains small and without child, even after several years of marriage. I know she wishes for a baby. I have heard her in the privy, crying over the arrival of her courses. Each month she approaches my lord Hades without news of an heir.

"Our heir will appear in time," he consoles her as she weeps. "I waited for you, and I can wait for our babe as well."

Persephone reaches for her perfume. She dabs the scent behind her ears and along her wrists. The rose and almond oil fragrance fills the room. "My black leather sandals, please, Selene," my lady says as she replaces her bottle. "I'll take a walk before the heat of the day is overwhelming."

I bend to fasten the strap around her ankle. "Would you like me to accompany you, Your Highness?"

"No, I shall not be long in this stifling weather. I'll stop at the cabin for the tincture and be right home. Please see to it that the table is set when I return." She sweeps quickly from the room, and I busy myself tidying the bed and closet. I pick up last night's discarded toga and notice the hem is dirty with spilled wine. I'll have to take it to the laundress. On my way, I request that the cook send Persephone's morning meal to her chambers, warm bread dipped in honey and watered wine. I drop off the dirtied garment and, after a stop in the kitchen for my own breakfast, return to my lady's suite.

It is empty. The bread and honey, both grown cold, remain untouched. I furrow my brow and knock on the privy door. "My lady?" I ask. There is no response. I glance outside and, by the heat in the air, can tell an hour or more has passed. The day is becoming humid and unpleasant. My lady would never stay outside in this temperature. As I head to the courtyard, hoping to find Persephone in the stable, I pass one of Hades's body servants.

"Have you seen Her Majesty?" I ask, hoping she was simply distracted by a new litter of pups.

"No, m'lady," he replies with a bow. "M'lord just returned from his morning ride and is now meeting with the new arrivals in the great chamber."

I continue to the courtyard but do not come upon Persephone. As I exit the castle and look toward the sky, I notice a storm brewing in the distance. Dark gray, nearly black, clouds move swiftly, and the air suddenly grows cooler. The wind picks up, the courtyard's dust swirling around me. A sick feeling settles in my stomach. It is not like Persephone to delay her daily routine without sending word to me. Looking around for a solution, I spy Hades's groom.

"I need my horse," I demand over the howl of the wind. While I am just a servant, my lady gifted me a gelding, whom I named Arion, so that I could accompany her riding. I think of how well I am treated by Her Majesty, and a lump forms in my throat. I should have gone with her this morning, I berate myself.

"M'lady, I cannot allow you to go out in this weather," he responds. "There's a storm brewing."

"I didn't ask for your permission, sir. Please saddle the horse immediately." Within minutes, I am racing away from the castle, the wind whipping my hair from its plait. As I have accompanied her several times on her visits to the cottage, I know the route she prefers to take, and I head toward the trail through the nearby forest.

"Mistress!" I call out, my voice swept away by the wind. I feel raindrops hit my face, thunder rumbling in the distance. Lightning flares through the sky, casting terrifying shapes beneath the treetops. The trees sway wildly, and under the canopy, it's nearly as dark as night. "Mistress!" Thunder roars above. I have to find her.

Just as I think about returning to the castle, I spy something on the ground. My lady's sandal. I quickly dismount and tie Arion to a tree. His eyes are wide, and as another stroke of lightning blinds us, he bucks in fear and pulls against the tether.

I bend to pick up the sandal and suddenly see her. Persephone. My mistress. She lies curled on her side, shivering and silently crying. I rush to her.

"My lady!" I exclaim, thinking she's stumbled, twisted her ankle, and become too terrified of the storm to move. I reach for her arm to help her up. But then I see the blood. I gasp and fully take in the scene before me.

Her chiton is torn, exposing her breasts. Her right eye is swollen shut, and there is a gash above her eyebrow. Bruises are forming around her neck, darkening from a maroon red into a sickly purple. Her hair has come loose, and her lip is bleeding. I try to pull her to her feet, but she is unsteady as she attempts to untangle her clothing and cover herself. I see blood on the inside of her thighs as she attempts to pull down her tunic.

"We must get you back to the castle," I manage to whisper. The wind is so strong, I don't know if she's heard me. I take her arm and point toward Arion, who has become agitated with the weather.

Her teeth chatter. She is shaking all over. "Can you ride?" I ask delicately. When she nods, I help her up onto Arion and we slowly return to the castle.

My lady lies in bed for days. She refuses to speak or eat. I tell Hades, and anyone who asks, that she has a fever from her walk in the storm, but no amount of poultices or salves will cure what truly ails her. Her body and mind need to heal. One will heal faster than the other. I bring her favorite foods, but they are left untouched. Hades sends flowers, trinkets, and fresh fruit from the Land of the Living. Nothing will rouse her. She stares into the distance, and tears slip from her eyes. While I know she's not seeing me, I worry about what she does see in her mind.

MELINOE

S elene gently pulls her hands away as my eyes slowly open. "Who is he?" I exhale angrily to the servant. She lowers her chin, her gaze flicking to my mother. I turn slowly, the rage building. "Who is he, Mother?"

"Selene, please leave us," the queen commands. Selene stands, performs a slight bob, and moves quickly from the room. My mother reaches again for her tea and takes a small sip. This time, her hand visibly shakes as she lowers the cup, and it rattles loudly upon touching the saucer. The noise is deafening.

I grit my teeth together. "Who. Is. He?" I punctuate each word with the rumbling thunder boiling inside of me.

"Melin—" she begins. I cut her off before she can finish, my fingertips tingling in pain.

My hands slam down onto the aged table. I rise with such a force that my chair tumbles behind me. The air in the room crackles with anticipation, darkening to match my mood. "I will not ask again," I hiss.

"Calm yourself," she commands.

"I will not!" We stare daggers at each other, both of us unwilling to cede to the other.

Her eyes flash a golden yellow as her own magic surfaces. The room grows warm and a breeze of almond and rose swirls around my body, calming me. "Don't use your magic to appease me." I try to put the edge back into my voice, try to fight the softening in my body, but my limbs lower to the now-righted chair against my will.

"Until you manage to control your emotions, I will keep you here." She stands and her fingers twitch at her side. A thick green vine appears as if from nowhere and coils itself around my leg, tying me to the chair. It quickly slides up my body, wrapping tightly around my calves and heading toward my forearms. Before the plant can fully secure me, I reach for the dagger hidden in my sleeve and slice the cords away, freeing myself. My mother inhales sharply and steps back, brow falling over her eyes, the spell broken.

"Enough of this, Mother!" I slap the dagger down on the table and hold out my hands, palms up, a sign of submission. "Please, just tell me . . ." I look into her eyes, silently pleading for the truth.

She sinks into her chair, releasing a long, slow sigh, but then goes quiet. The silence descends upon us as I wait for her to speak. I feel the tension rise from my shoulders, through my neck, and into my face. "Zeus," she finally admits. "Zeus is your father, Melinoe."

Somewhere within my brain, a tether snaps and I feel a surge of energy release with a roar. *Zeusssssssssssss,* a voice growls as my body goes from cold to burning hot in seconds.

My fingertips continue tingling, the pain almost unbearable. I feel a ball of emotion form in my stomach, growing until it swallows up my lungs. I can't breathe. The growling voice goes silent, but instead, a myriad of questions run through my mind. Why did she never tell me? Does he know about me? What will happen now? Ultimately, though, only one question truly seems to matter. "Does my fath—" I correct myself. "Does Hades know?" I whisper, my heart constricting, breaking open. I'm terrified of what this means for him, for our kingdom, for our family.

"Yes, he knows." She sighs heavily. "And before you can correct yourself again, he *is* your father. He's loved you from the day you were born. His love for you is unconditional." Tears well in her eyes and overflow, coursing down her cheeks.

"Melinoe, there's something else you need to know. Without magic of your own, you aren't safe against Zeus, or any of the other Olympians for that matter. Zeus himself came to me when I was in the Land of the Living."

My jaw clenches. *What did he do to her?* the voice inside rages again.

"He didn't do anything to me," she clarifies, as though she can hear my thoughts. "He promised that if you married Castor, he would ensure your safety, Melinoe. He wouldn't harm you, nor would any of the others. You'd be safe. Our kingdom would be safe."

I shake my head, not believing what I've heard. "And if you chose not to affiance me to Prince Castor, Zeus would come here, into our realm, and do what?"

Her eyes lower ashamedly. Why would she ever trust the man who brutalized and assaulted her? Something doesn't make sense.

She sighs heavily before meeting my gaze directly. "Despite what I believed about you, your magic refuses to appear." My heart shatters at her words, but she continues, "Hades and I made the arrangement—together. Sparta is a strong ally. A warrior nation beloved by the gods, beloved by Zeus. That's the end of it, Melinoe." The thin lines of her lips brook no argument, but I'm not one to give up.

"Has Zeus threatened you, Mother? Is this why you're doing this to me?" My eyes bulge from my head.

"Of course not."

I can't believe what I'm hearing. I stand quickly, heat and anger continuing to course through my veins. After all the work I've done, I'm still not powerful enough to run the kingdom alone without a means of protection. Whether it be Zeus or Prince Castor, I need to be protected because I'm weak. Powerless. My breath hitches and I grind my teeth, knowing that I have to escape and process what I've just been told or I'm likely to burn the entire palace to the ground, with or without magic.

"Melinoe." Her voice is tight. Defeated. I pause but refuse to meet my mother's eyes. "I still have hope that you'll become someone great. Your story isn't over."

I give her a contemptuous look and curl my lip in disgust. I grab my dagger from the table, sheathe it under my sleeve, and run from the room, my mother's words echoing behind me. *Your story isn't over.*

• • • ● • ● • ● • • •

In my attempt to escape the confines of the palace, I head outside to the orchard. Despite the time of year, the pomegranate trees are still in bloom, thanks to my mother's magical presence in the Underworld. The cool breeze instantly calms my heated nerves, but before long I find the atmosphere chilly. I shiver and rub my arms as I head farther away from the castle. The grass crunches underfoot, and my breathing increases as my legs propel me faster. My mind churns, and my heart aches at the new information. I can't protect myself, so how am I supposed to protect an entire kingdom? I wish there was an answer, but the gods are silent to my query.

Before I realize it, I've wandered into the Elysian fields. The sky has lightened to a beautiful peach hue, the grass has turned greener, and the air has warmed considerably. Elysium has always been my favorite realm of the Underworld, its similarities to the Land of the Living almost startling. I plop down in the soft grass and lie back, gazing at the sky. My thoughts turn to Prince Castor. How am I going to get out of this marriage? I need to work harder, my magic must appear before the ceremony takes place. Sighing, I close my eyes and recite the "Codes of Justice for the Deceased," my body instantly calming as I mouth the familiar words.

Sitting up, I notice a small brown cottage in the distance. My brows furrow, my mouth turning down. I'm certain this abode wasn't there a moment ago.

Standing and dusting off my skirt, I jog through the tall meadow grass, lifting my legs higher to spur myself forward. Looking around, I see only destruction. The hut is blackened, the wood tarnished and soot covered. I run my hand over the posts, ash darkening my palm. The ground beneath my feet, too, is burned. The devastation extends outward, stopping at an oak tree, which remains standing in the distance, its leaves a lush emerald green and the trunk a rich chocolate brown. The spiraling limbs reach for the destroyed hut, and for some reason the tree, so full of life, makes my heart pound and a shiver runs down my spine. Turning away from the tree, I walk around to the entrance and push at the aged door. It opens with an ominous creaking and I enter, my footsteps crunching on the charred floorboards.

• • • • • • • • • • •

"Selene, get the cloths ready," my grandmother, Demeter, demands. From the doorway, I turn and watch as the handmaiden rushes to the corner of the room and begins sorting the fabric. A fire roars in the hearth, with a pot of boiling water in a cauldron. I smell the healing herbs within. My mother's screams rip through the small hut. Heavy curtains cover the windows. To protect against the evil spirits of Thanatos, the death deity, entering the room.

My grandmother checks between Persephone's legs. My birth is near. As my soul inhales within my mother's womb, I feel the child gaining strength. Demeter need not worry about Thanatos's evil spirits entering the birthing chamber. My soul was formed the moment Zeus took advantage of Persephone, an evil act which spawned something sinister.

"Persephone, it's time for you to push." Grandmother rolls up the sleeves of her plain gown and beckons the handmaiden closer. A leather strap is placed between Mother's teeth, and she bears down, stifling her screams. Sweat pours down her face and her fiery curls cling to her forehead. Her green eyes flash brighter. "Push!" grandmother hisses. Mother inhales a ragged breath and her body tenses. She

29

pushes as the infant rips through her in a gush of fluid, black as night. The child enters the world as the hour strikes three, an unlucky number. My mother falls backward into the bedding, unmoving save for her heaving chest. Her eyelids flutter closed.

"The time, Mistress," the handmaiden notes quietly to Demeter. Grandmother nods sharply and sucks in her breath. Using the hem of her dress, she removes the black birthing fluid from the infant's mouth and nostrils and gently flips her over, combing back the downy ebony fuzz atop her head.

"Check the back of her neck," my mother croaks from the bed as she rises to her forearms. Turning the new babe gently, Grandmother's eyes snap up as she sees the markings.

"She has the markings of the witch." Their eyes meet, unblinking and wide. I lift my hand to the back of my neck. Superstition states that the markings mean danger, both physical and spiritual, will court me. Tempt me. Taunt me. What else could be expected, being the daughter of Zeus, I think. A flash sparks in the hut, blinding me. Backing away, I wince. Gone are the apparitions of my birth.

The bed has been freshly made and the hearth is cold. The infant is crying, screaming really. The hut's interior, the walls and floorboards, have become dark-ened, charred as if from fire. "You are a chimera, my daughter," Persephone states quietly, rocking the newborn babe in her arms. I do not know what the word means, only that it inspires sadness in my mother. A familiar voice whispers in my ear, I am the embodiment of Heaven and Hell. Light and dark. Good and evil. *I whip my head around, searching for the source, but the hut is now empty.*

MELINOE

My eyes snap open and I take in the scene before me: the sky, soft grass on my fingertips. I am still lying in the Elysian fields. I must have fallen asleep. I shake my head, clearing the cobwebs from my brain. The dream was so realistic. I stand and brush the grass and dirt from my dress before gazing into the distance, but there is no hut. No oak tree. Nothing left but the remnants of the vision. Thinking on the dream, I realize two things. The first is that I do, in fact, possess magic. As much as I am relieved to not be an anomaly in my family, one glance at my blackened fingers reminds me that I'm still unable to truly *summon* the magic, though. The second of my realizations is that my abilities have lain dormant since infancy. If I could just awaken my magic, all my problems would be solved. I exhale loudly and, spotting a wildflower at my feet, hold out my palms and recite a burning incantation.

"*Kápste to fos.*"

I wait.

"*Kápste to fos!*"

The flower dances in the breeze. My anger surfaces, my palms clench at my sides and my jaw tenses. I don't fight to hold my emotions in. Anger at my inability to spark magic spews from my skin. Anger at my mother's lies gushes from my pores.

"*Kápste to fos!*" I shout aloud, my hair whipping wildly as the wind picks up. I clench my fists so tightly that my nails dig into my palms, drawing blood. The warm liquid drips through my fingers, down my knuckles, and dots the ground beneath me. My anger boils over, and a scream of fury unleashes itself from inside my body. The force of my outburst blows me back on my ass as my scream propels itself forward, the energy wave both crushing and destroying everything in its path. I watch, astonished, as the wave turns the lush, moist soil to dust and blackens the trees in its path. The leaves turn brown, shriveling before my very eyes, and flutter to the earth. Overhead, I watch as birds scatter from the tidal wave, but a few fall to the ground in the distance, lifeless.

"Holy shit . . ." I whisper, horrified at what I've done. Standing gingerly, I stare at my hands, which are bloodied and caked in dirt from my fall. I backpedal, turning to make my way to the castle, and bump straight into the one person I can't handle seeing right now. Prince Castor.

"Princess!" he exclaims as I slam into his broad chest. He grabs my shoulders and steadies me, pulling me close. "I'm here." His voice tickles along my scalp. My muscles immediately loosen, and I sag against his solid frame.

"I . . . I'm so sorry," I mutter into his torso, my bottom lip trembling. I chide myself for apologizing, for appearing weak. Pressing my palm to his chest, I look up into his azure eyes, my lips parting even as my mind is still processing every-thing—my real father, the appearance of my magic, and our surprise upcoming marriage—when Castor notices my injuries.

"What happened?" He gently cups one of my hands in his and, with the other, reaches to the bottom of his tunic. With a swift dash of his hand, he tears a piece of fabric from the hem and presses it to my bloodied hand, dabbing at the mess. "You're shaking." Bending his tall frame, he meets my eyes. "Let me wrap this to stanch the bleeding."

"I'm fine, I promise," I insist as I attempt to compose myself. I just need to be alone with my thoughts. I force a smile and try to pull away, but the prince holds tightly to my hand.

"Princess, please." His voice is shaky. I find myself not wanting to let go. His captivating deep-blue eyes draw me in, and I feel a warm tingle in the hand he still holds. "I think we got off on the wrong foot, and I'd like a second chance to—"

"To what?" I cut him off, shaking my head as I remember why he's here in the Underworld. To align himself with *my* throne. I yank my hand from his, and this time he sets me free. "To make a marriage with the heiress of the Underworld? To claim what's rightfully mine?" My hands tingle painfully, and I rub my arms to distract from the uncomfortable feeling. Even if I'm not technically the true daughter of Hades, Prince Castor doesn't know that. So why is he really here if not to take what's mine?

He's shocked by my outburst, as is apparent by his raised eyebrows and open mouth. But before I can verbally attack him again, his expression changes. His eyebrows lower and his lips quirk up at the corner. He shrugs half-heartedly, cocking his head. His eyes darken, the ocean blue now cold and icy. "Let me enlighten you, *Princess*. My family home, Sparta, produces the fiercest warriors in all the lands. We are beloved by the gods. So when it was prophesied by the Oracle at Delphi that I would marry a daughter of Zeus, I wasn't surprised. After all, the king of Mount Olympus *owed* my family, owed my mother." He squints harshly. "What did surprise me was Persephone showing up on our doorstep this summer, begging for an audience *and* with a marriage proposal. A marriage proposal to the Underworld's heiress, who has no magic of her own, leaving her kingdom unprotected if she ever inherits the crown." His biting remarks hit their target.

I am shamed to my core by this man who knew the truth of my parentage before I did. I assess all that he's said and realize that, in order to save my kingdom and myself—to make the outside world see me as worthy—I have to make my magic truly work. Not just summon it when I'm furious. But I can't let this upstart think he's won my crown. Not yet. So I spin the truth, tossing my hair back and narrowing my eyes at him.

"For your information, *Prince*, I do have magic. Why don't you take a look for yourself?" I gesture confidently toward the blackened trees and scorched earth behind me. "In fact, I was in the middle of practicing before you rudely interrupted me." I watch as his mouth slackens and his eyes widen. Inwardly I'm terrified, but I force myself to project a calm demeanor. "I hope your bags are packed, *Sparta*, because you're heading home soon." I wink and walk past him toward the palace before turning and snidely remarking, "And don't for one second think you know *anything* about who I really am."

· · · ● · ● · ● · · ·

I stand on the edge of the great river Oceanus. In the distance lies my mother, Asteria, now called Delos, a small island lonely at sea. A tear leaks from my eye, trickling down my cheek, the wind drying it into a streak of salt that flakes away as I swipe my face, remembering.

My mother loved me, her only child. She married my father, Perses, who called her his "dear wife." Being offspring of the Titans, they made their home on Olympus, and until we became refugees, fleeing in the night to Crete, we were happy.

Inhaling the saltiness, the breeze tickles my nostrils as my mother's tangled curls did when I was young. She hated living on Crete, cut off from her family and the mainland. But we were in hiding, protecting one of our own, and she promised we'd one day return, triumphant as we again took our places on the mountain of Olympus.

A hiss from my traveling partner pulls me from my reverie. Turning to my heavily pregnant aunt, I inquire, taking her hand in my own, "Is it the babe?" Worry etches her brow, a trickle of sweat running down her face.

"Yes," she answers breathlessly, rubbing her palms over her swollen stomach. She squeezes her eyes shut in pain as another contraction racks her body. Her grip tightens, and I wince, clenching my jaw.

"Let me apply this poultice." I set down my satchel and dig within to produce a salve. After uncapping the elixir, I raise the hem of her dress and rub it onto her swollen belly.

Her breath hitches, and she exhales as the pain ebbs.

"Better?"

She nods, her eyes closing as she breathes out through pursed lips.

"Tell me how it happened." The words tumble from my mouth. She opens her eyes, searching my own, her brow creased. "I have a right to know what he did to her." I gesture toward the island of Delos, knowing it's the only safe place for my aunt to give birth. Knowing my mother, the island, will protect us both.

We walk along the shore, and she finally begins to tell me how Zeus turned my mother into the isolated and barren island in the distance, all because she refused his advances, refused to provide him information about me.

By the end of the tale, I'm not sure if it's the spray of the sea or my own salty tears that coat my face.

"We must go there," I say, pointing to the mass in the distance. "It's the only safe place for you to deliver, where you won't be found. We will protect you," I promise, taking her hand in my own. "I'll send a missive to the others, and we will protect you, Aunt Leto."

Staring into the distance, she finally agrees, and as we make our way to the island in a tiny boat, my heart breaks all over again.

· · · ● ● · ● · · · ·

"I swear my magic appeared," I tell Hermes the next day during my lessons. We stand in the Elysian fields, but the evidence of my powers has disappeared. I reach down and stroke the soft grass. The trees nearby stand tall, their green leaves again blowing in the warm breeze.

"Are you sure it wasn't part of your dream? You mentioned a hut and a large oak tree. I see neither of those." Hermes looks skeptically at me, pursing his lips into a fine line. I'd only told him about the vision from the Elysian fields, not the dream I'd had last night about the island of Delos, nor the others that continue to plague me each morning as I search for a thread to grasp, to remember.

Shaking my head, I clear the cobwebs from my brain. "I'm sure. This whole section was charred to dust, and those trees over there were blackened. Birds fell dead from the sky!" My voice becomes shrill, and my face heats in embarrassment. I wasn't dreaming . . . was I?

"There is no shame in your magic not appearing. I think we should prepare for the inevitable. My advice is to marry the prince. Find happiness with what you are, Melinoe." He sighs.

His use of my given name is a nail in my coffin. Not Princess. Not Mistress. Just Melinoe. I'm nothing special without the magic necessary to fulfill my duties.

"Are you saying that our lessons are over, Hermes?" I pinch my eyebrows together and reach for his hand, crushed by his advice.

He pulls away, tucking both hands behind his back. His face shutters, and my heart sinks. I won't get any more help from him. "Yes. I must return to Mount Olympus soon, Melinoe, and to my duties escorting souls between the Land of the Living and Underworld. It's time you moved on too." Hermes gives me a curt nod and, with a snap of his fingers, disappears.

Of course he would magic himself away as quickly as possible. Show off.

I sigh in frustration and decide to take a walk to clear my head. As I leave Elysium, I see the Lethe River in the distance, one of my favorite spots in all of the Underworld.

All new souls are forced to drink from the Lethe in order to forget, to completely erase, their previous lives. I've been warned since childhood to stay away from the river, for fear of falling in and losing all my memories, but there's something about the river that continues to call to me. I approach carefully, kneeling down and gazing into the flowing depths. Maybe I, like the incoming souls, should just take a dip and wipe my mind clean. Forgetting would be so much easier. I glance to the sky and close my eyes, wishing for a sign.

Instead, I hear a low growl nearby and my eyes snap open, searching for the cause. I stand and look around uncertainly, walking carefully toward the bridge to cross over the river. Spotting Prince Castor standing on the bridge, his back to me, I sigh heavily. "Not you again," I holler. "Can I ever have a moment alone or are you following me?" Castor doesn't acknowledge me or turn. How strange.

I press forward, the planks of the overpass creaking beneath my feet. "What are you—" I gasp, taking in the gigantic beast facing the prince. His black body is sleek, held up by four monstrous, muscular legs, while a serpent's tail extends from his hindquarters. Eagle talons extend from his paws, scraping against the timber as the hound flexes, ready to pounce. The nails alone could rip a man to ribbons in one swipe. The growl turns to a roar as I lock eyes with the creature. "Cerberus," I whisper.

My eyes take in the sheer size of the beast guarding the bridge's exit. His neck splits into three heads, each one with a lion's mane of snakes, hissing and striking at us with elongated fangs exposed.

"What the fuck?" Castor's eyes are wide as I slowly join him. He reaches back, drawing his blade from its baldric.

The movement upsets the hound, who leaps in the air, jaws wide open and snake fangs snapping.

"Princess, look out!" Castor shouts and shoves me out of the way, into the bridge's railing. I slam against the wood, losing my balance and flipping over toward the water. Before I can tumble into its murky, mind-clearing depths, I catch the beam and hold tightly, my legs dangling.

Looking up, I see Castor meet the beast midair with a swipe of his sword. A snake head is sliced off and flips past me into the water, its tongue nearly licking my cheek. I grimace in disgust, but manage to pull up, my arms burning as I hoist myself over the railing. Breathing a sigh of relief that I haven't fallen into the magic waters, I turn my attention to Castor and the monster, entangled on the ground. Castor's back is to the planks, the creature's jaws inches from his forearm. Snakes snap and swipe at Castor's face.

My fingers go numb, tingling as though they've fallen asleep. I flex and curl them into my palm, to no avail. The pain grows. My vision focuses, narrowing and dimming, and a golden leash cords itself around my arm, extending to the canine. As the leash coils around Cerberus's neck, the dog struggles against the chain, bucking and whipping his heads back and forth. He abandons Castor's arm and puts all his energy into breaking the invisible constraints.

"*To myaló sou eínai íremo,*" I whisper, blinking as the words come from within. "*I psychí sou tragoudáei me galíni,*" I continue the calming spell, slightly louder now, extending my hand and moving closer as the monster continues to arch against the leash. The energy in me strengthens, holding strong and pulling taut.

"Wh-what are you doing?" Castor whispers, standing and joining me at my side with his blade drawn. His shirt is torn to shreds, but his arm, miraculously, is uninjured.

"It's a calming spell," I whisper. I continue to inch closer, and as I near, Cerberus slowly begins to still. He drops his enormous head and sinks to his belly in submission. I lower to my knees and reach tentatively to his snout, stroking softly. "Good boy, hound. Good boy." Castor stares at me in amazement and I smile back, cocking an eyebrow.

He tilts his head slightly. "I guess you really do have magic, Princess."

"It would appear so, Sparta. I guess you'll be going home without a bride." I don't know if it's the energy leaving his body or the disappointment at not marrying my throne, but Prince Castor's shoulders sag noticeably as his face droops in apparent regret.

MELINOE

I spend the next few days attempting to hone my magical skills. But, no matter how hard I push my mind, the abilities have vanished as quickly as they appeared. Nothing I do restores the power I felt tying myself to Cerberus or scorching the earth.

I'm finally summoned to sup with Persephone and Hades on the eve of the ninth day, one day before my marriage is to take place. While I've briefly spoken to them of my stuttering magic, they now require an update and to bear witness for themselves. I pace my chambers in frustration, hand to my forehead and jaw clenched.

"Princess, it's time to prepare for the evening meal," Selene reminds me gently. She pulls a midnight-blue gown from the closet, holding it up for my approval. I shake my head.

"Fetch my birthday gown, Selene." If I am unable to summon my magic, perhaps I can yet change my parents' minds about the upcoming nuptials. I have to do something; I cannot marry the prince.

I slip into the dress with Selene's help and twirl in front of the mirror, my dark curls hanging loosely down my back. The black beaded bodice complements my ebony tresses, and the cormorant feather skirt, which shimmers between green and bronze in the room's candlelight, makes my pale complexion sparkle. I truly feel like a princess, the daughter of the Underworld. I assess myself in the mirror, my jaw set and muscles tightening. My eyes flash with strength, and I remember to strap my dagger to my thigh beneath the gown. I am a force to be reckoned with, even without magic.

"Good luck tonight, Mistress," Selene murmurs, bobbing a discreet curtsy. I give a curt nod and head to Hades's private rooms.

· · · • · • • · ·

As I walk the narrow hallways of the castle proper, it's as though I'm seeing everything for the first time. I run my fingers along the gray granite walls, formed ages ago from the underground volcanoes that helped create this majestic kingdom. I find that I'm following the same path Selene likely took the day she went in search of her mistress.

The rough stone scratches along the tips of my blackened fingers as my steps slow. I contemplate the terror Selene felt, the horrifying scene she discovered as her queen lay bloodied and raped, discarded in the depths of the forest. A ball of fury forms in my gut, and I grit my teeth as I feel it churn and grow—ever so slowly—as my fingers trace along the jagged archways.

Use that anger, use it for revenge, girl . . . The same feminine voice from before surfaces in my mind. I withdraw my hand from the wall as a slight warmth spreads from my nail through my palm.

Destroy him, the voice hisses seductively in my ear. I glance around and, noting no other courtiers nearby, hurry down the hall, as though I'm able to run from the woman in my head.

I approach the large doors of Hades's lair and, inhaling deeply, step into the room as the Tartarusian guards close the doors behind me. While my mother's boudoir evokes a lush summer garden in both color and decor, my father's chambers truly bring to mind death and despair. However, I'm at home in the darkened cypress wood interior, a scent of spice and evergreen soothing my tormented mind. Candlelight fills the room, flickering eerily and casting a dim

40

shadow across the table. A hearty meal of meats, cheeses, bread, and olives sits untouched in front of my parents, who both gesture for me to be seated.

I lower slowly, swallowing the lump in my throat. My mouth has gone dry and I reach, hand quaking, to the glass of crimson wine in front of me. Taking a strengthening pull, I down the juice and clear my throat. "Thank you for inviting me this evening."

"I see you've donned your birthday dress. It truly looks exquisite, Melinoe." My father nods his approval. "Have you deigned to try on your wedding gown?" He places a choice cut of meat on my plate, and I take up my cutlery.

So this is how it's going to be. If nothing else, Hades taught me to always fight fire with fire.

"I have not had the time, as I've been practicing my magic." I grip the knife, my knuckles going white.

"Ah, yes. The reason we are truly here, daughter." My mother finally addresses the unspoken tension in the room. "Hermes believes the appearance of your magic to be nothing more than the lingering effects of a dream from Elysium." She arches a brow, exchanging a knowing look with Hades.

"Unfortunately, Hermes is mistaken." I set my knife down and spear a piece of meat with my fork. "I was also able to tame the hellhound, stopping him from attacking Prince Castor."

"Hm . . . how lovely for you." Persephone offers a bemused smile. "Would you care to show us a bit of your magic now?" With the flick of her wrist, a yellow narcissus appears in my wine glass. "Turn this flower into ash, Melinoe."

I set my jaw and nod curtly. Taking a deep breath, I focus intently on the bloom before me and recite, "*Stis stáchtes*." The narcissus remains. "*Stis stáchtes*!" I stress the incantation and my voice lowers to a growl. "*Stis stáchtes*!"

Persephone shakes her head, mouth turning down. She turns to a nearby servant and whispers, nodding toward the door. I remove the flower and flick it onto the table, gulping the remaining wine from my glass. The servant rushes quickly to the entryway, and I choke on my drink, coughing loudly and taking a deep breath to clear my airway, as she escorts Prince Castor into the room.

"We've invited Prince Castor to dine with us tonight, Melinoe, so that you two may finalize the marriage arrangements that *will* take place tomorrow evening."

I open my mouth to interject, but Hades holds out his hand, stopping me. I swallow my words, wishing I had the ability to summon more wine. Instead, I gesture to my glass and smile in thanks as the nearest servant tops me off. Hades snaps his fingers and a chair and place setting appear across from me. "Prince Castor, have a seat please, and tell us what you saw when Cerberus attacked you."

Lowering my gaze, I wait for the prince to explain, in detail, how I leashed the unruly beast and saved his Spartan neck from being shredded to ribbons. A smirk touches my lips.

Castor clears his throat and turns toward my father. "Your Highness, I was beset by your magnificent hound, who did not recognize me as a royal visitor to your court. He attacked, as is his nature, to protect his territory."

Hades nods and twirls his hand. "Yes, yes, son, get on with it. Cerberus can be quite a pain in the ass, despite our best attempts at training him."

I stiffen at my father's use of the term *son*, but Castor continues, "Princess Melinoe came upon me and offered the beast her hand to sniff. He was immediately mollified, as he is acquainted with her, and left to, I can only assume, look for other intruders to the Underworld."

My eyes narrow. "How dare you spout such falsehoods to Their Highnesses? I saved you from Cerberus's deadly jaws and was almost thrown into the Lethe!" I spit venom at this Spartan traitor, my mind going wild as my lip curls back in disgust at the blatant lie this piece of filth has spewed from his mouth.

Hades's infamous rage bursts forth, white-hot and bright, and I wince as he directs it at me. "Daughter, calm yourself. It is clear that your magic has not appeared, no matter how much you've attempted to fool yourself. This is my kingdom, and I will have you kept safe as you assume your duties as heiress. You will marry Prince Castor whether you like it or not. We will not have this discussion again. I suggest you either come to terms with the arrangement or I will drag you down the aisle myself tomorrow evening."

I glare across the table, my teeth bared and my fingers stroking the dagger sheathed on my thigh as I meet Prince Castor's defiant gaze. He crosses his arms and leans back in his chair, and I swear I see a gleam of satisfaction sparkle in his traitorous eye. If this warrior prince wants a battle, then a battle he will get.

CASTOR

Princess Melinoe stares daggers at me across the table. She knows I've lied, but there's nothing she can do to prove that her story is the truth. I smirk, knowing that I have the upper hand in this battle, this relationship, or whatever it is, between the two of us.

The remainder of dinner is a tense affair. The princess sulks, refusing to eat another bite. Instead, she drinks her dinner, glass after glass. I lose count but notice, as her eyes start drooping and her movements become more free, that she is definitely drunk. I'm surprised no one else has made mention of it.

Her father and mother make stilted conversation with me across the table. "So, Prince Castor, tell me about Sparta." Hades lifts a piece of meat to his mouth and devours it hungrily. "I have not had the pleasure of visiting your fine homeland."

"Sparta is only a small portion of the beautiful city-state of Lacedaemon, Your Highness. It's the preeminent military force in all of Greece." I sit a little taller, proud of my roots, proud of the kingdom I may one day inherit if my plans align with the gods'.

"Mm-hmm . . ." he grumbles, taking a heavy drink. "What else do you do besides train and fight, or is that all there is to do in Lacedaemon?"

"Is that why you've come to claim the throne of the Underworld? You're *bored*?" the princess interrupts harshly, her eyes aflame and her palms splayed on the table that separates us.

"Melinoe," Hades warns, setting his fork down loudly on the table. "I will not have you disrespect our guest in my castle."

She rolls her eyes and lets out a derisive snort. "Excuse me, but I have preparations to make for tomorrow." The princess stands and flings her napkin roughly onto the table. She narrows her eyes at me and tosses her head as she turns, leaving the room. The temperature in the chamber instantly drops as her fire and hate disappear with her.

"I'll take my leave as well, husband." Persephone reaches for her husband's hand and gently brushes it with her thumb. Her eyes are bright with affection. True love. This takes me by surprise, as the rumors of Hades's abduction of Persephone continue to mar their reputation in the Land of the Living. She turns to me with an apologetic smile. "Have a pleasant evening, Prince Castor. Again, I apologize for my daughter's . . . dissatisfaction with our arrangements." She touches my hand gently before taking her leave.

I raise my napkin to my mouth and wipe, tossing it on the plate and looking to make my exit as well. Unfortunately Hades stills me by extending his hand.

"Stay a moment, son." The endearment strikes a chord and my chest tightens. "I'd hoped things would go smoother with Melinoe, but I can't say I'm surprised by her reaction. I raised her to fight, to question everything, and to always be ready to negotiate. I raised her to run a kingdom. My kingdom." He sighs heavily, swirling his glass of wine.

"I know you're aware of the truth of her parentage, but that girl is my daughter. No one else's. I couldn't bear to lose her. Her mother and I are trusting you to help protect her, even at her worst."

My cheeks flush and I lower my gaze, my heart nearly pounding out of my chest. Can Hades hear it from where he sits? "I hope you know I'll do my best,

Your Highness." I don't want to let this great man down, but a lump forms in my throat and I find it incredibly difficult to swallow.

· · • ◦ • · • · • ◦ · ·

After the terse dinner, I decide that a walk around the castle will clear my conscience before I settle in for the night. Tomorrow is the big day, my marriage to Melinoe will be complete, and I will begin fulfilling my end of the bargain. I inhale the crisp evening air, and a light breeze floats through the grounds, smelling of ash and bonfire. Looking for the source of the scent, I spy a town filled with revelers in the distance, likely celebrating their princess's upcoming nuptials. Thinking that a drink—anything stronger than wine—sounds nice, I head that way.

Plodding along in the dark, the faint bonfire in the distance lighting my way, I hear a faint sound—a grunt and then a quick squeal. Stiffening, my ears perk up at the unusual noise. Cerberus again? My insides go watery as I pause and listen.

"Come on, he'll never know," a male voice rumbles gruffly, followed by the sound of cloth tearing. A sharp smack on flesh. My fight response springs into motion.

I hurry toward the voice, spurred onward in the pitch-black night of the Underworld. The scent of ash has turned noxious as it coats my constricted throat, my mind running through what I might find in the dark.

Struggling to keep upright as I stumble over rocks and low shrubs, I slow my movement, careful to not make a sound as I approach. I keep a hand on the blade at my hip, my vision adjusting to the darkness. Two bodies are tumbling in the tall grass, a man and a woman. There's something familiar about the feathered dress, shining green and copper in the distant bonfire light. My stomach plummets as I spy my betrothed's curly dark locks, her milky-white skin gleaming even in the night. Have I stumbled upon a lover's tryst? One final way to ensure

46

that we aren't married tomorrow? Rage fills my chest, and I want nothing more than to stomp back to Sparta and raise an army in retaliation, but I refrain from acting and instead inch forward as I crouch down, waiting for my moment to catch them in the act.

"I said *no!*" A slap echoes through the valley, and as the man rears back unhurt, his meaty fist raises, the rage and desire in his eyes flickering bloodred as the fire's weak light shudders behind me. My soldier's training kicks in and everything slows. The man's burly paw held high, knuckles clenched so tightly that they've turned blindingly white. *My* princess's beautiful face, eyes squeezed shut as she prepares for the assault, flinching away as she cowers on the ground. Her gown torn and dirtied. A dagger tossed in the dirt, out of reach.

I spring into action, leaping and tackling the man to the ground, the look on his face echoing the surprise on Melinoe's. "How dare you try to take what's *mine*?" I rage as we tumble downhill toward the revelers' celebration. I ignore the rocks and clods of dried dirt digging into my back and body as we roll, then land on top and straddle the attacker, restraining him.

"What kind of man hits a woman?" I growl, my hand gripping tightly around his throat. He tries to land a few shots to my ribs, but I grasp his arm and pull, dislocating his shoulder with a wet pop. Howling in pain, he rolls over in submission, his useless arm landing at an odd angle.

Leaping off the offender, I run back toward Melinoe.

"It's me," I say as I drop to my knees next to her, unsure if she can see me in the darkness. "I'm here."

Her deep-blue eyes meet mine. Cradling her cheek in her palm, she shivers as she blinks back tears. I quickly take off my tunic and throw it over her shoulders, my fingers deftly buttoning the shirt over her exposed décolletage. I lift her effortlessly, holding her close to my own bare chest.

She curls into me, her breath tickling my skin as she whispers, "Thank you, Prince."

My knees nearly buckle at the desire that burns through my body, but I tighten my hold on her and continue back to the castle.

MELINOE

I stare at my blank features in the mirror, my dull eyes hopeless and my chin trembling. The crimson color of the wedding gown matches the tint Selene has applied to my full lips. Sparkling gray beads encircle my neck in a choker and fall away to expose my shoulders and biceps. The bodice hugs my curves, particularly my rear, and then flares out into a mermaid train. While my dress is beautiful, I know that my sallow complexion and sullen expression ruin its aesthetic. I look away, finding the image too painful.

I'm fortunate that Selene was able to cover up the bruising on my face, and as I reach my hand up to cup my cheek, I wince in pain. Shame knots itself in my belly as I think of how I spoke to Castor after he rescued me.

He stopped at the walls of the castle, and my fingers trailed down his exposed chest as he lowered me to the ground. I hissed in disbelief at his muscles, my hand refusing to return to my side, his torso as hard and defined as the stones of the castle. Looking at me through lowered lashes, he tensed his jaw and a low growl came from deep within his throat. "Who is he, Princess? I'll have his head by morning."

Yanking my hand back, the spell broken, I retorted, "You'll do nothing of the sort."

"He's your paramour then? Is that it? Is this your sorry attempt to get rid of me?" He grabbed my wrists as he pulled me to his bare chest. "Your plan won't work, you're *mine*, promised to *me*, Princess." Looking up into his face inches from my own, I was surprised by how broad his shoulders were, how this large Spartan prince dwarfed my own lean frame. I watched as his lips parted, his tongue darted out to touch his lower lip. Holding in my own breath, I became strongly aware of my heartbeat, the sensation of warmth flooding over me.

His arms snaked around my back and pulled me closer, and I tuned out the distractions of the evening. My failed magic, my argument with my parents, and Trophonius's unwanted affections and assault.

My body began to give in, feeling something catch fire within my soul, and I arched into him, forgetting everything else—

"Melinoe, there you are!"

I gasp as Persephone enters the room and stops suddenly, her mouth an O of surprise. "You look stunning, my daughter."

I blink back the tears that threaten to run over and ruin my kohl-rimmed eyes. Pressing my lips together and moving toward the vanity, I snatch earrings from the table and hook them into my ears. I have nothing to say to my mother and proceed to give her the silent treatment. Unfortunately, she doesn't take the hint.

She makes her way toward me and attempts to engulf me in a hug, but I shy away from her, curling into myself to avoid her repulsive touch. "I know you're upset with your father and me, but this is for the best. Prince Castor has signed the marriage contract. I need you to do the same." She unrolls a scroll and lays it in front of me on the vanity. With a twirl of her hand, a feathered pen appears. I refuse to take it and stare blankly at her, my lips pressing into a hard line across my face. "Melinoe, don't be such a child. If you won't sign it, I'll use my magic to force your hand." She raises an eyebrow, challenging me.

Like I'd give in so easily.

My nose is assaulted by her rose and almond scent as a vine swishes up the outer skirts of my gown. It coils around my stomach and maneuvers around my shoulder, down my arm. My muscles tense, determined to hold, but the vine's magic—my mother's magic—is too strong. I peek at my mother's fingers, bending at odd angles to control the crawling plant. I hold my breath and try to summon my own magic, but nothing appears. The vine breaks my hold and, with a flourish of my mother's hand, I have signed the marriage contract. My body releases, my hands landing on the dressing table as my body slumps and my chin falls to my chest, defeated.

"See? Was that so hard?" She plants a kiss on my cheek and sweeps from the room, her cloying scent vanishing with her. Sighing dejectedly, I sag into the vanity's chair. I close my eyes and pray to the gods for my powers to whisk me somewhere, anywhere, but here. But the gods, like my magic, are silent.

· · · ● · ● · · ·

Arriving at a corner of the castle I rarely visit, I'm unable to take in the surroundings as I'm instantly stripped of my gown and outfitted in a black lacy negligee. Luckily a fire roars in the hearth, or I'd be freezing my ass off in the silky concoction. Still holding a glass of wine from the wedding festivities, I move to the large bed and, after Selene pulls back the covers, am shoved in by my mother, who stands at my back. I glare as she takes the glass, setting it on the table across the room with a carafe and two clean, untouched goblets. Pulling the sheet up, I attempt to cover my exposed cleavage, just as the men enter the chamber. They make bawdy jokes and Castor, too, is pushed toward the bed. A man servant helps him undress to his undergarments, and he is soon under the bed covers as well. Staring at the expectant and giddy faces at the foot of the bed, my body and mind freeze at the thought of what's next.

While my father hadn't needed to carry me down the aisle, he very nearly dragged me, my wooden steps halting us along the way.

"Wipe that grimace off your face, daughter," Hades had whispered sternly as I attempted to control my breathing.

It felt as though I was being escorted to my death. Breathe in. Take a step. Breathe out. Take a step. I'd repeated the mantra over and over until I reached the dais and finally looked up at my intended.

His hair was swept back from his face, allowing me to take in his bright blue eyes. A look of pain flashed briefly in them, which startled me, but was quickly replaced with a mask of boredom. As he placed the ring on my finger, his hand visibly shook. Moments later, a chaste kiss on the cheek cemented our alliance, even as my heart plummeted at how soft and supple his lips were against my skin.

Looking at my husband now, I wonder if he truly wants this marriage. He catches me staring and offers a conciliatory smile. I lower my eyes, pulling the covers even higher.

My father blesses the marriage bed by sprinkling water from the River Phlegethon. "I anoint the coupling of my daughter, Princess Melinoe, and her husband, Prince Castor, with water from the river of fire. May passion and the heat of love join them in their union." Once the consecration is complete, he ushers the revelers into the hallway and back to the festivities, which will carry on until dawn. For the first time since last night, my husband and I are alone. His woodsy scent washes over me as his arm brushes against mine. A spark of heat spreads from my core, my traitorous body tingling all over at his mere presence. Grinding my teeth, I watch the threshold like a hawk.

The moment the last reveler leaves and the wooden door clicks shut, I leap out of bed as though the sheets are on fire, refusing to be any nearer than necessary to my new husband. Searching for something to throw at him, I spot a bronze candlestick within reach, and fling it at his head. He swiftly ducks, the candelabra embedding itself into the wall behind him.

Turning toward me, he looks at me with murderous eyes. "What the fuck, Melinoe?" he snarls, striding toward me as I begin to back away. When I'm flush against the wall, he looms over me as his bare chest presses against my breasts. Out of breath with anger, we heave against one another, refusing to break eye contact. His eyes flick briefly to my chest, and a blush creeps up his throat. He swallows heavily. As his gaze slowly moves from my cleavage, up to my neck, he sucks in his bottom lip, biting it. My insides burn with lust, but that doesn't stop me from attacking.

"How dare you force me into this sham of a marriage?" I'm a rabid beast unable to be contained, hitting and scratching anywhere my fingers find purchase. I manage to rake my nails across his cheek before he grabs my wrist and raises my arm above my head. Pinning it there, he wrestles to stop my other arm too. I land a punch to his jaw before that arm is also pinned overhead. Trapped and breathless, I thrash in anger against him as he slides his knee between my legs, holding me up. He's able to hold both my wrists above me with one hand as his other trails down my side, his fingers leaving delicious tingles in their wake. Ignoring the growing heat between my thighs, I bare my teeth. "Is this what you wanted? A wife who *despises* you? Will fucking me against my will make me *yours*?" I throw the words from last night back into his face.

Again, that look of pain briefly flashes in his eyes, but it vanishes with a single blink. Instead, he snorts with laughter. "You may find this hard to believe, Melinoe, but I'm not too fond of you either. I am a man of my word who promised Persephone and Hades I would wed their dear daughter, even if that meant aligning myself to a harpy who knows nothing of the real world, her own magic, or how to protect a kingdom." He slowly releases me and turns toward the bed. "And before you get the wrong idea about me, I'm not interested in forcing myself on you, nor will I share a bed with someone who has intentions of impaling me with a candlestick." He walks to his discarded clothes and pulls a blade from his belt. Ice fills my veins, and my heart stills. Is he going to kill me? Has this been his plan all along? Sign the marriage contract and then murder me? My breath hitches. What if he's working with Zeus?

My worries dissipate as I watch him slice deeply into his palm and smear the blood onto the sheets. I'm rendered speechless, knowing that the servants will check for my long-lost maidenhead in the morning and report back to

Persephone. I take a deep breath, my body and mind calming, and move toward the bed, ripping a piece of fabric from the bedding.

He stares at me.

"You bandaged my hand, and now I'm repaying the favor." Lifting his palm, I wrap the bandage around his wound, securing it tightly to stanch the bleeding. I keep hold of his hand, suddenly aware of my attire, or lack thereof, and heat creeps up my neck.

His eyes rake up and down my body, and goosebumps speckle my flesh. He leans in, our breathing synced, and I tip my face up toward his. My mind flashes to the almost-kiss from last night, before we'd been interrupted by a castle guard. My traitorous body is yearning for more, the passion from our fighting burning deep within me, but he breaks the spell by saying, "Take the bed, wife. I'll sleep on the floor." Grabbing a pillow and pulling off one of the blankets, he beds down near the hearth, effectively slamming the door on a goodnight kiss. I brush my thumb along my lips, desiring to feel his mouth pressed there, but also hating him for agreeing to this marriage. Nothing like being angry and turned on, I think as I stare at the fire burning in the hearth.

"Thank you," I mutter. Prince Castor mumbles something incoherently and turns toward the fire, effectively dismissing me. I make my way to the bed.

The knife, a mysterious male voice hisses from the hearth.

"What did you say?" I ask, turning toward Castor.

"I didn't say anything. Maybe it's all the wine you drank at dinner playing tricks on your mind," he comments from the floor.

Blinking, I note the bloodied blade has been left next to the wine carafe, discarded after Castor cut himself to spare me. I step toward it, my hand extending, fingers desiring the feel of the hilt and the weight in my palm.

Free yourself and become what you were meant to be—my little witch, the male voice rasps, its deep tenor vibrating in my gut and sending a shiver up my spine.

My steps falter and I bite my bottom lip. Shaking my head and turning toward the bed, I feel exhaustion and the effects of the wine wash over me. It's been a long day and I must be hearing things. I put the creepy voice out of my mind and climb into the plush bed, asleep before my head hits the pillow, the voice forgotten.

MELINOE

A knock on the door awakens me just as I'm violently shoved to the opposite side of the bed. The prince climbs under the covers. "Wha—?" I grumble sleepily.

He throws his arm over me, clamping his hand over my mouth. "Shh, it's the servants."

My eyes widen as I feel his muscular body line up with my own, then realize his morning arousal is also pressed against my hip, and my body temperature plummets. I bite into his hand.

Hard.

"Ow, what the fuck?" he hisses, pulling his hand back. The servants enter, bearing a tray filled with bread, jam, and mugs of hot tea. We both sit up at the same time, feigning yawns. They quickly deposit the sustenance and take their leave, passing knowing looks between themselves.

I turn to Castor, my eyes full of fury. "Don't you eve—" but I stop short, realizing that his eyes are staring straight at my chest, their depths deep pools of desire. Horrified, I look down and—*fuck*—my left breast is completely exposed, the flimsy negligee having supported *nothing* in the night.

Pulling the lacy concoction over myself, I quirk an eyebrow and flip back the covers, revealing his erection tenting his undergarments. He looks mortified, his face turning the color of the breakfast jam before he whips the blanket over his lap.

I roll my eyes and grab a robe as I pad to the table. Pulling out a chair, I inhale the aroma of the tea. Moments later, Castor takes a seat across from me, and I can't help but flick my eyes over his naked chest. He glares, wringing his bitten hand, and grabs a biscuit, smothering it in jam before standing, sans arousal, and beginning to dress.

"I suggest you make yourself ready. We leave in an hour."

My eyebrows shoot up. "Leave?"

"Nobody informed you that we would be leaving after the wedding?"

In the days leading up to the wedding, I hadn't exactly been paying attention to the information shoved down my throat. If anything, I'd purposefully ignored it all. My focus had been working on my magic; a lot of good that did. My blank expression is affirmation enough for him.

"We're going to Sparta. Hades arranged it."

I blink at him.

He exhales loudly and continues, "He'll travel with us to Cape Taenarum, render the earth, and we will arrive in the Land of the Living near the town of Taenarus. My brother will meet us there and escort us to Sparta." He slides his knife back into his belt. The same knife from last night.

Become what you were meant to be—my little witch, the voice from last night echoes in my mind. I furrow my brow.

Castor notices my expression. "What's wrong?"

I shake my head and take a gulp of tea, swallowing to avoid socializing with him. "I'll be ready within the hour."

• • • • ● • ● • • • •

I'm pulled awkwardly into a tight hug by my mother, her scent wraps around me. The rose and almond calms my nerves, but I keep my arms at my side, refusing to show affection to someone who's lied to me every day of my life. Someone who's sold me in the name of protection.

"I know you're upset with me now, Melinoe, but one day you'll understand." She wipes beneath her eyes where a tear trickles down her cheek.

I stare blankly at her, willing some retort to hurt her the way she's hurt me. Nothing comes to mind, and I turn to Selene. She sinks into a deep curtsy and rises, and I pull her in for a hug, my mother hissing through her teeth beside us.

"I'll miss you, Selene," I whisper in her ear. For her I will show emotion and love.

"Take care of yourself, Princess, and remember who you are. Remember *what* you are." She pulls away and stares deep into my eyes, nodding.

"We'll be off then," Hades booms behind me, beckoning to the saddled horse. I press my lips together and approach the familiar gelding. I whip back to Selene, who smiles widely.

"It's Arion," I tell her, the horse gifted to her by my mother.

"He's older and slower now, but he will give you strength on your journey, as he did for me once." I feel tears brim and they curl slowly down my cheeks. Sniffling, I nod my thanks and, with Prince Castor's help, climb into the saddle. I take the reins and set off behind the caravan. Goodbye, Mother, I think sadly. I don't turn back; I only press forward.

· · · ● · ● · · · ·

I stay quiet as we travel along the Cocytus, the river of lamentation. Our route is fitting, as I am holding in my own anguish, burying it deep down and thinning my lips to keep the sobs from escaping, but the souls' wailing from the waters seeps into the air, drowning out the rushing river. Castor's eyes dart around, trying to pinpoint the source of the sound, but I know the sadness comes from the Cocytus itself, the souls' anguish a constant drone beseeching forgiveness from those they've harmed. I keep a steely gaze forward and do my best to ignore the agonized keening surrounding us.

We travel for only a few hours before arriving at Cape Taenarum. The prince and I dismount and approach a hollow cave, its mouth yawning wide. While Prince Castor is new to this journey, I've made it several times in the past with Hermes as part of my training in collecting offerings to the deceased.

"How does this work?" Castor asks, eyeing the expanse in front of us. The servants unload our meager trunks while Hades dismounts.

I point to the two-pronged staff that my father holds. "Leaving the Underworld without the bident is impossible. The staff is able to sunder the earth, creating a passage between the Lands of the Living and Dead. The portal will open here"—I gesture to the mouth of the cave—"and we will cross through into Taenarus on the other side."

Hades approaches us, his eyebrows raised, and pulls me aside. "Are you ready?"

I smirk. "If I said no, would it matter?" I lower my gaze, ashamed that I've let him down.

He reaches for my chin, lifting it so my eyes meet his. "Melinoe, my daughter, this was not an easy decision for your mother nor for me, but it's the best one to keep you and our kingdom safe."

I swallow the lump in my throat and nod.

"You will meet the prince's family, acquaint yourself with their kingdom, and serve as my emissary until I summon you to return. Keep up with your training and continue working on your magic if you wish." He pulls me in for a hug, and as I'm pressed against his chest, tears pool in my eyes. Feeling a drop on my scalp, I pull away and glance up. The king of the Underworld, the mighty Hades himself, has a single tear streaming down his cheek.

For me.

His failure of a daughter.

His useless heiress.

My heart breaks in two at the damage I've done, my chin wobbling as I hold in the despair I feel.

"I'm so sor—"

"Don't," he commands, cupping my cheek. "Don't you dare apologize. I'm the one who's sorry. I'm sorry it has to be this way." His hand drops away, and I'm left feeling empty and broken.

I step back toward Castor and watch as my father unseals the doorway between the realms. He points the bident at the cave, the sky darkening around us. The air goes still and pressure fills my ears. "*Anoixe tin pórta. Fos anamméno,*" he intones. "*Xekleidóste tin pórta. Steílte to fos!*" The portal appears before us, dust circling the cave opening.

I peer through the opening and see a beautiful blue sky and lush green grass atop a cliff. Sparkling cerulean sea water curls in the distance. I gasp at the vibrant colors. Most of my visits to the Land of the Living have occurred in the middle of the night, and I am enchanted by the beauty I see before me.

I glance at Prince Castor, who smiles and holds out his hand. I find myself placing mine in his, and we step through the gateway. Together.

Welcome back, my little witch. The very same deep male voice from last night hums in my ear as I pass between the realms. I swing my head left and then right, but only see the tear in the earth. *Your destiny with me awaits.* Taking another step, I plunge into Taenarus, the sound of the ocean's waves in the distance drowning out everything else. I release the prince's hand and step away from him, drawing my brows together and looking around. The sun is so bright that I'm forced to squint and shield my face, my eyes watering.

While the servants quickly pass to-and-fro through the portal, loading our trunks into the waiting wagon, I find myself staring up at a rider on a massive mount. His golden-blond tresses furl in the gentle breeze and his chin juts out toward us.

"Welcome home, brother," he says, leaning from his horse to grasp Castor's forearm in greeting. "This must be her." He gives me a dismissive glance.

"This is Princess Melinoe, Pollux."

I draw myself up to my full height and dip a curtsy to Castor's twin. Pollux gives me the briefest nod before turning his stallion around. My blood boils at the affront.

"I've arranged a carriage for your wife, and your stallion has been saddled, brother." Pollux canters away and my mouth gapes open.

"I will not ride in a carriage, Prince," I hiss under my breath. "I will enter Sparta alongside you and your brother, not hidden away like a delicate damsel."

Castor shrugs nonchalantly. "Unfortunately my brother has only brought one horse, mine. You can either ride within the carriage or double with me on the stallion."

My shoulders fall, and I flick my gaze between the carriage and Castor. While I don't want to be seen as a weak woman riding in the carriage, the thought of my body pressed against the prince's makes my lip curl in disgust.

He taps his foot impatiently. "Which will it be, Princess?"

I sigh dejectedly and point to the horse. Castor smirks at me, chuckling under his breath. "You sure are stubborn. Not that I mind in this case," he mutters under his breath. He winks and my body goes warm.

I crinkle my brow in confusion, wanting to hate this man I've been chained to, but also wanting to see his naked torso again, run my hands along the sharp edges of his stomach. What is wrong with me?

He moves to assist me in mounting the beast, but I swat his hand away. I stick my foot in the stirrup and launch my other leg over the horse's back, settling in easily. I cock an eyebrow. He mounts himself onto the horse just as easily and presses his pelvis into my rear. Wrapping his hands around my waist, he adjusts the two of us, holding my hips as he presses his body securely against me, and a delicious warmth spreads through my chest. I'm lucky he can't see the flush creep into my cheeks.

"Are you ready?" he whispers into my neck, his breath tickling deliciously.

I cough, clearing my throat, "As I'll ever be," I respond, purposefully whipping my hair into his face and taking a strengthening breath as we canter toward my new home.

· · · ● · ● ● · · ·

We ride into the city of Sparta, and my eyes widen at the beauty around me. Built on the banks of the Eurotas River, the capital is magnificent. Castor points in the distance. "That's Mount Taygetus in the west, and over there"—he gestures with a pointed finger in the opposite direction—"is Mount Parnon in the east." He trails his fingers down my arm as he reaches around to take up the reins again. I hold in the shiver he's caused, but a delicious heat pools in my belly. I look around and note that the poisonous purple-flowering wolfsbane is bountiful, dotting the hillsides around the city. I make a mental note to acquire some of the herb to dry and preserve. The valley formed by the mountains is also abundant in almond trees, with their pink and white blossoms, and ash trees, which scent the air with the heady smell of the sweet sap called manna.

"It's beautiful," I admit begrudgingly. The sun kisses my skin, and for the first time in days, I feel like smiling. I'm not sure if it's the influx of sunlight or the beauty surrounding me, but I'm not thinking about my failing magic or feeling angry at my situation. I'm excited for a new adventure, eager to learn about Sparta and act as an emissary for my father. Maybe this won't be so bad.

We dismount in the courtyard of a grand palace. The white stone columns shine against the bright sun, blinding me as we walk up the steps. A welcome party has congregated, standing regally in a row, ready to be introduced. As I take in their faces, I stop on the girl at the end. She is the most beautiful person I've ever laid eyes on. She notices me gaping and offers a smile, dazzling me with her straight white teeth, bright blond hair, and her brother's ocean-blue eyes.

"Welcome home, son," King Tyndareus extends his forearm toward Castor, who clasps it.

"Father, I'd like to introduce Melinoe, Princess of the Underworld, and my wife."

Castor's father bends deeply at the waist, his head nearly touching the bright stones underfoot. As the immortal daughter of the king and queen of the Underworld, my rank precedes a mortal king.

"Rise, King Tyndareus." I smile broadly at him as I take his hand in mine. While warm, his palm is rough and calloused, his face weathered, both from his life of soldiering. He puts me at ease, and I sense kindness in him. Castor escorts me farther down the row to his mother.

"And this is my mother, Queen Leda." She lowers herself into a curtsy, and I nod accordingly.

"Welcome to our home, Princess. I hope you will feel safe and protected here."

I smile wanly at the barbed protection comment, drawing back to Castor's side. I'm further introduced to the Spartan children: Clytemnestra, Timandra, Philonoe, and finally, Helen, the beautiful girl on the end.

"I've been so excited to meet you," she gushes, launching herself at me for a hug. I'm taken aback and stiffen slightly before Castor breaks us apart.

He chuckles. "Careful, sister. There will be plenty of time for you two to form a friendship." Addressing his family he says, "Now, if you'll excuse us, I'm going to show the princess to our rooms." He bows and, taking my hand, pulls me along.

Our rooms? I flash him a questioning look, but he waits until we're out of earshot before answering.

Drawing me close, he whispers in my ear, "Seeing as we're newly married, *wife*, it would be unseemly and raise many questions to have separate quarters." His jaw tightens and he jerks me along, faster now. I struggle to keep up with his brusque steps and, before long, find myself winded.

"Will you slow down?" I plant my feet and yank my tingling hand from his. My anger flares and a spark shoots out of my fingertip. It hits Castor square in the chest, and he stumbles back with a bark. Startled, he clutches his chest, staring down in disbelief. The spark has burned out, leaving a scorched circle on his tunic. "I-I'm so sorry. Are you all right?" I rush to him and start patting his chest, assessing for injuries.

He grabs my hands and lowers them to my side. "I'm fine." He stares long and hard at me, unblinking, his eyes angry and cold. His gaze flicks around the room and he pulls me close, hissing in my ear, "Don't do that again." Turning on his heel, he proceeds at his previous pace, leaving me to run to keep up.

"I-I don't know what that was, Castor," I admit.

"It's fine, Melinoe. Think nothing of it. But please, *control* yourself while you're here. My family isn't exactly trusting of the gods or sporadic magic." His words bite at me and the air leaves my lungs.

Control myself? I narrow my eyes at his back and my nostrils flare. I feel the heat return to my fingertips and instantly my body goes cold. What is happening? Before I can spend too much time analyzing the situation, Castor suddenly stops in his tracks and gestures to a door on his right. "This is our room." He turns the knob and pushes it open, signaling me to enter first.

I step into the chamber and am awestruck by the opulence. A giant canopied bed with gossamer curtains takes up most of the space while a fire roars in the hearth, and a copper tub sits in front of a balcony that looks out to the mountains. I circle around in my examination of the room and find myself face-to-face with Castor.

"It will do." I nod, holding back that I'm impressed.

He quirks up an eyebrow and snorts.

I let out a heavy sigh. "It's very fine," I admit.

He smiles genuinely and turns to leave.

"Where are you going?"

"I have business to attend. Make yourself at home." He shuts the door loudly behind himself, and with that, he's gone and I'm completely alone.

CASTOR

I stalk away from our shared chambers as quickly as I can. I need to ensure that no servants saw Melinoe's magic, as our family is not keen on trusting the gods or their abilities. After all, once Zeus attacked and impregnated my mother—not once, but twice—a healthy distrust of the Olympians and their king is understandable.

When I'm satisfied that gossip among the staff is curtailed, I rush to the gardens, my boots pounding heavily on the marble beneath my feet. I need fresh air and to release some tension. Perhaps I'll stop by the training fields and knock out some of my combat mates. A fist fight and a couple of broken noses fixes everything.

Rubbing the back of my neck, I shake my head. This whole marriage was a horrible idea. I definitely did not know what I was getting myself into, *who* I was getting involved with.

When Queen Persephone begged for an audience with my father, he had no idea she wanted an alliance between our kingdoms. If anything, Father assumed she was here to ask for help in releasing her from Hades's shithole of a kingdom. It wasn't until she started describing her daughter in detail that it dawned on him. She wanted a marriage to align our two realms. Of course my father was ecstatic. Marry the daughter of a goddess and help her rule the second most powerful kingdom in the land? It wasn't even a choice. Of course *we* would accept. What *I* wanted was never a consideration.

I pass the gardens and keep walking, hiking toward the hills. My heart feels as though it will burst from my chest if I don't keep moving. I clench and unclench my fists, trying to think about anything other than the beautiful woman sitting alone in my room.

What was I thinking getting involved in this? I pull my sword from its scabbard and swipe mindlessly at vines and shrubs as I continue stalking through the hills. I'm no Zeus, I refuse to force myself on an unwilling lady, but I'm no saint either. Riding behind her had been torture. It'd taken all my control not to stop our horse and have her right in the middle of the roadway. If only Pollux hadn't been with us . . .

Who am I kidding? Melinoe is more likely to flay me from stomach to throat than fuck me. Taking advantage of her would be impossible. The more I learn about her, the more I'm intrigued. Stubborn but strong. Beautiful in her appearance, but brutal with her words. She truly is a dichotomy.

I hadn't been surprised when she refused the carriage, but I certainly did not know how my body would react having hers so close to me. Her tight ass pressed into my groin as the horse cantered from side to side was almost more than I could take. Her hair smelled delicious, and I know she felt something when I whispered into her neck to point out the various sights as we traveled. I could sense her body tensing, straightening in the saddle, each time. I chuckle, thinking maybe I've tormented her just as much as she's tormented me. I feel myself grow hard, the seam of my pants pressing painfully against my length.

Trying, and failing, to tamp down my arousal, I continue slicing through the foliage. I can't lose focus. I've been commanded to keep her safe until it is time for her to return to Olympus, and for my family's sake alone, that is what I'll do.

Melinoe

"Let's try another one, my dearest." Grandmother smiles gently, her soft palm cupping my cheek. My brow furrowing as I give a quick nod, I hold my tingling hands out in front of me and recite the words written on the scroll.

"Liónei," I intone, my muscles tightening all over my tiny body as I wait to see if I've melted the flower in the vase. When nothing happens, I slowly lower my hands, my body sagging in defeat, my face crumpling. I'm afraid I've disappointed Grandmama, and the worry etches itself on my face as I raise my watery gaze to hers.

Grandmother rushes forward, her eyes alight with worry. "No, no, no, dearest. There's no need for tears." She envelops me, stroking my wild curls as I bury my face into her wrinkled bosom. Grandmama Phoebe may be ancient, but her wit and wisdom are still known throughout the realm. She's taken charge of helping me hone my magic while Mother is away, assisting in the birth of Rhea's new baby.

I try to control my emotions, as my mother has always commanded, but, as the salty drops leak from my eyes, the frustration becomes unbearable, my throat tightening. "I can't do it, Grandmama," I whine to her.

She pulls back, her brows lowering over her eyes angrily. "Don't you dare say that! You can do anything. You are my special little witch. You are more powerful than you believe; you must simply work harder. Without hard work, how will you ever fulfill your own destiny, child?" She reaches for the scroll, unfurling it and *laying it flat before me. "Now, let's look at the enchantment." She points to the word on the paper. "Tell me how you pronounced it."*

"Liónei." I stretch out each letter, my tongue poking the gap of a missing front tooth. I raise my eyes to hers, swiping away the tears. "Liónei," I repeat.

Her eyes drop to the scrawled word, her finger dragging under it, as she points out my mistakes. "It's pronounced lee-oh-knee. The first i makes a long e sound. And the ei on the end also make a long e too. Liónei," she enunciates.

I smile slowly. "Liónei," I parrot back.

Her eyes widen and she claps. "There you go! You've got it now. Let's try again." She pulls me to the center of the room and, situating herself in the corner, nods encouragingly at the red rose in the vase.

Inhaling deeply, I close my eyes, imagining the flower as it melts, the deep color running down the vase, pooling on the table beneath. The green of the stem slicking the inside of the vessel like wax, its melted hue much darker as it congeals.

I open my eyes, my hands already extended, and, on an exhale, release the word from somewhere deep inside. "Liónei."

· · · ● · ● · · ·

I awake the next morning to a knock on the door, in an unfamiliar bed, staring at an unfamiliar ceiling. It takes me a moment to adjust and realize that I'm in Sparta, not the Underworld, despite the dream. I'd thought, even hoped, that once I was in the Land of the Living, the mysterious dreams would cease. Furrowing my brow, I try to grab threads of the dream before it's lost to the ether, but all I can recall is a woman I called *Grandmama*. I close my eyes and pull at the thread, wishing this woman's appearance to come into focus. Something in my gut tells me this isn't Grandmother Demeter, a goddess I've only met a handful of times during my brief visits to the Land of the Living with Hermes. If only I could visualize, could remember my dreams, then perhaps

I could analyze them, understand the messages hidden within, but nothing appears.

Dejected, I reach over and feel for Castor, thinking he must have sneaked in after I fell asleep. Finding nothing but the soft comforter, I sit up and check the floor. A pillow and blanket lie abandoned in front of the hearth.

"Good morning, Princess," the stout handmaiden greets cheerily as she enters without my command. "I've come to help you dress and then show you to Princess Helen's room. She has invited you to break your fast with her."

I go through the motions of getting dressed and coiffed. I'm outfitted in a completely ridiculous gown, suited more for a ballroom than breakfast, and am then ushered to the princess's chambers.

"Sister!" Helen pulls me into a tight hug before gesturing for me to have a seat at the table. I look around and my jaw drops. Everything, from bedding to curtains to carpets . . . everything is *gold*. "Do you like my rooms?" I struggle to admit how garish it looks compared to the darkness of the Underworld court, but her smile is blinding. I'm drawn into it, unable to be the reason it dims.

I sit gingerly, careful not to wrinkle the ruffled dress. "It's lovely." I offer a small smile and take a sip of tea to avoid saying anything else. "Have you seen Prince Castor this morning?"

She swats at the air. "Oh, he's off training with Pollux. They're always the first to rise. You likely won't see him until dinner, which is perfect because we can spend all day together!" I nod, unsure what I have in common with this beautiful, yet clearly vapid, creature.

"So what do you do all day?" I think on the schedule I kept in the Underworld. Between my magic courses with Hermes, my training with Trophonius, and the lessons from Father on running a kingdom, I never had time to just . . . be. How does a married princess, with no prospects of undertaking her duties anytime soon, spend her endless days?

"We weave, read aloud from Mother's favorite scrolls, and play the lyre. Oh, and we take walks about the grounds for exercise." I'm speechless, as it all sounds utterly boring to be honest. My ability to weave is even worse than my ability to summon magic, and I play the lyre about as decently as Cerberus would.

"Will we read petitions from the people?" This I may enjoy, as I'm a knowledgeable diplomat, thanks to Hades's training.

She giggles, her voice tinkling. "Of course not. Mother prefers to read poems." I try not to curl my lip in disgust.

"Do you ever train? Visit the villagers? Sit in with your mother and father when they hear concerns from the citizens?" I can't believe the sheltered life this beautiful, caged bird has lived. And, what's even worse, she seems *content* to be nothing more than a pretty decoration. My brows lower at the thought, knowing I could never just sit still and be admired.

"Of course not." She laughs. "Why would I want to do that?" I press my lips tightly together and sigh heavily. How am I ever going to survive here?

· · · ● · ● · ● · ·

Somehow Helen and I both make it to dinner. I've changed for the third time, even though my clothing never got dirtied, and I now don an evening gown, rather than a day gown or a walking-outside gown. After only a single day, the tedium has nearly driven me to insanity. I enter the dining hall and am escorted to my seat, finally coming face-to-face with Prince Castor. He is freshly bathed and the scent of orange and bergamot tingles my nose. His blond hair gleaming, he offers me a smile as I incline my head.

"How was your day, wife?" he asks quietly, cutting into his food, not meeting my eye.

Not one to mince words, I decide to be blunt. "Tedious." I hiss, laying the word out flat on the table for him. I raise my eyebrows and cross my arms, refusing to eat or drink until he acknowledges what I've said.

"Oh? Playing the lyre not to your liking?" His head tilts to the side, mocking me, as he chews his food.

Before I can respond, the table falls quiet and the family's eyes are all on me. My mouth gapes and I realize they're waiting for me to respond. "My apologies, what did you ask?" I smile sweetly at the table.

King Tyndareus repeats himself. "How did you find your first day in Sparta, daughter?"

"Quite a challenge, Your Highness," I admit loudly for all to hear, including Castor. I refuse to lie or play these courtly games. I've had enough of deceptions in the past weeks.

"How so? Did something happen today, Helen?" the king inquires of his golden princess.

She blinks rapidly, mouth agape. "No, Father. Princess Melinoe and I had a lovely day." Her brow furrows in confusion, and a look of hurt crosses her eyes as she meets my gaze from farther down the table.

Shit, I've hurt my only friend's feelings. I hurry to clarify. "I'm just not used to not being needed on the training field, in the advisor's council meeting, or at my various lessons." I lower my gaze in a show of contrition, which I don't actually feel at all. I'll not apologize for wanting to serve a purpose here.

The king lets out a jolly laugh, shaking the hall and startling me in the process. "Daughter, I had no idea you wanted to continue your training and learn the Spartan ways." He turns to Castor now, his expression darkening. "Son, why didn't you take your wife to the arena with you this morning? Do you care naught for her *desires* already?" My cheeks flame at the insinuation and I flick my eyes to Castor.

He opens and closes his mouth, clearly searching for something to say without giving away the truth of our marriage. I watch in amusement before speaking up, saving him. "Husband, I'd love to come to the training fields with you tomorrow. I very much look forward to it." I offer him a sarcastic smile and, finally, tuck in to my food.

• • • • ● • ● • ● • •

The Spartan training uniform for women is much less modest than my Underworld kit. A form-fitting tunic, belted at the waist, falls to my shins and is slit on either side up to my thighs. Leather cuffs slide up my forearms, while a set of leather caps cover my shoulders. Leather straps crisscross my chest to hold my weapon holsters in place on my back. Finally, bronze shin guards strap to my legs and are held in place by my laced sandals. As I step into the arena, I feel Castor's gaze travel up my exposed legs, and my nipples harden beneath the gear.

I feel completely at ease in my leathers; unfortunately, the Spartan helmet, forged in bronze, will take some getting used to. It's heavy, with only a single opening for my eyes, nose, and mouth. The plume at the top, also made of bronze, adds additional weight, causing my balance to be off. I roll my neck, attempting to get used to the extra heft, and lunge toward Castor with my blade extended.

He blocks easily, slashing across my middle and striking against my chest with his fist. The leather stops the knife from hitting skin, but I'm sent flying through the air and land hard on my ass, wincing with pain and embarrassment.

He stands over me, large hand reaching down, and I take it. "Again," he mutters stoically, lifting me effortlessly to my feet. Already, sweat drips from my brow and into my eyes. My hair has loosened from its braid and sticks to my forehead. I'm positive I look a fright, but I'd much rather be out here than weaving and making small talk over pastries with the beautiful Helen.

I try to slow my breathing and toss my sword from hand to hand, considering my maneuver. I dance from foot to foot, swiping left and then right, before landing a strike against his thigh. He laughs, and, for some reason, I feel the corners of my lips lift. I like when he smiles, the sound of his enjoyment.

"It's about time you got me."

I refocus, narrowing my eyes and baring my teeth, a fire igniting within. "Again," I snarl, now wishing to wipe that grin off his gloating face. We both step to the line and begin slashing. I lunge forward and am immediately blocked, my sword flying loose from my grip and landing out of reach. I deftly reach for the dagger in the metal shin guards and slice up toward the fleshy part under his arm, hitting my mark. Castor sucks in his breath, hissing.

I whip my head and swiftly sidestep, but a blinding pain sears through my scalp. I'm yanked backward into his chest. He fists my braid as he wraps it around my neck. Pulling tightly, he brings his blade up to my throat and whispers against the helmet, "I win." My body sags in defeat.

He releases my hair and I flip around, shoving him away. Without realizing it, I've summoned my magic, and he's thrown across the field, landing flat on his back in a cloud of dust.

My mouth drops open, and my heart falls into my stomach. "Aw shit," I mutter to myself, tucking my blade into my shin guard before I jog to his side, tossing the heavy helmet into the dirt. While I'm glad my magic is materializing more and more, I'm frustrated at my inability to control it.

As I stand over Castor's unconscious form, a cool breeze brushes past my cheek. *Now is your time, my little witch. End him. Free yourself and fulfill your destiny with me.*

The familiar deep male voice pierces my mind and my gaze snaps up, my hands shielding my eyes against the blinding sun to look around the empty training field.

"Who are you?" I shout into the air. Castor's body lies mere feet away. I watch, noting his chest rising and falling, but he doesn't stir.

I am your power, your magic, all your desires. Return to me.

A large shadow appears next to the prince. I squint my eyes, trying to make out a face to match the voice. "Stay away from him," I finally growl, taking slow steps forward. I reach for my dagger and keep my eyes trained on this phantom.

If only you had killed him on your wedding night with the knife, like I suggested. The phantom pauses, waiting, but I only narrow my eyes and reach for my sword.

Remembering Castor had knocked it from my grip, I mutter a curse under my breath.

What will you give me to protect him? What is this mortal prince worth to you?

"Leave him alone. It's me you're after, yes?"

Yes, it's you that I want. It's your soul. Your love. Be one with me. It's time.

I look down at Castor, but ultimately know there's no consideration needed. I would never let an innocent die to protect myself. Hades raised me better. I'm a fighter, a warrior.

I raise my chin, "Fine. Tell me what to do." I spit my answer at the shadow.

Make your way to Mount Olympus. I have the answers you seek to free yourself and your magic.

I blink, wanting to ask more. How does this shadowy figure know about my magic, or lack thereof?

I step forward, but the man disappears, melting into the air. The second he's gone, I scramble to Castor and pull up his shirt, leaning my cheek to his chest. My fingers hover over the trail of curls at his navel, and as I press my ear to hear his beating heart, I follow their path farther down into the deep V that disappears into his leathers. Gulping heavily, I find he's unmarked and still breathing. I move to his head, carefully remove his helmet, and gently brush his sweaty hair from his eyes.

"Castor . . ." My heart constricts as endless scenarios flash through my mind. If I hurt him, I'll never forgive myself. I lean forward slightly, checking for any wounds near his hairline, my fingers tangling in the blond tresses. My chest is pressed to his mouth, and I feel his breath through the material, my breasts tightening with desire.

Satisfied that there are no visible injuries to his head, I start to lean back onto my heels when his eyes flash open. I begin to speak—to apologize—but he reaches up and grasps the back of my head, pulling me down and devouring my mouth hungrily. I gasp in surprise against his warm mouth, but don't pull away. I can smell our sweat on each other and taste his saltiness in my mouth as he slides his tongue through my parted lips. I run my fingers through his hair, dropping my hands to his muscular shoulders as he pulls me on top of him. He lifts up, meeting me midway as our kiss deepens, his hands running along my back.

I feel him stir beneath my thighs, and with a heavy sigh against my mouth, he breaks the kiss as his head drops down to the earth. His eyes move from my swollen lips to meet my gaze. "I think that's enough for today," he says, flashing that annoying smirk. I'm not sure if he means the training or the kiss, but as I break eye contact and stand, offering my hand to help him up, I am unexpectedly disappointed.

· · · ● · ● · · · ·

Castor and I continue our daily training, but we never bring up our kiss or his injury from my magic. Instead, we both completely ignore anything that could spark meaningful conversation about either topic. Our sparring together becomes strained, our movements designed to never get too close to one another. His lunges and my subsequent blocks are shoddy at best, as it's clear he's trying to keep from touching me and I'm trying to avoid setting off my uninhibited powers.

It's not long before Pollux, deciding to join us for a day in the arena, calls us on our weak training. "What did I just watch?" He grimaces, looking between the two of us. Castor is hardly sweating, and my own breathing isn't even close to being labored. Neither of us has put in any real work today. I flick my gaze to my husband, who is eyeing me warily.

"Brother, you could have easily blocked her when she shot across your midsection and struck!" His brow lowers in frustration as he lectures Castor. "Princess, while you had a great shot setup and you struck with ease, there was no fight or strength behind it." I lower my eyes and my cheeks flush. I don't recall ever being lectured on my failures in the arena, and I'm mortified at Pollux thinking I'm lacking in skill or ability.

"Melinoe!" I see Helen gesturing for me as she makes her way across the lawn, and I hurry to meet her at the entrance to the ring. "Did you forget that we have to get ready for this evening's banquet?" She turns to her brothers and shouts, "Father says you have only a short time yourselves. The emissaries from Larissa arrived hours ago!" She watches on bouncing toes as I unhook and carry my weapons into the barn before she grabs my hand and pulls me along toward the palace. I sneak a glance back and catch Castor's gaze, offering him a small smile and a shrug.

Sniffing and making a sour face as we walk, Helen pushes me away. "You stink. We'll have to hurry if we're to make you presentable."

"If anyone can work magic on my appearance, it's you, Helen."

CASTOR

I watch as Helen and Melinoe saunter toward the castle before Pollux, having grabbed his own short blade, kicks my legs out and has me on my back, knife to the throat.

"Brother, what is going on with you and your wife? You're awfully distracted lately." Still holding the blade to me, Pollux searches my eyes. My own gaze flicks to Melinoe's retreating back as she hikes away, the Spartan leather skirt not hiding much of her pert ass. Her strong thighs and toned arms have turned a delicious golden tan from our time in the sunny training arena, and it's a nice change from the pale waif she was in the Underworld.

Turning back to my twin, I shake my head, refusing to answer. He presses the blade closer, adding a knee to my chest.

"You'll not escape until you tell me the truth." He puts all his weight onto the knee, and the air is sucked from my lungs.

"Fine!" I manage between gasps. "Let up, I'll explain," He releases me and I roll to my side, coughing into the dirt. He helps me up and, from his belt, tosses me a skin of water. I drink thirstily, attempting to stall the conversation.

"Well? Tell me, Castor, is married life all they say? Is that what's keeping your head in the clouds?" He's mistaken, but I don't bother to correct his error. If he thinks I'm distracted and a mess because Melinoe and I are fucking like rabbits, so be it. It's better than the truth.

I shrug and give him a wink, ambling toward the training barn to discard my weapons and clean up.

"You know, brother, I've been thinking of acquiring myself a wife."

I fiddle with my belt, frowning at him.

"Her name is Hilaeira," he adds.

"Isn't she betrothed to our cousin Idas? Or is it our cousin Lynceus?" It doesn't surprise me that Pollux would be sniffing around a woman already taken. As the youngest son, he's been quite spoiled, always given whatever he desires with little consequence.

"What of it? She doesn't love him," he replies, never mentioning to which cousin she's plighted her troth. "Besides, you'll be dividing your time between our realm and the Underworld soon enough. I need someone to keep me company." He winks, tossing his blades sloppily into the barn. As usual, I retrieve them, placing them neatly where they belong.

"You shouldn't get married just because you might get bored without me, Pol," I say quietly.

"So why'd you do it, especially to someone tied to the Underworld?" He crosses his arms, barring my exit from the barn. There's no way I can tell him the truth, but he won't let me leave until I appease his curiosity.

"Honestly? Who wouldn't want a part of the crown of the Underworld if something happens to Hades? It's about power. And have you seen her ass?" I smirk as Pollux lets out a loud laugh and slaps me heartily on the back.

"I knew it," he says, heading back toward the castle.

I'm left alone in the dim light of the barn, my breath hitching and my stomach in knots. I need to make Melinoe believe this is a real marriage, that I'm all in and falling for her, utterly and completely. She has to trust me. I'll tell her, and my family, whatever I need to, even if it's a lie. Even if the lies leave me feeling nauseous, eating me up inside.

MELINOE

"My gods . . ." I turn away from the mirror and find Castor standing in the doorway to our chambers, his mouth agape and eyebrows raised. Heat warms my insides, and I offer him a tight smile.

"Your sister is very talented." I meet his gaze brazenly and twirl. My emerald-green gown is dotted with sparkling sequins. It gathers in the front, accentuating my waist, while the deep V neckline draws attention to my perky breasts. The sheer side panels show off a touch of sun-kissed skin, while my shoulders are covered by a diaphanous drape down my back. My black curls are piled atop my head with some tendrils hanging loosely.

Castor strides toward me, and I back up slightly, my hand coming to my stomach. "My sister has nothing to do with your beauty, Melinoe." He's so close I can smell his cologne and my thighs tighten involuntarily. He tucks a curl behind my ear, brushing his fingers along my neck as he does so. A delicious shiver passes through me and I swallow, leaning into his touch. As one hand travels down the curve of my throat, the other grabs my hand, raising it to his lips and pressing a soft kiss to my skin. A smirk dances along my reddened lips. "I suppose we should make our way down to the banquet," he says, breaking the spell. I swallow the lump in my throat and nod, but I notice that he's still holding my hand as we leave the rooms, and I find myself smiling just a little wider because of it.

$$\cdot\,\cdot\,\cdot\,\bullet\,\cdot\,\bullet\,\cdot\,\bullet\,\cdot\,\cdot$$

"It's a pleasure to meet you, Princess Melinoe." King Pirithous bows as I incline my head in acknowledgment. I feel his gaze lingering on my breasts, and I try to keep my gaze lowered, but what I really want to do is raise my blade to his throat for the blatant ogling he's doing. I sense Castor stiffen at my side, noticing the leering king. Pirithous takes my hand and raises it to his lips, but I inhale sharply, pulling slightly away. "I would be utterly delighted if you would honor me with this dance." A smile lifts his mustached mouth, and I swallow down the bile burning the back of my throat as his gaze continues to roam over me.

"Of course, Your Highness," I demure, my skin crawling at his wandering eyes. I am not looking forward to being manhandled by some mortal king, but I take a strengthening breath and follow him to the dance floor. I feel Castor's eyes on my back, and when I turn, his gaze is dark, filled with the same rage as the night he rescued me from Trophonius. His expression is pinched, but a flush tints his cheeks and his mouth is turned down. Is that jealousy I detect?

There's a tightening under his eyes, but as he sees me bite my lip, his posture seems to relax. He leans back against the wall but keeps his gaze trained on me. King Pirithous takes my hand and leads me in an unfamiliar dance, his other hand inching lower and lower along my back.

I tear my gaze from Castor and throw ice into my voice. "Your hand will go no lower, Your Highness, else you want it broken." I smile sweetly and continue to follow his steps.

"My, you're a feisty one. I love your spirit. Once upon a time I knew your mother. She, too, was a lively one, so devoted to that barbaric husband of hers." He bends down to whisper in my ear, my skin crawling, "We in the Land of the Living know she could've done so much better than Hades."

My eyes snap up to Pirithous's face as my fists clench around his neck. "That 'barbaric husband of hers' is my father, Your Highness." I grind my teeth together, trying to keep my composure as this disgusting human speaks poorly of the greatest man I've ever known. Hades is an amazing father, even if I'm not his by blood, and he's my personal hero, the one man in my life whom I can trust above all others. I'll not stand to have his reputation besmirched by this upstart nobody.

"Your father, you say?" Pirithous's gaze becomes shrewd as his eyes narrow.

I attempt to pull away, but he tightens his hold, pulling me closer.

"A wife such as you would do well in my kingdom."

I blink rapidly, but keep a smile plastered to my face. "I'm afraid that I'm very much taken, as you are aware."

"I suppose that's a shame; if I couldn't have your mother, I would've loved a saucy little nymph like you for a wife."

I suppress the urge to claw at this man's face as I bare my teeth.

"I imagine you're an accomplished lover, what with that impudent mouth of yours." He reaches down and cups my ass, giving it a sharp pinch.

Disgusted at his forwardness, I yank my tingling hand from his and slap it across his face. The dancers around us pause their steps, and the hall goes still. "I believe we've had enough dancing." Stepping away from him, I raise my chin and make my way back to Castor, who quirks an eyebrow at me. I press my lips together and shake my head ever so slightly. I can handle my own battles.

His fingers brush against my still-tingling hand, heat shooting through my arm and up my neck. We say nothing as we stand shoulder to shoulder, observing the merrymaking that continues despite my outburst and making small talk with courtiers and visiting dignitaries.

I keep my eyes trained on Helen, who appears to be the center of attention at this banquet. She's gone from dancer to dancer, never taking a break, as she's twirled around the dance floor to each new tune. Her long golden locks are in a similar updo style as mine, with straight wisps framing her heart-shaped face. As she accepts a new partner, her pink-tinged smile dazzles the gentleman, whose cheeks flush with delight at partnering the beauteous Helen of Sparta.

But there's a hardness in her eyes, a fatigue that flashes in spurts as her father accepts the next dance on her behalf. She's exhausted. My heart pounds in my ears, a lump forming in my throat. Helen and I may be different, but I'm eager to have a new friend. A sister. And maybe we can both learn something from one another. I make it my mission to try harder to solidify our friendship.

Hours later, as the ball winds down, Castor finally turns to me and, shyly, asks, "Would you like to dance, wife?"

I look at him, those blue eyes hoping I'll agree, and nod. "It took you long enough to ask," I retort as I take his hand and, hips swaying, pull him to the dance floor.

"I wasn't sure if you'd agree, seeing as our last dance ended with you abandoning me in front of your people on the night of our betrothal."

I incline my head, admitting that I was a bit harsh. "Things have changed," I state simply.

His brows furrow. "What's changed, exactly, Melinoe?"

I blink, not sure how to admit to him all the thoughts running rampant in my mind. Instead, I just shrug. We dance quietly for a few moments. "I like it here. Your home. It's very lovely."

He smiles down at me, and I can see I've made him proud in some small way. My cheeks feel flushed, and I find that I like having this effect on him. I like making him smile. My breath hitches and it comes to me, unbidden. I *like* my husband. I roll my eyes and shake my head, thinking the gods must be laughing at me right now.

· · · ● · ● · ● · · ·

"King Pirithous certainly had a wandering eye." Helen chuckles as we sun ourselves the next day. I pluck a grape from the basket full of food and pop it into my mouth.

"And a wandering hand," I respond, swallowing the tart juice.

"My brother was not happy that you accepted a dance with that lascivious lecher."

"No, but I can take care of myself. I threatened to break his hand if he slid it any lower."

Helen snorts. "You did not!"

I chuckle and nod, and we both fall back in the grass, howling with laughter. It's nice to have a female friend, and I realize that I'm enjoying my time in Sparta. King Tyndareus's family is wonderful, and the landscape is breathtaking. I close my eyes and inhale the scent of manna from the ash trees bordering the palace grounds. With the sun shining so brightly, my closed eyelids appear red, and I'm reminded of the Underworld's crimson sky. As much as my heart calls for my home, I'm beginning to feel content in the Land of the Living and at the Spartan court. I continue to sun myself next to Helen, enjoying the warmth on my exposed skin.

Earlier today, Helen and I took a walk outside the palace, as I wanted to collect some wolfsbane. While I haven't spent a ton of time with my new sister-in-law, as I've been training daily with Castor and Pollux, I want to make an effort to grow my relationship with her, even if it means learning to sew and play the lyre better. As we walked through the lush forest bordering the castle grounds, she, too, collected various plants, sharing with me that she made an almond-scented perfume that drove her suitors mad. I laughed, but secretly wondered if that was the cause of her innumerable dance partners from the previous evening.

As I sit up to ask about her cosmetic tricks, a shadow falls over our blanketed picnic.

"Well what do we have here?"

I squint my eyes open, the sun blinding. The dark features of the two men standing above me are hard to make out. I don't recognize them as part of the court, with their blue-and-white tunics. I sit up and notice that Helen is trembling beside me. I reach for her hand and grasp it, holding tight.

"Who are you?" I demand, my voice stronger than I feel.

"We were sent by King Pirithous, Princess. Now get up before we yank both of you up by your beautiful hair."

I look down at my yellow day dress, wishing I had my training kit and blades on me. I stand and hoist Helen up, shielding her from the two towering men in front of us.

"Stay calm—" I start to whisper to Helen, but she unleashes a deafening scream, and as I turn to her, I feel my skull split open and everything goes black.

· · · · ● · ● · ● · ·

I've been living in the Underworld for quite some time, invited by the queen to stay and act as her adviser and companion, when I finally summon the nerve to make a visit to Tartarus, the storm-racked prison within the Underworld's bowels.

I tell no one of my journey, not my friend Persephone nor her husband, Hades, who controls the entirety of the Underworld. Instead, as I approach the bronze, gate-lined wall of the encampment, I'm accosted by one of the three Hecatoncheires. As I stare up, and up, and up even farther, I finally meet his gaze.

The myths surrounding this monster state he's hundred-handed with fifty heads, but as I behold his massive visage, I recite the disillusionment spell that will peel away his glamour.

"Ta mátia tou den vlépoun tin alítheia," I shout up to the giant, his windy roar turning into a simple face-spraying yell. He shuts his mouth and flinches away from me. Blinking the spittle from my eyes, I share my reason for visiting.

"I've come to see Coeus, my grandfather."

The giant grunts, realizing he doesn't stand a chance against the goddess of witchcraft, and, with a deafening grinding noise, opens the gates to the dungeon. I clasp my hands together to hide their trembling, hoping I am able to leave when the time comes. Taking a heartening breath, I push forward into the depths of the pit.

If the Underworld is full of sharp-edged grays and liquid blood red, Tartarus is a cold inky black, a feeling of emptiness and sadness that seeps into one's bones and exposes the fear within. I wrap my cloak tighter, but the frigid temperature seems to emanate from inside my body. I wonder if I'll ever be warm again.

Coeus is shackled to a granite table, and as I reach to touch his hand, he pulls away.

"If you touch me, the spells surrounding me will sap your magic, pull it straight from your marrow, and you'll be a prisoner here. Forever," he whispers under his breath, placing his hands back on the table as I lay mine in my lap. Terror snakes up my spine and I press my hands beneath my thighs to still the trembling—from both the cold and the horror at what I've risked coming here.

I look up into his graying face, the face of a Titan who hasn't seen the light of the sun in years. My heart breaks, but setting my jaw and lowering my voice, I ask the question I've come to get answered.

"Grandpapa, I've . . ." I gulp, unsure of how to voice what I've done. "I've hidden myself—protected myself, actually. From him." I refuse to utter his name, the one who forced me into this hopeless situation. The one who put my dear sweet Grand-papa in this horrible place. "But now I'm not sure I can set myself free again." My voice falls, and I look around, instantly feeling embarrassed for speaking of freedom in a place like this. "What if I'm not strong enough, Grandpapa? What if he—" The tears well in my eyes, stinging as my nose begins to drip.

Coeus starts to reach for me, then holds himself back, pulling his arms toward his chest. His eyes cloud over as his weathered skin trembles. "You have to keep fighting, Granddaughter. Keep fighting, even if the chains are stronger than you. You keep fighting. Every. Damn. Day." He punctuates the last words, pounding the chains loudly on the granite table. The grating sound echoes, and from a distance I hear the roars and hollers of his brethren, imprisoned here as well.

"That's enough!" A voice rains down on us, splitting my eardrums and nearly crushing my grandfather with some unseen magic. Giant Hecatoncheires ap-proach, hauling him up and carrying him away from me, even as he fights against

their strength. He roars in anger, pulling against the chains, but he's no match for the hundred-handed beasts that pull him away. Back into the pit.

"Grandpapa!" I yell, reaching out toward him, into darkness. My eyes search for his form, but I see nothing.

"Delphic Oracle," he manages to yell from the beyond.

"Delphic Oracle."

CASTOR

"What do you mean, my wife and sister have been abducted?" I growl at the servant who, bowing before me, trembles visibly. I run my hands through my hair to keep from punching the wall nearest me. My failure to protect Melinoe is going to cost me, and my heart plummets into my stomach at the realization that I've fucked up. Big time.

"Your Highness, I-I . . . I received word from our tower guards, who were knocked unconscious." I've yet to raise the messenger from his genuflection, so he continues to eye his shoes, the crown of his head breaking out in little dots of sweat as he strains to hold his bowed stance. His breathing has become shallow, whether from holding the kowtow or his fear, I don't know, nor do I care at this moment.

"What good are guards if they're incapable of protecting us?" I shout, the servant flinching at my outburst. I want answers. "Alert Prince Pollux immediately," I command the terrified servant. He rises on weakened legs and skitters away quickly.

As I grab my weapons, which I'd just discarded after coming in from my training exercises for the day, my mind goes wild. Has Zeus kidnapped Melinoe and, because she was also there, taken Helen as well? Did Hades find out about my true intentions?

Shaking my head and taking a breath, I force myself to revert to my soldier's training. One step at a time, with only known facts, is how I will rescue my bride and sister. The first step is to arm myself, preparing for battle. So, intending to stop at Pollux's room to grab a longbow and extra arrows as well, I strap my blades to my thighs, shoulder my scabbard, and add two daggers to my boot before heading to the door.

As I exit my chambers, I run straight into my brother, already prepared and outfitted with weapons. He tosses me the bowstring and shoves a quiver of arrows into my chest. "I knew you'd want more," he mutters bluntly, eyes focused as his boots echo down the hallway. I shoulder the additional weapons and run to catch up. "What do we know?" There's a murderous look mirrored in his eyes.

"The servants report that King Pirithous left unexpectedly this morning. Melinoe and Helen were taking a picnic just outside the palace walls when they were accosted. We've reports from the townsfolk that the two riders were seen heading north just over an hour ago." I can't believe that my wife, who I promised to protect, has been snatched right from under my nose.

I think back to our caresses last night at the ball. I'd been filled with rage when I saw that degenerate King Pirithous slide his hands suggestively down Melinoe's backside. My vision went red, and I wanted to throttle him right there on the dance floor until I witnessed the fury spark in his eyes at Melinoe's words. I didn't need to know what was said; she'd put him in his place, actually slapped the smirk off his face, and stalked off the dance floor, embarrassing him. My heart had soared with pride, but looking back, I know this is an act of retribution.

"I should've seen this coming."

"That traitorous bastard met with our father yesterday to sign a trade agreement between our two lands and then absconds with a princess of Sparta and an Underworld heiress. There's no way you could've seen this coming, brother." Pollux slaps my back heartily. "We'll get them back, I assure you."

I swallow the lump forming in my throat, hoping he's right. Hoping this isn't one of Zeus's little games. Hoping I'm still alive after he finds out.

89

MELINOE

My body is chilled, shivering in the darkness. I reach up to feel a gash at my hairline. Dried blood flakes into my lashes, and I wince in pain. Sitting up, I feel dizzy but manage to look around. Helen's unconscious form lies next to me, and I slink along the dirt in her direction.

"Helen," I hiss quietly, shaking her. "Helen!" I look around, noticing two horses tethered to a nearby tree and a fire crackling on the other side of Helen. She opens her eyes and blinks rapidly, her lip swollen and a purple bruise the size of my fist on her forehead. "Are you okay?" I keep my voice down as my eyes search wildly for the two men who've done this to us.

Her face crumples and tears leak from her eyes.

"Shh . . ." I soothe, rubbing her back as she sits up. I search for other injuries. "Can you walk?" She nods, sniffling. I stand and pull her to her feet. We've got to get moving, away from this encampment, if we have any chance of—"

"Just where do you think you're going?"

My blood runs cold and I turn, eyeing the man who appears across the fire. He's different from the men who took us from the palace, older and dressed in finer clothing.

His eyes are dead, devoid of emotion like the ghosts in the Underworld, and the red and orange shadows of the fire dance on his face.

"What do you want with us?" I raise my chin and force myself to meet his malevolent glare. I have no weapons on me, wearing nothing more than a dirtied yellow day dress, but I refuse to be seen as weak. I am a princess, daughter of a goddess, and I will fight to the death if attacked.

"You know what we want, Princess." He winks. My stomach drops. I swallow the bile rising in my throat. "We're going to make you our wives if you're well-behaved, and our whores if you're not. Either way, you belong to us now." He licks his lips, eyeing Helen lustfully. His partner comes up behind him, a venomous sneer crossing his face. King Pirithous. My brow furrows at the absurdity of the entire situation, and I snort in derision.

"Wait . . . You're behind this?" I gesture to the king. "That's impossible. You have no clue what you're doing. You can't kidnap us and expect to get away with it. You are aware of who my father is," I state bluntly. Hades would certainly hear about this; he would never allow his daughter to suffer at the hands of some presumptuous mortal royal scum.

Pirithous's gaze holds mine as his companion continues. "We know exactly what we're doing, daughter of *Zeus*." My body freezes and my heart stops. "Maybe you didn't realize, but we're going to make *two* daughters of Zeus our wives. And we're going to enjoy every minute of it. I'll take the pretty one." He gestures to Helen. "And my friend, Pirithous, has decided you'll be his, Princess. Apparently he enjoys breaking the feisty ones."

I stare wide-eyed at Helen, realizing too late that we share a father and that these two are going to take every advantage of our parentage if we don't fight back.

"Your plan is outrageous, but I assume you know this won't end well for you?" I cock an eyebrow, my lip curling in disgust. Despite not having any idea how to escape, I refuse to be cowed. As the king said while dancing with me last night, I do have an impudent mouth.

He advances around the fire and unsheathes a blade, holding it up to my neck. "Shut your gods-damned mouth, or I'll slit your throat right here and let your blood turn this mud into a patch of wildflowers when your mother weeps over your dead body." *Shit*. I swallow and lower my eyes, wondering how Helen and I are going to get out of this alive.

· · · ● · ● · ● · · ·

We don't stay long in the clearing. Helen and I are bound, gagged, and set atop the horses ahead of our jailers. I watch as Theseus, as I come to know him, rips Helen's bodice as he rides behind her. He sends me a look, daring me to stop him from touching her, and I grit my teeth. While Pirithous hasn't taken any liberties of his own, I know it's only a matter of time before both men claim what they believe to be theirs.

We ride through the night, my head pounding and my body sore from holding myself upright, refusing to lean against Pirithous. I try to summon my magic, but nothing sparks.

As we ride, I keep my mind alert and take note of landmarks. I mentally practice my training paces, fighting an invisible partner in my imagination. I imagine what I'll do to these kidnappers when my hands are free. It won't be pretty. When I've exhausted that outlet, I think of Castor and the night of the banquet.

The look on his face when I danced with King Pirithous. The murderous rage and jealousy I felt emanating from his body as he watched from the sidelines. The soothing touches he bestowed on me when I returned to his side. I close my eyes and walk with him back to our rooms, his thumb circling my palm, sending a delicious shiver up my arm. He escorted me to our door, reaching up with that same thumb to trace my bottom lip, and leaned in. Closing my eyes, I inhaled his delicious scent, a mixture of the wine on his breath and the almond blossoms that danced down from the trees onto the training arena. I wanted to feel his lips on mine again, to relive the unexpected kiss from the sparring courts. Waiting, my eyes closed, I sensed him pulling away. I opened my eyes and met his gaze. The lust was undeniable, his pupils dilated fully. Reaching up on my toes, I hoped to take matters into my own hands, but he stepped away. Crestfallen, I, too, retreated, pushing against the door at my back.

"I-I'm sorry, I have things to attend to. Goodnight, Melinoe," he said, his chest expanding as he inhaled. I nodded, blinking back the sting in my eyes, and reached behind me to open the door. I fled to the safety of the bedchamber. What was wrong with me? Didn't he find me attractive? I sat on the bed, wringing my hands.

I decided to slip into a silky robe and took down my hair, my locks flowing wildly as I shook them out. I applied a bit of rouge to my lips and sat up in the bed, awaiting his return. Maybe it was time we had a conversation and really tried to make this partnership work. I waited . . . and waited. He hadn't returned that night.

Now, with nothing else to do but think, my thoughts ultimately land on my new husband. Castor has been alternately hot and cold since returning to Sparta. One moment he's grabbing me, pulling me to his mouth in the arena, and the next he's pushing me away, spending next to no time alone in our shared rooms. I don't understand, and my body doesn't either. I hate that I'm tied to him, forced into this marriage against my wishes. Don't get me wrong, he's attractive. I want him to desire me. I want his hands on my skin. His star-illuminated hair, muscular chest, and ocean-blue eyes make me weak in the knees, send a lightning bolt of desire straight to my core. But looks are only half of the package. In spending time in Sparta, I've learned that he does care about what I want. He lets me train with him. He also cares about his family and the responsibility of his position as prince and warrior. We're actually a lot alike, no matter how much I hate to admit it. Sighing heavily, I think of the unexpected kiss on the training field, biting my lip and feeling a heat creep into my lower belly. I liked it. And I want more.

Unfortunately, I'm still stuck on a horse, in the middle of gods know where, with two disgusting pigs. And it looks like we're approaching a ship. Things couldn't possibly get any worse.

· · · ● · ● · · ·

Chained in the dark, moldy hull of a ship, I have to admit that things are much worse. Neither Helen nor I have seen the sky in a day and a half, and we've no idea which direction we've sailed. The rolling sea has upset Helen's stomach, and the stench of her sick assaults my nostrils, the remains plastered to the front of her dress as she slumps across from me.

I can't tell if we're in a storm, as the sound of thunder may simply be the waves crashing into the ship, but as Helen moans, I agree that the sea has become more tumultuous in recent minutes.

"Everything will be just fine, Helen." I move from a cross-legged position, stretching my legs out and touching her toes with my own, letting her know I'm with her.

"You don't know that," she manages softly.

She's right, I don't know anything right now. My fingers start to tingle, but it's simply from my hands falling asleep in the chains, not my magic appearing. I clench and unclench my fists, hoping the uncomfortable feeling will pass.

"You're right," I admit. My toe continues to slide along her foot as our bodies move with the ocean's undulations. "But I know we're in this together, and I'm thankful for that. I'm glad I'm not alone." Finding the bright side of things has become a strength of mine recently. From my magic failing to being married to a man I hardly know and effectively banished from my home, I'm nothing if not optimistic at this point.

Across the small hull, Helen is quiet, but her gaze is on mine, so I know she's listening. I need to get her to focus on something other than our miserable situation. "Tell me something about you, Castor, and Pollux." I look down, a smirk forming on my lips. "I feel I hardly know my husband at all. I don't have any siblings, so tell me about a time you three did something fun."

I watch as her eyes go glassy, thinking of an anecdote to share. She chuckles quietly to herself, and I sit up, crossing my legs again, ready to listen. "In Sparta," she begins, "war is part of life, part of becoming a man. We are always at war with someone, some tribe of vandals, or some small city-state. As is tradition, the king leads the army along with one brother while the other brother stays behind, securing the throne."

I nod, even as a large wave tilts the ship and we both pull painfully against our chains.

Helen hisses as the cuffs tear into her wrists, but she continues, biting out the words. "Pollux was always the twin to travel with the king, and Castor stayed behind, keeping the throne safe."

My brow furrows, wondering why my husband had to stay behind, but before I can ask, another wave pounds against the hull, and Helen squeals in fright.

"Focus on the story," I remind her, reaching my toe to her foot while my other leg remains tucked beneath my body. Helen's eyes are squeezed closed, her thin arms flexing against the restraints.

She blows a breath loudly out of her mouth. "One time, not long ago, a prince from Mycenae came begging for asylum while my stepfather and Pollux were away. This prince and his brother were exiled from their home but wanted Sparta's help to dethrone their evil ruler. Anyway, Castor agreed to let them stay the night and threw a huge feast in their honor."

"That was kind. What happened next?"

"Both of the exiled princes were . . . smelly." She crinkles her nose and I chuckle. "And so slovenly!" She shivers dramatically at the memory. "They ate like pigs at a trough, engorging themselves on our delicacies and belching at the table."

I laugh at the image, leaning forward.

"And then"—she barks out a laugh—"and then the younger one leans across the table to me and burps out, 'I'd like to take ye for a wife, ye pretty little thing.'" Tears are streaming down her cheeks as she giggles uncontrollably. I laugh, too, imagining these sloppy men sitting at the stately table in Sparta. "The older brother looks at Clytemnestra and says, 'I'll take this one then, she's fine enough to look at!'"

"What did you do?"

"Of course Castor was appalled and, seeing as he was the de facto ruler while Tyndareus was away with Pollux, he grabbed both men by the back of their shirts, lifted them from their seats as food spilled out of their gaping mouths, and dragged them straight out the front gate!"

I giggle, imagining my husband hauling two beastly men from the table, his biceps and chest muscles rippling with exertion. Helen shakes her head as the memory dissipates, her smile falling. "They've always protected me, my brothers."

I nod, not really knowing what it's like to have siblings but wanting to forge a relationship of my own with Helen.

"Helen." I lock eyes with her across the floor. Looking at her as fresh tears well in her eyes, her blond hair matted and stringy, I make a promise to her. "I'll protect you this time."

· · · ● · ● · · ·

"Wake up, woman." Pirithous shakes me from behind and my eyes snap open. Our horse continues its rhythmic canter, and I chastise myself for falling asleep against the brute behind me. "We've arrived at our destination."

I look around, the dawn breaking, at a small castle in the distance. Frost coats the ground, and my breath puffs into the air. We've gone north of Sparta.

"This is Aphidna," Theseus shouts from his horse, Helen swaying dead eyed ahead of him. "You'll both reside here with my mother until proper arrangements can be made."

We approach the castle, nestled in the foothills of a mountain range, and as we enter the courtyard, a stout woman comes out to greet us. "Mother!" Theseus dismounts, pulling Helen down beside him. He proceeds to shove her forward into a genuflection. "Bow to the woman of the castle, Helen." He grips her by the back of the neck, knuckles white and fingers digging into her delicate skin. Her face mere inches from the ground. My eyes flash angrily before I, too, am yanked down from the mount by Pirithous.

"Aethra, thank you for allowing us the use of your home." He bows and I stand, chin jutting, eyes narrowing, refusing to show deference to this criminal's mother. She glares and her mouth hardens, nostrils flaring.

"And who are you, so high and mighty?" Her sneer exposes a set of rotting teeth.

"I'm the nightmare that haunts your sleep," I hiss, leaning forward despite my bound hands, baring my teeth. "If you don't release us this instant, a rain of hellfire will come down upon this castle, the likes of which even Hades will fear." Heat courses through my hands, searing the bindings at my wrist. They fall away, and the woman lets out a squeak of surprise.

Arms free, I leap toward the beastly woman in front of me, hands wrapping tightly around her neck. She tumbles backward, my weight pressing wholly on her chest. As I squeeze, I feel her life-force draining from her body. I press even harder, desperate now. She gasps for breath. I press and press. The murderous rage flowing from my body unbidden. But before the death is complete, moments before her soul enters the Underworld, I am yanked backward by Pirithous as Theseus rushes to his weeping mother.

I am too slow to block the blow that Pirithous unleashes on me. My mind goes dark, and I slump to the ground, Helen's cries echoing in the distance.

CASTOR

"We'll stop here for the night, switch out our horses, and get a few hours of shut eye." I toss the horse's reins to Pollux and stomp into the inn, throwing down a bag of coins to the proprietor. Dumbfounded, he feels the heft of the purse, mentally calculating how much I've overpaid.

"My brother and I require supper, a room, and two fresh horses immediately. See that it is done and there's more for you in the morning." The innkeeper nods eagerly, pushing his waif of a wife toward the kitchen to obtain our meal. Pollux enters and takes a seat at an empty table. I cross to him and sit, both of us immediately draining the mugs of ale that are placed before us by the slight matron.

"Where to now?" Pollux nods his thanks as the matron returns with our stew.

"I recall that Pirithous is close with Theseus. That rake has a home in the north, I believe. Perhaps I can speak with some of the townsfolk and glean more information."

Pollux swallows his stew, watching me warily. "Have you tried to summon Hades?"

I shake my head, opening and closing my mouth, unsure of how to answer my twin. "No, he would be furious if he knew what's happened. But if I can't get any information, I'll be forced to make contact." There's a heaviness in my body, as though I've become weighed down with the lies I'm living.

We finish our meal in silence, mine hardly touched, and then head upstairs, both of us falling into our respective bedrolls without undressing or taking off our shoes. I lie on my back and stare at the ceiling, unable to sleep, as Pollux's snores fill the silence.

My mind races with what I've done. With what I *haven't* done. With what I've *wanted* to do since I met Melinoe. Instead of protecting her like I promised, I've allowed her to be taken, along with my innocent sister. I worry for both of them, for their safety.

As much as I've wanted to take Melinoe to my bed and consummate our marriage, I could never force myself on her. I'm not the type of man who gets off on forcing innocents into sex. Plus, I'm pretty sure that's not exactly allowed as part of my agreement. No tainted goods, and all that. Despite my rational brain, I feel myself growing hard just thinking about the kiss we shared on the sparring field, my cock straining at the seam along my pants.

Chuckling to myself, I think about her magic blasting me on my ass. I'd been knocked the fuck out, and when I came to and saw her leaning over me, her tits pressed against my chest and her hands searching my body for injuries, caressing me gently . . . well, I wasn't thinking clearly. I press my hand to my length, imagining Mel pressed against me in the arena, her body straddling my own as I pulled her to me. The lust that had awakened in her eyes could set a man on fire, and it took all my strength to pull away. Staying away had been even more of a challenge, especially after seeing her in that emerald-green gown.

I adjust myself, groaning with an inflamed urge, and roll over to my side. It's going to be a rough night.

MELINOE

I feel hot breath on my face, and my eyes snap open. My arms and legs are bound to thick wooden bedposts, my body spread-eagle. I yank at the heavy chains, an animal caged, and snarl at my captor, baring my teeth. Pirithous leans over me, a smug smile lifting his lips.

"You've brought this on yourself with your embarrassing outburst in the courtyard." He shoves his hands down his pants, tugging himself in front of me. "And now you'll pay."

I fight the urge to vomit.

His fingers trail down my arm toward my breast, and my body stills in terror. I feel my mind shutting down, and I'm somehow floating above, looking down on my imprisoned body. I try to pull away, my chin trembling. He continues the path, getting closer and closer to my breast.

Fight, Princess, fight! A female voice fills my mind as my fingertips tingle in pain. Blinking rapidly, I clench my bound fists, my blood boiling.

He massages himself as he pants heavily near my face. His hand skims over my shoulder and begins to move down my arm. Something inside me snaps, and I come back into my body, ready to fight. I turn my head and clamp my mouth down on his fingers. Blood spurts into my face as I yank. I refuse to let go of his digits and he screeches, attempting to pull away, but my jaw is as locked as Cerberus's. When I finally do release him, my teeth are throbbing from the exertion.

He rears his grisly hand back and slaps me. Hard. His blood smears and splatters all over my face. I blink through the red haze and glare savagely, refusing to feel the pain. "I *will* kill you," I growl.

Sneering at me while cradling his injured hand, his face turns beet red. "I'd like to see you try, chained like a beast. And if *you* won't behave, we'll just have to punish your *sister* instead." A feline smirk transforms his face as my body chills.

My eyes bulge, my body trembling in fear. I'm sick at the thought of Helen being violated, touched by these disgusting brutes. Helen isn't the fighter that I am, and my heart plummets at the terrifying images that fly into my mind. What have I done?

"Don't," I whisper, gulping heavily. My eyes widen. I'll beg. Do anything. "*Please don't.*"

"Too late, Princess." He rubs himself through his pants, his face slackening as he thrusts into his hand.

I roar, pulling at the chains and writhing, my heart broken at what I know is coming, and at what I've done to cause it.

He slams the door and I hear footsteps retreat down the hallway. Not so far away, a door opens, but doesn't close. Silence. Then . . .

"No, no, *no, no!*" I hear Helen scream, her terror apparent. My mind goes berserk with what I know is about to happen.

A slap and sobbing.

Muffled crying and the sound of choking, gagging. Coughing.

"Please don't, *please!*" Helen begs.

And finally . . .

Thumping of a bed against the wall.

My breath hitches and I, too, sob. Silently.

• • • • • • • • • •

I whip my head toward the door as it slams into the wall. My face is tight from the dried tears, my eyes sore and puffy, but Theseus's mother stands in the entry, a tray of food in her hands. The room has darkened as I've lain here, motionless, my mind closed off from Helen's torment. I've no clue how much time has passed. Seconds? Minutes? Hours? None of it matters now that Helen has suffered at my hands.

"It's time for your meal, girl." Aethra approaches haughtily, dropping the tray loudly on the side table. I roll my shoulders, the chains clanking loudly against the wooden bedposts. "I'll have to feed you, obviously, since you've been shackled like a wild animal." Her grimace doesn't cover the hesitation I see in her eyes as she pulls up a stool. Bruises darken her neck. She's afraid of me. I narrow my eyes at her, pulling at strength I don't feel.

"I'm not such a *beast* as your son, kidnapping innocent women and doing abhorrent things to us." I hold her gaze, willing her to acknowledge the horror her son and his friend have inflicted upon Helen.

Instead of embarrassment, a look of defiance passes over her features. She draws herself up, posture erect, and meets my gaze with a challenge. "You've no idea what I've done to secure a hero as my son, girl. What my family did to ensure that I bore a legend such as Theseus."

I'm silent as she extends a spoon full of stew toward my mouth, but I shake my head, pressing my lips together.

"Eat, or you'll never be free of these shackles."

My belly grumbles in hunger, and I tentatively open my mouth.

"Theseus is doubly blessed, the son of King Aegeus of Athens and the god Poseidon." Her head tilts to one side, cheeks going pink with pleasure.

I swallow, wrinkling my nose in disgust at her admission. "I'm sure you tricked both into impregnating you, which is why you have no clue which man is actually his father."

"Of course I tricked them, and I'd do it again. You'd do well to learn from me and my son. If you want power, you don't wait for it to come to you. You take it, as he did when he heard about the beauteous Helen. Her allure has been bandied about for years; it was only a matter of time before someone claimed her. My son deserves a wife such as her, but the pompous King Tyndareus wouldn't even meet to negotiate a marriage treaty. So, I encouraged Theseus to take what is rightfully his." She lifts a cup of ale to my mouth and I gulp heavily, liquid dribbling down my chin.

Sickened, I shake my head. "I'll take my power, but not at the expense of innocents. Perhaps you'd do well to learn from *me*." My eyes narrow in warning and Aethra drops the spoon with a clatter into the now-empty bowl.

She stands, eyes flashing at my boldness. "I'm glad my son chose Helen as his bride instead of you. But I can't wait to watch Pirithous break that insolent spirit of yours."

"He won't succeed," I spit at her.

She offers me a watery smile and inhales a few sharp breaths before exhaling slowly. She takes one step at a time until her face, rotting teeth and sour breath, is inches from mine. "If he does fail, my son is sure to succeed. I'll make sure of it . . . when he makes you his whore."

CASTOR

After attempting to talk to various townspeople and travelers, Pollux and I aren't any closer to finding the whereabouts of Helen, Melinoe, or Theseus's castle. The trail has gone cold, and if we wait much longer, who knows what shape either will be in when we do find them. I refuse to think on it.

Ultimately, I know what I must do before Pollux even insists. "Brother," he says bluntly, "we won't find them unless you summon Hades and ask for help. Do it. Before it's too late." I rub the back of my neck and head to the nearest temple, ready to swallow my pride and admit that I've fucked up.

As I approach, I look around, the beauty of the pantheon taking me by surprise. This temple, though ancient, is well cared for. Stone columns flank the entrance. I climb the worn stairs, and glance quickly at the frieze on the outer walls showing the battle between the Titans—the offspring of the sky and earth, the original rulers—and the gods of Mount Olympus. Upon entering, I'm guided to the altar by a hooded priestess, her robes quietly skimming the marble floor. I shove a bag of coins into her hand, whispering that I need to be left alone. She nods discreetly and bars the door behind her. I'm completely alone as my footsteps echo in the emptiness.

I slowly approach the shrine, breathing deeply to calm my pounding heart, and take a match to light a candle. Kneeling on a rough woolen rug, I utter words to call him forth. I'm not sure what to say, not that it would matter. He'll find me, already knowing what I've done. "I invoke the gods, seeking the missing daughter. Daughter and princess of the Underworld. Daughter of Persephone, daughter of Hades, daughter of Zeus. I invoke the gods, seeking the missing daughter." I pull out Melinoe's brush, which I've brought along for just this instance. I pull a few strands of her ebony curls from the bristles, quickly braid them, and then hold them over the candle, watching as they instantly ignite and disappear, the scent of burnt hair the only remaining evidence.

The candle sputters and I turn, startled, as the other sconces around the temple flare and then go dark. Thunder booms, quietly at first then growing in strength, echoing along the stone walls like waves pounding the cliffs of Sparta. White smoke billows slowly from each extinguished candle wick before melding into an apparition before the altar, swirling until the god is fully formed before me. His dark eyes stand out against the white vapor and his form sharpens, the cords of his neck taut and his nostrils flaring. I feel his violent and uncontrolled anger in the choking smoke and lower my eyes obediently.

"*Where is she*?" he commands, the boom of his voice vibrating my bones.

"I have lost her, Majesty." I bow from my knees, my forehead pressing into the cool floor. "I need your help to recover her and return her to you safely."

His voice rumbles, rattling the stones of the temple. My body stiffens, preparing to run should the structure collapse in his anger. "You were to protect her, keep her safe, until it was time for her to take her place with me on Mount Olympus. You moronic prince, couldn't manage the simplest task asked of you?"

I nod, ashamed, but keep to my bowed position.

My body spasms violently as my arms are thrown behind my body. I'm lifted onto my toes, my back arched and chest exposed. My mouth gapes against my will as he reaches down my throat, suffocating me. "You will find her in Aphidna at the castle of Aethra. She is held by Theseus and Pirithous, as you suspected. If you do not return her to me . . . well, I'll show you what will happen to you."

My mind flickers as the smoke enters my brain, burning a path up my nostrils. Horrendous images of my body sprawled out, belly ripped open and guts exposed, flash before my eyes. Tendrils of my stomach leach onto the ground and blood drips from my ears and mouth. I'm still alive, but the pain is excruciating, and I let out a guttural roar inside the temple, begging to be released.

"Bring her home to me or suffer the consequences, Prince." He releases me, and my body falls heavily to the ground. I hiss as my knees absorb the impact. The smoke dissipates into the air of the temple, candles glowing again.

I hesitate for a moment, catching my breath and feeling for injuries, before rising, needing to get out of this place as quickly as possible. After rolling up the rug and placing the candle back on the shrine, I hurry to the door, unbar it, and throw it open to the sunlight. I gasp, bowing over my knees, filling my lungs with the fresh air. I need to get away from this place as quickly as possible. As I rush down the temple's stairs, I glance again at the frieze adorning the outer walls. Something catches my eye and I skid to a stop, almost tumbling face-first down the steps. I move closer to examine the tableau, grazing my fingers over the etched figures.

A woman fighting alongside the gods of Mount Olympus. Long, curly hair. Graceful features. Large soulful eyes. Darkened hands spewing forth fire against the Titans.

My eyes widen, my mind racing. Why is Melinoe, my twenty-three-year-old wife and a giftless princess of the Underworld, part of an ancient frieze sculpted on this temple?

MELINOE

Aethra doesn't return to my room the next day. Instead, I watch with flames in my eyes and my lip curled back as Pirithous enters with a tray of breakfast foods. He, too, sets the tray on the side table and then, surprisingly, pulls a key from his pocket. He walks around the bed, unlocking each chain from my body. I immediately curl into myself, rubbing one wrist at a time, keeping my eyes on my captor.

"Now that you know what we're capable of, and how we will punish Helen for your impertinence, I assume you'll behave yourself." It's not a question. He knows he's found my weakness. I crawl to the opposite side of the bed, giving a wide berth. That same evil smile splays his lips. "Come here," he commands.

I shake my head. "Fuck you." My hands curl into fists at my side, my fingers beginning to tingle.

"If you refuse, you know what will happen . . . to Helen." A sob escapes unbidden from somewhere inside me, and I slink around the bed to his side. He turns to face me, running the back of his uninjured hand down my cheek. I grit my teeth, wishing for my magic to appear so I could launch him against the wall, watch his head turn to pulp against the stones.

"So beautiful, and so dangerous." He winds his fingers around my throat, lifting my chin as he grips harder. "What will I do with you once we're bound in matrimony?" I have trouble swallowing the lump forming in my throat as I run my eyes up and down his body, searching for a weapon. Unfortunately he has none, and I bite my lip in an attempt to control my frustration. I lower my gaze, hiding my anger from his eyes.

"I think I'll have you here, now, before our vows are solidified." He shoves me back onto the bed and climbs up next to me. I hold myself rigid, muscles tense, as he runs his hand along my exposed thigh and up to my hips, pushing the dirtied yellow dress higher and higher. I stop his hand just as he rises and straddles me, his weight pressing me deep into the soft mattress. I keep my gaze lowered, refusing to meet his eyes, as he leans down to kiss my mouth.

"Open for me, unless you want this to be painful." He grinds into me, pushing his weight onto my stomach. Swallowing back the bile rising in my throat, I take his mouth with mine, struggling to play the part and not retch. His hands paw at my breasts as though he's kneading dough. No wonder he couldn't find a willing wife. I inch my own hands along his back, feeling for a hidden weapon—anything—faking a moan and writhing my hips. "Oh, you like that, do you?" He grinds against me again and I feel evidence of his arousal press into my stomach.

I think to feign a cough, but it turns into a gagging fit at the terror before me.

Do it now, the feminine voice hisses in my ear. Batting my lashes, I ask if I may have a drink of the watered wine he's brought.

"Get it yourself," he sneers at me, jutting his chin toward the carafe on the table.

I inch my way off the bed and, adjusting my dress, pull a small vial of wolfsbane from my undergarments. I thank the gods that Helen and I managed to collect the poison, and that I was able to keep it safely on my person the past few days. Biding my time to use it has been excruciating, but I know my chances are running out. I glance behind me to ensure Pirithous is occupied. He's adjusting himself, stroking his flaccid member within his toga.

"Hurry up!"

I take a sip of the wine and, as I set down the glass, drop the potion in. I let the empty vial drop to the rug and kick it under the bed. "Would you like some, Your Highness?" I ask quietly.

He nods and grunts, still stroking himself, and I top off the glass before bringing it to his lips, tipping it so he's forced to gulp the entire contents down his throat. His eyes widen as I empty the glass into his mouth. Warmth infuses my body, and a smile stretches my face for the first time in days.

"Watch it!" he sputters, narrowing his eyes at me. "I'm going to teach you how to serve me properly." He wiggles out of his breeches, his penis springing free, still soft.

I take my time returning the glass to the table and, kneeling on the ground ever so slowly, begin by running my hands up his legs, watching his face for the poison to take effect. I unlace his sandals, rubbing his black-soled feet. Swallowing, urging time to go quicker, I realize I'm going to be forced to touch my mouth to his skin. My gorge rises, the wine threatening to come up. I try to look anywhere but at his limp member.

I climb back up into the bed, biting my lip, and continue watching his face. His breathing appears normal, and as he catches me eyeing him, he grabs the back of my head with his free hand. The other continues stroking his length, or lack thereof.

"You better get good at this, Princess, because you're going to be doing it an awful lo—" He shudders, loosening his grip as his body spasms violently, bilious foam spurting from his mouth. I leap off the bed, backing into the wall, as I watch him choke and seize, his eyes rolling back in his head as his hands reach toward me. My brows lower over my eyes, and my mouth thins, but I refuse to turn away.

"Die, you piece of shit," I hiss at him. His mouth forms an O, and then his body stills. "I told you I'd kill you," I snarl.

Now to rescue Helen.

• • • • ● • ● • • • •

Unfortunately, Pirithous didn't carry any long swords or daggers with him. I check his toga, but find nothing. Taking a strengthening breath, I quietly open the door and make my way down the hallway. I have no clue what I'll use to protect myself, but I know I have to get to Helen.

I follow the direction of yesterday's footsteps, listening at each door as I pass. I keep my steps slow. I'm three doors down from my own when I hear it. Sobbing.

I press my ear firmly to the door and listen.

"You fuck like a dead fish, Helen of Sparta. If you don't start getting me hard, I'll slice your cheek and ruin that beauteous face." Helen moans and the sobs increase in volume. My blood boils and a hiss whispers in my ear.

Princess.

Looking to my right I see a mirror, but instead of my own reflection, there's a dark shadow hovering closer and closer. I, too, step forward. Two dark pools shine out of a shadowed face, long curly white hair glimmering in the darkened hallway. As I raise my hands, I see that her hands and forearms are also shimmering white—like stars in the dark night sky—a contrast to my blackened fingers. She is my complete opposite in every way.

I feel my magic thrum in my veins as she moves toward her side of the mirror, toward me. I reach my hand toward the mirror.

I'm here. You summoned me with your prayers.

I gulp as I look into the abyss of her eyes, drowning in them.

Drink me in and save yourself.

Her voice is a balm, soothing me into submission, but I shake myself alert and mentally remove her from my thoughts.

"This isn't about saving myself. This is about saving Helen, so stay out of my head and out of my way," I hiss to the mirror, keeping my voice lowered and then returning to the door to press my ear against it. The bed is thumping, and

I need to get inside and stop it. I reach for the handle, but the vision covers my hand and halts me.

How the fuck did she get out of the mirror?

My eyes widen as I meet those deep pools, now right next to me, and she speaks into my mind.

Your powers are weak and no match for Theseus, king of Athens and Poseidon's son. He's stronger than you are. You will lose and Helen will die. She will die if you do not allow me in.

I swallow the lump in my throat and close my eyes. I feel the magic inside of me, growing stronger with my anger and hatred. Hatred at Theseus for his violation of Helen. Hatred at this phantom, doubting my strength.

"Fine. Help me," I growl at her and fling open the door. I've waited long enough.

· · · · ● · ● · · · ·

My eyes take a moment to adjust to the brightness of the room. The sun shines directly from the window, giving everything a garish and harsh appearance. I blink, my mind not grasping what my eyes are witnessing. Theseus is thrusting himself into Helen, whose arms are extended overhead, chained to the headboard. He clearly hasn't heard me enter the room, as he continues unimpeded. Helen's eyes are scrunched closed and her face is twisted in pain, moans escaping from her bruised mouth, tears leaking from the side of her eyes. I snap into action, grab Theseus viciously by the back of his head, and yank him off her. His naked body clatters to the floor before me. As I shake chunks of his hair from my hands, I frantically look around for his trousers, his scabbard and weapons.

He scrambles across the floor, finding them before I do, and unsheathes the short sword from its scabbard. Standing toe to toe, I tear my gaze from his genitals with a sneer. "Not man enough to find a wife the lawful way, and now I see why . . ." I draw my brows together and focus on the flush that creeps along his cheeks.

"Where's Pirithous?" He moves fluidly around the bed toward Helen.

"I promised your mother I'd rain hellfire down on this castle if we weren't released, the likes of which even my father Hades would fear. Now you and your mother know *I* am that hellfire." I watch with amusement as he grabs Helen, and with a squeak of pain from her, he pulls her still-chained body toward himself, lifting the knife to her exposed throat.

I snort in derision. "You couldn't find yourself a bride unless you kidnapped one, and now you can't even properly defend yourself. You're a sorry excuse for a man, Theseus."

"Shut your mouth or I'll slit her throat!" His eyes are wild, unblinking. I can feel his heart racing as though the air around him is pulsing with his fear and uncertainty. *Thump, thump. Thump, thump.* The rhythm speeds up as my fingers begin tingling painfully, the ache begging to be released. He has no idea what he's unleashed or what's about to happen to him.

My magic stirs, my fingers thrumming with adrenaline and energy. I feel my breath quicken and my eyes narrow, focusing on Theseus's rapid heartbeat beneath his skin. I slide my gaze to Helen and give an infinitesimal nod. She closes her eyes and takes a deep breath, and I instantly unleash my power.

I breathe it out. I set her free. The woman from the mirror. I watch from above, floating in the fetid air of the room, outside of my own body, as my skin goes shadowy dark, my power coming to the surface. My eyes turn translucent and my fingers, once inky black with immobile magic, bind Theseus with silvery strands that flow from my fingertips straight into his chest. He burns from the inside out, his skin igniting, and, in an instant, becomes engulfed in flames of white and blue. Hotter than the fire in the hearth. Hotter than the sun's rays. He is bound to me, unable to move, unable to scream as the pain tears through him.

Helen, only centimeters from the inferno, remains untouched and free of injury. Her chains release, and as she rushes to me, they clatter onto the floor. I return to my body, descending from above as my skin goes from dark to light, my vision clearing and focusing. My fingers are no longer stained; my magic has been set free. I look at my hands in wonder, turning them over and wiggling my digits, closing and opening my fist. Am I still me?

I hear footsteps thundering down the hall and turn to the doorway, ready to continue the destruction. My fingers tingle again and my body hums. I'm ready to wage war and get Helen and I out of here safely when both Castor and Pollux crash into the doorframe, splintering it. They take in the fiery corpse behind Helen and me, their eyes questioning and mouths agape.

I smirk as my magic retreats. "Thanks for coming, but I've got this handled."

CASTOR

I don't know what Pollux and I expected to find when entering the palace of Aethra, but it certainly wasn't my wife hugging our half naked sister while a dead body sizzled in the corner of the room.

Helen immediately runs into Pollux's arms, her body now tangled in a sheet. My brother lifts her easily and carries her from the room, her face buried in his neck as she sobs. As much as I want to comfort our little sister, I turn toward Melinoe. She's trembling, staring at her hands. I approach her slowly, bending my large frame down to make eye contact.

"I'm here." I slowly reach for her hands, as though she's a scared wild animal, but she yanks them behind herself, fear flashing in her eyes.

"Don't," she whispers, shaking her head. "Don't touch me." She curls her hands into her chest, her lower lip quivering as her eyes suddenly well with unshed tears. "I-I killed him." She glances past me to the body in the corner.

I nod gently, a mixture of pride and fear simmering in my belly. Is this what she's capable of with her magic? "You did what you had to do, Melinoe." I keep my voice calm and try to block her view of the charred body. "You saved Helen and yourself." I stand awkwardly in front of her, unsure if I should wrap my arms around her or give her a soldier's pat on the back. She solves my dilemma, launching herself into my embrace, wrapping her legs around my waist. I enfold her in my arms and, without even thinking, press my face into her hair. Thank the gods she's safe. I want to hold her like this forever, protect her from all the bad in the world.

"Is . . . is that Pirithous?"

She stiffens, and then I feel her shake her head against my chest. "That was Theseus. Pirithous is down the hall. I poisoned him." Her words are mumbled, her face still pressed into my chest.

I gulp, equally surprised by and proud of my wife. My *wife*. I'd nearly lost her, and she was able to keep herself, and my sister, safe. Without me. It dawns on me that she doesn't need me. This warrior princess does not need me. If anything, I'm the one who needs her. I hold her a little tighter, bury myself a little deeper into her hair, until I feel her pull away.

"We've got to get out of here," she tells me as the mask descends, her eyes closing off the emotional moment we just shared. She slides down my body as I lower her, letting go of the warmth. I feel empty and cold without her wrapped around me.

Taking her hand, I follow her out of the room and down the stairs, where we find Pollux comforting Helen, who's gone catatonic, her eyes staring into the nothingness. Her clothing is still missing, so I send Pollux to find something suitable until we can purchase new garments for both her and Melinoe.

Mel takes a seat next to Helen and cradles my broken sister's head in her lap. She strokes Helen's golden locks while rocking back and forth. Helen's face crumples, and Melinoe simply mutters, "I know, I know." I watch, useless, from the corner like an overlarge piece of furniture, while my baby sister breaks down and my strong wife, who just went through her own trauma, comforts her.

Pollux returns with something warm, albeit much less regal than Helen's normal attire. She doesn't even bother to scrunch her nose at the brown color and plain fabric. She takes it woodenly and leaves the room.

While we wait for Helen to get dressed, Pollux decides to raid the kitchen for provisions while I confront Melinoe. "I'm taking you back to the Underworld. I've failed to keep you safe, and it's clear that you don't belong here . . . with me." I lower my gaze, embarrassed that I wasn't the warrior and savior Hades and Persephone thought.

"No." Her steely gaze is resolute, her mouth pressed into a hard line.

I furrow my brow. "What do you mean? I thought you'd be glad to go back home. Get rid of me. Take your place as heiress and all that . . ." I trail off, unsure what's changed in her mind.

"I want you to take me to Zeus."

I pause, shaking my head. "I don't think that's a good idea." The last thing I want to do is bring her to Zeus. I need to get both of us somewhere safe, and the only place we are bound to be safe is in the Underworld.

"It doesn't matter what you think. I'm going to Mount Olympus, to Zeus, with or without you. But I'm asking for you to come with me." She reaches her hand out, waiting for me to take it. Waiting for me to agree to take her to the one place that could destroy her, to the one god who she definitely shouldn't be near. And frankly, neither should I.

Unfortunately, it's too late for me. I've made my deal and there's no going back. Now I just need to get Melinoe back to the Underworld, somehow, so she's safe with Hades.

"Will you come with me?"

I look into her beseeching eyes and know I can't deny her. I know, instantly and without a doubt, that I'd do anything to help her, to keep her safe, from this moment forward. Even if she doesn't need me, even if she can do it all by herself, I want to be by her side on this adventure. Gulping down the uncertainty and ignoring all the possible horrible outcomes, I want to be with this woman. The question is, will she want to be with me when she finds out who I *really* am?

MELINOE

At an inn near the Boeotian border, Castor unlocks the wooden door with a rusty skeleton key. Across the hall, Pollux and Helen bid us goodnight and slip into their own shared room, Pollux refusing to let our sister out of his sight. I take in our accommodations: a large bed, a copper tub filled with steaming water, and a fire crackling in the hearth. The pillows and blankets heaped on the bed look inviting, and I can't wait to put this day behind me, but I also need to wash the deaths of Pirithous and Theseus off.

"I'll go downstairs and scrounge up some dinner while you bathe." He closes the door quietly behind him, and I immediately disrobe and sink into the hot water. I let out a hiss at the temperature, my muscles instantly relax, and I lean my head against the rim as the scent of rose oil and eucalyptus wafts around me. I dip under, scrubbing until my skin is bright pink. I scour every inch where Pirithous touched me and swallow down the images of his life leaving his body. Blinking, I refuse to feel badly for taking the life of someone who was going to effectively take mine. I'm lounging in the water, trying to stay awake, when Castor walks in carrying our dinner.

"Oh, I-I'm sorry. I can give you another minute to finish up . . ." A blush creeps up his face as he tries to look anywhere else but at the tub.

I sit up, folding my arms over the ledge and lean toward him. "It's fine, I'm done. Close the door, you're letting out the warmth." I'm exhausted and my voice sounds low and sultry. He sets the plates on the bed and sits down, looking at his feet. "Can you hand me the towel?" I point toward the end of the bed, and with eyes still lowered, he tosses it my way. I miss and it lands on the floor, just out of reach.

"Sorry . . ." He stands and grabs the towel, holding it out for me. I meet his eyes and stand from the tub, water dripping down my naked body. My long hair covers my breasts, but everything else is exposed. I watch as he inhales, holding my gaze as he fights the urge to look down.

I reach for the towel and wrap it around myself. "Thank you," I murmur, quickly moving to the bed and unwrapping the dinner plate. Castor sits beside me and watches as I inhale the food.

I catch him staring at my wrists, which are black and blue from the chains. "Does it hurt?"

"I'm a little sore," I admit before taking a slug of ale.

"Here." He holds out his palm and wiggles his fingers. I set down the glass of ale and extend one of my wrists for him to examine. He gently turns my forearm over, checking for any broken bones. Noting that there are none, he uses his thumb to massage the area around the bruise. I inhale sharply.

"I can stop." His eyes peek through dark lashes, and I shake my head, enjoying his touch, the way his hands make my skin feel warm. He makes small circles with his thumb and forefinger, inching his way up my arm. I'm suddenly reminded of Pirithous's fingers running down my arm and yank my wrist back, startling Castor.

"I-I didn't mean to scare you."

I bite my lip and shake my head before tears pool in my eyes. "It's going to take some time . . ." A sob escapes my throat, and I dig my palms into my eyes, not wanting him to see me like this. Weak. A mess.

"I understand. It takes time to come to terms with your first kill, Melinoe." He hovers over me and presses me down to the mattress, flipping me to my stomach. My body tenses, ready to fight again, but then he gently pulls my hair to the side and begins kneading my shoulders and the muscles of my back. I lengthen like a cat, my hands palming the bed covers. With his large form covering my body, I feel safe, knowing he'll protect and care for me.

I'm aware of my nakedness under the thin towel, but it feels good to be massaged, the tension worked from my body. I take a deep breath and close my eyes, and it's not long before I'm sound asleep.

· · · · ● · ● · · · ·

"Ready or not, here I come!" I shout, peeking out from behind my palms and pushing away from the thick bark of the tree. Glancing around, I watch for a moment, waiting to see Zeus's bright white hair or movement from behind a shrub. When nothing appears, I purse my lips and start the short trek back toward the town of Zominthos. Even though the rules of hide-and-seek specifically state that no one may hide in town, Zeus is a habitual rule breaker.

It'll serve him right when I find him.

Though small and hidden on the plateau of Mount Ida, the village is filled with many courtiers, all here to serve Zeus. My parents, Asteria and Perses, like the others who live in the village, left home when I was a babe. We've remained refugees, hiding from the evil Cronus, who would kill his son Zeus as well as destroy all of us if he knew we were here.

I round the hut of Melisseus, the father of Zeus's nurses. He is digging in his garden, and I see he's built yet another wind chime. It tinkles in the warm breeze.

"Ho, Melisseus!" I call to him, holding my hand up in greeting. I approach the fence, dodging the bees that buzz in and out of the hives kept near the chimes.

"Ho, Hecate! How are you on this lovely day?" He shields his eyes, but a bright white smile lights up his wrinkled face.

"I'm well, thank you. Have you seen Zeus?"

He chuckles, a laugh that starts in his large gut and bubbles out of his rosebud mouth. "Trying to cheat at the game, are ye girl?"

Blushing, I withhold the fact that it's actually Zeus who is cheating by hiding in the village. Instead, I frown and bat my eyelashes playfully.

Laughing again. "Now, now, don't ye be using any of that magic on me, miss. He went past the Dactyls' place."

Shouting my thanks, I sprint along the path to the legendary metalworkers' hut, my brow growing sweatier and sweatier as I near the heated forges.

"Hecate!" A screech causes me to skid to a stop, and I look around. Seeing no one, I continue onward.

"Hecate!" The same scream again, full of terror and fear. Shielding my eyes from the midday sun, I kneel to check under the nearest stoop.

Nothing.

"Hecate!"

Zeus? Realizing the call is coming from inside my head, I still, closing my eyes and inhaling deeply. My magic isn't perfect yet, but with my grandmother's help, I've been honing it. Someone is summoning me, and I remind myself to listen not only to the words being said, but also listen for background noises while using my other senses to guide me.

With my eyes closed and my mind focused, I see a flickering, bright orange light. A fire roars, nearly melting the skin from my face, and the floor is blackened with soot.

The Dactyls' forge.

I race onward, rounding the corner and smacking straight into Celmis, the Dactyl of casting metal. He has liquid iron, heated to a bright orange, in a pot, held over my friend. Zeus is lying prostrate on the ground. His left eye is bruised, his lip busted. His toga is ripped, exposing a gash on his collarbone.

"What are you doing to him?" I spew at Celmis. He's always been an odd youth, an outcast drawn to hurting innocent animals, unlike his kindly brothers, Acmon and Damnameneus.

"Shut up, you witch!" Startled, Celmis tips a bit of the iron out of the pot, and I watch in horror as it falls toward Zeus's face.

"Piéste kai zestánete chílious ílious!" I cry, my body darkening as my vision flutters. Hearing a squeal and then a plink, I fall to my knees, the power sapping my strength.

I stay there for only a moment, the grit covering my sweaty palms, but it's Zeus who approaches me, running his trembling hand along my arched back, comforting me. Looking up, I furrow my brow and take in the brilliant diamond in his hand. "Where did you find—?"

"It's Celmis," he whispers, holding out the gem. "You did this, Hecate."

He drops the diamond into my palm. Turning it, my eyes widening in horror, I drop the glittering stone and cover my face, sobs racking my body.

"I didn—" I sob. "He was going to hurt you." I've killed someone. The weight of the words crushes me as my tears drop into the sooty soil.

Zeus pulls me to standing and engulfs me in his arms. "You did this, Hecate," he repeats, stroking my tangled curls. "You did this. For me. You saved me."

• • • ● • ● • • • •

I awake the next morning completely naked, the bath towel discarded on the floor. Startled, I reach my hand to the opposite side of the bed, but it's empty. I sit up, clutching the covers to my chest, and find Castor's sleeping form bunked down near the hearth. My heart constricts. He could have easily claimed the other side of the bed after tucking me in, but he didn't. I smile to myself, thinking that I might *want* him to claim his side of the bed someday. Exhaling, I flop back into the pillows, thinking on the events of the last few days.

I don't feel guilty for killing Pirithous and Theseus. I know that deep down. It had to be done. It was either me and Helen, our safety, or them, and as a trained warrior, I did what was necessary. I inhale deeply, promising myself I'll not think of them ever again. What's done is done, and the world is better off without rapists kidnapping innocent women for their sick pleasure.

My mind flits to Zeus and what he did to Persephone. He's no different from Theseus and Pirithous. He took sick pleasure in violating her, and the image of Theseus forcing himself on Helen flashes in my mind. Deep down I know that I cannot fight the king of gods and win, but I can't seem to let it go either. I promised the shadowy figure that I'd make my way to Mount Olympus to learn the truth of my magic, but I have other reasons for making the trip now.

Revenge.

A knock sounds at the door and I panic, whipping a pillow at Castor's head. He turns toward me sleepily, his face a mask of confusion.

"Get off the floor!" I hiss as quietly as I can. He registers the knock at the door and jumps up, tossing the blanket and pillow onto the bed next to me. He bounds to the door and opens it a crack to find Helen's beaming face.

"Good morning, lovebirds. I've brought Melinoe some new clothes. I'm pretty good at sizes, so they should fit." From the bed, I roll my eyes at what I presume is going to be a gaudy dress or some other frilly concoction that is not conducive to travel or ease of movement. However, when she thrusts the Spartan uniform, nearly identical to the one I had at court, through the crack in the door, I sit up, nearly exposing myself, and gasp with glee, a smile breaking out across my face.

"Where did you find them, being so far away from home?" Castor opens the door a little wider as he takes the outfit and tosses it my way.

She shrugs. "I have my sources. Now get dressed and meet us downstairs, unless you have something else to take care of . . .?" Her eyes flit back and forth between me and Castor, a suggestive grin pulling at her lips.

"Thank you for the clothes. We'll be down shortly." Castor ushers her to the door and slams it loudly. I chuckle from the bed as he turns to me, raising an eyebrow. "I'll turn around so you can get dressed."

I fling the covers back, eager to get into the clean and comfortable skirted uniform and start our journey forward, but something gives me pause. "Castor?" I bite my lip and he cocks his head my way, careful to keep his eyes averted from my nakedness. I struggle to find the right words and run my hand through my tangled hair, eyes downcast. "If . . . If you wanted to sleep in the bed next time we stop at an inn, I-I think that would be fine . . ." I trail off, feeling a heat creep up my neck.

He nods as he turns his back to give me privacy, but I swear I see a small smile beginning to form on his lips.

CASTOR

"How much farther until we reach Thebes?" Helen whines from her seat in front of Pollux. While we have been traveling all day and the sun is shortly setting, Boeotia is a large city-state, and thus we have decided to stop for the night at the Theban residence of General Amphitryon.

"Sister, the city's gates are just there." He points toward a haze in the distance. Robust ivy trails along the walls of the gates.

Melinoe is quiet in the seat ahead of me, and I brush her hair back, holding it in my hands. "Is everything all right, wife?" She stiffens, but nods, not saying anything. We canter down the road toward the city, and I enjoy the last few moments of silence with my thoughts, the sway of the horse on the meandering dirt path.

My wife is an enigma, a puzzle I cannot, for the life of me, figure out. I'm so thankful she was able to hold her own against those deviants, Theseus and Pirithous, but at what cost? As a soldier, I know the toll that killing can take on a person. I desperately want to take her and hold her, erasing the pain from her mind, but I know that's impossible. What stops me is not her terror at being touched, the memories coming back to her in spurts, but the unknown. I feel my anger grow at the thought of Pirithous touching her. *Hurting* her. My knuckles turn white and my grip on the horse's reins burns my forearms.

Melinoe can sense something amiss, and she withdraws her hand from the saddle's horn and lays it gently on my arm, caressing the tension away. At her touch, I exhale, my breath surely tickling her neck. From the side of her face, I glimpse a grin forming, but I hold in the urge to run the back of my hand down her cheek. Instead, I focus my thoughts back on the mystery that is Melinoe.

I have so many questions, but am afraid it would drive her away if I were to ask. Why is her magic only now growing in strength? Why did I see her image on an ancient temple frieze? Why does she want to seek out Zeus? *Who is she?*

And, if I'm honest with myself, I'm afraid the answers might drive me away too.

• • • • ● • ● • • •

"Welcome to our home!" Alcmene, wife of General Amphitryon, pulls open the door and ushers our group into the house. She is heavily pregnant and maneuvering around her takes some effort on our part. Amphitryon stands just behind her, grasping forearms with Pollux and me.

"It's nice to see you again, soldiers." His booming voice is at odds with his diminutive frame, and I know many who are surprised at his status as a distinguished military hero. He leads us into the open foyer complete with stone floors, where introductions are made.

Helen, ever the inquisitive guest, immediately probes at Alcmene's condition. "How much longer until the babe is born?" She reaches for our hostess's belly, stroking it gently and leaning in to plant a kiss. Startled at her forwardness, I raise my eyebrows at Melinoe, who suppresses a laugh, while Pollux yanks his sister back.

"I'm so sorry for our sister, madam." He narrows his eyes at Helen, and she pouts. Even chastised, she's still beautiful, and I know everyone in the room finds it hard to be upset with her.

"My apologies, but I cannot wait to be a mother someday. When I find my perfect husband," she adds, quirking her lip slightly and playfully rocking on her toes.

Alcmene gives us a wan smile and nods in acceptance of Helen's apology, her hand covering her belly protectively.

"Gentlemen, please join me for a drink while the women retire and refresh themselves." Amphitryon leads me and Pollux away from the stairs while the women ascend. Turning toward Melinoe, I watch greedily as her hips sway up the stairs, reminding myself that I need to stay focused, not get distracted by my wife.

MELINOE

As we ascend the stairs behind the tall, willowy hostess, the smell of fresh-cut flowers on a side table tickle my nose, and I'm eager to see the sleeping accommodations if the entryway is so lovely.

Alcmene shows Helen to her room first, a beautiful suite with a tray of delicacies laid out on a table. We approach and take a seat on the velvet cushions while Alcmene, her dark eyes focused, pours us each a cup of tart white wine. I nibble on a fig while Helen takes a serving of salted fish. Alcmene sits, her long legs extending beneath the table, and folds her hands in her lap demurely. Awkward silence quickly fills the room.

"You must be excited for the arrival of your first child, madam." Helen attempts to draw our hostess into conversation.

"Oh, I am." Alcmene lowers her gaze to her folded hands, sniffing. As she raises her eyes, I see unshed tears threatening to overflow. My gaze flicks to Helen's, who immediately rushes to console our emotional host.

"Whatever is wrong?" Helen gasps, reaching to take Alcmene's hand, who, biting her trembling lip, shakes her head before her body is racked with sobs. She raises her hands to her eyes, and I move to kneel by her chair.

"You can tell us, Alcmene. We will help you." I grab hold of her other hand and reach for a crisp cloth napkin to wipe her tears.

"Oh, it's just this silly pregnancy causing me to be overly emotional."

Helen and I glance at one another, both of us unsure how to help.

"I feel so foolish sharing my pain with you girls," Alcmene continues. "But it's been so long since we've had guests, and I've no one to talk to . . ."

I smile encouragingly, and I notice that Helen does the same.

"Please, feel free to unburden yourself, madam. Your husband has such a reputation as an excellent general, and my brothers speak very highly of him. We are like family."

She sniffs a few more times before dabbing her eyes and blowing her nose. "I'm so embarrassed. Shamed, really."

"Go on," I encourage, despite the feeling growing in my gut.

Alcmene takes a deep, shuddering breath. "I-I'm afraid this ch-child isn't Amphitryon's." Her eyes lower as her face flames red. "I was forced, you see, against my will."

My eyes meet Helen's, and I see a flash of rage, likely mirroring my own, before she composes herself.

Helen squeezes Alcmene's hand, raising it to her chest. "Alcmene, you must know that this is not your fault." She swallows, glancing at Alcmene and then quickly away. "As you know, my mother, too, was forced. Twice. My brother Pollux and I myself are the products of those horrific events. But she loves us unconditionally, and I know you, too, will love this babe despite its beginning." She presses a kiss to Alcmene's fist and bows her head over their joined hands as though praying. Praying for love to come out of a hateful attack.

Alcmene sniffles again and nods. "I knew you two, especially, would understand." She looks at me and I, too, bow my head, ashamed to admit that my birth is the same as Helen's, even if those in the Land of the Living are all too aware. My mother's pain, the same as Alcmene's. Instead, I offer the only advice I know to be true.

"Your son or daughter will love *you* despite who his father is. And if Amphitryon is half the man he is claimed to be, this babe will be so very loved by both of you and will grow to become something great." My eyes well as I think of my father, Hades, and how much he loves me despite my conception. I am his daughter, through and through. I reach and press my palm to her stomach, forcing a smile.

Alcmene nods, extending her arms, and we are pulled in for a hug. As I meet Helen's worried gaze behind Alcmene's back, I know, without a doubt, that we share the same father as this unborn babe. The desire for revenge against Zeus solidifies in my stomach, and I turn my face away from Helen's before she can see the hatred burning in my eyes.

• • • ● • ● • • ● • •

We are back in the saddle the next morning after a hearty goodbye breakfast with both Amphitryon and Alcmene.

"Where to now, Dioscuri?" Amphitryon had asked us earlier, using the infamous moniker to address both Pollux and Castor. I had glanced up from my honeyed bread as Pollux deferred to his brother.

"We're heading north, toward Thessaly and the border of Macedon."

"Hm." Amphitryon paused, chewing his bread loudly. "Not much up there except Mount Olympus." He flicked his gaze to me, an eyebrow arched. I met his eyes, refusing to answer the unasked question.

"That's exactly where we're going," Castor replied, shocking both Pollux and Helen into dropping their food simultaneously.

Now, saddled and riding through the gates of Thebes toward the city-state of Phocis, Pollux turns to us, anger simmering in the air between our mounts.

"When were you going to tell us that we're going to Mount Olympus, brother?" He reins his horse in front of ours, forcing us to stop suddenly. The tree-lined trail provides beautiful scenery, but I can tell by Castor's rigid posture that he's watching for potential attacks and doesn't like this unnecessary halt to our trip, leaving us out in the open and arguing loudly.

"Melinoe needs to see her father, her *real* father, and I've agreed to accompany her. You're more than welcome to escort Helen home if you'd like. Or the two of you can come along, seeing as he's *your* father as well." Castor maneuvers our horse easily around the obstacle and trots back onto the road. I feel his head turning left and right, keeping an eye out for bandits or thieves.

"I, for one, am up for the adventure, especially as I'll be stuck at home once Papa marries me off," Helen chirps. "C'mon, Polydeuces." She turns in her seat, using the family nickname to coax Pollux into joining us. I, too, turn, watching the scene unfold as Castor slows our horse.

Pollux is quiet for a moment, his horse stopped in the middle of the road while ours champs to carry onward. "Fine, I'll come, but only if we can stop in Aetolia on our way." His eyes meet Castor's and a wide grin breaks out on his face.

I feel Castor slump in the saddle, and he lets a groan escape from his lips. I turn to him. "What's in Aetolia?"

"The Calydonian boar is what's in Aetolia, dear wife."

I raise an eyebrow, wanting more clarification.

"It's a boar hunt held by King Oeneus of Calydon. We received the invitation just days before you and Helen were—"

"The winner receives the boar's pelt and tusks as a prize!" Pollux eagerly squeezes the horse's ribcage with his calves, cantering ahead of us.

I shrug against Castor and turn toward him. "What's the harm in a little detour?"

· · · ● · ● ● · · ·

I take in the single bed before me and bite my lip. Am I sure about this? I look back at Castor, who's standing at the door, eyes fixed on me intently.

"We don't—"

"I think—"

We both speak at the same time.

He stops and I continue, "I think we should sit down and talk, Castor." I motion to the bed, taking a seat against the headboard as he perches near the foot. "I didn't want this marriage," I admit, lowering my gaze to my fidgeting hands. I sigh heavily, fold them in my lap to keep them still, and look into his eyes. In the flickering candlelight, they appear darker than they really are, the blue sedate and dim, like a frozen lake in winter. The skin around his eyes bunches, as though he's in pain.

"But I'm glad you're here with me." I offer him a small smile to reassure him, maybe take away the pain I see on his face. "I think this"—I move my hand back and forth between the two of us—"could work, but there are some things I need you to know."

Castor suddenly stands up and slips his shirt over his head.

"What are you—"

He leans down, hushing me as his lips touch mind tenderly, his hands running along my throat and up into my hair.

I start to dissolve into the heat that flickers up my spine, but my mind snaps into place. I pull back, brows drawn together in confusion. "Cas—"

He closes the distance I've created, bringing his hand around the back of my neck and pulling me close again, our foreheads pressed together, nose to nose, as he inches forward before claiming my mouth.

Fuck it. I silence my brain and launch myself at him, toppling us backward. My hands snake down his perfectly formed chest, tickling my way toward his abdominals, which are rock-hard. A moan escapes from his lips, and I feel heat spread to my thighs as I straddle him, leaning down and pulling his mouth to me. I part my lips, letting my tongue push against his and drawing it into my mouth.

He pulls me down, crushing me to his tight body, and flips us both so he's now on top. I writhe against him, feeling his erection, and my toes curl. Muscular thighs flexing, he grinds into me and snakes his hand under my shirt, stroking my stomach until he reaches my breast. Finding my nipple hard, he smiles against my mouth before cupping my breast in his warm hand, playfully stroking and caressing. I let out a gasp and reach for his pants.

He tenses and pulls away, his jaw clenching as the cords in his neck jump. "Mel, I don't think that's a good idea."

I blink, trying to hide my hurt. Swallowing, I mutter, "Oh . . ." I sit up and adjust my shirt, scooching away from him. Embarrassment and shame flutter in my belly. Have I done something wrong?

He puts his hand on my thigh and leans down to meet my gaze. "Hey, I don't mean it like that. Trust me, I want all of you. *Badly.* But I don't want to rush this. I want . . ." He hesitates, moving his hand from my thigh to grab my hand. "I want this to work."

I nod and give him a small smile. "I want this to work too." I push my hair behind my ears and, in the silence that follows, feel a little silly. I bite my lip and look up at him.

"What?" He cracks a gorgeous smile and heat creeps into my cheeks.

"Does that mean we have to stop what we *were* doing?" A slow smile stretches my face as I wiggle my eyebrows.

"Fuck no," he growls, pulling me back into his embrace.

CASTOR

I'm breaking all the rules as I pull Melinoe toward me, demanding her lips part as my tongue slides through them. I taste her, savor her, and still want more. She straddles me and I thrust up, grabbing her hips and pulling her into me. I want her so badly, even though I shouldn't, and I know she can feel my desire through my leathers. A moan escapes her mouth, and I clench her hair in my hand, pulling her head back and exposing her throat. She smiles wickedly, her eyes downcast, meeting mine, and I reach up to bite at her neck. A shiver runs through her body, thrumming against my erection.

"Mel," I whisper in her ear. "We need to stop." *Before it's too late* hangs in the air. *Before I'm completely gone for you.* But I don't stop. I keep kissing her everywhere, her mouth, her neck, sucking all the way down to her chest. I yank at her shirt, and she raises her arms, wiggling free. I continue caressing her exposed skin with my tongue, heading for her breasts.

"More, Cas," she begs, and I become unhinged. I roll her over, situate myself between her legs, and press her down into the mattress, my cock straining at my pants. I lean over, nibbling her ear.

"Is this what you want, Princess?" I alternate between soft bites and licks in the whorl of her lobe as goosebumps pucker her skin. She fists my hair, pulling it and raking her nails along my scalp. A delicious shiver runs down my spine, and I grind against her as she groans.

"Yes, Cas, *yes* . . ."

Our mouths are entwined, our breathing synchronized, and I honestly don't know where she ends and I begin. I want all of her, *now*. She wraps her legs around me, and I'm seconds from undoing her skirt and taking all of her when my mind snaps back to reality. If I don't stop now, I won't stop. I have to show her, prove to her, that our relationship means everything to me. She has to believe that I'm all in on this marriage, all in on *us*. I can't let myself lose control. If I do . . . well, I don't want to think what he'll do to me. My stomach clenches as I recall the horrifying images of my body sprawled out, stomach ripped open and guts exposed.

Feeling nauseous, I slow my movements and lie down next to her on the bed, pushing her hair behind her ear, and give her a smile.

"I want us to work, you know. I just think we need to spend some more time getting to know one another, getting to know who we are *together*." The sweet nothings make her purr like a cat.

She smiles drowsily and mumbles something unintelligible, her eyes closing as she wraps her body around mine.

I trace my finger along her jawline and down her collarbone, along her shoulder and down her arm. She continues purring contentedly. I reach over and throw the blanket over us as her mouth drops open and her body slackens. In the flickering candlelight, I look at my wife, this woman I've been charged to protect by Hades. She's beautiful and—gods be damned—I think I'd do *almost* anything for her. But, as I lie back, tucking my arm behind my head, I can't forget about my bargain, the agreement that I've made. *Almost* anything . . . not *anything*, I chastise myself as I close my eyes.

MELINOE

I awake in a cocoon of warmth and, for the first time, don't remember dreaming. I'm truly refreshed. Wondering at the amazing sleep, I find that Castor's giant is arm thrown around my shoulders, my body pulled tightly to his. I feel his desire pressing against me, and I, too, am still wound up after last night. I'm still yearning for more as his breath tickles against the back of my neck, and I smile dreamily, inhaling deeply and turning toward him. My movements wake him, and I watch as his pupils focus on me, widening in slight surprise.

"Morning," he whispers, cracking a smile.

"Morning," I reciprocate, biting my lip and rubbing the sleep from my eyes. I turn toward the door as I hear cutlery and a swift knock, indicating our breakfast has arrived. As I move to leave the warmth of our nest and retrieve the sustenance from the hall, Castor grabs my wrist, pulling me back into his embrace.

"Not yet." He claims my mouth, running his hands down my back and gripping my hips.

I smile against him, slowly drawing away. "We have to eat and get back on the road, *husband*." I see the lust flare in his eyes at my use of our married status, and a heat pools deep in my core. "We have the rest of our lives to indulge in lazy mornings spent abed, but today is not one of them."

He gulps and stiffens, nodding as his eyes lower. I crinkle my brow in confusion at his change in demeanor, but the scent of warm tea and fresh bread—my stomach grumbles—lures me to the chamber door.

After filling our bellies and donning our Spartan gear, we meet Pollux and Helen in the stable, our horses already saddled and ready to depart.

"It's about time you two lovebirds awoke!" Helen chirps. "Pollux was able to purchase two more horses for our journey, so now we can cover more ground." She motions toward the new mounts, both stallions. One is pure white and the other a deep, smoky gray. She raises her eyebrows to me.

"Which do you prefer, sister?"

I nod toward the snowy beast, a memory of riding a white horse, a sense of fleeing danger, flickering in my mind before disappearing. Helen doesn't seem to notice as I frown, futilely trying to bring back the recollection.

"Good," she says happily, "I had already named the gray Ashes."

Castor assists me in mounting, the sense of déjà vu briefly returning as his strong arms easily lift me into the saddle. Caressing his large hands down my calf, he notches my foot into the stirrup.

"We'll ride toward Phocis, making a stop at the Oracle at Delphi," he announces to our group. I eye him suspiciously, wondering what business he would have with the Oracle. "I'm sure we all have some questions we'd like answered," he adds.

Swallowing the lump that has formed in my throat, I tighten my thighs and set into a canter after the others. What questions could my husband need answered?

· · · ● · ● · ● · ·

As we travel the narrow paths to Phocis and the Oracle at Delphi, I purposefully walk my horse near Helen's, as we haven't had much time together recently. I feel guilty that I haven't checked in on her after Theseus, but she seems stronger than I'd originally thought.

"What do you know of the oracle?" I ask her quietly, watching Castor and Pollux deep in their own conversation about the Calydonian boar hunt.

"Not much." She shrugs. "As babes, my parents had the oracle read our futures. It was prophesied that I would be a great beauty"—she snorts—"as if that's any surprise." I laugh along with her.

"What did the oracle say about Castor and Pollux?" I try to remain indifferent, not wanting to let her know I'm digging for information.

She thinks for a moment, biting her lip. "I don't remember what Pollux's prophecy was. The oracle said that Castor would marry a daughter of Zeus, which I guess worked out for you both!" She pauses for a moment, brushing Ashes's mane contemplatively. "My father has always hated that Delphi, and thus the oracle, remained neutral, not attaching itself to Sparta, nor Athens or Corinth. I imagine her only allegiance is to Apollo."

"The oracle is a woman?" I raise my brows, surprised by this.

Helen nods. "She's called a Pythia, but who knows if we'll even get a chance to hear her speak."

"Why wouldn't we get to hear her speak?"

"The Pythia is only available to consult one day each month, and it's said that Apollo leaves Delphi for warmer climates in the winter, so the opportunities to speak with her are very slim."

My lips thin at our chances, wondering why Castor is so eager to consult the oracle. Is it about our marriage? About me and my magic? What does he need to know so badly? I stare at his back, wishing I knew his thoughts.

As though he can sense my watching him, he turns in his saddle, briefly making eye contact. I offer a smile, but he turns instead to Helen.

"As we approach Delphi, we'll need to prepare ourselves in hopes that we are chosen to consult the oracle." His gaze flicks to mine.

"What do these preparations require?" *And why are you going through all this trouble?* I don't give voice to the question burning my tongue.

"We'll need to make sure the oracle is available and that the day was found to be auspicious. If so, we must purify ourselves in the spring water of the sanctuary. Pollux will purchase us a sacrificial cake as an offering while we cleanse ourselves. He will then assist in the burnt offering to the gods, and we will be ushered in to meet the priestess."

"You will not seek the oracle's advice, then?" I ask Pollux.

He shrugs, shaking his head. "There isn't anything I need to know about my life's thread, woven by the Fates." Pollux's eyes brighten and he gives me a genuine grin. "I prefer not to know the answers to life's questions and instead live spontaneously!"

I'm envious of his nonchalant attitude, and as I lift my hand to my chest, rubbing my sternum, I feel the worry inside me solidifying into an ache. Am I ready to know what the Fates have woven in my own life's thread?

• • • • ● • ● • • •

The sun is high in the sky as we stand in line for our turn with the oracle. The weatherworn stone pillars surround the waiting area as trees creak in the breeze. Luck has been on our side, as the day was found to be auspicious. We have cleansed ourselves in the sanctuary's cool waters, and Helen holds the ceremonial cake in her hands, purchased from a cart outside the temple grounds. I gulp and look away as Pollux appears with a small goat, our burnt offering for the gods.

"Thank you for obtaining our necessities, brother." Castor acknowledges Pollux with a clap on the back. "This goat is sure to please the gods." The beast screeches, its horizontal pupils flicking at the surroundings.

"I've named him Idas, after our cousin." A wide grin splits Pollux's face and Castor snorts. Helen and I glance at each other and then shake our heads, not understanding the joke between the two.

138

"How much longer will I have to hold this delicious cake?" Helen whines, her belly audibly grumbling. "I hope we don't have to wait too much longer. I'm starving!"

"It looks as though we're up next," Castor responds, gesturing for Pollux to take the goat to the altar nearby.

Pollux pulls the goat along behind him. "Say goodbye to everyone, Idas." The goat sticks out its tongue and bleats again as it blindly follows along.

I turn toward Helen and Castor, my back to the altar. I've never liked the gore associated with sacrifices. "Helen, what are you going to ask the oracle?"

She shrugs, still eyeing the cake with envy. "I suppose I could ask about my future husband, if he'll be handsome and a love match." I nod, knowing a love match is highly unlikely for a princess of Sparta. Or any princess married for political alliances, for that matter.

Lowering my lashes to slyly watch Castor, I see that he taps his foot impatiently. Why does he appear nervous? Is he afraid the oracle will speak poorly about our union? I remind myself to breathe, hoping to calm my own nerves.

"It looks like it's finally our turn!" Helen's eyes light up eagerly, and we are ushered up the steps of the temple.

I follow, glancing back at Pollux, who looks serious, his eyes meeting mine. I continue to inhale deeply and make my way up the steps.

Castor enters first, and I move to join him. Instead, he turns, placing his hand out, stopping me. I look up at him and blink, confusion knitting my brows together.

"I'd like to go in alone, Melinoe." His steely gaze offers no room for negotiation, and I take a small step back, pressing my lips together. My mouth goes dry.

"Oh," I utter, feeling very dim for my presumption that we would visit the oracle together, and search his eyes for an explanation. When he says no more, I find my voice. "I-I'll just wait here with Helen for my turn." I watch as she hands Castor the cake, blinking back the sting in my eyes. I'd thought this would be something we would share, and the worry in my chest slides into my gut.

He enters the temple without turning back, and I wonder what he's hiding.

CASTOR

I gnoring the obvious hurt I saw in Melinoe's eyes, I lift my chin and approach the Pythia. I lower the cake slowly onto the steps overlooking a small fountain, where more dishes have been placed.

Seated on a tripod in the middle of the temple, with a vapor wafting in the air from a small canister on the floor before her, the oracle is taking deep, sating breaths of the incense, eyes closed. Her white robe, made of sturdy linen, wraps tightly around her diminutive frame. Tiny wrists peek from the sleeves, long fingers forming a steeple.

"Welcome, son of Sparta." She exhales, slowly cracking open her eyes. The skin around them is wrinkled and thin, purple crescent moons circle underneath. She's tired. Her emotionless face watches me as I take a seat on the pillow before her. With a trembling, ancient hand, she retrieves a fresh packet of herbs from a box to her left, shaking them into the canister and then adding a clear liquid from a carafe. Lighting the burner beneath the case, she finally inquires of my journey.

"You have come to ask for peace, yes?"

Sitting cross-legged and attempting to keep my back straightened, I nod, my jaw tense. "Yes, Pythia."

She leans over the vapor, inhaling deeply, and closes her milky eyes as though entering into a trance. I wait patiently, the silence drowning out my own thoughts. Finally, after what feels like ages, she speaks.

"Apollo will be unable to prophesy your future."

My eyes widen, not understanding. "Wh-why not, Oracle? Why is Apollo unable to see my future?"

She stares blankly at me, swaying in her seat. "Your future is not set yet, Prince. You have yet to choose a path." She indicates the swirling smoke, which begins to form a road between us. I watch, transfixed, as the path suddenly divides and then disappears in the distance.

"Your path was set and your future clear until a few days ago." She indicates the intersection in the smoke. "Now I see a great choice to make, one which will not only affect you, but those around you." She narrows her eyes, meeting mine with a determined gaze.

"Can you help me make the choice, Mistress?" My voice is strained, my muscles tense as my mind tries to discern which course of action to take.

"No, son. You must make the decision. But no matter the choice, the outcome remains the same." She flicks her wrist and the smoke moves past the intersection, further down the timeline. I watch as a vapor-created figure falls to the ground and disappears into the air. Into nothingness.

"Death," she states. I gulp.

My thoughts race while I try to make sense of the situation. Opening my mouth slowly, I ask the question that, deep down, I already know the answer to.

"Whose death, Pythia?" I scan her face rapidly, wishing the words were different. My gut clenches, as if it already knows the answer to my question.

"Yours, Prince of Sparta." The smoke engulfs the room and, as I cough loudly while I try to gasp for air, a door opens to the left of the chamber, indicating my time is over. I flail my arms about, trying to clear the smoke from the air, but the Pythia's seat is empty.

She's gone.

MELINOE

I wait as Castor, then Helen, enters the temple to speak with the Oracle. Fidgeting and pulling at my lip, I pace outside the large wooden doors, thinking fretfully on the questions I seek to be answered. Deep down in my gut, something feels off, but I push the niggling feeling aside and continue my pacing.

Pollux ascends the stairs as he cleans his hands with a cloth, the goat's sacrifice complete, and rests his hand on my arm, stilling me from my paces. "What troubles you, sister?"

I shake my head, not wanting to voice my apprehension to him for fear it'll be shared with Helen or, even worse, Castor. Instead, I turn my attention to him. "Are you sure you have no questions for the oracle? No desire to hear your future?"

"No, I know what the future holds for me, and I do not need to hear it spoken from a drugged priestess."

My eyes widen.

"I have a full life of debauchery ahead of me." He chuckles playfully.

I furrow my brows, wondering at his ability to be so indifferent while I'm worried sick, the anticipation gnawing my insides.

"I can read your future while you wait . . . if you'd like?" He smiles mischievously and crosses his arms, then lowers his gaze to his boots as he toes the stone floor of the temple steps.

Smiling widely, I decide to indulge him, if only to take my mind from the impatience I feel at waiting for the real oracle. "Tell me, oh wise one, what does my future hold?"

Cocking his head as though listening to an invisible voice in the distance, he smiles roguishly.

I laugh, raising my eyebrows. "What do you see, then? Bags of gold? A large castle? Your brother with a new sword?"

He chuckles and shakes his head. "I see nothing so primitive from either of you. For you, I see many happy years married to my brother, the future king of Sparta, and ruling by his side as his powerful warrior queen."

My smile falters and I blink rapidly, inhaling a gasp. "What about the Underworld? Shall I give up everything, my place and my people there, to sit prettily by your brother's side and be a brood mare for the future of Sparta?" My voice is ice, freezing Pollux's playful grin.

Crestfallen, he shakes his head and replies, "I didn't mean anything by it, Melinoe. I was just pretending." His eyebrows furrow and a mix of confusion and hurt flicker on his face, making me feel horrible for my outburst.

I again fidget with my fingers, curling and uncurling them into fists, and lower my gaze, feeling like a genuine ass for taking his playfulness so seriously. "I'm sorry, Pollux. I didn't mean to snap at you. I just—" Suddenly the door to the temple opens and the attendant beckons me forward, into the darkness within.

I turn toward Pollux, my stomach fluttering with nerves. I grab his hand. "I—"

But he cuts me off. "I know, sister." He smiles and squeezes back, gesturing for me to enter the temple. "Good luck," he calls behind me, and I walk toward the entrance, one step at a time, ready to hear my destiny prophesied.

The temple feels familiar, yet I am still in awe as I enter the inner sanctum. Glancing around as I approach the oracle, I'm astonished by the beauty. Trees blossom, flowers grow wild, and a babbling fountain flows in the corner. Butterflies float lazily on the scented vapor that fills the chamber with an equally sweet and spicy odor. Light shines from a skylight opening in the roof, and I blink, surprised by it all. My eyes finally come to rest on a tiny woman resting in the middle of the room on a large circular slab atop a low dais.

Her white-blond hair is covered by a bloodred scarf, and her dress is so sheer I can see the dark outline of her nipples, her perky breasts visible through the material. As I take in her cross-legged position, I notice that her entire body is on display. Lowering my gaze to the ground, I approach and immediately kneel in supplication, pressing my forehead to the stone floor.

"Rise, daughter of the Destroyer and Falling Stars, We will not be bowed to by One as honored as You."

I raise my eyes and, now that I'm closer, fully take in her features. Her pale hair is offset by the ochre color of her skin. Her youthful eyes, a brilliant maroon color, are unlike any I've ever seen, even in the Underworld. Set below white brows and rimmed with thick lashes, they meet my gaze with equal curiosity, examining me. Her plump lips, colored a blood red to match her tunic, break into a smile and I watch, mystified, as her pupils flash from small circles into vertical slits, like a cat. Startled, I step back and raise my hand to my chest.

"What are you?" I ask, equally inquisitive and horrified. I swallow, taking a step forward again.

"I am the Pythia, Oracle of Apollo," she states bluntly. She blinks, the vertical pupils slowly appraising me from head to toe. "As you are one of Our Family, I am able to shed my guise and appear to you in my true form." She extends her arms straight out from her body, unashamed at her nakedness.

I nod slowly, unsure what she means by "one of Our Family," but push it to the back of my mind as I focus, instead, on my reason for consulting her. "I have come—"

"You have come to discover who you are, Princess."

"No, I wanted to—"

"You cannot 'want' to do anything until you know who you are. And, I imagine, you do not know the truth of who you are, do you?"

Her voice, combining with the smoky scent blooming from a basket on the floor, becomes muffled in my brain. I fight to stay alert, focusing on her lips, squinting to comprehend.

"Do you want to know who you are?" she hisses in my direction, her eyes flashing brighter.

"I want to know what's wrong with me. I want to know why I can't summon my magic," I clarify, holding out my palms to her. Since entering the temple, my fingers have again blackened. I crinkle my brow and run my thumb along my digits.

She glances briefly at my fingers, a smirk forming on her lips, and then turns to her right to refill the canister at her feet. She gently adds a spoonful of herbs to the basket, grasps hold of a carafe, and pours in a thick red liquid that resembles blood. A coppery tang coats my nostrils, burns its way down my throat.

"Light the burner," she commands, gesturing beneath the canister.

I shake my head, mouth gaping. "I-I'm unable to use my magic. It doesn't work," I tell her, feeling heat creep up my neck.

"Light the burner," she repeats.

"Didn't you hear me? I can't. Look." I lazily wave my hand toward the basket, and as expected, it remains unlit.

Her eyes flash a bright red, blinding me, and I squint as I raise my hand to protect my face from the heat emanating from the oracle.

Her voice becomes a rumble, thundering from within her tiny body. "Light. The. Burner."

Holding my hands out, palms up, I yell back at her, "I can't!"

"Εκάτη, ανάψε τον καταραμένο καυστήρα," she commands one last time.

As she utters the name *Hecate*, my body heats, a tingle spreading from my fingers up my arms, the pain growing stronger as it moves through my chest.

"Kápste to fos!" Pointing to the canister, I feel magic surge from my finger as the whole damn thing goes up in flames.

The Pythia's eyes flutter in ecstasy as a feline smile breaks out on her face. "*I knew it*," she hisses aloud as I gaze in amazement at the flames before me.

"Welcome back, Hecate."

· · ● ●· ● ●· · ·

"What did you just call me?" Other than a hard thudding in my chest, my body has frozen. I blink slowly, letting my eyes refocus.

"I called you the name you are." She shrugs, leaning in to inhale the smoky vapor now pouring from the canister.

"That is *not* my name." My breaths are coming in short bursts, and I swallow rapidly, trying to slow everything down. Trying to slow down the pounding in my chest.

"You wanted to know who you are. She is who you are." The Pythia blinks at me, tilting her head to the side as her cat eyes continue to watch me, assess me.

"H-how can that be? How can I *be* someone I'm *not*?" I don't understand, and as I raise my hand to my chest, I find that it's trembling uncontrollably. I cover my face with my palms. Surely this is just another dream.

"You have always been Hecate. You have just been in denial. Your soul is older than you think, and has been on many journeys. Throughout them all, you have been Hecate." She says this as though she is informing me the sky is blue or the grass green.

"Why me?" I whisper.

"Why not you?" She lets out a bark of a laugh at my question. "And now that you know who you truly are, you can take your place on Mount Olympus."

I snap my gaze to hers, horrified by what she's just said. "My place on Mount Olympus? Why on earth would I want to live there?"

"It is where you belong, Hecate."

"Stop calling me that. My name is Melinoe."

"Regardless"—she waves away my protests dismissively—"as a Titan, you belong on Mount Olympus. You are older than the gods. You are more *powerful*, more *ancient*, more *divine*. It is in your *blood*. It is where you belong."

I sit quietly for a moment, thinking on these . . . allegations. "How do I . . . summon her? How do I bring her back?" I ask, holding my palms up again, the blackened fingers now free of their coloring.

"Once you stop denying who you truly are, you will invite her into your heart and you will simply . . . become her. I imagine it has happened before, has it not?" Again, she cocks her head and blinks.

I slide my eyes away from hers, my mind a rush of unanswered questions and a web of confusion. My mouth opens and closes as my brain fights to comprehend.

"I believe we are done here." As she dismisses me, the large wooden door opens to her left, and smoke fills the chamber.

"Wait, what happens to me—to Melinoe—when I invite her in?" I gasp through the smoky room, waving my hands around to clear the air. I flap my arms wildly, moving forward as I search, trying to find the Pythia, to call her back, but she's disappeared.

CASTOR

The temple door flings open and Melinoe stumbles out, coughing wildly and flailing her arms in a panic. I grab her, moving us away from the smoky vapors pouring from the doorway, and smack her back to help her clear her lungs.

"I'm here." I tell her as I pull her closer, her fingers holding tightly to my tunic as she struggles to pull in air. "Breathe, Mel." Helen is at my side, holding forth a jug of watered wine from her satchel.

"Take a drink." She shoves the flagon into Mel's face. I stand back and watch as Melinoe drinks heavily, liquid dripping down her chin. "Are you all right?" she asks, worry etched in her features.

Melinoe continues gulping the liquid, while Helen's eyes meet mine, and I see a flash of worry flicker in them before she turns her focus back to Melinoe.

Melinoe returns the wine and proceeds to take deep, settling breaths. "I-I'm fine. The smoke . . . it was just unexpected. I think I inhaled too much." She gasps as her breathing continues to slow.

I rub her back and nod as Pollux jogs our way. His gaze flicks between mine and Helen's, but I shrug him off, guiding Melinoe and our group toward the horses.

"How about we grab sustenance before finding accommodations for the night? We've had a long day."

Helen perks up, her eyes widening. "I'm *starving*! I almost ate one of the offerings in the temple!" She jokes, laughing to herself.

Melinoe's eyes remain unfocused, and she doesn't acknowledge Helen's jesting. I frown, holding her back and gesturing for Helen and Pollux to go on ahead.

My hand tightens on her arm, and I pull her to me. "What happened in there?"

She looks everywhere but at me, and my chest constricts, worry speeding up my heartbeats.

"You tell me," she says, her gaze finally meeting mine, wide and unblinking.

My stomach plummets. What did the oracle say to her?

"Wh-what do you mean?" I stutter, my brow furrowing. I take a step back, putting some distance between us in case things turn violent. I know how volatile Melinoe can be when her magic appears, especially when emotions are involved.

Her nostrils flare and her gaze hardens. "Why are you moving away from me? Are you hiding something?" She stabs the air between us with her finger, demanding an answer. One I can't give her. I can't utter those words to her until I've done everything in my power to stop it from happening.

"What would I have to hide, Mel?" I am terrified at where this conversation is headed, my mind going in a thousand different directions, none of which show the possibility of solving this amicably.

"Why didn't you want to speak with the oracle together, Castor? Are you questioning this? Us?" She gestures at the space between us.

My heart rate instantly slows and I exhale, my shoulders falling. The oracle didn't reveal my truths to Melinoe. I let a lazy smile lift my lips and shake my head, allowing out a small chuckle of relief. "Mel, of course I'm not questioning us." I pause, thinking quickly.

"I only . . ." I gulp, the lie burning my tongue as I taste it take form. "I only wanted to make sure we're making the right journey. Toward Mount Olympus and Zeus." I lower my head, hating myself for the deception.

She blinks, the anger clearing from her face, replaced by confusion. "You don't think we should continue onward?"

I shake my head, grabbing her hands and squeezing. "It's not that. I'm just . . . I'm just worried. I don't want anything to happen to you." That, at least, is the truth. How I'm going to stop something happening to her—happening to me—is beyond my brain's understanding. I push the thought away. I'll deal with it later.

She smiles, and my heart splits in two. Biting her lip, she flexes onto her toes and pressing a quick peck on my mouth. My breath hitches. Everything is fine. Or so it appears to her.

"Don't be worried. We'll be fine." She pulls me along, following after Pollux and Helen.

I don't realize until later that she doesn't mention her time with the oracle, nor what she learned.

MELINOE

"Welcome, hunters, to Calydon and the boar hunt!" Meleager, the crown prince, shouts from his mounted perch. Seated beside him on a magnificent ebony steed is his father, King Oeneus, the reason the boar has been unleashed onto his people. By forgetting to honor Artemis with the annual harvest sacrifice, he upset the fickle goddess, who in turn loosed the rampaging beast on the Calydonian people. Looking around, I can see the destruction brought about by this monster, the vineyards destroyed and the crops decimated. The Calydonian people are starving, but these hunters are here to stop it.

I stare out among the others gathered, seeing a few familiar faces. Sons of gods and other royal offspring, ready to show the world that, like me, they are able to step out of their parents' shadows and achieve greatness. At my side, Castor and Pollux flick their gazes around the assembled congregation as well, making note of the men who are eyeing Helen as though *she* were the prize. Rolling my eyes, I realize that, one day soon, she will be if King Tyndareus has any say in her marriage.

My wandering glance lands on a familiar face, and my heart drops, ice instantly freezing my veins. Stiffening, I let out a gasp and Castor, hearing me, follows my gaze out into the crowd, his own eyes widening in recognition.

Castor's jaw clenches. "*Pirithous*," he growls quietly, avoiding alerting anyone else of our enemy. From my horse, I can hear his teeth grinding, and I flinch, worrying what this means for our journey. "I thought you'd finished him off." His words are curt, cold, accusatory.

Gulping, I refuse to balk at his tone, instead narrowing my eyes. "I thought I had. There was enough wolfsbane in that cup to fell the Cretan Minotaur."

Pollux glances at us, his eyebrows raised. When Castor juts his chin toward Pirithous, who miraculously still hasn't noticed our group, Pollux's face goes red with rage. "What the fuck is he doing here?" He hisses, his anger alerting Helen, who hushes us as Meleager continues to announce the rules of the hunt, as well as the prizes. Luckily she hasn't seen Pirithous and is unaware of our nemesis's presence in the crowd.

"Apparently he's immune to wolfsbane, or *someone* interfered with his descent to the Underworld," Castor bites back at his brother, swinging his horse around and trotting toward the makeshift tented village in the clearing.

Someone interfered with his descent to the Underworld? My eyebrows squish together. What did Castor mean by that? Does he think Hades would stop a kidnapper and potential rapist from entering the Land of the Dead?

Frowning, Helen, Pollux, and I follow, drawing the attention of the crowd. As I turn my horse, I catch Pirithous's eyes. His face hardens as he acknowledges me. I refuse to avert my gaze, refuse to weaken myself as I straighten my back, sitting taller. It's then that I notice him leaning toward a man at his side. He whispers something to the man and nods in my party's direction. As I move my mount, I am afforded a clear view of his neighbor.

Euphemus, son of Poseidon, and Theseus's brother.

• • • • • • • • • •

"What do you suggest we do, brother?" Pollux inquires as we dismount near our shelters. He helps Helen from her horse and then stomps after Castor into our shared tent. I make to follow, but Helen stops me, grabbing my arm forcefully and pulling me to the side.

"What is he doing here, Melinoe? I thought you took care of everything?" Her voice is shrill and I watch as she takes shallow breaths, terror flashing in her eyes.

I grab her hands and squeeze tightly. "Helen, Pirithous was *dead* when I left that room." My mind flashes back to the image of his body laid out on the bed, bilious foam spurting from his mouth, his eyes rolling back in his head as his hands reach toward me, his mouth forming that deathly O as his body stilled. "He was dead. I'm sure of it, Helen. There must be something else at play here. We need to figure out what happened and how he's alive. Who would want *Pirithous* alive?" I ask incredulously, shaking my head as my lip curls in disgust. "He's nothing but a menace."

Helen reaches her hand up and tucks a loosened curl behind my ear before she grazes her palm down my cheek, offering motherly comfort. I try not to wish Persephone was here, but I do wish I could ask her for advice. "Maybe it's not who wants *Pirithous* alive, but who wants *you* dead, Melinoe." She slows her breathing and bites her lip. "Would Hades ever . . .?" She cocks an eyebrow and I still.

"No." My blunt answer is enough to stop the mere suggestion, but I elaborate anyway. "Hades is my father. He would never hurt anyone, despite what everyone in the Land of the Living believes of him and my mother."

Helen is quiet, her steely gaze probing my own. "Who else ushers souls to the Underworld?"

My stomach drops and my mouth goes dry. "He wouldn't," I whisper, my eyes widening in horror.

Helen reaches for my hand, squeezing it in comfort. She gulps, realization dawning on her face. "Hermes," she breathes.

I take a step back, covering my mouth with my hand. She's right. I'm speechless, but I know she's right. This isn't about Pirithous at all. This is about me, about Hecate. I feel it in my bones, in my gut. I turn and flee into the tent, smashing into Castor's broad chest.

"Whoa, what's wrong?" He pulls my hand away from my mouth and tilts my chin to meet his gaze. I'm instantly calmed by his presence, but the fear has settled in the pit of my stomach, curling and twisting into something dark and ominous.

"I saw Euphemus with Pirithous, Castor. He's—"

"I know who Euphemus is. Poseidon's son. But why would that frighten you?"

"I met Theseus's mother. She mentioned that Theseus was the son of Poseidon, which makes . . ." My voice trails off.

" . . . which makes Euphemus and Theseus brothers. Poseidon is their father," Castor finishes the sentence, nodding in understanding.

"You think Euphemus wants revenge for what you did to his brother?" Pollux inquires as Helen enters the tent.

"If not Euphemus, then certainly Poseidon might want revenge," I add, fear tickling the back of my neck. I've angered an Olympian. Shit.

"Theseus deserved everything Melinoe did to him," Helen snarls from behind me. I turn slowly, trying to push away the memories from that day. From what I saw Theseus doing to Helen. She makes her way to me, wrapping her arms around my shivering body. I hadn't even realized I was cold, and her warmth and closeness soothe me. I hug her back, squeezing tightly.

"Pollux, you may not get that boar's hide or tusks as a prize." Castor's lips thin as he addresses his brother.

"Oh, I'll get my prize, brother, and I can guarantee it will come from a pig." Pollux's words give me strength, and as we lock eyes across the tent, he nods fiercely. I'm so grateful for my new little family.

· • • • •• • • • ·

Stoking the fire outside our two tents, I enjoy a moment of peace alone, as Castor and Pollux haven't let either me or Helen out of their sights. Instead, one of them is always present, hovering like a clucking mother hen. Pollux, before plodding his way down to the nearby stream in an attempt to catch dinner, makes sure Castor and I are aware that Helen is lying down in their shared tent and implores us to check on her every few moments in case a philanderer, or worse, were to intrude upon us.

My mind has been going nonstop since I realized Hermes's deceit. The pieces of the puzzle are clicking into place. As my tutor, the sole person responsible for helping me hone my magic, he must be the reason my skills never appeared. He improperly trained me and then refused to lead Pirithous to the Underworld. But why? Why would my teacher—a trusted adviser to Hades and Persephone—commit such deception?

I take a seat closer to the fire and pull my wrapper closed around my shoulders. The air has turned chilly beneath the canopy of the trees. I keep my gaze focused on the fire, my mind in a tangle, as Castor sits next to me, our thighs brushing. He, too, remains quiet, the flickering fire illuminating his chiseled features.

Holding my breath, I peek at him through lowered lashes, thankful for the opportunity to focus on anything else at the moment. Taking him in, I'm surprised at how my heart thuds in my chest. His chin is dotted with day-old stubble, giving him a surprisingly rugged appearance. It's a pleasant change from the smoothness of his clean-cut princely appearance. I imagine that rough stubble against my neck, and my thighs clench beneath my skirt.

"Are you cold?" he asks, his gaze trailing up my bare legs. It's as though I can feel his eyes caressing my skin. Goosebumps pepper my limbs, not from the chill but from the desire snaking up my body.

I blush, shaking my head, and smile slowly. "I-I'm not," I stammer, embarrassment flaring in my chest. If anything, I'm liquid fire, dripping wetness all over the wooden seat. I attempt to scoot farther down on the log, but he turns toward me, whips off his cloak, and slings it around my shoulders. He pulls me onto his lap as though I weigh nothing, fingers trailing up my legs as I snuggle against him. A warmth dips down into my core. I turn toward him, our noses nearly touching, and without thinking about it, I reach for his scruffy beard, my fingers tickling along his jawline.

His lips part as his breathing increases, our chests heaving in tandem. I rake my fingers higher, along his temple and into his hair. His tongue flicks out, licking along his bottom lip, and I melt further into his warmth.

"Melinoe," he growls quietly, his large hands moving from my hips up my back. My breasts press into his chest, our breathing erratic as we start to move against one another. His hips thrust up into me as I tangle my other arm around his neck.

"Cas—" I begin, my voice cracking. We're writhing against one another, him grinding up and me pressing firmly down into his lap, where I can feel him hardening beneath me.

He looks into my eyes and then slowly lowers his face to mine, claiming my mouth and sucking on my bottom lip. I let out a whimper, and with a low rumble in his throat, Castor lifts me effortlessly, my legs wrapping around his waist as he circles his hands around my ass, and turns toward our tent.

Parting the flap, he hauls us both inside and slowly lowers me onto our makeshift bed, covered in soft, warm furs. I gasp as his mouth moves from my lips to my neck, the stubble tickling and likely to leave a noticeable rash, but I don't care and writhe my hips against him. I want this. I want him. I want to silence the chaos in my mind and enjoy the feel of his body pressed against me. Unfortunately, he interrupts my reverie.

"Are you sure this is what you want?" He pulls back, seductively meeting my eyes as his hand starts to move beneath my top. I don't like this little game. I don't want to think, I don't want to talk, I only want to play. My breath hitches as he fingers the waistband of my Spartan skirt, untucking the blouse and inching his way up my stomach. I bite my lip and nod my head as his hand finds my nipple.

"I need to hear you say it," he demands, yanking the fabric up over my head and sinking his mouth to my breast, flicking his tongue around the sensitive flesh.

"Yes," I cry as I arch into him.

While his mouth tastes my flesh, his hand slides beneath the band of my skirt, pulling it low around my pelvis. I continue rolling my hips, eager for him to touch me, but suddenly his hand stops and his mouth releases me. I stare at his darkened, lustful eyes, and my heart stops.

CASTOR

Her hardened nipple pops out of my mouth with a delicious smack, and I stare deeply at her, my stiff cock pressing into her thigh. I shouldn't be doing this, but I can't help myself. When she looked at me by the fire, I was possessed, with only one thing on my mind. *My wife.*

"Princess, I'll ask you one more time." I smirk, dipping and licking her neck in between each word. "Are you sure you want this? Want me?" I smile impishly, enjoying teasing her. Based on her frown and refusal to answer me, she's hating it. But her body says otherwise as she trembles beneath my caresses.

My mind is screaming at me to stop, that I'm breaking all the rules of the bargain, but my body isn't listening. I've known since the day I met Melinoe that I wanted to take her, fully make her mine, the gods be damned. The second I saw her, I knew she'd be my downfall, and as I inch her skirt higher, exposing her, I'm ready to fall headfirst into the abyss. She moans so softly, barely a breath escaping those swollen lips, that my cock throbs against the seam of my pants. I'm done for, completely lost in her and the moment. I slowly move my face lower and lower, kissing her sternum, down to her navel, and along the tops of her thighs. I can smell her sweetness, and it makes me want to drink her in. As I tongue lower toward her apex, I stop once more, smirking as she sighs loudly and glares at me.

I say nothing, only stare from between her pale thighs. She huffs indignantly, eyebrows lowered over those dark eyes. Finally, I say, "You'll get no more from me until you admit that you want me to fuck you. Hard." I make to rise, adjusting myself, but then she stills my hand.

"I want . . ." She swallows. ". . . you." A blush tints her cheeks, and my heart stutters in my chest.

"What do you want me to do to you?"

She blinks, confusion knitting her brow, and I instantly know that she's never been pleasured the way I want to pleasure her. I chuckle aloud, glee mixed with desire shooting straight to my cock at what I'm about to do to her, and then attempt to thin my lips and contain my mirth as her eyes betray hurt at my reaction.

"Don't laugh at me!" she exclaims, trying to swat me.

Instead, I lunge toward her, grabbing her face between my hands, and kiss her fully on the mouth while I grind my hard length into her. She shudders, and I move quickly back to my position between her legs, ready to lap at her wetness.

"Wife, no woman has ever made me feel the way you have," I say as I part her wet flesh with my fingers. This time, I'm not lying. There's something about her, about this woman I've promised to protect. Even if I'm lying to her every day about a plethora of other things, I'm not lying about how much I desire her. She gasps as I swipe my tongue gently into the valleys of her sex, her legs shaking on either side of my shoulders.

"You, my sweet, wet, princess, are the only one I want." My fingers flicker back and forth over her folds, taunting that bundle of nerves, her hips bucking against my hand. "I want to taste your sweetness." I plunge my fingers into her and pull out, drenched with her desire. Meeting her gaze, I slowly lick each digit, savoring the taste of her in my mouth.

"Cas," she gasps, biting that damn lip and driving me mad. She pulls me up to her mouth and kisses me, tasting herself on my lips. I drive my fingers back into her pussy, pushing in and pulling out, gently tweaking her sensitive skin.

"Let me taste you," I beg, pulling away from her mouth. I lower myself and lap at her skin, savoring each drink I take from her. She gasps louder, her hands digging into my scalp and hips bucking into my mouth as she grinds herself into my face. Her ass writhes against the furs, her heels pressed into the bedding. I feel her muscles tighten around my fingers and plunge them deeper. My own body seeks release, and I reach down to undo my leathers, sliding in to stroke myself, gripping my length tightly as I pump my hand up and down. The scene before me is one from a dream, and I fist myself harder as her shrieks of ecstasy fill my ears. My hips jerk against my hand and she comes with a shudder, her body arching against the bed. I collapse next to her, massaging her thighs and snaking my hands around to her ass, cupping it as I rise up to her, my cock standing at attention.

Her lazy gaze meets mine and a faint blush tints her cheeks as she shivers with the aftershocks of her sated desire.

"Now it's your turn," she says, smiling wickedly as she pushes me onto my back. My length throbs, eager to feel her mouth.

Suddenly, a shriek tears through our tent, and my heart stops. It's Helen.

MELINOE

Cas laces up his leathers and I wrap a fur around my naked body as we tumble from our tent and barge into Helen's. She stands over a small creature cowering in the corner of the hut, its eyes beady and brown fur matted.

"What the fuck, Helen?" Castor snarls, short sword drawn and pointed in front of him, ready to slay an intruder.

She points to the elongated body, her hand trembling. "I-I didn't realize it was just a weasel," she admits, eyes wide with fear.

"It's okay." I crouch down and extend my hand to the pitiful beast, but it emits a low growl and hisses, scooching farther into the darkness of the corner.

I feel Helen stiffen beside me as she notices our attire, or lack thereof. "I'm so sorry to have interrupted . . . I promise I didn't realize what it was," she repeats, plunking down loudly onto the furs of her own bedroll. She sighs heavily and fidgets with her fingers. "I guess I'm just nervous about every little sound," she admits.

Turning my attention away from the creature, I move to sit next to her, wrapping my arm around her shoulder. "Helen, you don't need to apologize. We're both a little jumpy with Pirithous showing up like this." I look at Castor, who has finally lowered his sword, and widening my eyes at him, I dip my head toward his sister.

Startled, he clears his throat and plops down on the other side of Helen, crossing and uncrossing his arms. "Everything is going to be fine," he adds rather unhelpfully. I meet his eyes and roll my own, shaking my head.

The weasel, feeling brave enough to leave the corner of the tent, jumps into my lap and joins us, pawing at my makeshift dress before circling and settling among the furs.

Helen chuckles. "Looks like we've got another adventurer. Let's keep her!"

Castor sniffs and crinkles his nose. "It stinks, are you sure you want to keep it?"

Helen and I both cry out, demanding to keep the beady-eyed beast, and shove Castor off the bedroll, laughing at his shocked face. Unperturbed in her nest on my lap, the weasel sighs contentedly.

· · · • · • · · ·

Later in the evening we gather around the fire, roasting the fish that Pollux caught. In the nearby camps, more hunters sit around their own fires, the sounds of jolly merrymakers in the distance making me feel safe.

"Get off me, rodent!" Pollux screeches as our new friend tries to snatch a bite of fish. The pitiful creature slumps her shoulders and hisses, baring her tiny fangs.

"Hey, leave Gale alone!" Helen scolds, holding out a piece of her meal to the weasel. Gale greedily snarfs up the food using her tiny paws, licking her chops when she's finished. She sniffs, looking around expectantly for more, and we laugh at Pollux's disgusted face.

"It's not a pet, Helen. It's a giant rat."

I grab hold of Gale, and she snuggles into my lap. "She's a *girl*, Pollux. Not an *it*," I emphasize, scratching behind her ears.

"Why'd you name it Gale anyway?" Pollux asks us.

Helen turns to me, and we both burst into a fit of giggles. "At General Amphitryon's castle, we were spending time with Alcmene. Her midwife, Galinthias, kept interrupting to check on her charge—"

Helen interrupts me. "Remember when she came in and told us to stop hugging Alcmene or we'd harm the babe?" We both burst into laughter.

"So anyway," I continue, "the midwife had these beady little eyes, just like our weasel friend here. So we've named her Gale!"

Pollux gestures to Castor. "Are you going to allow this . . . this smelly thing into your tent?"

I eye Castor and make a pouting face at him, pushing out my bottom lip and widening my eyes sorrowfully. He chuckles and takes a bite of fish before addressing his brother.

"My wife can do whatever she wants, Pol, and if she wants a smelly weasel for a pet, so be it." I smile sweetly at him before turning back to my own meal.

We sit in companionable silence for a bit, each of us enjoying our full bellies and the crackling fire. Castor, scooting closer despite his aversion to Gale, traces his fingers up my arm. Delicious shivers run down my spine, and as I look at him, a heat rises to my cheeks at the memory of his face between my thighs. I clench my legs together and reach for him, running my fingers through his hair as he leans down and nuzzles my neck.

"Knock it off you two, we're trying to eat." Pollux tosses a piece of fish our way, and as I pull away, embarrassed at my blatant display of affection, I notice Meleager, the crown prince, approaching.

"Good evening, Dioscuri." He nods quickly as he walks past our group. Castor shared with me earlier that the twins had known Prince Meleager since they were children, all tutored together in Thessaly. Now the prince is trailing a beautiful woman, who pauses and inspects our foursome, her wild brown hair held back by a leather cord. Barefoot with a large bow strapped to her muscular back and a green tunic barely covering her rear. She wears no leggings beneath. Helen widens her eyes at the lady's muscular thighs.

"I'm Atalanta," she says, smiling. "Oh my, who have you got there?" she asks, pointing to Gale.

"This little weasel just joined our group." I smile as I ruffle Gale's fur. "She's pretty tame if you'd like to pet her."

Atalanta nods eagerly and comes forward, bending down and gently massaging Gale's elongated body. "Where I'm from, we call them polecats." The weasel purrs complacently and paws at my tunic, her eyes scrunched closed.

"Why don't you join us?" Helen gestures to a vacant log next to her.

"We'd love that." Atalanta smiles at Meleager as she takes a seat. He awkwardly sits beside her, his rump settling on the very edge of the log just to be near her. Castor passes around two more cups and Meleager, a cheeky smile on his face, pulls a bottle of wine from beneath his tunic.

· · • • · • • · ·

I take an instant liking to Atalanta, especially after she quickly puts Pollux in his place by feeding Gale a treat from her pouch. The polecat is now lying across Atalanta's ample chest, snoring lightly, a complete traitor to our earlier bond. I chuckle as Meleager finishes telling us a story about a time he had to root out a weasel who'd dug up some of his family's grapevines.

"That damn polecat was about three times the size of your Gale and had fangs the size of my fingers!" We all laugh as Gale sleepily lifts her head, sneezes, then immediately falls back to Atalanta's bosom.

"She's a lucky one, has the best spot for a nap." Meleager nods toward our pet, and Atalanta blushes.

"How'd you two meet?" Helen inquires, sipping her wine slowly. I'm surprised by Helen's overall attitude toward Atalanta. Often beautiful women are mean to those seen as competition, but not Helen. She loves everyone, and a sense of pride swells in my chest as I watch my newfound sister. She is the embodiment of sweetness and everything nice in this world, and I would burn it all to the ground to ensure she's never hurt again.

"I simply answered the call of the hunters, as did you all." She lowers her gaze, and I notice Meleager staring at her, unblinking. He's clearly taken with the stunning woman by his side, and I wonder if the feeling is mutual.

"Aye, and I'm glad you did, Mistress." He covers her hand with his own and smiles shyly at her. It feels as though I've intruded on an intimate moment, so I avert my eyes and, instead, turn to look at my own lover. He's deep in conversation with Pollux over the best strategy for slaying the boar.

"We've got to flush the beast out with smoke," Pollux notes, but Castor shakes his head. I watch as my husband's face is enlivened by a passionate disagreement with his best friend, and my heart constricts, fluttering as I remember the moments before Helen's terror interrupted us. A blush spreads across my face, heating my cheeks and sliding lower into my belly. I reach for Castor's hand and pull it into my lap. He stiffens slightly as his eyes slide to mine, but a small smile touches his lips.

I lean over and whisper in his ear, "I think it's time we retire, husband." I feel his skin shiver against my lips. "I didn't get a chance to repay you earlier, and I'd like to now . . ." My mouth waters as desire snakes through me.

His face whips toward mine, nearly smashing into my nose, and I laugh out loud at the reaction I so effortlessly caused just by being a woman. His woman. His wife.

He downs the rest of his wine and pretends to stretch, addressing our group while feigning a yawn. "I think we're going to retire, mates." Grabbing my hand, he pulls me along toward our tent.

"Keep it down in there!" Pollux yells jovially, and I let out a gleeful shriek as Castor tosses me playfully onto the fur-covered bedroll.

CASTOR

Melinoe lands in the pile of furs with a throaty laugh and immediately sits up. I want to bury my face in her again, but she gestures for me to have a seat next to her.

"It's your turn, husband." She leans in and licks the whorl of my ear, sending a delicious shiver down my spine. I shouldn't be doing this. I should stop while I'm ahead before I've really pissed off the gods, but as I hum my pleasure, she's spurred onward, kissing down my jaw and nuzzling into my neck.

"Be careful. I don't want your face to get all scratched up from my stubble," I caution her.

She sucks and nibbles her way around my neck, and I stretch out, exposing my throat. *Stop it*, my mind is yelling. I shouldn't be doing this, shouldn't be letting *her* do this to me. Unfortunately, my brain isn't getting much attention right now, so it quiets and lets the rest of my body take over. I focus on Melinoe's hands trailing over my chest.

"I kind of like the scruffy look," she says against my skin. I swallow deeply and she reaches for my shirt, tiptoeing her fingers under and caressing my abs.

I sit up, stripping off the tunic, and toss it into the corner, noting the way her eyes sparkle in the darkness.

"Take off your pants," she demands.

I unlace the tie and wiggle out of the Spartan leathers, my hard cock springing free. Her eyes widen, desire tinting her cheeks, as she takes in my length. She bites her bottom lip, and dazed, I watch as she lowers herself to my stomach, kissing and licking her way downward. My cock fits neatly in between her breasts, and I nearly come before taking a deep breath and counting to ten.

"Do you like this?" she whispers against my skin, her breath tickling my torso. An alarm goes off in my brain, but it's immediately silenced as the feel of her lips on my lower abdomen causes an ache to spread all the way up my shaft, a small bead of precum forming on the tip.

I nod, hissing through my teeth, and throw my arms behind my head so I can watch her work. She moves her hand lower, cupping my balls and massaging them gently in her soft hands. My thighs tighten, and a moan escapes my lips as the pleasure moves from my toes straight to my groin. She hasn't even touched my cock yet, and I'm already so close. My eyes roll back. This woman . . .

As if she can hear my thoughts, she lifts her head and smiles wickedly at me. "We're just getting started, Castor."

She worries that damn lip between her teeth as she lowers herself to my cock. Her hand grasps the length, and I visibly throb in her palm.

"Oh!" she exclaims, her eyebrows raised.

"You do that to me, Melinoe," I whisper to her. She blinks a few times, pleasure flashing in her eyes, and lowers her mouth to me.

I writhe into the furs as her slick tongue slides over the shaft and up to the tip, flicking the sensitive head and causing me to gasp with pleasure. She alternates between licking and stroking with her soft hands, and it's not long before I'm nearly ready to explode.

"Mel, stop," I manage to utter before she goes any further. She pulls away, confusion knitting her brow, and wipes at her lips. I'm about to become unhinged just by watching her. I need to stop this. *Now.*

"Was I doing something wrong?" she asks. "I haven't had a lot of practice . . ." She lowers her eyes seductively and my body takes over, damn the consequences.

I reach up and grab her chin, bringing her mouth to mine and covering the smile I feel tickling my lips. She's so damn hot. It's time for me to be honest with her. "I want you. I want all of you."

She blinks at me. "How do you want me, Castor?" she asks, her voice turning husky as she trails a finger down her neck toward her cleavage.

"It doesn't matter as long as I'm inside you, *fucking* you," I clarify boldly. My palms start to feel clammy, my body tingling all over with anticipation.

Her eyes lower as a small smile plays at her lips. She tangles her fingers in my hair and pulls, yanking my head back as she straddles me, taking the lead. Leaning down, her upper body flush against my own, she pulls harder, and I don't know what's more pleasurable, the sweet pain at having my hair pulled or her wetness slicking the base of my cock. She leans in, her swollen lips inches from my jaw sending shivers straight to my cock, and whispers in my ear.

"So fuck me."

MELINOE

"Fuck me, Castor," I repeat as I pull away from his ear, my stomach fluttering with a mixture of desire and nerves. In an instant my mind stalls, my brain creating awful scenarios that flash before my eyes. Is this the right thing to do when I have so many other things to worry about? I need to focus on my magic, my inner Titaness, and getting to Mount Olympus. I need to focus on *revenge*.

But, for the first time, instead of dwelling on everything else in my life, instead of being the responsible, perfect princess—which has gotten me nowhere—I silent my worries and go for it. I shake my head, knocking the negativity away, and pull his face to mine, crushing our mouths together and parting his lips with my tongue.

"I *want* you to fuck me, Castor," I whisper into his mouth, grabbing his hard cock and stroking it from root to tip. He pulls me against him, twists us so he's now on top, hands on either side of my shoulders, and proceeds to brush my hair out of my face.

Looking me in the eyes, his length pressed into my stomach, he asks, "Are you sure? I don't want to pressure you into something you're not ready for . . ." His eyes are shadowed, a frown creasing his lips as he pulls away slightly. Does he want to stop or is he simply giving me a chance to?

I shake my head, watching him brighten with pleasure. "I'm ready. *We're* ready." I make it clear to him. This is about us. *Together.*

He swallows, his eyes flickering slightly, the lump on his neck bobbing. He sits back on his knees, and as he helps me undress, I notice his hands are shaky. Is he nervous? I keep going, tossing my tunic onto the floor with his own discarded garments and stand to wriggle out of my skirt, shimmying it down over my hips and kicking it aside.

I stand before him, bare and confident in my body, my hair pushed behind my shoulders as his gaze caresses my nakedness. I raise my hands to cover my chest, but he comes to stand in front of me, raising my arms above then trailing his fingers downward. Finally he takes my head in his large, calloused hands and brings his mouth down to mine. My fingers rake through his hair, and I hook one leg over his hip, pressing my entire body against him. His hands lower to my neck, my shoulders, and finally down to my breasts. His mouth follows suit, kissing each place his hands just touched, until his lips settle on a peaked nipple.

He swirls his tongue around one hardened nub before tending to the next one, but his hands continue their trail down my body. First they settle on my hips. He then lowers his palms to my ass, pulling me against his length. I melt into him, pushing him back toward the fur-covered bed.

As he collapses, he tugs me along with him. I straddle his muscled thighs, his cock seated between us, and continue stroking him as I lean over, pressing my breasts into his chest.

"I'll never tire of this view, wife," he manages to say before I rise higher to my knees, sitting tall and giving him the full view of me. The way he says it makes me think he's in this for the long haul, and so am I, I realize, running my hands over my breasts, toying with my own nipples. I slowly move down to my stomach, inching lower and lower.

Castor grinds into me. "Touch yourself," he demands, eyes flickering with desire. I do as he asks, delving into myself and swirling my fingers into my crevices. Pushing inside myself. I give off a soft moan for his pleasure, leaning back so he can see it all.

Eyes flashing, he flips me over onto my back, and my fingers are drawn into his mouth as he sucks each one before sliding his tongue into my mouth.

"I want you inside me. *Please*," I beg, arching my back, thrusting my chest up as I writhe against him. His gaze softens while goosebumps pucker my flesh. Consummating our marriage, finally becoming true husband and wife, turns me on, and I meet his gaze. I can feel how ready I am, my wetness slicking my thighs, and he positions himself over me, his cock teasing my entrance. I'm ready for this, for us. I'm ready for this man to be with me—by my side, beneath me, inside me—I'm ready for it all.

"I want you, Melinoe," he whispers, catching my gaze again as he finally pushes into me. I gasp, not at the pain, but at the pleasure. I'm so wet that he has no trouble sliding in and out, over and over, and the rhythm feels perfect, like I'm where I'm meant to be for the first time. I match his thrusts, raising my hips to meet his, as the pleasure builds. His cock presses deep inside me, and I feel it to my core. The ecstasy. The feeling of rapture.

His pulses increase in intensity, and when he throws my legs over his shoulders, he drives deeper. I can tell he's almost there, almost. He begins hammering into me, my wetness covering his cock. The noises our bodies make are obscene, but as he sinks himself to the hilt, I see stars, cease to care about anything but the pleasure. I try to be quiet, but I can't contain myself as I come, crying out in ecstasy as he hits a spot within my core. He roars along with me, and I feel his cock harden as he releases inside me. We collapse together, our bodies a tangle of sweat and ecstasy.

My mind, unfocused, drugged with passion, slides into darkness as a smile touches my lips.

· · • · • · • · · ·

"We'll break into two groups and root out the boar from the underbrush," Pollux commands our small coterie the next day. As I sit astride my horse, my tender flesh pulses with lightning as I catch Castor's gaze. I blush and smile, lowering my eyes. Last night was perfect and waking sated in his arms this morning only solidified my feelings for my husband. He's the one for me, and I don't have to be alone, an outcast in the Underworld, anymore. We'll be together, live our lives happily side-by-side, and have both desire and love in this marriage. My heart skips a beat at the realization, and I can't wait to tell him how I feel later tonight when we make love again.

I turn my focus to our group, which consists of Pollux, Meleager, Atalanta, Helen, Castor, and myself. Meleager has also invited his friend, Ancaeus from Arcadia, who keeps making eyes at Helen. I laugh inwardly, as Helen would never be interested in this brute. I'm sure he reminds her of those two piggish princes from Mycenaeum. His slovenly appearance is made worse by a pair of blackened teeth, which we viewed as he let out a wet belch earlier, Helen crinkling her nose in obvious disgust.

"As there are seven, our groups will be uneven," Meleager notes, and I can sense that he's concerned about being split from Atalanta.

"Let's stay together, then." I widen my eyes at Castor and Pollux, nodding slightly to Ancaeus, who is leering at Helen's chest.

Pollux blinks and immediately moves his mount in between the two. "Ancaeus, tell me about Arcadia," he inquires, pulling the ogre away from Helen. I motion her closer to me, and she smiles with gratitude.

We commence the hunt, Atalanta and Meleager leading us forth into the deep forest. Our horses' hooves crunch the dead pine needles and twigs underfoot. Weathered trees rise out of the earth to brush against the sky, and the cool breeze tickles my cheek. I reach up and touch my skin, trying not to think about Castor's rough hands brushing against me last night, his tongue exploring my mouth.

"What's gotten you so unfocused today, Mel?" Helen asks from her mount next to me.

I blush, shaking my head at her. "Oh, nothing." I notice Gale's head pop out of a saddlebag at her side and give a snort of amusement. "I'm surprised Gale will stay put in that pouch!"

Helen turns slightly, taking in the creature, before turning back to me. "Don't try to change the subject. We all heard you last night." She wiggles her eyebrows suggestively and bursts into laughter, causing Meleager to shoot a warning look our way.

"Shh!" I admonish her, my face surely the color of a pomegranate. "I have no idea what you are talking about anyway." I set my lips in a thin line and stare straight ahead.

"I'm teasing, sister!" She reaches toward me before lowering her hand. "I'm happy for you both. I'm glad my brother has *finally* found some happiness."

My heart stutters. "What do you mean *finally*?" My eyes slink toward hers, and I find the smell of pine and fresh air suddenly insufferable.

She's quiet for a moment, stopping her horse. I, too, bring my mount to a standstill and look at her expectantly.

"It's just that . . ." She pauses, rolling her eyes as she thinks of the right words to say. "Castor isn't like Pollux and me."

I frown. "What do you mean?"

"He's not a demigod like us, or in your case, a goddess," she clarifies. I don't bother to tell her that, according to the Oracle, I'm actually a Titan. Instead, I probe further.

"What does any of that matter?"

"Haven't you realized? We"—she gestures between us—"age much slower than normal, and you probably age hardly at all!" She bites her lip, eyes widening at my stupidity. "Castor is completely human. He'll die, Melinoe. Way before any of us."

I'm quiet as I contemplate the future, or lack thereof, with my husband. Only moments ago I was so certain that this man would be by my side forever. We would help rule the Underworld, together, and create a life of our own. Instead, our short time together flashes before my eyes and I see a vision of him, old and gray, drinking from the Lethe, forgetting about our bond as he becomes just another soul in the Underworld. My heart nearly stops in my chest as the realization—how dumb I've been—smacks me right in the face.

"Listen, Melinoe, I'm sure he's come to terms with it. You'll have a few happy years together." Helen shrugs as though this is not a big deal.

I thought I'd finally found my person, my place, and for the first time felt happy, but I'm now watching it all crumble in *a few happy years*. Tears well, stinging my eyes, and my chin trembles.

"Although," Helen adds with a derisive snort, "he's likely to go much sooner with the way death follows you around."

She turns her horse toward the group, galloping away without a backward glance.

Stricken and mouth agape, I slap my forehead, disbelieving that I never thought of my husband's mortality. Being part of the Underworld, with parents who are pure god and goddess, it'd somehow escaped my knowledge that Castor wasn't like me. Like us. I walk my horse farther into the forest, letting the beast take me along as I sit numb in the saddle, my mind at a loss.

I look around, realizing I've traveled out of sight of the group. I dismount and tie my horse to a nearby tree, taking a seat against a mighty oak. I cover my face with my palms, dropping my head to my knees. The rough ridges of the tree's bark dig into my back, like Castor's hands did last night as we pleasured each other. While Castor does have many years of life ahead of him, I can't help but feel helpless about our future.

A stray raindrop drips from the canopy onto my scalp, and I'm suddenly aware that the forest has become eerily quiet. The calling birds and rustling of leaves have stilled. I sit up straight, alert, and then I'm pulled back against the tree as something soft encircles my throat, choking me, the air leaving my body.

I struggle against the leather cord, tearing my nails against my neck as I try to wiggle my fingers under the rope. I gasp for breath, my head starting to pound as the blood makes my eyes bulge. My legs kick free in terror, working to gain traction, expending energy I don't have as my vision blurs. The smell of the forest's musty moss and rotting wood become fainter. My face feels as though it will explode, and I'm moments from certain death.

Princess, the familiar voice hisses, seemingly next to me. I am unable to look, but I know she's here. Hecate.

I growl unintelligibly in response, still kicking my feet and struggling to dig into the cord. A warm liquid drips down my neck, the copper scent sliding into my nostrils. Blood.

We can save each other, Princess.

Trying to let out a shriek, I feel myself going under. Deeper and deeper into the darkness. I welcome it at this point, if only so I can finally take a breath and the pounding in my head will cease.

Say the words. Bring me forth.

Unable to speak the words swirling in my brain, I think, *Why can't you just help me like when I destroyed Theseus?*

It doesn't work like that anymore; the longer we are parted outside of the Underworld, our home, the weaker I become. You cannot have magic without me, Princess. You cannot be whole without me. I cannot be whole without you. We must become one. My soul and your body must align. Say the words. Save us . . .

My mind flicks through all the spells and enchantments I learned from Hermes. Collective mind spell? No. The merge ritual?

Yes, she hisses in my ear. I thrash and recall the incantation. Gasping for air, I attempt to recite it aloud before I pass out from lack of air.

"To aíma mou eínai dikó sou . . ." I barely choke out, still twitching and grappling against the cord at my neck. My eyes drop and I feel my life ebbing

away. A bright light stutters in front of me, and I focus on it, attempting to eke out the last few words.

"*Tóra eímaste . . . éna . . .*" My head drops as blackness engulfs me.

178

HECATE

I can breathe. Inhale. Exhale. Inhale again. Let out a deep exhale. I'm no longer tethered to the tree, and as I continue to take deep, sating breaths a few more times to calm my pounding heart, I reach my mangled hands up to my neck. Slimy, sticky blood covers each digit. Turning side to side, I wince in pain. From my seated position against the tree, I flip to my knees and peer around the trunk. The leather cord is discarded on the ground. I grab it and wrap it around my wrist, managing to tie it into a sloppy bow. A memento. I smile, my eyes soaking in the scene behind the tree.

Lying flat on his back as though shoved by a force—*my force*—is Euphemus, son of Poseidon. I tsk and shake my head, the implications of his death looming over me. I can't afford to piss off Poseidon, but he should have taught his sons better manners. First Theseus and now Euphemus. Poor Papa Poseidon. I smirk, looking at the corpse in front of me. Euphemus's entire front, from his face down to his ankles, is charred as though he fell face-first into a fire. Serves him right for trying to kill me.

I don't even bother covering up the body, but I do recite a quick healing spell to mend my neck. I can't have Castor or the others knowing about this.

"*Tha*," I recite, wiggling my fingers. "*Xanagennithei grigora kai grigora.*" My neck tickles slightly, but as I reach up to touch it again, I find the pain has disappeared. I circle my head forward, backward, and side to side. Healed. My lips lift in a smile. So much easier now that I don't have to fight against my magic by denying my true self.

As I make my way toward the horse, a rustling nearby causes me to pause.

"Who's there?" I boom, my eyes searching, my body on alert. Muttering an invisibility spell, I immediately catch the culprit attempting to hide behind a now-transparent tree.

Pirithous.

Narrowing my eyes, I stride toward his cowering body. He looks up, chin trembling, face ashen. I laugh, extending my fingers. As I raise my hand, the crouched mortal rises in conjunction with my movement, his body hanging in the air as his toes dangle in the leaves. His soft belly expands as his breathing increases. His throat bobs.

I think back on my time as his captive. His dirty fingers touching my breast as he pleasured himself. My rage ignites.

My vision focuses on his pitiful face as my fingers burn white-hot. "You thought you could kill me."

He gulps, terror flashing in his eyes, clearly holding back a scream.

"I want you to run and tell Poseidon that I have killed another of his sons, and tell him *why* I did it. He has done a shit job parenting them, and the world is a better place without their criminal antics. Tell him he can meet me at Lake Trichonida in four days' time if he demands justice."

"*Ypakoúo stis entolés mou*," I command, and the compliance spell washes over Pirithous, making him obedient like a dog to my orders.

Dropping him to his feet, I watch with mirth as he stumbles, hauls himself up, and runs away from me in terror.

I turn and stride back to my mount, ready to rejoin my group.

CASTOR

I follow Atalanta and Meleager, trying to outpace Pollux and his damn demigod strength. Turning, I see Helen and Melinoe stop, likely taking a drink from their skins and having a chat. I'm glad they've got each other, and hating to break up their girl talk, I speed toward the other hunters.

I'm focusing my attention on the riders before me when Atalanta calls out, "Ho!" She charges forward at breakneck speed. I catch Pollux's eyes, and there's a determined glint as he smiles wickedly at me, spurring his mount onward.

"Oh, no you don't!" I shout after him, kicking my own horse ahead. I'm transported back to our childhood, thinking of how competitive we were, the pity on his face when he inevitably beat me. Swallowing, I push back the memory and ride faster, encouraging my horse to accelerate. I won't be beat again.

Just then Atalanta pulls up her mount and stops short before notching an arrow in her bow and taking aim. The wild beast runs across our path, charging at the warrior woman. Without hesitation, she releases, and the weapon strikes true, hitting the massive boar in its left flank and throwing him off course. She smiles widely and Meleager, never far from her side, claps her proudly on the back. I watch as his palm lingers, lazily tracing down her spine.

Heat strums through my veins as I recall Melinoe's nakedness and the pleasures we took together. I can't wait to taste her flesh again tonight, and the thought sends a shiver of passion straight to my groin. Adjusting myself in the saddle, I turn around, finding Helen trotting toward us.

Atalanta draws my attention back to the hunt as she dismounts, tossing the reins to Meleager. Pollux and I follow suit, but the brute Ancaeus appears from nowhere, charging forward on foot. I watch as Atalanta holds her fist up, giving us the signal to proceed slowly and quietly, and Pollux and I obey. After all, as she has inflicted the first wound to the beast, we must follow the hunters' code. The orders are hers to give.

Unfortunately Ancaeus, acting foolish as he attempts to show off for Helen, presses ahead of Atalanta into the brush. The boar's blood coats the leaves, and a loud snarl comes from within the darkness. Nevertheless, Ancaeus, pulls his short sword from his belt and stabs into the undergrowth, thus exposing his side body. As Ancaeus thrusts into the bush again, the beast shoots out and plunges its massive tusks into the man, goring him from armpit to hip.

Pollux's face goes ashen as we watch Ancaeus's guts burst forth from the gash. We rush to his aid as he falls back, the boar taking flight. Atalanta, her brow furrowed in anger, contains her admonishment as Meleager comes forward, placing his hand on her forearm and offering comfort to her. She yanks away, her jaw clenching in anger as she watches the boar flee into the forest.

The garbled noises coming from Ancaeus spur Helen into a jog from the distance, and I finally notice that Melinoe isn't with her. Looking around, I see nothing but empty forest.

"Where's Mel?"

She shakes her head, slowing her approach as her eyes take in the bloody scene before her. Raising a hand to cover her gaped mouth, she stills. The man is dying at my feet, but all I can think is my wife isn't with my sister. She's gone.

"Helen, where's Melinoe?" I prod louder, grabbing her shoulders and peering into her face. Her eyes glaze over, shock freezing her as she watches Ancaeus's blood seep into the dirt, chunks of his innards losing their slimy sheen as they hit the open air.

"I-I-I . . ." she stutters before turning away and vomiting the contents of her stomach all over her sandals.

I growl, turning away from the bloodshed, and sprint back to our horses. I've seen death on the battlefield before. I've watched men bleed out with a knife stuck in their head. It makes putting this all behind me and focusing on my wife's whereabouts that much easier. I am a soldier, after all.

Mounting my stallion, I retrace our trail at a gallop. Where could she have gone?

"Mel!" I shout into the forest. It's eerily quiet, the birds having ceased singing and the breeze stilled. "Melinoe!" I call again. My horse jerks sideways and I nearly fly off as I take in the scene in the middle of the trail.

Melinoe. Her throat and fingers caked in dried blood. Smiling oddly at me as her eyes flutter closed and she topples to the ground.

MELINOE

"__M__y dear friend, I'd like to introduce you to someone. Please, follow me." Persephone's voice, much higher than normal, beckons me forward. I traipse behind her as she leads me through the wedding reception, her marriage to Hades completed mere moments ago. I'm pleased to see her so happy, her cheeks rosy and her smile genuine. She belongs here, and I'm glad to have ignored her mother's demanding letters the past few months.

"Where are you taking me?" I grab her, slowing her pace, and tilt my head to the side. Her conspiratorial smile says it all, and I playfully squint my eyes at her. "You're up to something!" I laugh.

Grabbing my hand, she places her finger to my lips. "Hush and come along." I'm yanked forward like a petulant puppy on a leash.

As we weave and maneuver through the large crowd of guests, including various gods, goddesses, mortals, and the souls from Hades's kingdom, a sense of community swells in my chest, the likes of which I haven't felt since leaving Crete many moons ago. Before I can get too emotional, Persephone suddenly stops, and I slam into her back, my nose landing right in between her shoulder blades.

Turning, she pulls me forward as I scrub at my face. "Hermes, this is Hecate, the Titan I was telling you about." Her eyes widen briefly before returning to their normal size, a smile touching her lips. "Oh, I think I see my . . ." She points into the distance and smiles, arching a perfectly manicured brow at me, before rushing off.

I assess Hermes as he dips his chin in greeting. While handsome, he's incredibly thin, almost gaunt. His dark hair is braided, which makes his youthful eyes appear even larger in his bony face. I wonder when he's last eaten. His job as messenger to the gods must keep him active as the poor thing has not a single ounce of fat on his bones.

"Would you care to eat?" I blurt out as I feel my cheeks burn in shame.

He crinkles his brow, a frown touching his lips. "No, thank you, unless you're hungry?"

I shake my head before looking around, feeling incredibly awkward in his presence. "Tell me about your time in the Underworld. I haven't been here long, and I don't recall seeing you around much," I offer.

"I'm Zeus's emissary to the court of Hades, and I often guide souls here on my travels from the Land of the Living."

At the mention of the king of gods, I wince, wondering how much this bony man knows about my friendship with the man who now sits on the throne at Olympus. I keep my mouth closed and continue perusing the guests in attendance.

"He knows you're here."

I rear back as though I've been slapped, my eyes burning with anger. "I don't know who you're referencing, Hermes." My tone is cold, chilly. He'd be brazen to continue on with this conversation.

He grasps my arm and pulls me to an alcove, away from the eyes and ears of the party. "You know exactly whom I speak of, witch. If you don't return to your rightful place with him, he'll make sure your reputation as a Titan is ruined."

I hold his stare, challenging him, as I draw myself up to my full height. I'm still much shorter than he is, but as I roll my shoulders back and toss my head side to side my stature magically increases so that I'm looking down on him, my nostrils flaring as plumes of smoke billow from them.

My voice deepens. "You tell Zeus that he knows where to find me, and I'll be waiting. Growing stronger. More powerful." Blinking, my body now returned to its normal size, my lip curls in disgust.

"You wouldn't be so strong without your magic," he sneers at me.

I don't even bother responding to him as I turn and fade into the crowd, my thoughts only on celebrating my new queen.

· · · ● · ● · ● · ● · ·

My brain wakes before I open my eyes. I sense that I'm back in the tent, and I hear Castor's soft voice near the opening.

"Pol, I know that Helen is worried, but she cannot bring that rat into the tent. Tell her—" He's cut off by Pollux, who seems to be standing just outside the flaps, whispering something. The rustling of the leaves on the trees carries his response away, but the tone sounds urgent.

"Fine, give me a moment," Castor replies. I sense him turn and approach the bedroll, leaning closer. He brushes a stray strand of hair from my brow and I fight the urge to let my eyelids flicker. Keeping as still as a corpse, I maintain my steady breathing. He needs to believe I'm asleep.

Satisfied with my acting, he leaves the tent with hurried steps. I recite the "Codes of Justice for the Deceased" three times before finally peeking through squinted eyes. I'm alone. Releasing a sigh of relief and carefully sitting up, I peer through the tent flap and gauge if Helen is tending the fire and monitoring me. She's staring into the fire, her body shaking as she cries quietly into the blanket wrapped around her shoulders.

Feeling slightly guilty, but not enough to stop myself from my mission, I stand up. Ignoring the vertigo, I pull on my boots, strap a bow and arrow and short sword to myself, and quietly duck under the back of the tent.

Shifting onto the balls of my feet, I keep low to the ground and avoid the quieter tents, where my movements are likely to be heard. I sneak away from camp, my feet guiding me while my brain fills with questions.

What am I going to do?

How am I going to explain who I've become?

Hush, the voice within whispers. *I've got us.*

My mind quiets, my feet continuing to propel me toward the unknown.

· · ● ●· ● ● · · · ·

The sun has traveled a third of its position higher into the sky, and yet my feet continue to traipse through the terrain, no sanctuary in sight.

I need to stop and take a drink, I tell her. I know who she is, I know who is navigating, but I do not know to where.

I find a cool spot under a lone tree and settle down, uncorking the skin on my belt. The water, though warm, refreshes me, and I suckle until I feel rejuvenated.

I stare out at the landscape, noting that the lush forest has become rocky hills with low-lying shrubs. My posture perks up and, pausing to examine my pale fingers, I simply imagine lighting one of the bushes on fire, and it happens.

My eyes widen, my hand dropping to the dirt. I leap up to my feet, giddy with excitement, a smile spreading across my face.

"I've done it!" I exclaim aloud.

We've done it, the voice inside corrects me.

I swallow the lump in my throat, lowering my chin to my chest, and flop back down against the jagged trunk.

We're one now, the same, the voice reminds me. *You cannot fight me. You cannot leave me behind. I am you. We are Hecate.*

"*We* are Melinoe," I correct, speaking aloud to the nothingness. "And *we* cannot keep wandering with no destination in mind."

Glance over the hill, and you will see that we have arrived.

Startled, I straighten up and move toward the edge of the cliff. Looking down, I gasp in awe. The Temple of Artemis.

· · • • · • · · •

"I wondered how long it would take for you to journey to my temple, cousin." Artemis's voice booms loudly, echoing from the stone columns of her temple. A small girl-child, much younger than I, appears from a chamber door. As she walks toward me, I glance around at the pantheon, its beauty. The walls are darker than that of the Oracle at Delphi, a deep brown. The floor is made of dirt, with trees and grass sprouting freely, reaching toward the open air above. Birds and butterflies coast on the breeze that blows from above. I squint through the sunshine as the goddess approaches.

She walks slowly, assessing me with her wide eyes set off by dark locks complemented with a crown of cypress leaves. We share similar features, the unruly curls and full lips, but her eyes are light brown, almost yellow. They remind me of dried wheat or the fur of a deer.

"I-I am honored to meet you, Goddess." I lower to my knees, supplicating myself as she nears. From beneath lowered lashes, I notice a dark brown pelt draped across her shoulders.

"Rise, Hecate, for we have met before. Do you not remember?"

I flinch. I don't dare correct her, as she is the high goddess of Calydon and Aetolia, worshipped above all others.

"You were with my mother when my twin Apollo and I were born on the island of Delos." Circling me, she continues to appraise me. She takes my hand, opening my palm and examining my fingers. "No more black then?" How does she know about my broken magic, my blackened fingers?

I shake my head mutely, afraid to utter anything to upset her, as she is the one who unleashed the boar on the Calydonian people. Her anger is infamous, but so is her kindness. Instead, I swallow the lump forming in my throat and return my gaze to the floor.

She smiles, but the warmth doesn't reach her eyes. "Are you afraid of me, dear cousin?"

My vision flickers, my voice becoming raspy, and instead of admitting that I am, in fact, terrified of her, the voice inside utters with a derisive sneer, "No, why would I be afraid of you? As a Titan of Mount Olympus, I outrank you."

Artemis throws her head back and laughs, the throaty cackle bombastically piercing my ears. Snapping her head forward maniacally, she meets my gaze, hers a pool of darkness as her mouth twists into a sneer.

"What do you want, Hecate? I tire of this." She looks at her nails, frowning.

My body moves lazily around the room, taking in the various offerings from the Aetolian people. "First, cease this nonsense with the boar. It's beneath you, and everyone knows Atalanta is your pet, destined to slay the beast, winning the tusks and hide as the prize." I swirl my finger along the lip of a vase, tipping it over and watching with a mischievous grin as it crashes to the ground. That's the least of what she deserves for putting innocent lives at risk of starvation over her hurt feelings.

"Fine," Artemis hisses through clenched teeth, her eyes crackling with anger at the smashed offering.

"Second"—I turn, sweeping my arm above my head and catching a hanging tapestry alight with fire, just because I can—"tell Zeus I am returning to Mount Olympus."

The goddess rolls her eyes, purposefully ignoring the smoke filling the temple sanctuary as the tapestry burns. "Enough with the theatrics. Zeus is aware. He's been watching you. In fact—"

Arching an eyebrow, I smirk, interrupting. "Oh, he knows I'm coming. But he doesn't know I seek revenge. And," I add, "that I need *your* help."

Artemis's eyes widen in disbelief before crossing her arms. "I'm listening, cousin," she says, a mischievous smile lifting her lips.

CASTOR

There are but a few times in my life where I've felt truly helpless. Years ago, as young soldiers, Pollux and I were aboard an Argonaut ship. As we sailed to fetch the fleece of the winged ram with our captain, Jason, there arose a great storm, and as the mast fell and the ship's hull was sure to be leaking, Orpheus, one of our brethren, offered to the gods prayers for our salvation. Immediately, the wind died, the thunder and lightning ceased, and a star shone down on Pollux's head, the favored son of Zeus by our mother. Watching in awe and completely helpless, I witnessed my brother save those sailors that day. And now, years later, sailors still send up prayers for safe travels to Pollux, visiting him in Sparta before their voyages, while I watch from the distance, utterly useless. I couldn't protect those sailors, and I cannot protect my wife, either.

"You had one task, Helen!" I roar at my sister, whose eyes are welling with tears that threaten to overflow at any second.

"Cas, I'm so sorry! Gale was—"

I cut her off, angry that a glorified rat would take precedence over keeping an eye on my wife. It takes all my effort not to grab the damn rodent and throw it across the encampment. Fortunately, terrorizing animals is not in my repertoire, but I am pissed at Helen's incompetence.

"What if she's with Pirithous or Euphemus? Do you have any idea what this means?"

She lowers her chin to her chest, the tears dripping down her cheeks. "I know . . ."

Just then Pollux rides up on his mount, stopping so abruptly that dirt and debris splatter into the fire, nearly putting it out.

"Did you spot her?" I don't bother hiding the desperation from my voice.

Shaking his head, he dismounts and ties his horse to the nearest tree. "No, but some of the hunters from Thrace noted a woman wandering alone nearly four hours ago. She matched Mel's description."

My eyes widen at the news, but just as quickly I furrow my brow. "But that means . . ." My voice trails off.

"It means that she left on her own accord, brother," Pollux completes my thought aloud.

"Why would she leave us?" Helen asks, cradling Gale in her arms. Her gaze flicks between mine and Pollux's, and I know it's time for me to admit the truth to them.

Turning toward our tent, I beckon them inside. They sit tentatively on the bedroll while I stand, pacing back and forth, the anguish churning in my belly.

"There's something I never told you . . . about Melinoe," I admit, raking my hands through my hair as I circle the small area, unable to keep still.

I stare at Pollux, who, despite the circumstances, nearly blurts out an inappropriate joke about my marriage. Helen, knowing our brother just as well as I do, silences him with a death stare. Swallowing his words, he has the gall to look contrite.

Shaking my head and sighing heavily, I spill the truth that I've been holding in.

"I don't think Melinoe is who *we* think she is." And then I share the details of the temple frieze, and my wife's mysterious magic.

MELINOE

Stumbling through the tent flaps hours later, I'm greeted by silence. The tent isn't empty, though. Castor sits on the bedroll, his elbows to his knees and his head in his hands. Hearing my entrance, he looks up, his face transforming from surprise to anger in no time at all.

"Where the fuck have you been?" He stands, his rage permeating the tent. I stumble back.

"I went to the Temple of Artemis," I admit.

"Why would you go there? What aren't you telling me?"

I inhale deeply, crossing to him and taking a seat at his side. "The oracle finally told me the truth about who I am."

Blinking, he waits for me to continue.

He listens with rapt attention as I explain the oracle's truth of my soul's extensive history, my true identity as a Titan, and my magic being tied to accepting who I really am: Hecate.

Castor's mouth hangs open. He continues to blink at me, appearing to absorb the information I've laid out for him, and finally speaks. "Why didn't you tell me?"

My brow furrows as anger simmers in my belly. "Why didn't you share what the oracle told you?" I counter.

He swallows, his throat bobbing as his eyes lower. "When Pollux and I were looking for you and Helen, I went to a temple to . . . ask the gods for your location." His eyes raise, and he fidgets with his fingers. "There was a frieze on the temple's outer walls. You were in the frieze, Mel—I mean, Hecate."

I worry my lip with my teeth. "Why did you never tell me?" *What else is he hiding?*

He continues fidgeting with his fingers, and I narrow my eyes. "I don't know. When we found you both, you immediately wanted to travel to Mount Olympus, for a reason you still haven't shared with me, and it just became something I tucked away for later."

Funnily, I was doing the same with his nervous behavior right now.

"So I—I mean Hecate—was on an ancient mural. What was she—or I—doing?" I shake my head and growl in frustration, confused at how to phrase something so simple, but Castor clearly understands what I've asked.

"It appears that you were fighting against the Titans during the Titanomachy, the War of the Titans."

"Why would she have fought *against* her own people, her own family, and *for* Zeus?" My mind races, searching for answers, but nothing comes. For the first time in days, my inner Titan is silent.

• • • ● • ● • • •

"So let me make sure I have this correct," Helen states hours later over smoked fish while we sit around the fire. Pointing to Atalanta, she says, "You inflicted the first wound on the boar, but it's Meleager who gets the tusks and hide as the prize?" Helen cocks a single eyebrow as she chews her fish, shaking her head in disbelief.

Atalanta, for all her beauty and athleticism, simply shrugs her shoulders and smiles nonchalantly. "Helen, if you haven't figured out that men will take

193

whatever they want from you without a single thought in their head for your own merit or well-being, you've got a lot to learn, my friend."

"Hey, not all men are like that!" Pollux proclaims from his seat next to Helen. Raising a piece of fish and flailing it about prophetically, he says, "I, for one, always think of a woman's well-being before my own."

He waggles his eyebrows suggestively at the group, but it's Helen who tosses a fish head his way. "You're gross!"

Gale, ever the thief, grabs the errant remains and, tucking herself behind a log, begins licking them clean.

We continue our meal in companionable silence, enjoying our last feast before continuing our journey in the morning. Nobody has mentioned my little disappearance, but that doesn't mean I don't notice their questioning stares, the accusatory looks. Frankly, I don't owe anyone an explanation, but I do feel rather guilty for worrying Helen. I remind myself to apologize to her and ensure our friendship is still solid.

Meleager saunters up behind Atalanta, carrying the boar's tusks and hide.

"Come to gloat, have you?" Atalanta asks as she turns back to her plate.

Meleager, for all his princely attitude, looks crestfallen. "No, I have come to deliver your prize." He holds the treasures toward her, a small smile lifting his lips. An amends, perhaps?

Atalanta's mouth drops open and her eyes widen. "I can't take those from you! You're the hunter who struck the killing blow, Your Highness." Her use of his formal title doesn't bode well for him, and I see his eagerness dissipate before my eyes.

Taking a seat next to her, he drops the prizes on the ground at her feet. "You struck the first blow. I wouldn't have felled the beast without your initial hit. The prizes are yours to keep, Mistress."

Atalanta's eyes take in the prickly hide and shiny tusks, oiled and gleaming white in the fire light. "Meleager, I can't accept this gift." She glances up at him, her eyes meeting his.

He takes her hands in his, eyes imploring. "Please accept your rightful prize and put me out of my misery by accompanying me to my tent so we can toast to your victory."

We all wait with bated breath as she looks around at our group, focusing on both me and Helen foremost. We both smile eagerly at her and nod our encouragement, gesturing for her to go with our blessing.

Biting her lip, she agrees with a chuckle and stands, holding her hand out to him. He grabs up the hide and tusks and, beneath the load, manages to take her hand and follow along like a lovesick dog.

Pollux, ever the charmer, hollers, "Don't forget about her well-being first, Meleager!" Atalanta shakes her head and makes an obscene gesture his way, confusion lighting Meleager's adoring face.

Muffling our laughter, we turn back to the fire, planning tomorrow's departure. It's time for me to seek out Poseidon.

$$\cdot \, \cdot \, \bullet \, \cdot \, \bullet \, \cdot \, \bullet \, \cdot \, \cdot \, \cdot$$

The next morning we're tearing down the tents and loading our mounts when Atalanta sprints through the wooded encampments toward our party. Her face, streaked with tears, is flecked with blood, as though sprayed from afar, and her eyes are wild with terror.

She crashes into Helen's arms before collapsing to the ground, sobs racking her body.

"What is it, Atalanta? What's happened?" Helen's eyes are full of concern, her lips pursed as she kneels down to Atalanta's level.

Castor and Pollux, hearing the commotion, rush from their packing and, taking in the scene before them, pull their swords from their scabbards, eyes searching the horizon for threats.

Gasping as she explains, Atalanta tells us how, early this morning, while bunked with Meleager, she was awoken by two bodies entering the tent.

"Your Highness." She playfully poked him. "Your servants are here." She didn't bother reaching for her weapons.

Meleager, rolling over to dismiss his body attendants, gasped in surprise. "Uncle Cometes, Uncle Prothous, what are you doing here at this hour?" Atalanta pulled the sheet over her exposed breasts, her jaw clenched with unease.

"How dare you give the prized hide and tusks to this . . . this whore?" The man unsheathed his sword and, with a fell swoop and no warning, slit Meleager's throat. Atalanta, horrified and covered in the spray of blood, shrieked for help while the men laughed heartily, leaving the tent as though nothing had happened. She tried to stanch the bleeding, but it was too late, so she held her lover's hand as his life ebbed away.

"Why on earth would they . . ." My voice trails off, wondering why someone's family member would commit such a heinous act.

"They wanted the hide and tusks," Atalanta explains. "They thought the prize should go to them since Meleager didn't want it, as they were next in line as his kin." She shakes her head, swiping at her face.

"All this death over a prize," Helen mutters to herself, shaking her head in disbelief, tears staining her cheeks.

"Come with us, Atalanta." I grab her hands in mine and draw her to stand. "It's not safe for you here. Pollux and Castor will return to get your things and your horse." I nod my head to my husband and his brother, and they immediately take off.

Leading her to the dying fire, I dip a rag into our bucket of water and begin cleaning her face of the grime, blood, and tears. She clenches her fists in her lap and works her jaw while Helen combs her hair, braiding it tightly. Gale settles in her lap, snuggling close.

With dazed eyes she says, "I can't come with you. I must take the hide and tusks to Artemis's sacred grove in Arcadia, my home. Artemis set this curse loose on the people of Calydon, the boar and all this death. I must end it by making the proper offerings to her." Her jaw is set, determined.

"Are you sure?" Helen asks, tying the braid with a cord.

Nodding, Atalanta tells us, "I'm sure. But thank you. For everything." She moves to hand Gale back to Helen, but I shake my head.

"Gale stays with you. She's a comfort, a friend. And you're clearly her favorite." I smirk.

"I couldn't keep her. She's your pet." Atalanta meets my eye, and I see understanding. She knows the real me.

Sighing, I take her hand in mine, patting it gently. "We've a long journey ahead of us, and I don't know if we'll make it back. Will you please keep her safe until a time when I can return for her?"

She nods. "I will make an offering to Artemis for your continued safe journey and to repay all your kindness." She stands, gives us each a hug, and after Castor and Pollux return with her horse and the boar's skin and tusks, she mounts up effortlessly and takes her leave, her grim expression and unnatural stillness an indication of her warrior mentality.

CASTOR

As we ride toward Trichonida Lake and our inevitable rendezvous with Poseidon, I glance warily at Melinoe. At Hecate? Swallowing, I realize that I don't even know who she is at this point. Or where we're really going. Instead of continuing our journey straight to Mount Olympus, she's shared that we must detour to the lake and rendezvous with Poseidon. But why? I have an uneasy feeling about all this, especially since I'm to protect her.

I eye her warily, noticing nothing different about her outward appearance. Regardless, something within her has changed. I can feel it in the way she talks, the way she carries herself. What does this mean for our marriage, the love I felt developing between the two of us? The intimacy we shared? Shaking my head, I wonder if this is for the best. I shouldn't be thinking of her as anything more than part of an agreement. I press my lips together, frowning slightly.

She catches my glance and holds it, waiting for me to speak. Instead, I avert my gaze back to the trail ahead of us as I clear my throat to mask my embarrassment. Am I scared of her? No, simply on my guard, as any good soldier would be.

Pollux, on the other side of her, inserts his question effortlessly. "Explain to me how we're *not* going to die by Poseidon's hands. He's a god of Olympus, for crying out loud!"

Melinoe simply thins her lips and pauses before speaking. "Poseidon should be worrying about us. About me," she corrects. "His ill-mannered sons have terrorized this land for long enough. If he seeks vengeance for my actions, so be it."

Gulping back a retort, Pollux states that we should give our mounts, and ourselves, a rest at a glen just over the next hill. As we dismount and lead our horses to a stream, I sidestep Melinoe but stay attuned to her expression. I feel as though we are simply circling one another, and I miss the comfort we were starting to develop before . . . well, before she disappeared and resurfaced as Hecate.

Pollux ties up the horses while Helen lays out a fur and then pulls several pieces of dried fish from her saddlebag.

I beckon for Melinoe to take a seat next to me on the blanket, but she shakes her head. "I think I'll take a walk," she says quietly, her gaze unfocused and distant.

I choose my words carefully, my gaze probing. "Would you like company? The trail isn't safe for a woman alone, and I'd feel better if I came along."

Her eyes flash to mine, anger searing in them. My breath hitches, knowing I've said the wrong thing to her, insulted her strength. "Mayhap I should stay here to keep *you* safe," she hisses, her eyes taking in our sorry group of powerless individuals. The air around us stills, the birds falling silent. When none of us utter another word, she retreats slightly, blinking and raising her chin. "No? I didn't think so." She turns on her heel and vanishes into the woods, the leaves returning to their rustling and the birds to their chirping.

"Well then . . ." Pollux widens his eyes at me as he chews his salted fish. "Care to elaborate on this new development?"

I look down at my own snack and shake my head, weary at the web in which I've entangled myself. How can I fulfill my duty when now I can't even protect her? What use do I serve?

As if reading my thoughts, Helen reaches over and tentatively rubs my shoulder, her thumb caressing maternally. "It's all right, Cas. Melinoe is still figuring it all out. This is new to both of you. You just need to be there for her."

I offer her a wan smile and, on second thought, decide to keep my wife company on her walk, whether she needs me or not. I have to make this work or else *both* our lives are forfeit.

MELINOE

Walking alone in the woods, I finally have a moment to myself again, something I have come to treasure more and more the past few days. It's when I'm alone that I can truly focus on my magic and speak with Hecate, who I've come to realize feels like home. Her guidance, which has become my inner voice, is what I've been missing my entire life, and as I learn to accept us as one, my magic has grown in strength. If only I hadn't been fighting against her for so long, maybe I wouldn't have needed to marry . . .

"Castor!" I exclaim, whipping around at the sound of snapping twigs behind me. I stalk angrily toward him.

He stands in the distance, hesitating at my approach. "I didn't mean to interrupt your . . . whatever this is"—he gestures wildly in the air—"but I'm here, and we need to talk."

Rolling my eyes, I stop midstride and assess him, my eyes narrowing. "Fine." I exhale through gritted teeth. With a flick of my wrist, I clear the detritus from a patch of soft, dry moss. His eyebrow cocks in admiration, and he nods his thanks while taking a seat.

I plop down next to him, toying with a leaf. "Well . . .?" I inquire, prodding him to begin.

He clears his throat, which I've come to realize indicates his discomfort, and I press my lips together to hide an emerging smile.

"Mel, talk to me." He grasps my hands as his imploring eyes meet mine. "We were doing so well before . . ." He trails off, leaving the sentence unfinished, even though we both know what he wants to say.

"Before I became Hecate, my true self?" I tilt my head.

He lowers his gaze, dropping my hands, and scoots back slightly. "You know what I mean. Something has changed. Did I do something wrong?"

I exhale slowly, looking up to the canopy. How do I tell him that I know he's embarrassed about his mortality? My thoughts flick back to my conversation with Helen and the boar hunt.

"Castor is completely human. He'll die, Melinoe. Way before any of us."

My goal should have been getting revenge on Zeus, not falling in love with a mortal. I've lost my destiny, what I'm meant to do, all because of some attractive man who makes my heart pound a little faster.

"How is this going to work, between us?" I ask him, finally meeting his gaze. "You're mortal and I'm . . . well, whatever I am."

Shaking his head, he moves toward me again, this time kneeling in front of me as he takes my face in his hands. "That's what you've been worried about this whole time?" He chuckles, his body seeming to relax.

I furrow my brows. "Yes, how are we supposed to make this work when you're going to d—" I can't bring myself to finish the sentence.

"Die?" he asks.

I nod my head, lowering my gaze. "Maybe it would be easier if we parted ways now, before things get too deep, Castor."

He pulls my face toward his and lowers his mouth, gently taking my lips and wrapping my body into a hug. "I hate to tell you, but I'm already in too deep, Mel. There's no way I could let you go now."

He presses more kisses to my mouth as he lowers me onto my back, pressing his hips into mine, grinding against me. A soft moan of ecstasy escapes my lips, and I tangle my hands in his hair, pulling his face into mine and deepening the kiss.

My mind stutters and goes blank, which is a gods-send. For the first time in days, everything is quiet and I can just *feel*. I roll Castor to his back, straddling him. Since gaining my magic, I haven't needed to use weapons, making it easy to strip off my top, my breasts bare against the warm breeze. He reaches up and fondles my flesh, playfully twinging my nipples until they are swollen and hard. I arch back, moaning, and raise my arms up, undoing my braid and letting my locks flow around my naked torso.

"Gods, you're beautiful, wife." He reaches for my clit, massaging it under my skirt, and I feel myself becoming wetter as his thumb circles my sensitive flesh. I, too, reach for his leathers and untie them, setting his cock free. My hands instantly snake up and down his length, jerking him smoothly. He moans, hissing through his teeth, thrusting against my hand.

"You need to take off your skirt. Now," he demands. I stand, turn around, and lower it ever so slowly over my ass, bending down to give him a full view of me from behind, shimmying as I go. Looking through my legs, I see his cock straining against his stomach, his eyes on fire with yearning.

He stands up, lifts me from behind, and pushes me toward the nearest tree. I catch myself, propped up with my shoulder against the bark and my leg hooked around his hips, as he enters me from behind. He drives into me as I grip the tree, and my cries of pleasure spiral out into the empty forest.

He thrusts deeper and deeper until I'm so close, and as I orgasm, my fingers flexing against the tree's ragged edges, I feel the power flow out of me and into the bark, torching it from trunk to treetop, the whole oak going up in flames.

Pulling me away from the embers, Castor lowers us back to our mossy blanket, and I take the lead, slowly lowering myself onto his engorged length. He fondles my breasts, lowering his wandering hands to my clit, and begins exploring my folds while I ride him, grinding him into the soft green cushion. Grabbing my hips, he pumps into me, bouncing me up and down on his cock, and with a final thrust up into me, he, too, comes, roaring into the forest like a beast who's been tamed.

Lying back on the mossy carpeting of the forest floor, Cas and I linger, completely naked to the elements as we explore each other's bodies, touching and tickling. The burning tree provides enough warmth, and the falling embers are like shooting stars streaking through the forest's shadows.

"How did you get this scar?" I ask, pointing to a long shimmery gash across his collarbone, down toward his sternum.

Pressing his hand to the puckered skin, his eyes go distant as he thinks back to the event. "When Pol and I served as Argonauts, and we were accompanying Jason to find the Golden Fleece, Pol got into a boxing match with the king of the Bebryces, a tribe near Thrace."

"If Pollux was boxing, how did *you* get the scar?" I lean in to kiss the lightened skin, noticing that my lips leave a trail of goosebumps along his flesh. A warmth rushes to my belly as Castor traces his fingers over my hip bone.

"Being that Pol was the best boxer on the ship, he defeated King Amycus, but his men attacked us. We narrowly escaped with our lives, and this scar was my only wound." He smiles, tapping the skin proudly.

I brush my mouth against his and sit up, ready to head back to Pollux and Helen. A chill rushes through my bones, as though I'm being watched, and goosebumps break out across my back. My scalp tingles, and as I turn, I discover a group of men, swords pointed at us, staring me down.

Licking his lips and smiling, his gaze trained on my naked breasts, the leader beckons his men to detain us. "Feel free to take what you want from her, boys. Poseidon's orders." He grunts at me, letting his men know that my body is now theirs to ravage.

My blood runs cold, and as I meet Castor's malevolent stare, I know he's holding in his rage as one of the henchmen cups my breast in his calloused hands. Another attempts to lead me away, pulling me behind a tree. My knees lock and I try to hold myself still, but I'm pulled along, sliding against the wet leaves underfoot.

"Mel," Castor begins as he struggles against the brutes, his teeth grinding. His scabbard lies discarded out of reach. The scene before me darkens—my body going from cold to warm to burning. I see red.

"It's *Hecate*," I correct him with a malicious grin, my fingers tingling as I set my powers free.

CASTOR

The man who was fondling Melinoe's breast is now alight with fire, his face melting as he runs, hands flapping wildly as he tries to stop the burning. The smell of cooked meat fills the air, and another man, the one who was pulling her behind a tree, seems to burn from within, the smoke billowing out of his mouth, ears, and nose. Their high-pitched screams sputter out within seconds, and their bodies drop to the ground with solid, finite thuds.

Helpless, I watch as Melinoe's eyes turn into dark pools, her body darkening to the same color as the burnt tree. She's become the night, a void that is filled only with the twinkling stars on her skin, as she lifts her star-touched fingers, which match the blinding light of the sun, intoning a spell toward the other men.

"*Lýthikan ta névra*," she chants, her body floating off the ground as she points toward the group. Her long dark curls float above her head, and I gape in horror as the men become immobile, only their eyes moving. I'm released by my captor and immediately stoop to gather my clothing, tugging my leathers over my legs hastily and taking up the sword from my scabbard.

Her body hovers toward the men, touching each one at a time, as she sings in a high-pitched, otherworldly voice, "*Tha se vasaníso.*"

I torment.

Once the words have been spoken into the breeze, the men emit wailing noises from immovable lips. Their pain is deafening, and I fight the urge to drop my sword and raise my hands to my ears.

Instead, watching her torture these paralyzed men, I know what I must do.

I stalk to the group and, one after the other, slice their throats, ending their agony. They drop lifelessly to the ground. Thud. Thud. Thud. Their lifeblood seeping into the soft, mossy bed Melinoe and I just vacated.

I turn to look at her, and my body stills as she maintains her Hecate aura.

Tilting her head as she still levitates above, she asks, "Why did you do that, husband?" The deep, unblinking pools bore into my soul. I gulp down the fear, meeting her empty gaze.

"I couldn't let them suffer needlessly, even if they were the enemy. They were following orders, as any soldier would be required to do." I toss my blade to the ground at her feet, ready to supplicate myself to her power, should the need arise.

Instead, the darkness seeps from her skin, and with a few blinks, the sky-blue color of her eyes returns. She lands like a cat on the ground and, still naked, throws herself in my arms, sobs ripping through her.

"I'm here. It's all right, everything is all right," I soothe, running my palm up and down her bumpy spine, pressing my mouth to her neck.

I hold her tighter until her body collapses against mine in exhaustion. Laying her gently on a pile of leaves, I quickly dress her and then, lifting her easily, begin our trek back to Helen and Pollux.

As I walk, my wife's lifeless body in my arms, I realize that none of us should be worried about Poseidon. Instead, we should all be worried about Hecate.

MELINOE

"*R*end the earth, witch," *Demeter commands. Rolling my eyes at Demeter's inability to use my name, I approach the cave. My travels from Crete have not been what I expected. Sailing to the mainland left me feeling so seasick that even preparing a tincture of lavender and licorice hadn't worked. Since I was retching daily, I arrived malnourished and dehydrated, but eager for life outside of the island. Unfortunately, Demeter, who met me at the docks, immediately treated me as a servant, informing me that my duties would include preparing her meals, as well as dressing her and treating any ailments she may acquire. My skill set only includes alchemy and witchcraft, though, so as I continued to fail at the additional tasks, she has taken to simply calling me "witch."*

I inspect the cavern near the Cape of Taenarum. The boundary is solid, reinforced. Lowering my palms to the ground, I recite a quick destruction spell, hoping it might work. "Kai tha vréxei páno sou. Kai tha vréxei páno sou."

I wait, but nothing happens, so I press on. "Kai to spíti sou! Kai to spíti sou!" Blinking one eye open, I watch Demeter's face transform from tolerant to furious. I exhale, refocus, and begin the third incantation.

"Tin katastrofi sou!" I push my palms into the dirt, but still nothing.

Demeter stomps over to me, pointing an accusatory finger in my face. "You've failed? What good are you if you can't rend the earth and get me access to my daughter?"

Sighing, I stand, brushing the dirt from my knees. I turn to her and raise my chin. "Goddess, the entrance is clearly indestructible. I would expect nothing less from Hades."

"You stupid, insolent witch!" She slaps me across the cheek, and I hiss in pain, cupping my face. "How dare you speak that name to me?"

My eyes flare, my palms tingling with rage. I clench my teeth together and attempt to control myself, lest this goddess be turned into a toad and thrown into the cape. An attack on one of the Olympians would certainly be cause for my powers to be bound, never to be used again. I inhale a calming breath and push my anger down. "I have another plan, if I may be so bold, my goddess." I bow my head in supplication, keeping the devious smirk from my lips.

"Speak up, then!"

"If I were invited to the Underworld, I could then cross the threshold, as well as open the portal at my leisure." At this point, I'd do anything to get away from this bitch, even go so far as to live in the gloomy Underworld. Sitting on Mount Olympus be damned, especially if Demeter's around.

"And how long will this plan of yours take?"

I shrug, biting my lip. "It's hard to say, but it's honestly the only way to get passage to the Underworld, outside of my death."

She eyes me up and down, and I go cold, my heart pounding, that she'd believe my death would be a better solution. She's fucking crazy if she thinks I'll let her near me again.

"Fine," she concludes. "I expect an update within three months' time on your progress from the Underworld. You can direct the missive to Mount Olympus." Her aura of superiority is so nauseating that I could really use some lavender and licorice root right now.

"Yes, Goddess." I bow to her, my smile finally breaking. I'm free of her. Now all I have to do is earn entrance to the Underworld.

• • • •• • •• • •

I come to in a small bed and, looking around, find Castor asleep in a chair in just his undergarments. Smiling, I reach out my hand and caress his leg, playfully tickling his bare skin. He stirs, blinking awake, and, on an inhale, sits upright.

"Come join me," I invite from under the mound of furs.

His throat bobs as he swallows, woodenly standing from the chair and sitting on the bed next to me. I roll into him, snuggling down, and inch my palms up his chest.

"Where are we?" I ask, sliding my hands under his tunic.

"Just outside of Trichonida Lake." His answer is clipped, the air suddenly feeling chilly, even as the fire burns in the hearth across the room.

"Hm . . ." I purr, inching his shirt higher. But, as I press my face to his exposed chest, his hands come to my shoulders, gently halting me. Biting my lip, I lock eyes with him and playfully pout. "You don't want to play?"

"Melinoe, what is going on with you?"

"What do you mean?" I try to keep the irritation from my voice but fail miserably as my tone clearly sets him on edge.

"What do I mean? I mean, what the fuck happened back in the woods? What were you thinking, senselessly torturing men who were only following orders from a superior? A god?"

I stand, my emotions moving quickly now, unable to settle. Grinding my teeth in anger, I seethe at his naivety. "Only following orders, Castor? When their leader, their god, insinuated that those beasts could take what they wanted from me? When that lecher fondled me in front of you, was he only following orders?" The fire within me rages, and I feel it forming in my fingertips, ready to light the whole inn aflame. I pace the floor, the urge to torch the building coming on stronger.

Ashen and wide-eyed, Castor begins to backtrack. "Mel, calm down . . . That's not what I meant. I know you, and torturing people needlessly isn't who you are . . ."

Narrowing my eyes, I meet his gaze. I can feel my pupils enlarging, my vision hyperfocusing. "Those men deserved much more than what you gave them—an easy way out and a quick, painless death." My rage vibrates the wooden planks of our room. "How dare you question me, *mortal*?" Castor shakes his head, the fight instantly going out of him, as two red spots dot his cheeks. But I don't bother caring.

As I advance toward the bed, I watch gleefully as Castor scrambles away from me, terror flashing in his eyes.

"This isn't you." He shakes his head, eyes filling with disgust, his lip curling as though a foul stench has permeated the room.

"For the first time, this *is* the real me," I hiss, flicking a flame his way. It burns out before reaching him, but not before I see him flinch. Laughing, I turn toward the door, barrel through it, and leave him behind.

It's about time I found my own way to Zeus.

· · • • · • • · • · ·

"Faster!" I urge the horse, digging my heels into his sides. We seem to fly through the forest as if carried by wings, and it's not long before I've arrived at the tranquil lake, ready to meet Poseidon.

As we reach the shore, the horse dips his head and takes a quenching drink. He's coated in a sheen of sweat, and froth blooms from his mouth. As he lifts his nose, the water crashes into us, and his hooves begin to sink into the now-flooded, muddy silt.

I dismount, hoping to remove my weight and free him. I start to pull his reins as he continues to fight against the suction, but the struggle only causes his hooves to sink deeper into the soft earth. The muck makes a terrifying squishing noise each time the horse tries to pull his hooves free before sucking him farther into the sludge.

"No!" I yell, terrified as the horse's neighing becomes shrill, splitting my ear drum. "I can't lose you!" Kneeling down, I drop my hands into the mud and begin digging, clawing at the muck and pulling his hooves free, only for him to readjust and sink farther.

Wild-eyed and feeling helpless, I stand, the weight of the clay heavy on my soul.

"Think, think!" I shout to the horse, whose terrified eyes dance in the moonlight, his head shaking back and forth. He's sinking faster, nearly covered to his thighs, and as my breathing becomes panicked, I realize I've failed yet again.

As sobs rack my body, the horse's struggle abates too, as though he feels my despair and has also given up. I lay my head on his warm side, tears of sadness washing both of us. I couldn't keep Helen safe from Theseus. I couldn't make my magic appear without losing myself and becoming someone Castor was disgusted by. I can't even save my poor horse. Looking at my hands, I crumble against the beast, his white coat now irreparably darkened by the inky sludge of the lake's coastline.

"I'm so sorry, Horse. I couldn't save either of us . . ." I sob against his snout, dirtying the soft velvet of his nose. I never even bothered to give the poor beast a name. I've been so self-absorbed, not caring about anyone but myself. "I don't know what to do to fix this. The earth is too wet . . ."

He blinks, grunting.

I furrow my brow. "The sludge is pulling you under. I don't know how to help you!"

He violently shakes his head to-and-fro. What the . . . ?

Is this horse trying to tell me something?

Pulling back, I try again, my eyes wild as I communicate with a beast. "The earth is too wet! I can't help you!"

Whinny. Snort.

"What do you want me to do?" My shrill voice cracks, and despite how ridiculous I feel, I will do anything, even talk to a horse, if it involves saving the creature from a certain death.

He flings his hide side to side. Confused and lost, I release a frustrated scream to the sky. I hurl obscenities to the gods, damning them. This poor creature is dying before my eyes and I can't even figure out how to help him. I'm completely and utterly useless!

My hands pound into the muck, and I unleash a string of curses. As the tears mix with snot, spit, and spray from the water, the sandy soil solidifies around my clenched fists, and it finally hits me.

Fuck . . . If I can manipulate fire, why didn't I think about my magic's ability to manipulate the earth? The horse harrumphs, blowing air from his nostrils and shaking his head.

I back away, my feet squishing into the muck as I mentally flip through my spells. Sinking my mud-covered hands into the ooze, I focus, a small bloom of hope warming my chest.

"*Afíste ta stoicheía na katevnastoún, eíte eínai gíini dýnami eíte pýrino neró kai parádeisos, ákousé me, fónaxé me!*"

I invoke the power of the elements: earth, fire, water, and air.

"Hear my call! Protect my chosen!" I yell into the emptiness of the lake. I'm exhausted, both emotionally and physically, and as the spell wafts away, I pinch my eyes closed, hoping that it works.

The water in the lake bobs once, as though a giant turtle is poking its head out, immediately disappearing below the surface. It bobs again. And again. And again. Until the ripples churn together and begin twirling, turning into a swirling whirlpool. The horse whinnies next to me, his grunts and snorts coming faster. The water moves quickly, and the ground beneath my feet begins to rumble. I stand, steadying myself, and try to pull at his hooves, but he's still stuck.

In the darkness, with only the light of the moon to shine on his body, Poseidon rises from the water's vortex, his body glistening in the moonlight. As he strides closer, his skin wiggles and cascades. What the . . .?

His torso is covered in slimy black leeches, their round mouths sucking, their tails writhing across his skin. A few fall to the ground and he steps on them, their greasy bodies squelching as they're smashed underfoot. My eyebrows shoot up into my hairline as my mouth frowns. A bit of vomit bubbles up from my stomach, and I swallow heavily.

Fuck.

He comes to a stop in front of me, pulling the last few leeches from his body and dropping them to the ground, grinding his bare foot over each one. I look down, the leeches' bloody remains coating the sandy dirt, and the back of my throat burns.

"I've been waiting for you, Hecate."

CASTOR

I don't even have to summon him this time. He appears from the hearth, as though a portal opened in the flames, and steps loudly into the room, filling the void Melinoe left.

Before I have time to bow, to supplicate myself as befits his status, my mouth gets the better of me and I spout off. "What the fuck are you doing here?"

His anger is palpable. I feel it snake up my spine, twist around my neck, and press into my temples, threatening to squeeze the life-force out of me.

"How dare you speak to me in that tone, mortal prince of Sparta?" His gravelly voice demands justice, expects answers that I don't have.

I fight the urge to flinch, and as I've had enough drama at the hands of these gods, goddesses, and Titans, I meet his gaze. "Melinoe—whoever she is—has turned into a nightmare, thanks to you."

"We both know she's Hecate, Titan of witchcraft, boy." He squeezes his fists together, and the throbbing at my temples grows stronger, my vision blurring.

I grind my teeth, refusing to yell out in pain, refusing to bend to his will. For her, I will fight. Despite my anger at her, I want to fight for her. For us.

"You had one task, to control and bring her back to me. It seems you have failed miserably."

"I haven't failed," I manage through gritted teeth. The pain is unbearable, but I won't back down.

He tilts his head. "Where is she then?"

"With your brother, Poseidon," I hiss, expelling a loud breath. My wife might not think I know her, but I'm starting to. I knew the second she left she would head to Trichonida Lake and to Poseidon. She wants to fight—to win. Just like me.

With the mention of his brother's name, his grip on me loosens, and I cradle my head in my hands, rubbing the aching spots and attempting to maintain the Spartan warrior mentality when all I really want to do is thrash him. A lot of good that would do, though. I'd be dead in seconds, sent to Tartarus or worse.

"You must free her from Poseidon; he cannot know who she really is. If he has her in his possession, my place as king—and our bargain—is forfeit. She's too powerful to be in the hands of my brother, my enemy."

Feeling myself moments from snapping, I lash out. "What makes you think I, a mere mortal, could rescue her? She's clearly a Titan with magic stronger than most gods, right? You expect me to rescue her from Poseidon, one of the strongest Olympian gods to ever exist?" The ridiculousness of the entire situation makes me laugh maniacally.

Assessing my outburst, he blinks. Eyes narrowing, he stalks a circle around me slowly, eyeing me up and down. Coming back to my front, he snaps his fingers.

"There." He nods his head, obviously pleased with himself, and crosses his arms.

I shift my gaze, looking around. "There? There what?" I open my palms, confusion knitting my brow. Have I missed something?

"You wanted to be immortal, now you're immortal."

My eyes widen in disbelief. Well that was fucking easy.

He continues on, "But only if you fulfill your end of the bargain. If you don't deliver her within seven days, your immortality wears off and your life is forfeit."

"Wait, that's not what we agreed upon! We agreed I'd bring Melinoe to you, to Olympus, in exchange for immortality. For safety." Suddenly my life will be forfeit? I shake my head. Dying wasn't in the contract!

He chuckles, the laughter shaking the wooden panels of the room, just like her. "I've upped the ante since you seem to be having so much trouble. I didn't expect to be so . . . involved. It's rather time-consuming, don't you think? To be honest, I expected more from a Spartan."

I narrow my eyes, clenching my fists at my side, and remind myself that attacking a god, let along the king of gods, would surely forfeit my life. Immediately.

As an afterthought, he turns to me and adds, "And, let's be honest with one another, I know you've been having a change of heart. I can smell it on you." Sniffing me, he makes a face of disgust. "But let me be clear, falling in love was never part of the deal. You will return what's *mine*, Prince."

Turning toward the hearth and the flames, he glances back one last time.

"Seven days."

MELINOE

I watch in awe as Poseidon places his trident to the earth and rends it, freeing my muddied horse from his would-be watery grave. The stallion scampers away from the shore, stamping his feet to clear his hooves of the sludge. I sigh, but my relief is short-lived as I watch the mighty god look on the horse with affection. He approaches the dirtied beast, reaching his hand to rub his snout, and I see a flicker of something flash in Poseidon's eyes. It's the same way Hades has always looked at me, with pride and love. *Fatherly* affection. My eyes prick with tears; I wish I was back home in the Underworld where things were easier.

Patting the mount on the neck, Poseidon notices me. "Pegasus is my son, Hecate." He smiles slightly as he leads the muddied horse to a tree some distance away from the shore. Tying him securely, Poseidon scratches his son's forehead and returns to me, holding his hand out.

"Come."

I back away slowly, shaking my head, my gaze on his open palm. "No."

Narrowing his gaze, his lips tilt up into a smile that doesn't reach his eyes. "It wasn't a question." He grabs my wrist and pulls me onto the water. I gasp as my feet don't sink, but rather walk atop the waves.

As he yanks me over the water, I continue to fight back, trying to pull my hand free. I plant my feet, but it's useless as I slide along the slick surface with him.

"Stop! I'm not going with you!" I start to summon my magic, the incantation bubbling inside me to be released, but I'm thrown onto the hard surface.

Pain explodes in my shoulder, and I feel as though I've hit solid rock, yet I'm still over the water. He points his trident at me, winking in the moonlight. "Do you know what this is made of, witch?"

I shake my head, staring at the shiny metal.

"It's made of adamantine, the same material as the pillars of Tartarus. You're familiar with Tartarus, no?"

Before I can answer, a memory flickers through my mind. Someone I love is held captive in Tartarus, but I can't remember who or how I know this . . .

"Yes, your kind is *very* familiar with Tartarus," he hisses, his large body sidling next to me. The trident barely skims along my forearm, but the touch causes a blinding pain so white-hot that I stiffen, grinding my teeth as a moan escapes unbidden from my belly.

My vision swims as I wish I could be back in the Underworld, even in the land of Tartarus with the worst of the worst, but I blink back the tears, refusing to show any weakness.

"So you're aware that this trident is made of the only material capable of slaying, say, a *Titan*?"

I swallow the lump in my throat, lowering my eyes and nodding. A Titan. He knows exactly what I am. Who I really am.

"Now get your fucking ass up and walk, or this trident will sail straight through your heart."

I widen my eyes and stand, feeling my magic flicker in my fingers. I fold my hands in my cloak and follow him across the seemingly frozen lake, to a destination unknown.

· • • ● • ● • • • ·

We travel for what seems like hours, trudging over the windy lake's solidified waves. As much as I want to know how he's managed to stop the lake's undulations, I refuse to make small talk with him. Instead, I walk with my head down, eyeing the life beneath the hardened surf. They, like me, are prisoners, caught beneath the ceiling of Poseidon's magic. We walk until dawn breaks in the sky, the fog beginning to burn off with the sun's rays.

Finally, we reach a small fishing village. Climbing through the sandy soil, I follow in Poseidon's wake as we trudge directly to a tiny hut, and after I'm shoved me through the door, I'm met by a woman, her eyes widening in horror as she looks upon the burn on my arm, the despair on her face matching my own.

"We have a guest, Amphitrite," Poseidon states flatly as my eyes roam the cabin. It's small, too small for the god of the sea. My heart pounds in my ears as I realize that being brought to such a tiny home, and not his seat of power, doesn't bode well for my situation. I swallow, noticing the bare walls and lack of furniture. My gaze finally lands on Poseidon's wife.

She blinks at me, a flicker of terror passing over her features. It's gone in an instant. Her frizzy white hair resembles the ocean's waves, and her indigo eyes the horizon at twilight. I'm hypnotized by her movements, fluid and smooth as she moves about the small cabin, divesting me of my muddied clothing and drawing a warm bath in an alcove with a simple flick of her wrist. Naked and shivering, I step into the bath, luxuriating in the warm water despite the fear that still chills my bones. My exhaustion becomes evident as my eyelids feel heavier and heavier.

I drift to sleep, the water lapping at the side of the tub with my breaths, and slip under, blissfully lost to sleep.

CASTOR

I have seven days to rescue my bride and bring her to Olympus, or else my life is forfeit. I repeat the words to myself, over and over again, as I pace outside Pollux and Helen's rooms.

"Hurry up, you two!" I bellow, pounding on the door.

Pollux stumbles out, his tunic untucked and his sandals unlaced, a sneer smeared across his face. "What's the rush? Last time she up and disappeared, she came back. The time before, she very damn well took care of herself, brother. I'm sure she's fine." He reaches out and clasps my shoulder, shaking me from my worried furor. "Face it, that wife of yours can handle her own." He tosses his knapsack over his shoulder and stomps down the hallway toward the stables.

I peer inside the rooms, searching for Helen. She's braiding her blond locks and humming to herself. I raise my arms at her, widening my eyes and shaking my head.

"What?" she inquires, blinking slowly.

"By all means, take your time," I reply, my attitude dripping with sarcasm and anger that, I know, is not fair to direct toward my little sister. Unfortunately, she's the only one here.

"Castor, Melinoe left of her own volition. And we all know she can handle herself, much better than you can." She snorts in derision.

"What's that supposed to mean?"

Helen stands, runs her hands down her peplos, adjusts her belt, and inhales, her gaze meeting mine.

"Brother, I shared with Melinoe that you've always been a bit . . . worried about your mortality. I told her that I was glad you'd finally found happiness." She smiles as though she's done something magnificent, but in reality, all Helen's done is laid bare my deepest and darkest secret. The jealousy I've felt for years as I watched my brother fight valiantly, without fear of death or injury. The envy I've felt at watching Helen, knowing she would become queen of Sparta while my bones were buried six feet deep. While their legacies would last for centuries, mine would be a mere whisper in time.

"Helen"—I reach for her hands, grabbing them and pulling her close—"wh-when did you tell this to Melinoe?"

Furrowing her brow, she tucks her lip under her teeth and thinks. "I think it was the first day of the Calydonian boar hunt. Why?"

It dawns on me. Is this the reason Melinoe's left? Does she somehow know about the arrangement I made? I panic, my eyes growing wider, and I yank Helen out of the room.

"Wait! I need to gather my things!" she protests, pulling away from me.

"You have five minutes! We've got to go—now—before it's too late!" I sprint down the hall and rush out to the stables, ready to catch up with Melinoe before I lose her for good.

MELINOE

I awake splayed out on a hard bed, a heavy feeling weighing down my arms and legs. Trying to lift my head, I find that it, too, is weighted. Languid. As though my body is being held underwater. I blink my eyes open wider, unable to fully sit up or move.

My rustling causes a visitor to appear, but it's not until the form moves closer that my vision clears enough to recognize him. Poseidon moves from the doorway to the bedside, and reaching down to move my hair away from my face, he leans closer. His breath smells of cooked fish, and my stomach roils against the stench. I try to roll away, pushing my head against the bed, but my body won't cooperate.

"Don't try to fight against me, witch. You've become sick from the water here. Your system isn't used to the type of magic Amphitrite and I exhibit. This refreshing herbal tea will help soothe the symptoms of lethargy you're feeling. Take a drink." My mind tries to understand. Am I sick from the water? Or his magic? My head pounds just being awake, and I'm so thirsty.

He holds a warm mug up to my lips, and I drink greedily. My body is parched; I'm not sure how long I've been asleep, but it feels as though it's been days. I gulp the liquid, spilling a few drops down my chin, but Poseidon cleans me with a cloth, wiping at my mouth.

"There, there. Rest now. You will feel better on the morrow."

I lie back, my eyelids drooping and my breath slowing, and sink gratefully into the darkness.

· · · ● · ● · ● · · ·

I run toward Zeus, laughing as I tackle him to the ground, his body thrown backward into the sand.

"Hecate, stop it!" my father yells from the blanket near the dock. Our faces sticky with the jam rolls from the picnic, Zeus and I tussle in the sand, spitting the grains from our mouths and blinking the sunlight from our eyes.

"Let's take a dip and clean ourselves off." Zeus nods toward the surf, pulling me to my feet. I shake out my long hair, sand spilling from the dark tresses. Zeus, too, flings his head side to side like a dog.

I grab his hand and tug him toward the azure water, our knobby-kneed legs leaping over the waves, only letting go of his touch when I dive forward into the salty Terranean Sea. I glance back toward the dock, my mother and father reclining in the shadow of a palm. Smiling, I turn toward Zeus, who's swimming farther out than we're allowed.

"Zeus, wait!" I shout, paddling slowly after him. My strength is no match for his. At the age of eleven he's already muscled like a youth twice his age. My spindly arms and legs flail uselessly in the water, my hair sticking to my face and entangling itself in my mouth.

He pauses and stands, eyes cast toward the horizon. "Do you think I could swim to the mainland, Hecate?" His voice is thick with emotion.

I swim up beside him, unable to touch the bottom, and tread water as the waves furl around us. He presses his lips together before letting out a sad sigh. Does my only friend want to leave me? "Why would you want to go to the mainland?" I worry that I've done something wrong, that I'm not enough for him, that I'm making him want to go away. I cough as water shoots up my nose, burning my nostrils. "Zeus, can we go back? I can't touch here." I am breathless from treading for so long. A larger wave rushes over me, and I fight to keep my head above the water. The undertow pulls at me, threatening to suck me beneath the salty spray.

He doesn't seem to hear me, his gaze still fixed on the horizon. I'm not even sure if the mainland is in that particular direction, but I don't remind him of that.

"Zeus!" A wave crashes over me, pulling me under. Beneath the crystal waters, I catch a glimpse of him turning toward me, reaching down into the foam and yanking me upward into his strong arms.

"Let's go back," he says, cradling me against his chest. I blink the salt from my eyes and look over his shoulder to the distance, where I swear I see a flash of light glisten through the sun's rays.

·　·　·　●　·　●　·　●　·　·　·

A voice whispers my name. It tickles my ear, and I try to adjust and roll my shoulder forward, but my neck is frozen. Stiff.

"Hecate," the voice purrs. My eyes open, squinting against the candlelight. It's Amphitrite. I recognize her, but from where, I don't know. From the past?

I try to form words with my mouth, but my lips are glued together from disuse. My tongue feels heavy and thick. Swollen. My mind flickers back to what Poseidon said about the water, the magic harming me. I can't form a cohesive thought, and I try my hardest to focus on Amphitrite's form in front of me. Where do I know her from?

She leans closer, her voice no more than a whisper against my ear. "Hecate."

I blink at her, and she reaches for my hand. Her touch is painful, my muscles atrophied and burning from the lack of movement.

She pulls a chair up with her other hand and sits down, rubbing her thumb over my palm. I swallow, grunting for something to drink.

"No, you cannot have anything to drink."

I frown, but I cannot form the words to ask why.

"The tea, the water, it's all poisoned. It's why you're unable to move, my dear. It's the only way Poseidon can control you and your magic, to keep you drugged. He's afraid of you," she whispers.

I let out a small groan, and a tear slips from my eye, crawling down my face. I'm so thirsty. "W-w-why?" I manage to breathe through parched lips.

Her brow furrows as she bites her lip. "Poseidon knows how strong you are. He knows that, with you and your magic in his control, he can take Mount Olympus or even the Underworld. He's not satisfied with just the sea, he wants more. It's why he sent Pirithous and Euphemus to find you at the hunt. He wanted you brought back alive, to use you. They weren't meant to hurt you." Her eyes darken in anger.

I attempt to clear my throat, to speak more, but my mouth is so dry that I only end up retching silently.

"I know this is difficult, but the poison needs to leave your system."

I flare my nostrils and blink my eyes closed for a moment, acknowledging that I've heard her warning.

"Play the part, Hecate. It's what I've been doing for years. Play the part until you can cut the head off the snake." Why is she talking about snakes at a time like this? My mind can't comprehend, and my eyes droop heavily. She stands and, still holding my hand, squeezes it heartily before turning to leave.

· · ● · ● ● · · ·

My throat burns, the pain nearly unbearable, and my stomach rumbles from the lack of food or water. Even standing takes its toll, my legs wobbly from disuse. As Poseidon brings me mug after mug of tea, I fight the urge to gulp greedily and, instead, place my lips on the cup and swallow nothing. I pretend my body is still drugged, my arms and legs leaden weights against the bed, but when he leaves, I'm finally able to fling the sheet back and stand, albeit carefully.

I'm still weak, too weak for my magic to do more than create a spark, my mind fuzzy and unable to recall even the most basic spells. And, seeing as I don't want to die in the process, I have to come up with some other plan, without magic.

I wander the small room, assessing all the decor and items that could potentially be used to escape. Curtains. Bedding. Candles. Woven rug. There's not much here, and I collapse back on the bed, exhausted from my simple pacing.

CASTOR

We race to Trichonida Lake and find Melinoe's horse tethered to a tree on the edge of the water.

The horse whinnies and stamps his hooves, agitated at having been confined. Judging by the picked grass around the tree, it's been at least a day since Melinoe left him behind. I look out to the lake as though a clue will magically appear from its depths.

"People in town said Poseidon, along with his wife, has a small hut near the fishing village of Myrtia," Pollux states as he pulls up beside me, following my gaze across the waves. "We'd have to travel around the lake to get there. It'd likely take at least another day or so, as the trails will take us farther away from the shore."

I worry my lip between my teeth, remembering the time limit. Seven days.

"We'll need to make it there in one day, even less if possible." We can't waste any time if I want to keep my life—which I do.

Pollux swallows and nods. While he may not understand the reasons, he's nothing if not a soldier, able to follow orders from his commanding officer.

"We'd best saddle up, then."

We race toward an invisible force, Melinoe's mount in the lead. He seems to know where he's going, which is odd, but I shrug it off and, instead, check on

Helen. I'm proud of my sister's horse-riding abilities, grateful for both her and Pollux's silence as we ride through the night to Myrtia.

When we do finally arrive in the small village, we take care to keep to the outskirts, making a camp and staying away from the main thoroughfares.

Pollux, ever the consummate conversationalist, does reconnaissance at the local tavern and determines which hut belongs to Amphitrite, Poseidon's wife.

"I was only able to watch the house for a little while today, but Poseidon leaves early in the morning and returns just before dusk. We'd need to make our move then."

I nod, thinking, devising a plan to rescue my wife. Devising a plan to keep myself alive.

. . . ● . ● . ● . . .

Over ale at the local watering hole that night, Pollux and I go over our plan one more time while Helen, standing between the wooden stools lined up along the counter, orders another drink.

"Listen, it's not perfect, but it's the best shot we have at rescuing her, brother."

Helen returns, dropping loudly into her seat and slamming her cup on the table.

I cock an eyebrow. "Did the bartender say something to upset you, sister?"

She huffs, sitting back and crossing her arms. Glancing at the bartender, his sleeves rolled up as he moves from one end of the counter to the other, I confer with Pollux, and we both decide we can take him.

We make to stand, ready to pound him for insulting our sister, when she shouts, "Stop!"

Creasing our brows, we sit back down. "What's the matter, then?" Pollux inquires, taking a pull from his mug.

"Aren't you both exhausted, tired of all this?" She sweeps her hand through the air.

"Drinking?" I snort. "No, I'll never tire of ale or wine, sister." Pollux and I clink our mugs together and chuckle.

She slams her palms down on the table, the liquid in our cups nearly spilling over the rims. "Enough! I don't mean drinking, you fools." Her eyes blaze with irritation.

"What do you mean then?"

She lowers her eyes, scratching her nail along the table. Exhaling loudly, she finally relents. "I'm tired of being the pretty one, the one whom everyone needs to protect, the one who has no purpose other than to be a pawn for our family's alliances."

I'm silent, stunned at Helen's outburst, but Pollux speaks for the both of us. "What's brought all this on?" He reaches across the table, stilling her hand.

"I've just . . ." She pauses, throwing her eyes to the ceiling and finding the courage to speak. "I've just seen how strong Mel has been—how you both look at her with pride—and I want that too. I want you to be proud of me for my strength, not for my beauty."

The words spill out of my mouth, unbidden. "Helen, we are both so proud of you, especially after . . ." My throat tightens as I watch my little sister's eyes well, her chin tremble. To know how she truly feels about herself, to know that she isn't proud of herself after all she's been through, is heartbreaking.

"I won't let what Theseus did to me"—she abruptly closes her mouth before opening it again—"what happened to me . . . I won't let it define who I am." Her eyes are steely as she presses her lips together.

"You've come through all this with more strength than either of us has in a single finger, Helen," Pollux adds, reaching for her.

She suddenly stands, taking Pollux and me by surprise as we eye her warily. "I just need a moment, a bit of fresh air. I'll be fine." She gestures to the shiny, unused dagger she's taken to wearing at her hip, a gift from Melinoe to apologize for her disappearance at the boar hunt.

I nod as she heads out the front of the pub, and as Pollux goes to the bar to get another round, I take a step out back to relieve myself.

I finish and lean against the outside wall of the tavern, wondering why I can't get Melinoe out of my head. Wondering how she's become such an important part of my life in only a few short weeks. What's caused me to forget my mission, my one goal, throwing it all away over some stubborn princess?

It's because she challenges you, dumbass, I think to myself. I knew from the moment I saw her dancing with King Pirithous at the Spartan ball, his fingers sliding lower and lower along her backside, that I didn't want anyone else to have her. Then, dropping her off at our room and not touching her? Turning away from her parted lips and the desire that had been dripping from her? I'm hard just thinking about it weeks later, how stupid I'd been to not take her right then and there, have my way with her. Now that I've had her, I only want more. The feel of her wrapped around me, her blue eyes darkening with desire . . . I've got to get her back. No, I want to get her back. No, I simply want *her.*

I turn toward the door when I hear it, a woman's loud grunt, as though she's lifted something heavy and needed to release the breath loudly from her body for extra strength. Hurrying around the pub, I see a figure lying on the ground, a knife stuck in his neck. Helen, my little sister, stands over the body, her jaw clenched and eyes wild. Her hands are fisted, and as I approach, she raises them, on her guard.

"W-what the hell happened?"

She lowers her fists when she sees my face emerge from the shadows, and as I slowly drop to one knee and turn the bloodied man to his back, I see his face.

Pirithous.

My eyes quickly flick up to Helen's, and instead of fear or horror, I see pride in them. Strength. A small smile lifts her lips. "Helen, what happened? Where did he come from?"

The adrenaline coursing through her body leaves her breathless, as though she's just run a marathon, but she explains through breaths, bouncing on her feet, "I wanted some fresh air and he came around the corner—from over there." She points to the opposite side of the pub. "And then when I saw his face, that *disgusting* face of his, I stabbed him before he even opened his dirty mouth."

Just then, Pollux comes barreling out of the bar, his eyes wild with drink. He stumbles over Pirithous's body, and as he looks between Helen and me, he slaps me on the back.

"Well, good job, Cas! You finally got 'im!"

I shake my head as the skin around Helen's eyes tightens, her lips thinning. "Actually," I speak up, "it was our dear baby sister who slew him."

Pollux's mouth drops open, and he emits a guffaw, his face beaming with pride. He sweeps Helen into a hug, twirling her around as he rumples her hair like a child. As he sets her down, he assesses the situation, his hand on his hips and his face dropping, becoming serious.

"So our sister killed a king." His head bobs as the wheels begin turning in his mind. "I think it's best we get rid of the body before we've another bit of drama on our hands then, yes?"

Looking at Helen, I watch as her face falls, paling as the realization sets in, and simply say, "You wanted to be strong, to be one of us." I shrug. "Getting rid of the evidence is just part of it." I move to hoist the body over my shoulder when she reaches her hand out.

"Wait," she says, moving toward Pirithous. I watch her face, waiting for it to break, waiting for the guilt to set in. "I want my dagger back," she states plainly, yanking it noisily out of the bloodied wound and wiping it on her dress before sticking it daintily back in the scabbard at her waist.

Pollux and I widen our eyes at one another before breaking out into a laugh. We trudge toward the lake, eager to finally be rid of this lecherous king.

MELINOE

"Hecate, I have something to tell you." Zeus reaches his hand out to me, and I frown, my eyebrows lowering in consternation.

We are walking in the lush forest, a goat leashed at Zeus's side, on our way to make a sacrifice to the Titans for favor and prosperity in the coming season. I gulp, trying not to make eye contact with the goat, my belly tightening at the death I know awaits her.

"Hecate, stop, please. I need to talk to you." He pulls me toward him, and I crash into his hard chest, his sweat slicking my nose. I frown in displeasure, wiping at my face.

"Ugh, you're so sweaty. What is it already? I want to get this over with!"

He takes a deep breath and looks up at the canopy. I see his throat bob as he swallows. "I'm leaving the island."

My eyes widen in dismay and my mouth falls open, no words coming out.

"Before you try to stop me, my mind is made up. It's time for me to fulfill my destiny."

"What destiny? Why can't you fulfill whatever it is here, on Crete? Why must you leave?" The shrillness of my voice is startling. I yank the goat's leash out of his hand and stomp onward, continuing on the way to the altar.

He jogs to catch up with me, but I push forward, refusing to stop. "Let me explain!"

"There's no need to explain, Zeus. Your destiny, your life, is somewhere out there. I've watched you for years, knowing this island was too small for you." I approach the altar, tie the goat to the shrine and step back, motioning for Zeus to take over. I've never been able to handle the killing. My skills lie in summoning the fire for the offering and casting enchantments to keep the goat calm before her demise.

I kneel, supplicating myself on the holy ground, refusing to watch Zeus slit the goat's throat. I press my eyes closed, but something touches my back, caressing down my spine. Shivering, I shift to my knees, looking up to meet Zeus's eyes.

"Come with me," he pleads, his eyes full of hope.

• • • ● • ● • • • •

I press my lips closed, fighting Poseidon's grip on my jaw.

"Drink, you stupid little witch." He fumes, digging the cup into my clenched teeth. The pain is unbearable, especially with how weak I've become over the past several days. When Poseidon found me passed out at the window, with the bed dismantled, he knew instantly that I'd been dumping the poisoned liquids into the chamber pot.

Now, as I fight against him, I know my cause is lost. Poseidon curses and rears back, sloshing the warm brown liquid onto the bedding. He releases me, and I fall back against the pillows, my breaths coming in gasps. I know he won't kill me, but I'm sure he'll use my incapacitation to threaten Zeus and any other god who wants my blood. My abilities. I have to be tough enough to hold my own against him, but my strength is fading. Fast. My eyes grow heavy, and I feel myself slipping into oblivion again. I don't bother fighting it. What's the point?

• • • ● • ● • • • •

It's been years since Zeus left, leaving me behind on this gods-forsaken island. That night, the night he left, I rushed home, hoping to quickly pack my belongings and escape into the night, my future with Zeus all but assured, when my mother, Asteria, discovered my plan.

"You'll not last one month with that boy, Hecate," she said, a sneer curling her lip as she watched me with disdain.

"You don't know what you're talking about. He wants me to come with him to avenge his legacy, to fulfill his destiny. He needs me."

As I rushed around the room, heedlessly flinging items into a bag at my feet, my mother grabbed my wrist, stopping me. "What about your destiny?" she asked quietly.

I paused. Shaking my head, I turned again, ready to continue my packing. "He needs me," I repeated to her.

"That boy needs nothing except himself, and you're a fool to believe otherwise. Have you completely ignored everything the townspeople say about his liaisons? He would never be faithful to you. He will never love you the way you think you love him, Hecate."

I swallowed, lowering my eyes in shame. As much as I hated to admit it, my mother was right. Zeus was a known philanderer. Women threw themselves at him, and he partook willingly. I'd seen the broken hearts he left in his wake, and I hardened my heart, refusing to be one more of his conquests. Refusing to be one more broken heart. My mother enfolded me in a hug, and I sobbed. I released the anguish that'd been building up for years.

"He'll never love you the way he loves himself, my daughter."

Now, a decade later, I'm finally summoned off the island. I've been asked to assist Demeter, goddess of the harvest, in locating her daughter Persephone, goddess of spring, in the Underworld. As the Titan of witchcraft and ghosts, my abilities have become widely known, and Demeter believes I can assist her in rending the earth and entering the Underworld through a cave near a place called Taenarus.

This time, as my mother watches me pack my belongings, there is warmth in her eyes, a smile lighting her face.

"I'm so proud of you, daughter. All your hard work, your studies in honing your gift and dedication to your craft, have led you to this moment. To be summoned by a goddess of Olympus is a high honor, indeed."

I accept her praise, even as my mind worries over the adventure before me. I must travel to the mainland before entering the Underworld near Cape Taenarum, and as my life has consisted of the simplistic island of Crete, I am obviously nervous.

"Remember, Demeter is a fine goddess who will lead you down the rightful path of justice and truth. Learn from her and maybe a place on Mount Olympus will be yours!" Nothing would make my mother happier than me becoming an Olympian, but I have other plans in mind.

Mainly, finding my old friend Zeus.

CASTOR

Pollux wasn't able to determine what time Poseidon leaves for his duties, but we know it must around the high tide, so we watch Poseidon's abode from afar, waiting for him to take his leave. I glance toward the lake's coastline, noting the height of the water, then look back to the hut's door. Sighing, I run my hands through my hair, my foot tapping in annoyance. I'm running out of time. I'm now down to five days, four and a half if I'm being technical. My foot tapping has progressed up my leg, my nervous energy spewing off me like a stench. Pollux, sitting rigid next to me, puts his hand on my leg, stilling my anxiousness.

Helen has stayed behind at the encampment, preparing odds and ends in case Mel is injured or . . . I shake my head, refusing to think of what else this bastard could have done to my wife in order to incapacitate her. I know her strength, her drive. And I know she's feet away from me, unable to rescue herself. Something isn't right. She's in real danger.

My thoughts stray to the last time I was with Mel, in the woods. The feel of her body against mine. Her hand on my cock, stroking me until I was near bursting. The softness of her breasts as I palmed them, her body arching into me. Feeling my face grow hot, I shake my head to clear my thoughts. I need to focus, and I can't very well just wait around while my wife sits across the lane at the hands of a deranged god.

"I've had enough of waiting," I snarl to Pollux, standing and pushing away from him. I stride across the street, Pollux snapping into action and following me.

"What are you doing?" He grabs my collar, yanking me back, but his strength is no match for my determination.

Turning, I shove him off. "I'm not sitting around; I'm rescuing Mel before it's too late." I meet his eyes, not saying what we're both thinking.

It might already be too late.

Pol nods once, sliding his blade from its scabbard, and trails behind me.

As I approach the door, I, too, pull my sword from its sheath. Sidling up to the side of the hut, I crouch down below a window. Pollux follows suit, and we continue to communicate through a series of hand motions learned in the Spartan army. He stands, while I stay crouching, and peers into the window above us.

Empty, he signals, and I follow him around the side of the cottage to the next window. This time, he crouches while I peer inside.

My heart stops as I take the briefest glimpse before pulling back to hide behind the shuttered frame.

Pollux catches my eyes, and he knows we've found her. He nods and stands on the other side of the frame. Peering in, he quickly assesses the room and pulls back.

Clear, he signals to me.

We use our blades and edge the grate off the window, silently pulling it to the ground. Pollux moves beneath the window, ready to help me climb through. Then, we count together.

One.

Two.

Three.

Pollux lifts me through the frame, but someone immediately grabs me around the throat, pulls me through the window, and then throws me against the wall. Dizzily, I blink, my gaze focusing on the imposing figure above me.

Poseidon.

MELINOE

My small cabin in the heart of Elysium is filled with innumerable potions, mixtures, elixirs, and draughts. I've finally found a home of my own, right here in the heart of the Underworld. I look toward the red sky, eager for the time when my new friend, Queen Persephone, will visit. She usually stops by on her morning walk, and I have a new tincture prepared for her. When she shared her and Hades's troubles conceiving, my heart warmed that she trusted me enough to assist. She now regularly visits my cottage, and I am often invited to the castle for dinner and entertainments.

A knock sounds at the door, and I distractedly flick my wrist to open it, not even bothering to wonder why the queen would be knocking.

"Hello, Hecate." The deep, booming voice takes my breath away, and I spin, my eyes taking in the hulking figure in the doorway.

Zeus.

I swallow, my mouth suddenly dry, my eyes wide. "What are you doing here?" I tentatively step forward, holding my forearm out for a friendly shake. Instead, he lifts me off my feet and swings me around in an all-encompassing hug.

"I figured it was about time I paid you a visit." He surveys my small abode, nodding in appreciation at the simple decor. "It suits you."

"I didn't realize you knew I was here . . ."

He strolls toward my workbench, picking up and discarding various vials and tools. "Of course I knew you were here. I've kept tabs on you for years, you know." His eyes meet mine, a flash of something sinister darkening his look. Does he remember what happened on Olympus?

"Let me get you some refreshments." Gulping, I move into the kitchen where I quickly brew a Cretan tea from our homeland. I hand him a mug, and he swallows the liquid, his grin stretching wide.

"Ah," he sighs contentedly. "It reminds me of home!"

"I've very nearly perfected it, so I'm glad you like it." I gesture to a chair, where Zeus plops down heavily. I, too, take a seat across from him, but keep my eye on the door.

"Expecting someone?" While his grin stays spread across his face, the merriment is missing from his eyes. I plaster a grin on my face, pretending everything is fine, when in actuality I'm terrified. Terrified he'll remember.

"Queen Persephone visits from time to time. She was meant to stop in today for a tincture."

"I see. Tell me how you became friends with Persephone after working so closely with Demeter to return her daughter to the Land of the Living."

I shrug, wondering myself how I became such fast friends with the goddess of spring. "Demeter was wrong. Persephone was in love, and she chose to come to the Underworld. She chose to live here with Hades. She's happy." Telling Demeter the truth of her daughter's absconding had not been easy, and it had effectively severed our working relationship. Severed any hope of becoming an Olympian when I'd shared that I would not assist in returning Persephone to the Land of the Living against her will.

Silence fills the cabin, settling heavily over us, filled with years of unshared truths. Seeing as I've lived alone for some time, I'm comfortable with the lack of noise, the calm. I crave it, sink into it. Zeus, however, clearly isn't as he fidgets with his hands, running them through his silvery hair and tapping his foot impatiently.

I finally put him out of his misery. "Why have you truly come, Zeus?"

His foot stills and his body goes rigid, only the vein in his neck throbbing. "I came here for you, of course."

My forehead crinkles in confusion. "I'm afraid I don't understand."

He stands, his arms encircling my hut. "Why are you here in this hellhole when you could be with me on Mount Olympus?"

I blink slowly. "I like my home. I like it here. Are you asking me to ascend as an Olympian?" I think back to my mother and how proud she will be to hear of this offer, even if I don't intend to take it.

Zeus barks out a laugh, shaking his head. "Of course I don't mean for you to ascend. I can't just go around making every goddess an Olympian, Hecate. I want you to be with me."

I inhale, steeling my nerves. "But I'm not a goddess. I'm a Titan." I meet his eyes.

He approaches, running his large fingers up and down my arm. A tickle of pleasure settles in my belly, but it's quickly replaced by fear and anger. He laughed at the thought of my ascension.

I narrow my eyes at him. "You mean that you want to use me, is that it?" I try to keep the disgust out of my voice but filtering my emotions has never been my strong suit.

He coughs, but covers it up with a chuckle, clearly taken aback by my bluntness. His hands come up to my face, pulling me closer to him, and I stiffen. "Be with me, Hecate."

I pull away, shaking my head. "No, you're married!"

He laughs again. "That hasn't stopped me in the past. I am the king of gods. I do what I please."

I'm well aware of his past. His first lover was Metis, mother of the Olympian Athena. Then Themis, Mnemosyne, Leto, Europa, Io, Semele, Ganymede, Callisto, Dione, Nemesis, and innumerable mortal women. The list will continue to grow, whether or not my name is included.

I shake my head again, as though doing so will repel his words from my mind. "No, Zeus. I'll not be your little pet—your witch—only there to give you more power." I back away from him, feeling safer with distance separating us. "My mother was right. You've never loved anyone the way you love yourself."

Anger burns in his eyes, and I know he's considering what to do next. I'm sure he's never been turned down before, but I meet his gaze, steadying myself, firm in my decision. He remembers, he remembers what happened on Olympus, and he knows he can't force me to do his bidding, not with my powers at their peak.

His jaw works, muscles clenching. "You'll regret this, Hecate. And you'll wish you'd answered differently."

He turns and stomps from the cabin, slamming the door in his wake.

CASTOR

"Fuck," I growl as Poseidon yanks me to my feet, throwing me across the room. I slam into the stone wall and slide back to the ground, groaning the entire way.

Pollux flops through the window clumsily, and Poseidon easily plants his booted foot to my brother's neck, pressing the air from his throat. Coughing, Pollux fights against Poseidon's massive calves for release.

"Stop!" I roar, my vision swimming. Rising like a drunkard and swinging my sword wildly, I catch Poseidon against his forearm. He hisses, blood spurting from the wound. Luckily, the distraction caused him to step back from Pollux's throat, and he now sweeps Poseidon from his feet. He lands on his back with a thud, and Pollux holds his sword to the god's throat, pressing until I see the skin give way and a drop of blood appear. The blood instantly boils, burning Poseidon's skin. He howls in pain, a grimace lighting his face.

"You think we weren't smart enough to coat our swords in adamantine, you fucking fool?"

I hope we can hold him off long enough to rescue Mel. I finally take a moment and glance at her body, slumped on the bed.

"I'm here, sweetheart," I murmur as I approach her lifeless body. She doesn't stir. She's breathing, but just barely. "What the fuck have you done to her?" I roar at Poseidon.

"Like I'd tell you," he spits out. Pollux quickly swipes his blade against Poseidon's bare chest, the blood bubbling from the wound, before returning the tip back to his throat. The god roars in agony, his eyes filled with pure malice.

"You will tell us or we will end your reign, but not too quickly."

The door flings open and I turn, my sword pointed at the intruder.

Amphitrite.

I point my blade to her throat, ready to draw blood should the need arise. She fans the room with her eyes: Poseidon on the ground with welts quickly growing larger by the minute as the poison works on his exposed skin, Pollux standing over him, and Melinoe's lifeless body on the bed. Eyes softening as she takes in my wife, she meets my gaze.

"I'm so sorry," she says, raising her hands in submission.

"What's he done to her?" I demand.

"You keep your mouth closed, bitch," Poseidon yells from the floor. Pollux swiftly kicks him in the jaw, and Amphitrite snorts in derision.

I turn to her, surprised by her reaction.

"You think I wanted this?" she asks him. Turning to me, she explains, "I told him this was a foolish idea, kidnapping Hecate, the strongest witch to exist, and drugging her." She turns to Poseidon. "You're a fucking buffoon."

"What's he drugged her with?"

"He's concocted a tea of blue water lily," she admits, keeping her eyes on me. "It's kept her sedated for days. I tried to warn her, but he found her trying to escape and has been force-feeding her larger amounts each day."

"You traitorous—"

This time I turn my sword on Poseidon, the tip of my blade sliding along his cheek, blood bubbling from the wound. His cries of pain spur me to slice deeper. Seeing Amphitrite wince from my periphery, I pull back.

All four of us turn as a trumpet sounds in the distance. Amphitrite's eyes widen, and Poseidon's expression morphs into one of pure delight.

"What's that?" Pollux inquires to Amphitrite. Biting her lip, she slides her gaze to Poseidon.

"It's my son, Triton, alerting our army when I did not show up for an important meeting," the god snarls. He laughs deeply, the wounds on his chest and cheek coagulating to a dark red crust.

I flick my gaze to Pollux, who nods in silent agreement. Grabbing Melinoe and hoisting her over my shoulder, I run through the hut and out into the street, Pollux fast on my heels. It'll be a miracle of the gods if we make it out of this mess alive.

MELINOE

"Please come to the palace immediately. She needs you."

-Selene

I read the missive quickly, my heart constricting, and immediately pack a satchel of various remedies: a bundle of mint for stomach issues, ingredients to make Greek mountain tea for wounds, a packet of fennel and saffron for digestion, licorice root for breathing difficulties, root of the mandrake for pain relief, and last Balkan peony for women's ailments. As I leave my home, I cast a binding spell around the door, inhibiting any unwanted visitors from entering. I press my lips together and, with the red sun high overhead, flick my wrist and arrive at Hades's castle.

I'm met at the gate by a worried Selene. Her brow is furrowed, her lips blistered from being picked. Hoisting my satchel around my shoulder, I quickly fall into step with her.

"What's Her Highness's ailment?" I lower my voice, hiding my worry as the handmaiden leads me through shortcuts and passageways designed for the fastest route to the queen.

Selene looks around, assessing the emptied halls, and pulls me close, whispering, "Her Highness went out for her morning walk. When she didn't return with the coming storm, I went in search of her. I . . ." She inhales deeply, raising her hand to pull at her lip, *"I found her in the woods. Badly accosted. I believe she was raped, Hecate."*

My eyes widen, my stomach plummeting to the floor. Ice runs through my veins, and I immediately know. Zeus. Zeus has done this. When I rebuffed him, he didn't just return to the Land of the Living. No, he purposefully hurt my friend, my friend he knew was on her way to visit me. My eyes well, but I gulp down the guilt, my jaw clenching. He'll pay for this, but first I must tend to my friend. I pull Selene along as we now run to Persephone's chambers.

· · · · ●·● · ● · · ·

I stand over my workbench, weeks later, combining elixirs and tonics. I know what I must do. I've seen to the healing of Persephone's outer wounds, but the inner ones remain. They will always remain.

As I plan my revenge on Zeus, I know this for certain: I would never get close enough to Mount Olympus, to him, to cast the spell needed to stop him. I need a different approach, one he would never suspect. He doesn't truly know my strength, but he would realize my intentions, as I'm constantly watched by his spies. Unfortunately for him, my witchcraft is no match for him or his lackeys, and I'm willing to do anything to stop him. Including reincarnating myself and becoming her.

"Agapití kardiá . . . énas ángelos pou koimátai. Sikotheíte apó ta vathiá sto fos, xýpnioi apó ton vathýtero ýpno. Anadýetai apó to neró pou anavlýzei, eínai sto fos tou matioú! Ela piso!"

"To the beloved, who is sleeping. Our bond is formed. Get up from the depths, into the light! You may arise again out of the abyss, in the light of the eye exists! Come back!"

My eyes snap open and I sit up, bile and hot liquid pouring from my mouth, burning my throat as tears rush down my cheeks.

Next to me, Castor jumps into action, holds my hair back, and presses a cool cloth to my neck. "I'm here. I'm here, sweetheart." The relief in his voice is obvious, and after emptying my stomach, I sit up and wipe my mouth with the back of my hand, furrowing my brow at him.

He holds a cup of warm broth toward me, and I greedily accept it, pulling deep swallows from the mug. When I've sucked down the hearty juice, I flop back onto the pillows, taking a deep breath and finally assessing my surroundings.

"Melinoe, we're—"

I cut him off, placing my palm to his chest. "Hecate," I state flatly. "It's Hecate."

Something flickers in his eyes. Confusion? Anger? Whatever it is, it's gone before I can decipher it, but he nods in acceptance. "Can I ask what happened?"

I'm silent for a moment, remembering our argument, but then start to explain, filling him in on the meeting at Lake Trichonida, traveling across the seemingly frozen lake, and the subsequent fever dreams. The dreams that filled in the gaps of who I am. Of *what* I am.

Castor nods, taking my hand in his. "Poseidon was drugging you with blue water lily infused in a tea. Amphitrite confirmed it to us when Pollux and I rescued you."

At the mention of Poseidon's wife, my eyes widen and my body stiffens. "Amphitrite tried to help me, Castor. We must return the favor; she won't be safe with him."

Smiling at me, Castor runs his hand up my arm. "Amphitrite helped us escape, and she's safe with Helios, her son-in-law. She's on her way to be with her daughter Rhode."

I exhale in relief, leaning back against the pillows. I drink in my savior, the dark circles under his eyes, the scruffy facial hair growing along his chin. He looks as though he hasn't slept in days. Lowering my gaze, I feel guilty at the trouble I got myself into, embarrassed at needing a mortal—no—needing *my husband* to come to my rescue. Gulping, I force my gaze higher, force myself to utter the words that are so foreign to me. "Thank you. For coming for me. For saving me."

My throat aches with emotion, and my bottom lip starts to tremble.

"I'm here. I'm right here." Castor pulls me toward him, my head coming to rest in the crook of his neck. He strokes my back, and I lean into him. "I'll always be here for you," he says again, and I reluctantly pull away. He stands and takes my hand. I finally notice the steaming bath in the corner of the chamber.

"I was going to bathe while I waited for you to wake, but now I think I'd like my wife's company, if she'll have me?"

My eyes meet his and I nod, ready to sink into the scented water and feel whole again.

· • · ● · ● ● · ·

Castor takes his time helping me undress, my body sore from disuse. He pulls the loose nightdress over my head and discards it. His hands skim up my thighs, over my hips and stomach, and finally cup my breasts. He leans down, pulling one hardened nipple into his mouth, swirling his tongue around the areola before releasing it and moving to the next breast. I hiss in pleasure, my body already trembling from standing for so long.

He lifts me effortlessly, lowering me gently into the scented water. The warmth soothes my limbs, and I purr like a cat, arching my back and rolling my shoulders.

"Join me," I invite, my eyes meeting his. He bites his lip and, in one fluid movement, pulls his dirtied and torn tunic over his head before lowering his leathers over his thick thighs. I watch, transfixed, as his hardened length springs free, the bath's warmth no match for the heat simmering in my lower body.

I pull my legs into my chest as Castor steps into the tub. The space barely enough for one person is now occupied by his long limbs and wide muscular

250

chest. We laugh as our bodies become entangled, and as he reaches for me, I switch positions, turning into him with my ass pressed into his thighs. I relax into the water, and as Castor begins massaging my neck, I close my eyes. He reaches around and cups my breasts, my nipples puckered again from the cool air hitting my skin, and rolls each bud between his fingers. I moan, the tension releasing from my body as he continues to explore with his large hands.

"Should I keep going, M—I mean, Hecate?" he asks, lowering his hands to my hips and grinding his cock against my ass.

"Yes," I whisper, moving my body in time with his. His fingers continue their descent, moving from my hips to my slick thighs. His hands rub inward, massaging the muscles of my legs and grazing my sex. A whimper escapes my lips, and I lean my head back to trail kisses along his jaw. "I want you inside me."

He obliges, slipping a finger into my folds and instantly finding my sweet spot. While he plays with my clit with one hand, the other seeks my entrance, his fingers delving deep into me while his thickness pulses between my cheeks, and I let out a cry of ecstasy, my own heat warming the water.

I may be stronger, more powerful now that I've accepted who I really am. But this man . . . this mortal man will be my undoing.

CASTOR

Finger fucking my wife while she grinds her ass against my cock feels amazing, especially after almost losing her to Poseidon. I shift, moving on top as I grab her around the waist, turn her to face me, and dip her deeper into the bathwater. Lifting her hips out of the warmth, I sink my mouth into her pussy. My mind is full of nothing but Hecate. The name still feels foreign on my tongue, but her body tastes the same.

I lick against her wet skin with the flat of my tongue, lapping at her sweetness, dipping into her valleys, until she's screaming my name. Her hands fist my hair, nails scraping along my scalp, and I feel my cock throbbing for my own release beneath the water.

"Fuck me," she begs, as though she can read my mind. I growl, not wanting to tear my face away from her sweet clit, but she yanks me up against her chest. I get a glimpse of her glistening breasts bobbing out of the water, and I'm gone. I sink my cock into her in one motion, and as she gasps, I begin sliding in and out, faster and faster. Her muscles squeeze around me, and combined with the warmth of the water, it won't be long until I'm spent.

"I've got to slow down or this will be over much too soon, sweetheart."

Her eyelids lower and she smiles wickedly, licking along the curve of my neck. I'm transfixed by the feel of her pussy wrapped around me, her tits bouncing out of the water as I slam into her over and over.

"Touch yourself," I demand, the finish line within sight. She seductively dips her hand beneath the clear water, and I watch as she parts her folds, playing with the bundle of nerves at her apex. She arches her back, further pressing into me, and water sloshes over the lip of the tub.

"Fuck," she mutters, whether at her own touch or the mess on the floor, I'm not sure, but it sends me over the edge and my vision tunnels, the sounds of the water dimming as my only focus is fucking her until we both come in a torrent of slickness and warmth.

As my seed spills into her, the most amazing feeling in the world turns to intense pain, tearing my chest apart as my heart is ripped free, and gasping for breath and looking into Hecate's horrified face, I drop into the water.

HECATE

Fuck, fuck, fuck! I scream silently in my head as I watch Castor drop into the bath, his lifeless body splayed out. I stand and yank his slippery body from the tub, laying him onto the floor. I work to flip him over, hissing, "Gods damn it!" as his weight and the slickness of both his skin and the water-soaked floor make the task nearly impossible. Rushing to the bed, I slip, landing my entire weight on my knee. I cry out in pain but manage to grab the blanket from the bed and hobble back to his body, racking my brain for what happened.

Laying out the blanket, I'm able to roll Castor's body over easily. I grasp his wrist and feel for a pulse—none—when I notice the effects of magic along his arm. Where his veins should be blue, they've now darkened to a gray soot color. My eyes widen and I drop his wet wrist before checking the other arm. It's the same. As I trail my eyes over his chest and down his torso and legs, I notice the charcoal map of his body's blood.

Gasping, I press my hands to my mouth, horrified at what I've done. In the heat of the moment, and with my powers now strengthened to their full potential, I must have summoned lightning into the water. Looking at my own coal-colored hands, I confirm my suspicions. My face crumples, and I lean over Castor, sobbing at my own stupidity. Why did I think things would get easier with magic? I couldn't control my power before, I still can't control it, and now the only person I truly love is dying.

Searching my brain, I spew forth random incantations, hoping one of them sticks.

I sob through the six incantations of the healing spell.

"*I pligí epoulónetai.*

"*Gia aftá, parakaló, giatrépste tis pligés.*

"*Kánte ton ygií.*

"*Éna ygiés sóma.*"

I wait. And wait.

Nothing.

"Fuck!" I scream aloud, pounding my fists against his chest.

Breathing deeply, I focus and try to calm myself and recite a relief spell.

"*Tha xanagennitheí grígora kai grígora.*"

I wait.

Nothing.

My fingers dance over his chest, my eyes squeezing closed as the tears continue to fall.

"Please," I beg the empty room. "Please!"

My mind continues to work for a solution, landing on a restoration spell. I utter the spell, keeping my fingers on Castor's chest to seal the magic. I wait. Again, nothing.

Defeated, I slump over his body, my sobs echoing, my desperation amplified. It's the Pegasus situation all over again. I can't save Castor. Am I really reliving this yet again?

My cheek pressed to his chest, I hear a dull thump. I sit up, startled. Was that . . .? I lean over his rib cage, the thump hitting my cheek again. A heartbeat. I swipe at my eyes and lean over again, needing to confirm that Castor's heart is beating. The thumping continues.

Lub-dub. Lub-dub.

As I sit back on my heels, Castor's eyes blink open and he takes a full breath, the darkened road map disappearing before my eyes, his veins returning to their purplish hue.

How the—?

My eyes widen, and I utter the words I never thought I'd say to my mortal husband as I meet his gaze, understanding dawning on me.

The spells were useless. Ineffective. Because, looking at Castor, I know. "You're *immortal*."

. . . ● ● . ● ● . ● . .

Castor meets my wide eyes and swallows. Trying to sit up, he groans, and I push him back down before standing up and grabbing another blanket to wrap around my now-shivering naked body. Still limping from my bruised knee, I turn, my gaze accusing, angry. The fury and confusion simmers under my skin like a fire needing oxygen, ready to explode.

"When were you going to tell me?" I demand.

He rolls slowly to his side and manages to make his way to his feet, taking the sopping blanket and tying it around his hips. "I didn't know how to tell you," he admits, having the gall to look chastened. "He—"

"He? Hades? You mean that, in addition to my hand in marriage, you got immortality and failed to mention it? My father made you immortal *weeks* ago?" I rage, feeling the sparks flying from my fingers. I direct them at the ground, where they quickly burn out against the wet floor.

Castor opens his mouth to say something, but then closes it, a flicker of confusion flashing in his eyes, but I'm too upset to think on it as I continue my tempest. "Husbands and wives aren't supposed to keep secrets from each other, Castor. How could you lie to me?"

"I didn't necessarily lie . . . I just didn't tell you the truth." He tries to smirk at me, cockily quirking an eyebrow up and shrugging his shoulders.

"Stop!" I demand, pointing my sparking forefinger at him. The magic lands directly in the center of his chest and immediately burns out, not affecting him in the least. Mouth falling open, and in spite of my better judgment, I launch a fireball at him. Instead of incinerating his mortal skin, it knocks him off his feet and he falls to the ground, otherwise unharmed. I grit my teeth and clench my fists. "What else are you keeping from me, husband? What other secrets aren't you telling me?"

He regains his footing and stands, blinking at me. Raising his arm, he scratches the back of his neck, biceps flexing as I get an eyeful of his muscled stomach. I shake my head, avoiding the lustful thoughts invading my brain, but he strides toward me and takes me in his arms.

"Think of all the possibilities my immortality brings to our relationship, my powerful wife." He leans down and licks the shell of my ear, sending a pool of desire to my belly. "No more holding back, no more restraint."

A moan escapes from me when he sinks his teeth into my collarbone, then nips along my chest. "I want to take my anger out on you," I state bluntly, my eyes tingling with heat.

"So do it," he responds, ripping the blanket from my body and lowering his mouth to mine. I claim his lips and, swapping places, shove him onto the bed with all the fire, lightning, and desire I can muster.

For the first time, my husband is going to feel all of me.

· · · • · • · · · ·

Breathing heavily, Castor and I collapse on what's left of the bed, our eyes taking in the destruction around us. The window coverings are incinerated. The bed frame broken and the mattress uneven. There are various holes and cracks in the walls, evidence of my anger mixed with the desire I feel for my husband.

I stand and approach the now-cold bath water. Sticking my finger into the liquid, I mindlessly mutter a heating spell. A moment later, the water is steaming, filling the room with humidity. My hair sticks to my neck as I dip one foot in, sucking in my breath at the warmth. Sinking down, I enjoy my second bath of the day, keeping my eyes trained on Castor, who watches me with his arms thrown behind his head.

"We'll be on our way to Mount Olympus in the morning, Hecate."

I nod, soaping my hair and dipping my head under the water to rinse. "A stop in Thessaly is required, husband." I watch his eyes take in my breasts as I rise from the steam, water dripping down my back. I do love that I have this effect on him. He can't take his eyes off me, even after having me twice already. I purposefully push my chest forward, smiling inwardly as he sucks in his breath. To be fair, as I take in his naked body, I, too, feel the familiar tingle as my breasts tighten.

"What's in Thessaly?" he inquires, moving to the bath.

I stand, taking the towel he holds out, and wrap it around myself. "A means to destroy Zeus."

CASTOR

"You've arrived at the perfect time, Polydeuces!" Peleus, a friend from our days as Argonauts, roars, clapping Pollux on the back. "Tomorrow is my marriage to the beautiful Thetis, so tonight we celebrate my last evening as a bachelor!"

I look back at Helen and Hecate, both trying to hide their smiles as it's clear that Peleus is drunk on the ale he continues to offer to us.

"Now where's my future wife?" he slurs, looking through the crowd of attendees. "Thetis!" he roars good-naturedly.

A tiny sea nymph springs forward from the group, flitting to her man's side, and plants a kiss on his cheek. "You called, my almost-husband?"

I feel Pollux stiffen at my side as he does his best not to gape at the beautiful woman in front of us. Her bright blond hair hangs in loose waves down her back, while deep-green eyes stare lovingly at her fiancée. She's small, only coming up to Peleus's shoulder, but her pointed nymph ears and full breasts are certainly not childlike. To be fair, she is rather striking, but as I pull Hecate from behind me and wrap my arm around her shoulder, I know my eyes will never stray to another woman. My heart, fully revived and beating louder as I glance at her, belongs only to her. A smile lights my face, and it's not until Pollux clears his throat that I realize I'm holding up the conversation.

"What brings you here to our wedding feast, my fellow sailors?" On unsteady feet, Peleus eyes our group.

"My wife, Hecate, brings congratulations from her parents, Hades and Persephone, and also wishes to speak with her uncle, Hephaestus."

Using her new name brings a slew of widened eyes from not only Peleus and Thetis, but also Helen and Pollux. It's the first time I've introduced her as befits her status as a Titan, and I feel her shoulders relax as she stands taller, straighter. A sly smile plays at her lips, and I feel something besides desire snake through me. *Pride.* I'm still not sure how I found myself aligned with this woman, but I plan on keeping her, even if it kills me.

"Come." Thetis beckons Hecate away from our group, and as she follows, she glances back at me, subtly nodding to communicate I should learn all I can by spending time with Peleus while he's in his cups.

I wink and turn toward my old friend and ask, "Another round on this the eve of your marriage?"

HECATE

As we travel away from the festivities, Thetis tugs me along a worn path. While she, too, is unsteady on her feet, I assume it to be the darkness of the path, not her ale consumption.

"You know," she says quietly as she slowly makes our way, "as the daughter of Hades and Persephone, you've likely heard rumors about me."

I feign confusion. "Oh?"

She nods, a laugh escaping her lips. "Prior to becoming engaged to Peleus, I was courted by both Zeus and Poseidon. Can you believe it?"

I snort, not surprised. Thetis is incredibly beautiful, perhaps even more so than Helen. "What happened?" I ask nonchalantly.

"Oh, you know, there's an old prophecy about me which states my son will become greater than his father. Once Zeus and Poseidon heard the rumors, they vanished without a trace." She laughs bitterly.

I lower my eyes, shaking my head. Of course Zeus would never risk becoming less powerful than his son. The same prophecy was said about his own father and look what happened. Until the day he eventually returned to the mainland and his Titan father Cronus, Zeus had been banished, raised alone by nursemaids and surrounded by courtiers, like my family, on Crete.

"Peleus doesn't worry about the prophecy?" I ask.

She snorts. "Of course not. Peleus can't wait for me to have his sons and prays to the gods they become greater men than he. That was how I knew he truly loved me." She bites her lip, a blush visible even in the darkness of the trail.

We approach a small hut lit only by the light of the moon. In the night, I hear clanking and smell the scent of bonfire and molten metal, and I know this is Hephaestus's forge.

"I'll leave you here, but please return to the feast when you're done speaking with your uncle." Thetis gestures toward the door before turning on her heel and making her way back to the party.

Instead of knocking on the door, I take the path leading to the back of the cottage, knowing without a doubt that Hephaestus will be working. I don't want to stop him from his task, but my need to speak with him makes me impatient, and my steps lead me quickly to the open forge.

As I step into the light, into the oppressive heat, I smile at my uncle.

"Hecate," he says, his lips raising to match my own. "I knew you'd come."

. . . • ● • ● ● • . .

Hephaestus strides forward with a limp and engulfs me in a hug. His sweaty arms hold me tightly, raising my feet from the ground. I laugh as he sets me down and takes my hand in his, his rough calluses, hands of a worker, reminding me of Hades's.

"It's good to see you, old friend."

"It's been a long time," I amend. "Hades and Persephone's wedding, I believe?"

"Yes, many years. Although they've been kind to you?"

I smile, purposefully ignoring the question. My travails to reincarnate myself aren't something I'm comfortable speaking about just yet. Instead, I squint over his shoulder at his newest project. "What are you making?" Just peering into the forge makes a sheen of sweat break out along my hairline.

"I've decided to cast a knife for Peleus and Thetis's wedding present." He approaches the blade and holds it out for my inspection. I smile, knowing anything that Hephaestus makes for his foster mother will be treasured. After all, it was Thetis who raised him after he was thrown from Mount Olympus by his birth mother, Hera, for his deformed foot.

"Will you attend the wedding?" he asks, placing the knife back on his work bench.

"I believe we will." I lower my lashes, waiting for the question I know he'll ask next.

"*We?*"

I blush, nodding as I bite my lip to prevent my obnoxious smile from becoming too much. "I've married. The prince of Sparta, Castor."

Hephaestus's face falls flat, and I furrow my brow in confusion. "Do you know him?"

He swallows and blinks away the pain I briefly see flash in his eyes. "I have heard things of the Dioscuri, particularly Pollux. He's a real rogue, that one." His gaze doesn't meet mine, and I tamp down the unease I feel in my gut. He knows something more, so what isn't he telling me?

"Pol isn't so bad. He's quite charming, once you get to know him."

Rubbing his chin, he asks, "So how can I help you, Hecate?"

I move toward the fire, my eyes drawn to the dancing flames. Holding my hands out against the chill in the night air, I rub them together. I raise my gaze to Hephaestus and, by simply thinking of fire, am able to summon flames to my own fingertips. Flicking my digits back and forth and playing with the flames, I finally say, "I need to know how to hurt Zeus, *really* hurt him."

Hephaestus doesn't seem surprised by my request, so I go on, feeling emboldened by the flames dancing on my fingers.

"And any other helpful details you may want to add about my husband might be beneficial, too, my old friend."

• • • • • • • • • •

"Dance with me, wife?" Castor extends his hand, and rising from my seat at the wedding banquet, I take it. A small group of musicians plays tunes in the corner, and several other couples have taken to the floor, including the bride and groom. My dress, borrowed from Thetis, trails behind me, swishing delicately on the ground. "You look amazing. That necklace is especially lovely." His eyes darken as his fingers trail along the golden chain at my neck.

I glance down, feeling completely naked in the concoction that Thetis thrust upon me. The black fabric, silky smooth to the touch and light as air, skims my curves. The deep V cuts down to my sternum, leaving my cleavage exposed. A belt, matching the gold necklace, cinches at the waist, where my dagger is hooked. "It's definitely a new look," I say, meeting his eyes.

He twirls me around the dance floor, the mermaid train of my dress fanning out around me, his hand slipping lower and lower on my back until he's pulled me tightly against him. I can feel his arousal pressing against my stomach, but it's his other hand tracing circles on my exposed flesh that gets me hot.

"Did you learn everything you needed to know, talking to Hephaestus?" he whispers in my ear. I hum noncommittally, closing my eyes against his chest.

"Good," he says, taking my answer for a yes. "We need to be on our way soon."

My eyes snap open. "Why's that?"

I notice the knot in his throat bob as he swallows. "No reason, I just know this journey is important for you. We shouldn't waste time when we—I mean you—have a mission."

"We're not wasting time," I contradict. "We're at a wedding, enjoying ourselves?" I ask, raising my eyebrows.

He clears his throat. "Of course. Of course we're enjoying ourselves." He pulls me into his chest, his arms tightening as he rests his chin on my head. We sway to the music, the other guests around us following suit. Looking around as I'm pressed into his muscular frame, I watch a golden orb fly through the air.

"What's that?" I squeak against Castor's chest. Pulling apart, we track the orb as it falls to the ground. Eris, the goddess of discord, strides onto the dance floor.

Thetis, closest to the orb and appearing a bit tipsy with drink and celebration, picks it up and examines it. "An apple." She chuckles. "Why, Eris, it's beautiful!"

Instead, Eris meets Thetis's merriment with hatred dancing in her eyes and a scowl on her face. Snatching the golden apple from Thetis, she holds it aloft. "Behold, this golden apple is to be awarded to only the fairest!"

Clapping her hands together in excitement, Thetis looks around at the guests. "Oh, a game!" The uncertainty in her guests' eyes does not match her jovial tone.

The crowd's eyes float between Thetis, Helen, and several other guests. I keep my gaze trained on Helen, who has paled considerably, her hands shaking as she holds her mug of ale.

"I think it's time to go, husband," I say as I tug him toward Pollux, who's also making his way toward Helen.

"Agreed, let's get out of here before more Olympians show up. Where Eris goes, Hera shan't be far behind. We don't want to draw more unwanted attention to ourselves."

Pollux pulls Helen into his embrace, and we follow them out of the banquet, everyone's attention turned back toward Eris, who's announcing a judgment to be held in a few days' time.

"Please, get me out of here," Helen hisses, her body now shaking all over. "I have a horrible feeling." I pull her toward me, and we make our way to the stables as quickly as possible.

CASTOR

There are no inns nearby, and seeing as we'd planned on staying with Thetis and Peleus, we ride through the night, all of us bleary-eyed and exhausted.

"We've got to stop somewhere and get some sleep and food in our bellies," Pollux tells me while we're giving our horses a break just as dawn is breaking.

Pressing my lips together, I look toward Helen, lying back in the grass and fighting to stay awake. "These trails aren't safe, and we don't know the area well enough to camp."

Pollux grunts in agreement. "We do know someone else in the area, though, brother."

I crinkle my forehead, trying to recall who we know in Thessaly, and then it dawns on me. "Chiron? Our old tutor? That's right . . ." I'd completely forgotten my and Pollux's days as youths under the tutelage of the wise centaur.

"I'm sure he'd welcome us for an evening." Pollux trots toward Hecate and Helen, telling them of our plans.

I watch his retreating back as I stand next to my mount. It's been years since we saw Chiron, half brother to Zeus. As the others join me, I voice my concerns. "I think it's best that we keep our journey a secret from Chiron." I meet Hecate's eyes, and she nods in understanding. "Seeing as we are closing in on Mount Olympus, we need to lie low and keep our purpose hidden, even from those we trust." Helen blinks while Pollux furrows his brow. "We wouldn't want word to get out that we're intending to visit Zeus bearing a witch in tow," I clarify for their sakes.

Hecate exhales, giving me a stern gaze. I'd almost fucked up and blurted out the truth of our visit. Gulping down my exhaustion, I mentally chastise myself to stay focused and watch what I say. Even around my wife.

· · · · ● · ● · · · ·

"Welcome, my friends!" Chiron greets us as though we are family. He wraps both me and Pollux into a hug, and when we introduce Helen and Hecate, he pulls them both in as well. I can tell that Hecate is already taken with the hybrid beast, but Helen is more wary. Her life, unlike Hecate's, has been much more sheltered. I swallow guiltily as I think on how well she's handled this journey, a sense of pride swelling through me as I watch my little sister come into her own in the last week's trials.

"Helen." I beckon her toward me as Chiron's staff leads us to our rooms. She holds back, meeting my gaze.

"Yes, brother?"

I smile, laying my palm on her shoulder and squeezing affectionately. "I'm proud of you, you know? The changes I've seen since we began our journey have really brought out your strength."

Her eyes lower as a blush creeps up her neck. "Thank you," she murmurs, falling into step with me. "That means a lot."

While the others continue on, I saunter toward the hearth, where a crackling fire burns brightly. As we've traveled north into Thessaly, the weather has cooled. Neither Helen nor I are used to the chilly nights; Spartan evenings tend to be balmy, the air smelling of the salty ocean's breath. We both thrust our hands forward, savoring the fire's warmth.

"Do you miss home?" I inquire, rubbing my palms together.

Her lips thin, then pull into a frown. I watch as she inhales, as though readying to speak, but her mouth parts and then immediately clamps closed again.

"Helen, what is it? What's wrong?"

This time, there's no hesitation. "I look at what Mel—I mean Hecate—has done. She's so strong, so sure . . ." She trails off quietly. "I know I . . . killed"—she whispers the word—"Pirithous, but I wish Father had trained me to lead, had given me a purpose outside of being a prize to be married off for the good of Sparta."

My chest feels as though it's been stabbed as I watch my little sister struggle to admit that she wants more from her life. Truthfully, I can't believe I've not noticed it before our trip, before she mentioned it in the tavern, and I mentally kick myself for being so blind to her plight.

She continues on, "I thought being looked upon was enough. Now that I've been on this wild adventure"—she smiles wryly at me—"I know that going back to life as it once was will never be enough for me."

I reach my warmed hand out and pull her in for a side-hug. "When all this is over, perhaps you could ask Father to train with Pollux or take on more duties as an ambassador? You are more than just a beautiful face, Helen. You can do more if you fight for yourself."

She looks up at me and smiles. "You're right, brother. I think I need to start fighting for what I want, just like Hecate's done." My body stiffens at the mention of my wife. She's been acting strangely since Peleus's wedding and her meeting with Hephaestus.

My mind is pulled back to Helen as she says, "Now, if you'll excuse me, I'm exhausted and ready to see the bed I was promised."

I release her and turn back toward the fire, not ready to retreat to my shared lodging yet. The closer we get to Mount Olympus, the closer I am to revealing my deception and losing something I've come to value: Hecate. I stand for a few more moments, mustering up the courage to face my wife. Just as I'm about to leave, I notice a shift in the flames as the smoke begins to take shape.

"Fuck," I mutter under my breath, my body sagging as my shoulders drop. I already know what's to come. I stand back as the god takes shape before me.

Smirking at my obvious discomfort, he steps forward, invading my personal space. His gaze roams up and down my body. "Looking healthy. Immortality seems to agree with you, no?" His laughter booms, seeming to rattle the entire abode.

"Keep your voice down," I admonish, catching myself too late.

"How dare you chastise a god, you—" His attention pulls away from me, his eyes flicking toward the door. "Aha." He licks his lips, a chuckle bubbling from his mouth. "Look who we have here."

My stomach plummets and I slowly turn, hoping that I'll find Chiron behind me. But when I raise my eyes, I see the one person I know will be crushed by this revelation.

Helen.

CASTOR

Helen refuses to meet my eyes. Instead, her gaze is trained fully on the god standing in front of the fire. Zeus.

"Come forward, daughter. Let me take a look at your beauty."

She steps, one foot in front of the other, as if in a trance, but the skin around her mouth is tight, her eyes full of scorn. I curse the predicament I've put her in and clench my fists, feeling helpless to stop this scene from unfolding.

"The rumors are true, I see." Zeus closes the remaining distance and takes Helen's chin in his hand, tipping it up to assess her. "I've created the most beautiful woman in the world." He turns to me, a devilish look on his face, and my stomach falls. What is his game? I need to outmaneuver him before I lose Helen too.

"Leave her be. It's me you've bargained with." I push out my chest, hoping to appear braver than I feel.

Zeus drops Helen's chin and stalks toward me. I'm forced to raise my gaze, his height having extended several inches over me. "That's twice you've made demands of me, Castor. You've yet to learn your place, but I am sure it will happen soon." A wicked smile plays along his mouth, his eyes turning red enough to match the fire in the hearth.

I gulp down the fear and bare my teeth. "My seven days aren't up yet, so why are you even here?"

Shrugging, he crosses his arms over his barrel chest. "I like to keep track of my family."

"Funny, you've never spared a visit before," Pollux shouts from the door. The three of us turn toward the interruption, my eyes widening.

"And here's my strapping son, grown into his manhood and ready to strike down anyone who stands in his way!" Zeus roars, gesturing toward Pollux. I run my hands through my hair, terrified that this god will destroy my siblings over my stupidity.

Pollux strides forward, his hand on the hilt of his blade, ready to draw and flay Zeus from naval to neck. "Get the fuck out of here or—"

"Or what?" Zeus roars. He laughs, the noise settling deep in my bones, rattling me to the core. "You're as arrogant as your mortal brother, my son. Except you should know better, being part god, that you are no match for me. Your swords, your strength, cannot stop me from destroying you or your sister."

Pollux lowers his hand and moves cautiously toward Helen. He reaches her, pulling her small body behind his own. Protective, as a brother should be. I curse myself for getting my family involved in this.

Zeus turns his gaze toward me. "As entertaining as this family reunion has been, you've got two days left, Prince Castor. Get what's mine to Mount Olympus or you'll rot in Tartarus, the deepest abyss of the Underworld. You'd fit in well with the Titans as your prison mates." With that last warning, he steps back into the hearth's flames, crumbling in a sprinkling of ashes.

I immediately rush toward my siblings. "I'm so sorry." I exhale, needing to pull Helen close and soothe the terror I see flashing in her eyes.

"What the fuck have you done?" Pollux replies, his sword unsheathed and pointed straight at my throat.

• • • • • • • • • •

I hold up my hands, tightness forming in my throat. "Pol, you don't under-stand."

His eyes narrow, his lip curling. "What wouldn't I understand? You've sold your soul to Zeus in exchange for your *wife*. Do you realize what you've done?" The anger does little to hide the terror in his eyes.

Helen's body goes rigid at Pollux's admonishment. Suddenly, she turns to him, her brows lowering over her darkened eyes. "He did what he had to do, Pollux."

My eyes widen in disbelief. Did she just stand up for me?

"Put the sword down," she commands Pollux, who lowers the blade slowly. Helen moves toward the fire, thrusting her hands toward the flames. She must feel the same chill I do; my body is shaking, whether from the cold or fear, I can't say.

"How can you justify his actions? Zeus is going to kill him. He's likely to kill us all!"

She whips around to face him, finger stabbing the air with a darkness and determination I've not seen from my little sister. "We are Spartans, Pollux. We do what we have to do. We stick together as a family. Now," she says, assessing me from her place near the fire, "explain yourself."

I lower my eyes, the guilt weighing on me heavily, and shake my head. "I don't know why I thought this was a good idea, but what's done is done. The deal is Melinoe . . . er, Hecate, in exchange for immortality." I raise my eyes to theirs. I'd rather they think me a liar than know the truth of what I've really bargained.

"Do you love her?" Pollux asks me, his expression pained.

Yes.

"Of course not." The lie tastes sour on my tongue.

Pollux snorts in disgust and stalks toward me, his fist raised. He cuffs me in the ear, like our father used to when we'd been out of line or failed at our training paces. "You're an embarrassment to our family; I can't believe you would renege on the marriage treaty with Hades and Persephone for something as stupid as *immortality*."

The rage builds within me, and finally, I feel it burst forth. "Do you know what it's been like living in your shadow all my life? Knowing that, no matter how great a warrior I am, how fantastic my fighting skills, I'd never measure up to the immortal golden son?" I pause for a moment, watching as Pollux's features turn cold.

"Quit feeling sorry for yourself," he sneers.

"That's enough—the both of you!" Helen hisses. She strides away from the fire, her long blond locks absorbing the reflection of the flame. "We haven't the time to argue right now. We need to decide how to proceed before it's too late. Before Castor's time is up. How do we continue deceiving Hecate and get her to Mount Olympus?"

"Continue deceiving her?' Pollux jerks his head back as though he's been slapped. "You must be out of your mind, sister. We must tell her in order to save ourselves from certain doom!"

"No!" We both cry in unison. Eyeing each other, I proceed. "I've made it this far without her knowing. We've only got a little longer until we reach the mountain. Then, she's Zeus's problem." If I can let her go.

Pollux's stare is incredulous as he starts to shuffle backward toward the door. "I can't . . . I can't be a part of this treachery against our kingdom, against our father's wishes, against the treaty, or against that innocent Titan." He shakes his head. "I won't allow it."

"What won't you allow, Pollux?" Hecate asks innocently from the doorway.

We all freeze, wondering just how much she's heard.

HECATE

"Did I miss an important family meeting?" I inquire, cocking my head slightly as my lips tilt up at the corners. Strutting around the group, I make eye contact with each traitor. Beautiful, perfect Helen, her body rigid and shaking. I walk toward the next one. Loyal, rakish Pollux, the only one to make eye contact with me, thins his lips. Finally, my gaze lands on my husband. Castor . . . oh, Castor. I proceed slowly to him and run my finger from his navel to his throat before pressing my palm to his muscular chest.

Pouting and keeping my eyes widely innocent, I ask, "What's going on, *husband*?"

I sense him tensing against my palm, his heart beating wildly, and my eyes narrow. Has he been working against me this entire time, meeting with Zeus and then fucking me to keep me pliant, malleable? Did he really think I was that naive, that I wouldn't find out? Well . . . he's not the first to underestimate me.

Pollux steps forward, answering for Castor. "We were discussing returning to Sparta, Hecate." The deception slides effortlessly from his lips, and I smirk, admiring his tenacity. He's just protecting his twin, his best friend. It's admirable really, but does he know I can smell the lie the second it slips from his mouth?

Keeping my gaze trained on my husband, I whisper seductively, "Is this true, Castor? Do you think we should return to Sparta?" My fingers walk provocatively along his collarbone. The fingers he's seen destroy a man with a simple snap, a lazy flick of my wrist.

I watch his throat bob as he swallows. Biting my cheek, I wait for his response. As he answers, his voice quakes. "No, we should proceed, wife." He licks his lips, and as much as I want to pull his mouth to mine, run my tongue along his jaw and thrust myself into his warm embrace, I also want to destroy him.

"It's settled then." The blood rushes into my ears, but I force a smile that I'm sure looks horrifying. My face spreads unnaturally, my vision narrowing, and as the tingling returns to my fingers, I clench and release my fists, knowing that I have to play the part to get to Mount Olympus. Only then can I release the rage, the fire that's burning me from the inside.

But until then, I must contain myself. Conserve my strength. And use my so-called family as pawns.

· · ● · ● · ● · · ·

I don't sleep. Instead, I pace, back and forth across the floor. Hearing the doorknob turn, I still, watching and waiting. I've locked the door to Castor, not trusting myself to be near him without lighting his ass on fire and scorching this entire castle to the ground.

"Hecate, let me in," he finally hisses through the wooden door, jerking angrily on the handle.

I hesitate and, not feeling any castle-destroying tingling or uncontrollable outrage, move to unlock the door. Standing before him in only my leather bustier and undergarments, I enjoy the shock on his face as he takes in my outfit, or lack thereof.

Eyeing me, he walks to the bed and begins to strip down, discarding his weapons and boots first. I follow him, stalking my prey, and shove him backward onto the mattress. If I'm going to keep him believing that I'm deluded and ignorant of his plans, I need to ensure he's *occupied*. At all times.

"Here, let me help you, darling." I bat my eyes and lift his foot into my waiting hands. I warm my palms using my magic, and he lets out a subtle groan of pleasure as I begin massaging, pressing into the tender flesh. I continue my ministrations, moving from the ankle down to the toes before switching to the other foot. I finally make my move. "I never did thank you, husband, for saving me from Poseidon." Watching him through lowered lashes, I assess him as he keeps his eyes closed, but notice that his breath hitches slightly.

"Of course. I wouldn't let anything bad happen to you. I swore I'd protect you, and I intend to keep my word," he replies.

Liar.

I let out a small sigh before continuing. "You never did share with me how you found me. How you found that tiny little hut, secreted away in that nondescript fishing village . . ."

He's quiet for a moment. Thinking of a lie. "I suppose it was luck. Pollux has always been a steadfast scout. We must have spoken with the right people." He shrugs.

Fucking liar.

I try to keep the sarcasm out of my voice. "How lucky for you. And for me," I add a slight girlish giggle, even though I feel like I could vomit.

Dropping his foot from my hands, I ignore how he furrows his brow at my abruptness. "I'm exhausted. I think it's time we get some sleep. Tomorrow will be upon us before we know it."

If he catches my innuendo, he doesn't say anything. Luckily for me, he also keeps silent as I slide under the blankets and scoot to the edge of the bed, my back turned to him, and squeeze my eyes closed.

Before I drift off, I wonder if I'll ever trust anyone again.

• • • ● • ● • ● • • •

I crest the hill and see the zenith. Mount Olympus. My heart soaring, I pick up my pace and rush to the gates, walking through with nary a question. I smile for the first time in days, at least since I rid myself of that horrible Demeter. Hoping I don't encounter her on my visit, I continue walking briskly.

"Pardon me." I smile politely at a soldier who appears ready for battle. "I'm looking for Zeus. Can you show me where he might be?"

Looking me up and down, the soldier scoffs and juts his chin toward the stable. As I make my way toward the elaborate structure, I shout my thanks, but the soldier simply shakes his head.

I approach the beautiful building, gaping in awe at the wondrous woodwork. Made of solid oak, the beams are sanded to a sheen, with whirls and curlicues decorating the frames. Each stallion has a separate latched stall, a golden nameplate adorning the entrance. I walk along the aisle, my fingers dancing as I peer into each cell, note the fresh straw scattered across the floor, searching for my old friend.

"No . . . Stop it!"

My heart plummets and I freeze. The sounds of a struggle fill the entire barn, but I'd been so eager to find my friend that I hadn't heard. I curl my lip, backing away, scared to be caught. I trip over a water bucket and, cursing to myself, hope I haven't been caught.

"No, I said no!"

I breathe a sigh of relief that I haven't been heard. As I continue tiptoeing out of the barn, I pass a cell, but its inhabitant is not a horse.

It's Zeus. And he's thrusting into a tiny woman, a goddess? Leather cords wrap around her slight wrists, holding her to the hooks at the back of the stall's wall. We catch eyes, hers widening as she gasps. This alerts Zeus, who, glancing behind him, meets my horrified gaze and . . . smiles? He smiles at me. My heart crumbles, my eyes sting as tears begin to well, and I stand there, utterly horrified with my mouth agape, shaking my head as I keep my gaze averted.

"Hecate, it's not what it looks like." He pulls out of the woman, who curls into herself as best she can and begins to sob. Zeus, ignoring his unwilling partner, covers himself with his discarded clothing.

I continue backing away, my body trembling as my fingers begin to tingle. "Stay away from me," I growl. "Don't come any closer!"

"Let me explain." His suave smile stretches his face, his eyes sparkling maliciously under raised brows.

"I said, stay away from me, Zeus." My back hits the door to a stall, and I'm trapped. Sacks of oats block me on either side. Still stalking toward me, Zeus eyes me, licking his lips.

"Come join us, Hecate. My paramour doesn't mind sharing." A horse's tail swishes from a stall behind me.

As dust and chaff float in the sunlit air, I close and open my fists, preparing myself. My grandmother's training has kicked in, and lifting my chin, I make sure to use an even tone. "It looks like your paramour was telling you to stop, Zeus."

Blinking, he snorts, his eyes squinting at me. "You're mistaken, friend. Selene loves to share, don't you, Selene?" he calls back to the woman. He looks at me, those eyes dead and terrifyingly set on taking me, forcing me to join him. He reaches his hand up to my face and asks, "Are you scared of me, Hecate?"

"N-no, I'm not scared of you." My voice cracks as I cringe, trying to make myself smaller against the planks of the stall door. The wood digs into my back. My hair sticks to the splintered pieces. Flies whine in my ear, and I shake my head. Whether to rid myself of the flies or to prove I'm not scared, I'm not sure.

He leans toward me, his face inching closer, the creak of the floorboards the only sound in the silent stable.

This isn't what I want. "Stop it," I whisper, my eyes stinging again as a tear leaks down my cheek, sweat trickling down my back.

Taking my hand, he entwines our fingers, pulling me toward the stall where the sobbing woman is still held fast by the leather straps, trapped against her will.

I blink. No, not still tied up anymore. She stands in my line of vision, behind Zeus, a shovel held aloft. Shrieking, she brings it down on his skull with a loud thunk, and he collapses at my feet. My jaw drops as my eyes widen.

"Let's go." Selene grabs my hand, pulling me away from Zeus's prostrated form.

"Wait." I pull back, needing a moment to think, to formulate a plan. I must always think one step ahead, as my grandmother taught. "He'll remember we were here—what happened—and he'll come looking for you. For us."

She chews her lip between her teeth. Her eyes well, but before she can pull her hands up to cover her face, I have an idea.

"Ah, I think I can fix this." I stand over his body and recite a memory wipe spell. "Mou díneis ti mními sou." It's simple enough, but it should do the trick.

"Will that work? What did you do?"

I nod, grabbing her hand again, and as we run through the stable, looking for any horse, I explain the incantation's power. At the very last stall, I peek inside to find a beautiful snow-white mount. My mouth drops open at his height, and as I glance to the nameplate on the plank, I read it aloud. "Pegasus." He's perfect.

"Let's go!" I pull Selene into the stall and help her up. We've no time to get the tack, so we will have to ride bareback. She uses what's left of her strength to pull me onto the horse, and as we gallop away, I finally ask the question that will change my life, allowing me entrance to the Underworld. "Selene, where are you from?"

CASTOR

I'm not sure how I get any sleep, what with my brain completely certain that my wife is going to cut off my cock, or worse, use her magic to shrink it to the size of my pinkie finger, but the next morning, I wake to find Hecate's side of the bed deserted. Sitting up, I warily glance around before patting myself down, checking all the appendages.

I sigh with relief as I realize nothing is missing. It's still just as big as before too.

I tilt my head and listen. Laughter is floating from an adjoining room. I climb carefully out of the bed and dress quickly, sauntering out of the room to find a large group sitting around the table, including Helen.

"Come, sit with us, Castor," Chiron beckons from the head of the table. While the centaur cannot fit into a traditional chair, he has fashioned a table to fit around his half-beast body.

I nod to Helen as I take a seat beside her, and she gestures around the table. "Brother, let me introduce you to Aeneas, Diomedes, and Odysseus." I smile a greeting at each young man and, as I drink lustily from my cup, catch Chiron staring at me intently.

Helen, ever the effervescent flirt, continues to enjoy the attention of the three admirers while I dig in to my morning meal. As I gulp down my first helping, I notice that both Pollux and Hecate are absent. I lean forward, my eyes flicking around the table, but it's Chiron who causes my pulse to increase.

"Castor, a moment in my study." It's not a question. It's a command. Helen stills next to me, her throat bobbing as she swallows heavily. I excuse myself from the company and follow Chiron into the large room. The study is filled with floor-to-ceiling windows that remain uncovered and open to the mountainous air, and I'm reminded that, as children under Chiron's tutelage, we were never allowed to enter this private sanctuary. Therefore, I gaze around in astonishment at the shelves of scrolls and rotuli.

Chiron is silent while I turn, taking in the scope of my tutor's academic legacy. He nurtured the royal youths of various city-states, teaching us medicine, herbology, archery, hunting, physical fitness, and courtly etiquette. Pollux and I weren't the only royal charges sent to study with Chiron. Jason, our friend the Argonaut, was a fellow pupil. I approach a shelf filled with ancient vases and, as I reach out a shaky hand, am instantly pulled back to the present by Chiron brusquely clearing his throat.

"Castor, even though I'm no longer your tutor, you will always be my pupil."

Making a noncommittal noise, I rub my stubble-covered chin and keep my eyes trained on the exit.

He continues, "The same applies to your brother, Pollux."

At the mention of his name, my mouth goes dry.

"I think you should be aware that your brother and wife are no longer with us."

My mind goes blank, as if my brain has stopped working. I see spots and, afraid that I will pass out, make my way to the nearest chair and fall into it. I cover my face with my hands, wondering how this has gone so incredibly wrong. How have I managed to fail at protecting Hecate and also alienate my twin at the same time?

Years ago, as students under the instruction of Chiron, Pollux and I were quite the deviant pair, but nevertheless the best of friends. We pulled pranks, switched identities, and even went so far as to sneak off in the middle of the night. On one of our evening adventures, Pollux suggested we make our way toward Mount Olympus. He wanted to see where his father, his *real* father, lived. Eyeing him warily, I agreed, only because I wasn't going to allow my twin, my best friend, to get into trouble without me there too.

After lights out, we ducked out of our dorm window and sneaked to the barn. As the best horseman in our legion, I was able to saddle a mount, using only my hands and instincts to guide me in the pitch darkness of the stable. As we traveled to Olympus, trying not to show our fear as various noises haunted our imaginations, we shared our hopes and dreams for the future. As the eldest, I hoped to be an accomplished Spartan king who rode into battle with his troops. Pollux wanted to go on sailing adventures and see the world. Hours later, as we neared the gates of Olympus, Pollux, for whatever reason, chickened out.

"Turn around, this is a stupid idea," he said, sitting behind me in the saddle. Concerned, I hopped down near a tree and tied up our mount.

"Why must we turn around, brother? We're on an adventure!" I was eager to continue onward in our devious expedition, Pollux's disgruntled attitude be damned.

Instead, my twin, too, dismounted and sulked by the tree, his arms crossed over his chest, refusing to move. "I want to go back," he grumbled.

"And I want to go onward. Quit being such a baby," I admonished. As the moon peeked through the clouds, I saw tears streaming down his face, his chin quivering as he swiped under his nose. "Ugh," I snarled. "You *are* a baby, crying so!" I pointed, laughing in his face, until he ran off, disappearing into the dark depths of the forest.

I rolled my eyes as I nuzzled the horse's snout. "He'll return," I grumbled to the horse aloud. I lay down on the soft moss near the tree's trunk and curled into myself, waiting for my brother's return.

When I blinked at the shining sun the next morning, having fallen asleep, my brother was still nowhere to be found. Alarmed, I called out to him, but he didn't answer. I mounted the horse and decided to go searching, continuing to call his name. It wasn't until midday, when the sun was at its peak, that I found Pollux, puffy-eyed and dirtied, shivering on the banks of a stream.

"Why'd you run off like that?" I screamed at him, running to his side and roughly shoving him. I'd been worried, terrified, but couldn't utter those embarrassing thoughts to my immortal twin. He was the perfect one. The brave one. The golden child.

"Leave me alone, Castor." His voice was dull, emotionless. He didn't even bother shoving me back. Something was wrong, so instead of calling him on his babyish behavior, I did the grown-up thing. I sat down and listened.

That day, Pollux confessed that he was too afraid to meet his father, the magnificent and powerful Zeus. When I questioned him, he explained that, not once had his real father ever been to Sparta to visit him. Not once had his real father cared enough to know him, know the man he was becoming. As he sobbed, I tried to be a good brother. I reminded him that we had our father, King Tyndareus, raising us, watching over us, and loving us. But then, as Pollux squinted at me and said, "You don't get it, Castor. It's not the same," I was confused. I hadn't understood. To me, it was the same.

Now, looking back at that moment, I understand that Pollux was right. It wasn't the same. No matter how much our father doted on us, Pollux had needed reassurance that he was enough from Zeus, his real father. And, as the mortal twin who would never measure up, I needed to feel worthy too.

Snapping out of my reverie, I turn to Chiron. The only way I'm ever going to feel worthy is if I fix this. "Where are they?"

He clomps around to a pitcher and pours me a cup of watered ale. Handing it to me, he replies, "They left in the middle of the night. With my help."

My head jerks back as though I've been slapped. My hands clench around the chair's armrests. "You know not what you've done, Chiron," I hiss between my teeth.

"On the contrary, Castor, I know exactly what I've done. Hecate told me everything. Why would you bargain with my brother Zeus?"

My skin tingles, a sudden coldness hitting me in the gut.

She knows.

HECATE

I bend forward to place my hand on the dry, cracked earth. Inhaling deeply, I close my eyes, waiting for the earth to share its memories with me.

"*Oi amarties sou tha apokalyfthoún,*" I begin, whispering the recalling incantation under my breath.

"What are you doing?"

Taking another deep breath, I crack my eyes open slightly and then squeeze them shut again. Concentrate. "*Oi amarties s—*"

"Hecate! What are you doing?" Pollux is now standing behind me, his hand on my shoulder, shaking me out of my reverie.

Turning to him, I snap, "I'm trying to cast a recalling spell. It will allow me to see the last moments witnessed by the Titans here, on the Plain of Thessaly, where the Great War took place." I press my hands back into the hardened soil and close my eyes again.

"Wait." Pollux pauses, his eyes widening in disbelief. "The Great War took place here?" His voice is filled with awe as I blink my eyes open and watch him stare into the vast expanse of the empty field.

"Yes," I mutter irritably. "Now if you'll be quiet—"

"Were you there?"

I let out an annoyed groan and plop to my butt, crossing my legs. "Sit," I command.

He lowers himself to the ground, and after he crosses his legs, I find myself smirking at him.

Explaining to him like a child, I speak slowly. "The Great War was also called the Titanomachy, the battle between the Titans and the gods of Mount Olympus, led by Zeus." He rolls his eyes, and I continue, "Both my paternal and maternal grandparents fought, and they were all sent to Tartarus when the Olympians won."

Pollux swallows, then looks hesitantly at me.

"What's your question?" I ask, sighing heavily at his childishness.

"Why did Zeus start the war?"

I hesitate, knowing the answer but not wanting to say the words out loud, to give them power. But, if Pollux is going to accompany me to Mount Olympus and help me, as he said he would, he needs to know the truth. The truth that I kept from Castor to protect him. What a fool I was, believing that my husband needed protecting when he was the one working with Zeus to lure me to Mount Olympus. I scoff aloud.

"Zeus started the war because he wanted to destroy everything, and everyone, I ever loved."

· · · ● · ● ● · · ·

Seated across from one another in a tavern in the middle of Larissa, Pollux and I hungrily feast on a delicious lamb stew. I'm exhausted from my recalling incantation and know that I need to conserve my energy for the last part of our journey, so Pollux agreed to stop for the evening to sleep in a real bed rather than on the ground. We were lucky to find an inn with a room to spare, and Pollux's coins mixed with a little bit of my magic has allowed us to secure overnight stabling for our horses and the hearty stew and ale.

"Tell me what you saw on the Plain." Pollux's eyes beseech me.

I laugh. "You mean after you stopped with your incessant questions and finally let me cast my spell?" I find myself enjoying the ease with which Pollux and I are able to converse. We are more alike than Helen and I, and it shows in how we interact.

He drums his feet against the floor, waiting for me to continue.

"Fine," I concede. I lean in and lower my voice. "I saw the Hecatoncheires and the Cyclops freed from the depths of Tartarus. Using both the earth and weather as weapons, they hurled lightning and boulders as they fought on the side of the Olympians."

Pollux blinks.

"That means Zeus knows how to free someone from Tartarus. He can free my grandparents," I explain.

"Ooh, I get it."

I roll my eyes at him again. I've been doing that a lot since we set out together, but it's nice to have someone on my side. For once.

"Can I ask you one more question?" he asks, taking a swig of his ale.

I nod.

"I know you're, like, this great Titan, heir to the entire Underworld, and the goddess of magic, but why did you decide to reincarnate yourself instead of fight Zeus all those years ago?"

I open my mouth to contradict him, but then close it. What am I supposed to say? I was terrified that the king of gods was going to end me like he'd done to so many of my loved ones? That he would somehow use me for my powers—making himself all but invincible? That, despite my own power, I was, and still am, terrified of him?

Instead, I gulp down my fear and terror and say what I think Pollux wants to hear. "It was all part of my plan to outwit the motherfucker and take away the only thing he ever wanted but couldn't have. Me."

. . . ● . ● . ● . . .

Pollux heads up to our shared room while I wander to the stables, needing time alone with my thoughts. The moon's bright face shines on the path, and a chill has seeped into my skin. The night air feels refreshing, like home. I learned from my time training to collect offerings to the dead, I do my best work, my best thinking, in the darkness. Alone.

I knew that Castor had been working against me, had an agreement with Zeus, ever since my conversation with Hephaestus. An outcast himself, Hephaestus still maintained a home on Mount Olympus. As he created beautiful weapons and accessories for the gods and goddesses, he was able to quietly gather information, secreting it away for a time when it could be used as its own weapon.

"Your husband, as you call him, has been working with Zeus behind your back, my dear," he shared as I stood in his forge.

Suddenly, the downcast eyes, the fidgeting hands, the bitten lips and sidelong looks, all made sense. My heart plummeted. I stepped farther into the forge, picking up Hephaestus's creations and immediately discarding them, not seeing anything as the truth sank in. My thoughts were blank, my brain stopped working.

"Tell me everything," I demanded. "I want to hear it all." Even as the blood rushed to my ears, I heard everything. How Castor agreed to bring me to Mount Olympus in exchange for immortality. How I was a means to an end. How our marriage meant *nothing* to him.

Wiping my tears, I check that Pegasus is fed and watered and then make my way to the room, ready to turn in for the night.

Approaching the door, I hear talking within. I press my ear to the wood, but when that doesn't allow me to hear perfectly, I run through my list of spells, settling on a simple collective consciousness spell.

"*Oi aiónes mas eínai deménoi metaxý tous. Kai tha se akoúso,*" I mutter as a translucent sphere appears just outside the door. I step into the bubble, allowing me to hear the conversation occurring inside our room.

The words immediately amplify around me, bouncing off the bubble's stretchy walls. "And what do you want in exchange for your loyalty, son?"

I gasp, realizing that the voice belongs to Zeus. Clenching my fists, I make ready to burst through the door and scorch his ass to ashes when Pollux responds.

"I told you, I want nothing from you. I refuse to participate in your sick games, Father. You may have been able to trick Castor into selling his soul for immortality, but as your son, I'm already immortal."

When I hear Pollux's refusal, my heart swells. At least someone cares enough to go to battle for me.

Zeus laughs, a noise that freezes me to my core, my spine stiffening. "This is the last time I'll ask, boy. Either you work with me and bring Hecate to me, or you work against me and I'll destroy you."

It's Pollux's turn to laugh, which infuriates Zeus. I hear choking from within the room; he's hurting my friend. I'm moving to turn the handle of the door, to stop whatever's happening to Pollux, but Zeus's next words make me stop.

"If you refuse to help me, I think I'll just have to make my way back to Sparta and help myself to your mother . . . again." My heart stops beating, but my blood boils with the flames of a thousand fires.

Without thinking, I pop the bubble and shove open the door, coming face-to-face with my enemy, the one person whose power is stronger than mine. Zeus.

His eyes are colorless, only a small black dot within each orb shows me he's focused intently on my entrance into the room. His snow-white hair, once cut short as a youth, now hangs in long tendrils down to his muscular chest.

"Let Pollux leave, and I'll willingly come with you to Mount Olympus." I swallow in anguish. This isn't how it was supposed to happen, but I couldn't let another innocent victim be tortured, namely Leda, Pollux's mother, because of my obstinacy.

Pollux, looking at me with his fists clenched, silently shakes his head, his eyes pleading. I lower my own, knowing that I'm giving him something I never got, the ability to protect his family from Zeus. I bite my lip and finally meet his gaze, his eyes glistening with unshed tears as he comprehends what I'm doing, and he nods in acceptance.

"Fine," he says, turning to Pollux. "Leave, my boy. Run home to your mother before I change my mind." Zeus's eyes never leave me, and I do my best to avoid his lecherous stare. That he would threaten violence, rape no less, is exactly what I need from him. It ignites my fury, and I feel my magic thrumming under my skin, ready to be set free.

But I wait.

As Pollux passes me, I reach out and touch his hand, one last touch from my beloved brother-in-law, my friend. I offer him a wan smile and a nod and, once he's gone, turn my eyes to Zeus.

"I've waited a long time for this, Hecate."

I bark out a laugh, knowing the way to irritate Zeus is to laugh at him, laugh at his power. He always did think too much of himself, and it's time he knew my feelings have never changed. "You've waited a long time for this? Funny, I haven't waited for you at all."

Zeus snorts and my stomach roils. "That's right, you've been spending all your time with that poor mortal husband of yours. What's his name again?"

I narrow my eyes, knowing he is fully aware of Castor's name. But, instead of feeding his ego, I respond calmly, "His name is Castor, and I screamed it every night he made me come, Oh Mighty One." A laugh bubbles unbidden from inside me, echoing off the bare walls.

Zeus's lips pull back, and he bares his teeth. Heat emanates from his body. He points to the fire, through which a smoky mist has engulfed the hearth. "Get in there before I send you to Tartarus with your other relatives, you fucking whore."

Snickering as I approach the hearth, I can't help but innocently respond, "Ha, calling me a whore is a bit hypocritical, isn't it?"

The force with which he shoves me through the smoky mist causes me to catch myself with my hands on the other side, the cold granite and marble floor bruising my knees and palms. I glance around. Olympus. I'm finally here.

"Ah, Hecate, it's so very nice to meet you."

Looking up from my position on the floor, I meet the coldest eyes I've ever witnessed, colder than even Zeus's colorless depths. The deep-gray pools pull me in, and I'm drowning, unable to breathe. I crash to the floor, choking as the air is sucked from my lungs.

"My dear, this toy is not for you. She's all mine," Zeus issues from behind me as he, too, appears from the mist.

Before me regally stands the one woman I have been terrified to meet. Her reddish-brown locks are held in a demure chignon at her nape, a frown touching her thin lips. She's plainer than I imagined, the mother of gods. Gray eyes blink, instantly turning to a deep maroon with catlike slits. Blinking again, the gray eyes return. She grins, the evil transforming her face and features into a familiar one. White-blond hair, white brows, thick dark lashes, and bright red lips. But it's the maroon eyes with vertical, catlike pupils that cause me to gasp.

My voice comes out shaky. "You're the Pythia?"

She laughs heartily, throwing her head back and exposing a long, pale neck bedecked in jewels. "Oh, no, Hecate, I'm simply Hera."

CASTOR

Helen and I race our horses toward the town of Larissa, the only stopover between Chiron's home and Mount Olympus. It has to be where Hecate and Pollux were headed, and luckily we should outpace them as they'll need to stop and rest if Hecate is to conserve her magic.

After Chiron shared that he helped Pollux and Hecate leave in the middle of the night, I grabbed Helen, and within minutes, we were on the road.

"I still can't believe Pollux chose to leave us," Helen manages to call from her galloping mount.

I keep silent, swallowing down the guilt I feel at causing a rift between my siblings.

"Why would he choose Hecate over your life, Cas? Doesn't he realize that, without Hecate, your life is forfeit to Zeus? Hecate can damn well take care of herself!" Helen can't seem to comprehend that I'm the villain in this scenario. I may not be the one who initiated the deal with Zeus, but I'm the one who's followed through, carrying it out and agreeing to his terms. This entire mess is all my fault.

"Oh my— Is that?" Helen points, her eyes wide and jaw hanging open.

I squint, staring into the distance, and my heart plummets. It's definitely Pollux, riding quickly toward us, and he's alone.

Helen and I both draw our horses up short and wait for Pollux to do the same. We stay atop our mounts, but I keep my palm on my blade, just in case. As much as I love my brother, I would be foolish to trust him. I know how he feels about Zeus. Pollux is angry I've allowed the king of gods into our family once more.

"Ho, Pollux," Helen cries, as he nears. I see the sweat dripping from his brow, the crazed look in his eyes, and know something bad has happened.

Pulling my blade from its scabbard, I use it as a barrier between us, gripping the hilt to keep him from getting too close. "Where is she?" I demand, my teeth grinding out the question.

"What do you care?" he snarls back, glancing warily at Helen. Her nose wrinkles at his attack.

"We care," she adds, giving me a stern look that tells me to play nicely. "We're also glad you came to your senses, returning for Castor before it's too late."

"I didn't come back for *Castor*," Pollux sneers. "Zeus found me." He reddens, lowering his gaze as I lower my sword.

"What happened? Where is she? Tell me everything." I return my blade, knowing that we're all fucked if Zeus has the upper hand.

And since he has Hecate, he has the upper hand.

HECATE

It would be no surprise if I was held in the dungeons of Mount Olympus, but that isn't where I'm taken. Instead, Hera summons an old friend, Hermes, to lead me to my chambers.

As we round a corner and travel up a narrow stairway, Hermes finally drops his stately mask. "It's been a long time, Hecate," he says, pulling me close.

I snicker. "Not long enough if you're still working with Zeus." I push away from him, disgusted that he would attempt to touch me.

His eyebrows raise in confusion as he reaches for me. "Whatever do you mean, my darling? I've only ever been on your side."

"The fact that you believe there are sides tells me everything I need to know about you and your loyalty, Hermes."

"Come now, Hecate, we have been friends for a very long time."

I narrow my eyes at him as I bite the inside of my cheek and tilt my head. "We have been friends for quite some time. Tell me, is that why you improperly trained Melinoe? You certainly weren't hoping I'd fail at reincarnating myself, were you, *friend*?" The sarcasm drips from my lips as he pales.

Clearing his throat, he turns back toward the hall, leading me onward to my suite of rooms. I'm in a den of snakes, so I must keep my wits about me as I gather information. Can I use Hermes in any way to gain the upper hand on this gods-forsaken mountain? It's best not to burn all my bridges just yet, even as a tingle simmers in my fingertips.

"Listen," I trill lightly, walking my fingers up his arm. His pupils dilate and a musky aroma emanates from his pores. He's no different from the rest of the Olympians, so easily toyed with, so weak when it comes to sex. "Let's put the past behind us, friend. After all, I can put the past behind me—if you can do better in the future," I add with a wink. My voice lowers into a seductive rasp on the last word, and I push my chest closer to his lithe body. Even after all these years, he's still sporting the gangly, malnourished teenager look. Glancing up, I watch him lick his lips, his pulse throbbing wildly in his neck. The urge to slice him across the throat flicks through my mind, but I tamp down my murderous urge and focus on gaining useful information instead.

"I'm glad you see how misguided you've been about Zeus. He'll be happy to hear all about you putting the past behind yourself at dinner tonight." Before I can react, Hermes grabs me by the back of the neck and guides me through a door. As I enter the chamber, I feel a wave of dizziness crash over me, my senses going upside down.

"What magic is this?" I thrash against his hold, trying to claw my way back into the hallway.

"See you at dinner, Hecate," he says, shoving me away before he turns and locks the door behind himself.

I rush forward and turn the knob, but hiss in surprise as it burns my hand. Leaning forward and examining the handle, I glide my fingernail over the metal orb. I'm able to dig out a few flakes of white powder and, holding it to my nose, retch as the smell hits the back of my throat. Adamantine, the same poison Poseidon used to coat his trident when he abducted me across the lake. The same element that lines the gates of Tartarus, leaving the Titans, my family, captive within.

Fuck. How am I going to get out of here?

CASTOR

Helen and I both agree that Pollux would do best to return home and keep an eye on our mother. But before he departs, the two of us take a walk in the foothills. As the older brother by mere minutes, I know I've wronged both my baby brother and sister. It's time to set things right. There may never be another time.

Pollux, for all his familial love, doesn't take returning to Sparta lightly. "I'm not sure I trust that you're going to do the right thing, brother." His glare fills me with unease, and I know it will be a long time before I earn back his trust, if ever.

I pull a twig from a low-hanging limb, needing to hold something to keep my hands busy. Leaf-dappled sunlight dances on the ground. "Pol, I promise that I'll follow your instruction explicitly. She's my wife." I break off a piece of the twig and toss it into the foliage as we walk.

He rolls his eyes and snorts in derision. "You wouldn't know it the way you've treated her. Selling her out to Zeus? Are you even sure your marriage is valid? You married Melinoe, not Hecate. Are there rules for reincarnated brides?"

I catch the gleam in his eye and chuckle, shrugging. "I don't know about her, but I know what I feel. There will never be another woman like Hecate, and I can't let her slip through my fingers now that I've found her."

Pollux bites his lip, his eyes looking out into the distance at nothing. "If the plan doesn't work—"

I stop him before he can continue, clapping him on the back. "It'll work. It has to work." I put on a braver front than I feel, needing to convince him to return home and watch over our mother.

We stop at the bank of a river, the same river where I found a younger, sadder Pollux lamenting all those years ago. My twin proceeds to kick a few stones into the water. A pair of ducks swim in the shallows, dipping under the water in search of a meal. I toss a piece of the stick I've been snapping into the frothing abyss, but hesitate before throwing in the last piece. A lone crow calls from a nearby tree. "Pol, if I don't come back from this . . ." My voice trails off, leaving the worst outcome hanging in the air.

"I know, Castor."

"No, you don't know." My voice grows urgent with the need to say all the things I've kept pent up. Watching my mother's eyes light with worry each time I left for battle. Watching my immortal brother become a war hero while I stood idly by, barely managing to stay alive. As much as it hurt my pride, I never should've bargained with Zeus. I've lost not only the trust of my brother and sister, but also the only person who ever might've loved me for who I am, not who I thought I needed to be. "If I don't come back from this, I need you to tell her that I love her." I narrow my eyes, hating the pain I've caused everyone. Finally throwing the last piece of the broken stick into the water, I watch it float away as my brother pulls me in for a hug.

· · · ● · ● · · · ·

"Who the fuck are they?" I ask Helen quietly, raising my chin toward the two naked women dancing and chanting in the light of the moon. We lie shrouded in a field of violets, our bodies pressed into the hard earth. A set of golden gates glitter in the distance, but there's no way through without disrupting the ritual taking place before us.

Helen shrugs, biting her lip as she watches the women with curiosity. I glance around, taking in the luxury of our surroundings. Beyond the gates stands a magnificent palace, complete with a courtyard. A massive stable stands erect in the distance.

"Any ideas how to get inside, Helen?" Her gaze never leaves the dancing duo. "Helen?" I shake her shoulder, but she doesn't respond. She doesn't even bother to look at me. My brows lower in concern when her mouth begins to move, and as I glance between the women and my sister, I realize she's miming the dancers' words.

"Good Order, Justice, and Peace," Helen murmurs, her voice growing louder as she stands.

"Quiet!" I hiss, trying to pull her back to the ground where we've crouched out of sight. Her voice grows louder, her strength increasing as she pulls easily away from my clutches and moves toward the dancers. I reach my hand out to her, but she's already gone.

"Good Order, Justice, and Peace," she continues to echo, walking rigidly toward the pair. It's not until she's standing right next to them that the women notice her. They quiet, welcoming Helen into their circle, their arms widening as they pull her into a shared embrace. I lean forward, hoping to catch pieces of their conversation, but when Helen turns and points in my direction, my stomach plummets. They turn their twin gazes toward me, and I curse and flee, attempting to crawl out of sight, staying hidden under the sparse foliage of the mountain. Rocks and thorny twigs dig into my knees, and at one point, my tunic gets caught on a branch. I'm scratched up and sweating my ass off, but I think I might be in the clear. My chest heaving, I wait, listening to the silence around me.

Just when I think I've moved far enough away to stand and make a run for it, I sense something—or someone—approaching. The moon's light disappears as a cloud covers it, and I'm left blind, using only my other senses to guide me even farther away from the golden gates. Hunched over and creeping slowly, one foot at a time, I hold my breath, waiting for the apparition to appear. It's not until I'm grabbed from behind, a rope looped around my neck and pulled taut, that I realize there aren't only two dancing women guarding the gates.

There are three.

HECATE

I pace, back and forth, and back and forth again, until I swear I've worn a path in the floor of the chamber. The windowless inner room isn't square or rectangular as most bedrooms. Instead, it's round. I'm surrounded by gray stone, circling me from the ceiling to the floor. After realizing that the door was sealed with adamantine and impossible to penetrate, I attempted to cast various spells to free myself from the luxurious prison.

The doorway unsealing spell hadn't worked. Neither had the room isolation reversal spell. From there I tried the destruction incantation, and when that didn't work, I attempted the bilocation spell, which would have allowed me to be in two places at once, in both body and soul, but my strength was already sapped from the earlier spells.

Tossing myself on the bed and screeching into the pillow's downy fluff, I attempt to release all my rage and anger. Instead, I'm left with a raw throat and depleted energy, unable to even lift my head from the softness of the cushion.

As I lie there, my life forfeit to Zeus, I wonder what the Fates have in store for me. Have I traveled all this way, from reincarnation to marriage to Mount Olympus, only to be defeated at the hands of Zeus? Why put me through the paces if my fate thread was only to be cut short by Zeus? Why not put me out of my misery decades ago in my tiny Underworld hut?

I sit up suddenly, the reality of my situation becoming brighter. Zeus isn't going to kill me; if he was meant to end my life, it would have happened in the Underworld. No—I smack my forehead—he's going to seduce me in hopes of finally getting what he's always wanted. He knows my powers are stronger than his, which is why he's always been unable to kill me. Instead, he goes after those I love. He knows he can't force himself on me either. In order to truly win at this game, I have to go after the power *behind* Zeus.

I have to get the others on my side.

· · · • · • · • · · ·

Perched on the edge of the bed, I'm dressed and ready to be presented to the Olympians. Inhaling deeply and centering myself, calling to my magic, I do my best not to fidget with my hair, my necklace, or the dress, or lack thereof. I received the invitation hours ago, accompanied by a sheer toga, and, reddening in embarrassment, had been unable to meet Hermes's eyes as he handed me the filmy material.

"Servants will be sent up shortly. You'll be ready by sunset." His tongue darted out, slowly licking his lips, as he eyed me up and down, likely imagining my nakedness which would soon be available for all of Olympus to witness. Shivers of disgust broke out along my spine.

Now, primped and readied, I glance down at my body, completely on display through the diaphanous material. I inhale deeply as the door opens and immediately roll my eyes. Of course, as if parading my nakedness throughout the court wasn't enough, Zeus has to go and embarrass me further with his choice of attendant for this evening. My escort is none other than Demeter, who barely manages to hide her sneer as she takes in my dishabille. My shoulders sag slightly, but I still hold my head high. She's never been one to respect a woman's choices, and I'll not give her cause to believe that my outfit is anything but my choice.

"Good evening, witch." She assesses me as I stand and approach. Dressed demurely in a virgin-white toga that falls to her sandal-clad feet, I'm not surprised at Zeus's games. I snort and shake my head at the irony.

"You approve of Zeus holding me against my will, but not the love that Hades shares with your daughter." Her lips thin as anger flares in her deep-green eyes. The same eyes she shares with Persephone.

"That bastard Hades holds my daughter hostage for half the year, thanks to you," she grits out between clenched teeth.

I shake my head, hardly able to believe that Demeter still believes this old tale. "You'd think otherwise if you ever bothered to visit the Underworld. Instead, you lounge here on your golden stool, fawning over Zeus and his lies, too afraid to see the truth."

I attempt to stalk past her and into the hallway when she grabs my wrist, yanking me forcefully around. Since I'm standing beneath the doorway, my magic is stilted due to the adamantine coating the threshold, otherwise she'd think twice about angering me. My vision swims and I dizzily sway, trying to keep my gaze trained on Persephone's mother.

"I look forward to this evening's festivities, witch," she hisses as her eyes trail up and down my naked form, a smirk threading her lips.

"So do I," I retaliate, managing to yank my arm free and step into the hallway where my power surges back to life.

· · · · ● · ● · · ·

I don't take two steps before Hera appears before me, her Pythia glamour gone. She gazes at me intently, unblinking, as her stiff posture outlines her tense muscles.

"Follow me."

I'm unable to swallow the lump forming in my throat, the dryness instead causing me to cough. She arches a perfectly manicured eyebrow, and I see the slightest amusement flick over her face. She stalks off and I follow like a well-behaved duckling.

As we maneuver silently through the palace, I'm able to take in the opulence around me. The high ceilings are painted, a portrait of Zeus surrounded by beautiful, busty nymphs, their breasts exposed. Gasping, my gaze falls on his engorged manhood, and I hurriedly lower my eyes.

Hera snorts. "Like you haven't seen the real thing."

Eyes widening, I shake my head, my lip curling in disgust. "I certainly have not!"

She narrows her eyes and shrugs, tossing aside my outburst as we carry onward toward our destination. The sound of the outside fountains carries through the open windows.

Watching wistfully as we pass the castle's exit, I'm led down a narrow, dark stairwell seated at the back of the palace. My footsteps halt at the hole in the ground as I refuse to take another step. "Where are you taking me?"

Turning, her eyes boring into my own, she summons the mask of Pythia. The familiar face of the oracle heightens my sense of unease, and as I back away from her, she breathes out, releasing the same cloying scent from the temple. The smoke permeates my nostrils, choking me. I wave my arms to clear the air, but it's useless. The mist fills my vision, and gasping for breath, I drop to my knees.

When I stand, the smoke now cleared and my vision restored, my ankles are shackled together and I'm in the dungeons, down the dark hole I'd refused to descend. I sense Hera's presence at my back, and as I look around at the small, cramped cells dark with shadows, my stomach roils.

Her melodic voice calls out, "If you don't give me what I want, witch, this will be your home. Not Tartarus, where your ancestors reside, not the Underworld, where your precious cottage lies untouched, but this cell, where I will sap your magic from you daily, and as I'm sure you can figure out, my husband will use you for his pleasure . . . at my bidding, of course." I wince as she laughs bitterly, a shrill bark.

I peer through the iron bars at the dirty straw scattered across the floor, likely filled with fleas and rats. I scratch at my arms, my eyes climbing the black-mold-covered walls.

"See those shackles there, my dear?" She gestures to the chains fixed to the walls. "They're coated with adamantine."

Hearing a moan from the next cell, I avert my gaze from my future home and stumble toward the noise. "No . . ." I mutter, a pain growing in the back of my throat.

"Yessss," Hera hisses in my ear. "Your lowly mortal lover stumbled in here last night and quickly found himself—well, I'll let you be the judge of that."

The sound of Castor's labored breathing hits my ears as his limp form hangs chained to the cell wall. Dried blood crusts along his upper lip, and his hair is matted.

"Castor!" I exclaim, rushing to the bars. I hiss as the poison burns my palms. Horrified, I raise my hands and see they've crusted and scabbed over, the adamantine singeing my skin. "Castor, open your eyes!" He obliges, but the person I see within his dilated pupils is not my husband. The dead gaze lands on me, and chills rack my already cold body. "What have you done to him?" I demand, unable to take my eyes away from his.

"Exactly what I'll be doing to you, should you not agree to my terms."

Staring at Castor, I remind myself that he sold me out to Zeus, he made an agreement to trade me for his own chance at immortality. He's just one more villain haunting the halls of this infested mountain, one more person who wants to use me for their own gain. I blink, and my mind goes to the last time I was in chains, in the ship's hull with Helen. My friend. From Helen my brain flits to Pollux, who stood up to Zeus for me. Regardless of how I feel about Castor, I can't allow him to be hurt. For Helen's and Pol's sakes only, I tell myself.

I raise my fingers to my throat, my burnt thumb grazing my collarbone as I imagine Castor's lips playfully tracing kisses there. How did he come to be in this dungeon? Did he think he could rescue me, that he wouldn't get caught and killed? My heart softens slightly. *No, he lied to you*, I tell myself, my eyebrows lowering angrily. Eyes stinging and blood rushing to my ears, I grasp the heavy, cold necklace around my throat, the reverie broken as I force myself to behold the horrors in front of me.

"I'll do whatever you want, but you must let him go," I say, the chain around my throat as heavy as those around my ankles.

Hera nods once, an ugly twist lifting her mouth.

CASTOR

I enter the banquet hall, in cadence like a good little soldier, behind the Horae, the three sisters who attacked and locked me in the dungeon. They are the goddesses of time, as well as guardians of the gates of Olympus. Ironically, they're also the daughters of Zeus by a Titan named Themis. Who isn't this bastard related to?

I enter the ballroom, my body not my own, and when I try to halt my steps or look around at the guests, searching for Hecate, it's as though my muscles belong to someone else. I'm a puppet on a string. My mind, however, is still free, and it continues to push against its prison.

When I awoke, my neck sore and bruised from the choke hold that the one called Dice inflicted upon me, I found myself in the dungeon of Mount Olympus. While never a prisoner of war before, my Spartan training prepared me for the possibility. After peeling my sore body off the dirt floor, I slowly and methodically searched every nook and crevice of the cell for any loose stones, my fingertips gliding over the smooth surfaces and prodding each cranny. Nothing. I examined the bars, attempting to loosen each one as I turned and wiggled the metal. My shoulders and chest were much too wide to squeeze through, and finally, I collapsed onto the floor, my head pounding from the exertion.

Despite failing to find an escape, my training also taught me to stay mentally strong. I could not, under any circumstances, fall into the typical pit of despair.

Once I started to feel sorry for myself and my situation, my mind, and therefore my body, would instantly become weaker. Instead, I forced myself to stand, and I exercised by completing basic calisthenics, from push-ups to sit-ups, lunges, and squats. Anything to keep my mind from spiraling into its own dungeon of depression.

Food was brought to me by a pretty goddess, Dice's sister, Irene. She wore a white gossamer gown, her hair pulled back in a demur plait that trailed down her back. While nowhere near as beautiful as Hecate or as striking as the sea nymph Thetis, Irene's features were captivating, but her state of dress rather plain. Regardless, part of the prisoner of war training also included how to manipulate the minds of my captors, getting them to feel sorry for me and appealing to their sympathies, and as I gulped down the meager rations, I realized that meant flirting with Irene.

"Thank you for this," I whispered, keeping my eyes lowered as I accepted food through the cold metal bars of the cell. I gorged myself on the meal as she watched, then smiled sadly up at her. She needed to believe I was truly grateful for her kindness. She needed to believe I was broken, needed her to fix me.

It's not hard to believe that she was starved for attention, being a common goddess relegated to guard duty, and the next time she brought my food, she held a honeyed cake tied delicately in a napkin through the bars. As I took the treat, I made sure to caress her hand, letting my fingers linger on her soft skin. She inhaled, and a blush crept up her neck. I knew then that she was taking the bait.

That evening, she sneaked a woolen blanket and pillow through the bars. I thanked her and pretended to shed a tear of gratitude, watching in hidden amusement as she bit her lip while I swiped under my eye. My plan was working.

The next morning, as I heard her footsteps skipping down the hall to my cell, I smirked at how easy it had been to trick her and wondered how much longer until she offered to release me.

"My dear Irene, I've been waiting—" The sickly sweet greeting died on my tongue as I took in the additional visitors. Her two sisters, Dice and Eunomia, plus Helen, stood in a row peering through the bars, their eyes filled with malice. Matching smiles stretched their faces, as though they were cats ready to pounce. My gaze flickered to Helen, but Irene's snarl brought my attention back to her.

"Did you really think me so stupid, Prince?" Her cackle echoed, the stone walls amplifying the grating noise, as her face transformed from plain to grotesque. Her straight teeth elongated to pointy fangs, her dull brown eyes turning dark as curly fur sprouted from her perfectly arched eyebrows. "It's time for you to join your sister, despite your pathetic efforts to woo me."

I retreated farther into the cell, my fists clenched as I felt a power surging through me, my body calm even as my mind raged.

"Good Order," Eunomia recited.

"Justice," Dice followed.

"Peace," Irene hissed, drawing out the word. The trio repeated their phrases, the spell cast and descending over me as I crouched down and held my hands over my ears.

"Hecate, Hecate, Hecate," I intoned over and over, first in my head and then roaring the name aloud, as if I could summon her with just a wish. I needed to focus on anything other than the spell overtaking my body.

Instead, as my mind protested, my body stood rigid, and my muscles began to move with a mind of their own. As I walked through the bars that were pulled open by Irene, a smile of amusement touched her once-again plain lips.

Now, as I enter the dining hall behind the three sisters, I finally lay eyes on my wife. My Hecate.

My eyes travel her body, taking in the sheer clothing she must have been forced to wear. From behind, Zeus eyes her backside with greedy lust as she sits erect on his knee, her body giving away her distress. Her ankles are chained too, but she has them tucked under her in an attempt to hide the shackles, her weakness.

She meets my gaze, looking at me as though she could hear me calling for her. If my body were my own, I would run to her, throw myself over her nakedness and shield her from Zeus's hungry eyes. I'd admit to her all the wrongs I've done, tell her the whole story. How Zeus approached my father and threatened Helen's and my mother's lives if I didn't agree, how I would be confined to the pits of Tartarus if I didn't accept the deal. Then, once I was made immortal, how I would die within seven days if I didn't deliver her to his clutches. I would admit that I never expected her, that I believed the lies Zeus spewed about her before our very first meeting. I would tell her everything. That I hated myself more than she ever could for what I'd done.

But instead, unable to tell her what's in my heart, my nausea returns as my feet lead me to the center of the floor, where I join in a dance with Irene, whose own eyes devour me hungrily as she raises her head and laughs maniacally.

Hecate.

Hecate.

Hecate.

I continue to repeat to myself.

HECATE

It's clear that my entrance is part of the evening's entertainment. As I'm announced and shoved into the brightly lit dining hall, a banquet table full of guests turns, collectively gasping at my exposed body and adamantine-shackled ankles. Hera quickly takes her place while I'm escorted to the seat of honor—a small stool next to Zeus. She sits at his right, her face devoid of color as her eyes watch him appraise my nakedness. I meet her gaze and jut out my chin. Her long, elegant fingers coil around her cup, and I begin to wonder if she'll snap the golden stem in rage.

Sitting next to Hera is the beautiful but vapid Aphrodite, whose glare is focused on her paramour, Ares. Her rose-gold hair curls down her back, and as she swings to look at me, her hair follows. A sneer of disgust touches her bright pink lips as she notices Ares eyes are focused directly on my nipples, which have hardened to sharp peaks in the cool air. He licks his lips and reaches down to adjust himself, making sure to wink as he notices me watching. I'm horrified but force myself to keep a placid expression. *Play the game*, I remind myself.

"Sit, Hecate," booms Zeus. Behind me, the guard pushes me onto the stool. My knees give out as I sink down, my eyes lowering in shame.

I ignore the nervous butterflies fluttering in my belly, which are made worse when I don't see Hephaestus at his seat. I wish that I had at least one friendly face to look upon. Instead, I watch Hera out of the corner of my eye. She dotes on Ares, her rumored favorite child, and I can see why. His golden hair gleams in the candlelight as his chiseled jaw chews his food. His blue eyes look lovingly upon his mother, and he even reaches a muscular arm across the table to stroke her hand. Aphrodite, for all her beauty, sulks as Ares continues to ignore her.

For the next hour, I watch silently from my perch as dinner is served, followed by dessert. The wine flows freely, despite Dionysus's absence. Very few of the Olympians in attendance acknowledge my presence, as though they're used to Zeus's theatrics. Athena and Apollo stay in a heated debate about an arrogant satyr named Marsyas, while elfin Artemis, my cousin, quietly listens to her twin and nods along in agreement. I've tried to make eye contact with her several times, but she refuses to glance my way. Does she remember our conversation in her temple? Did Atalanta ever share the boar's tusks and hide as offerings? Will she help me?

My gaze is torn away from Artemis as, finally, the plates and cups are cleared. Zeus claps his hand and nods to Apollo, who listlessly twirls his wrist. Musicians enter from the antechamber, and a jaunty tune fills the hall. Zeus stands from his golden chair and, yanking me up from the stool, pulls me toward a raised dais where two thrones sit. He collapses in one while Hera, appearing from behind me, takes the other. I stand awkwardly, unsure of my place, before Zeus yanks me down onto his knee. My jaw tightens as his fingers trail down my spine, goosebumps breaking out along my skin as I try to hold my hatred and fear in check. I try not to glance at Hera, who I can sense is irate, her long red nails digging into the arms of her throne.

More and more immortals enter the chamber, but as I watch from my uncomfortable seat on Zeus's knee, I notice their eyes—devoid of all emotion, even while their faces appear jubilant. Are they in some kind of trance? Just then, Zeus moves against me, pressing his mouth to my ear.

"Dance for me, witch."

Gritting my teeth and wanting nothing more than to burn this place to the ground, I stand, my body writhing to the music as much as my ankle-bound feet allow. I keep my wits about me, but in the sheer dress my nakedness is on display for everyone. I refuse to feel shamed and instead use my time to surreptitiously scan the faces of the guests entering the banquet while I snake my hands down my exposed skin, drawing Zeus's attention away from my face.

Three graceful goddesses join the party, and Zeus thrusts his chest out as a gleam sparks in his eyes. "Ah, my daughters, the Horae, have arrived with two very special guests." Zeus pulls me back to his knee, his arm protectively circling my waist.

I lower my arms, crossing them over my chest, and purse my lips. As the last daughter enters, she turns and crooks her finger toward the entrance, where Helen appears. A sour taste permeates my mouth as I watch her move stiffly toward the Hora. Ares can't seem to take his eyes off Helen. Aphrodite, flares her nostrils, glaring at the beauty who's stolen Ares's attention.

"Oh, another special guest," Zeus whispers in my ear as my gaze turns toward the entrance again. I hold in a gasp as Castor follows, beckoned by the crook of the Hora's finger.

Without tearing my gaze from my husband, I hiss at Zeus, "Why have you brought them here?" Hera promised . . .

He snorts. "I didn't bring them. They came on their own, and they'll now enjoy the festivities along with you." He roars with laughter, clapping to the musicians to play louder, faster. My jaw tenses, grinding my teeth to stumps, as I snap my eyes to Hera. Clenching my fists, I stare as her lips tilt up into a smile at Castor's appearance. Then, ever so slowly, she turns to me, meets my murderous stare, and winks.

My body tingles all over, the desire to burn her from the inside so painful that my hands start to glow with magic. I attempt to step forward, but Zeus's massive sandal-clad foot stomps on my chains, holding me hostage at his side. A growl escapes my lips, and Hera chortles at my discomfort.

Visibly shaking with rage, I turn back to the guests and try to catch Castor's gaze, but his face doesn't turn my way. Frowning, I watch as, instead, he is drawn into a dance by one of the Horae. As Zeus's hand rests on my hip, I fight the urge to move away, my body held stiff as a rod. My husband's dance partner is beautiful. Her shiny blond locks fall down her back to complement a pert behind, where Castor rests his hands. My eyes blaze in fury, my breathing shallow as I watch her lean in with glossy lips and whisper something in his ear. A smile tilts his lips, but his eyes remain cold. Blinking, I bite my own lip, ignoring the lazy circles Zeus swirls on my lower back, sinking lower and lower. The Hora laughs, the cackle echoing off the walls, and leans back, exposing her pearly throat and breasts. Castor's fingers trail around her hips and over her stomach, then rove upward. My own body heats as I recall the way those same hands caressed me, and the familiar tingle lights the surface of my own fingertips.

I can't tear my eyes away as his hand continues to explore her body, her lips parting and her eyes glossing over. I can smell her desire, and I curl my lip in disgust, my anger growing stronger and stronger. As I feel the heat rising in my body, my fingers tingling painfully as my power is poised and ready to be unleashed, I hear it.

Hecate.

Hecate.

Hecate.

I see it all. I see *everything*. And then Castor's hands finally make purchase around his dance partner's neck, and he squeezes.

• • • ● • ● • ● • •

Hecate.

Hecate.

Hecate.

I hear my name called, and I'm pulled into complete darkness, an empty void. Castor has summoned me into his mind, and as I look around the desolate cavern, I spy various moments in time playing out before me like actors on a stage. The void is endless, stretching before me into nothingness, and as I turn, taking in the scenes around me, I grow cold. The temperature chills me to my very bones. I huff out a breath, the frozen fog dissipating into the nothingness. This place evokes despair, hopelessness. Ruination. I shiver, wrapping my arms around myself.

Then it hits me. These are Castor's memories. I slowly step toward a familiar scene, my silent steps rippling through the abyss.

As I take in the familiar tent, our oasis from the Calydonian boar hunt, I smirk. The moment we consummated our marriage. The warm furs, my naked body writhing as pleasurable waves undulate through my body. A warmth spreads through my abdomen as my face grows hot. I watch, a voyeur of my own experience, as Castor's thoughts are laid bare. Our naked bodies are entwined, my face in the throes of ecstasy, and Castor's familiar voice surrounds me. "This woman—my *wife*—is amazing. I can't wait to do this for the rest of our lives." We both come together—our cries echoing against the despairing darkness—and collapse into one another. I bite my lip, embarrassment warming my cheeks. I reach out, wanting to touch him, to run my hands through his hair, but the voices fade out and the memory disappears, smoke dissipating into the darkness of the cave. A familiar scent coats the air, but I can't quite place it, so I move onward, my feet guiding me to the next vision.

I look around at the gray stone facade. Castor is in an unfamiliar place, a temple. My heart pounds loudly. This place, though it's supposed to be one of reverie, has my husband feeling only fear. I watch as his body is bent at an odd angle, his toes dangling on the floor. His knees buckle and his chest is thrust forward, exposed. I hiss through my teeth, noticing Zeus standing over him, his hand outstretched, reaching for Castor's mouth. "Bring her home to me or suffer the consequences, Prince!" the god roars. Castor's cries of agony fill my ears, and I cover them with my hands and drop to my knees, sickened by the pain I feel in this memory.

"I must find her." Castor's memory disappears as his voice whispers into the void.

Before I can move to a new memory, before I can pull myself up from the ground, another one appears before me, replaced again with Zeus and Castor. They stand in our shared room just outside Trichonida Lake, squared up against one another. Castor's fists are clenched, his face furious with emotion, while Zeus's air of indifference is apparent from his smirk. "And, let's be honest with one another, I know you've been having a change of heart. I can smell it on you." Zeus barely leans toward Castor and sniffs, his lip curling in disgust. "But let me be clear, falling in love was never part of the deal. You will return what's *mine*, Prince." As the god steps into the burning hearth and disappears, Castor crashes to the floor, his head in his hands.

"What have I done? What have I done?" he repeats to himself. I crawl toward him, reaching out to touch him, to comfort him, when the memory explodes in a burst of smoke, and again, the familiar scent.

I'm hunched over on the ground, my chest heaving, fighting back the tears that threaten to spill over when a scene flickers in the distance. I see it before I hear it, and as I stand, the scene brightens, coming closer, flooding me. I squint against the brightness of the vision.

The throne room in Sparta appears, and I watch from outside the moment as Castor, Tyndareus, and Persephone stand on the dais, presumably negotiating my marriage contract. My brows lower over my eyes and my jaw stiffens as the queen speaks.

"Hades and I have agreed with Zeus's demands. We will marry the princess to your son, and Zeus will not invade the Underworld. The marriage shall take place on my return to the Underworld, with Prince Castor accompanying me." Her eyes are steely, her lips thin.

"Very well, Queen Persephone. We look forward to the match between your daughter and my son," Tyndareus replies. "Castor?" He beckons to his son, whose arms are crossed as he stands, feet apart, outside of the group.

Castor's voice reverberates loudly in the chamber. "Father, I don't trust Zeus and his demands. Why would we negotiate with him, after all he's done to our family? Are you mad?" He turns to Persephone, addressing her directly. "Hades certainly shouldn't trust his brother!"

The goddess's face hardens and her voice cools. "Do not dare speak of what you do not know, Prince of Sparta." They stare at one another, neither conceding, until finally Persephone's voice softens. "The situation is hardly ideal, child. But Zeus is a better ally than enemy." She lowers her gaze, ashamed. My heart constricts as I watch her admit defeat against her rapist.

The memory flickers, a candle sputtering, and Tyndareus and Persephone are gone. In their place stands a solitary Castor, pacing back and forth. He's agitated, his hands raking through his hair and his jaw clenched. I reach out, wanting to calm him, soothe away his frustration, when suddenly Zeus appears. I wince, stepping back into the darkness of the void, and watch as the god stalks toward Castor.

"Prince of Sparta." His voice booms, and Castor immediately drops to his knees in supplication, his mouth agape as his eyes take in the formidable size of the king of gods. "Now that you've agreed to the marriage, it's time to discuss the part you'll play in returning Melinoe to me."

Castor's gaze goes dark, his body stiffening. "I'll not align myself with you, nor will I take part in this sham of a marriage." He pulls a small dagger from his boot, but before he can lift and strike, Zeus has Castor on his back and is standing over him. He lifts his arm and the air crackles.

"If I summon the bolt, you will die."

Castor's face goes white and he nods, his grip loosening on the dagger.

"You will bring Melinoe to me on Mount Olympus," the god commands. "And in exchange, I'll grant you that which you most desire—immortality."

"And if I refuse?" I gasp at Castor's question. Is he *trying* to get himself killed?

Leaning over, his face mere inches from Castor's, Zeus hisses through gritted teeth, "Let me show you what happens to those who refuse me."

I watch in horror as Zeus terrorizes Castor with atrocious depictions of what he'd do to Helen, his own daughter, and Queen Leda. My gorge rises and I look away, refusing to commit the visions to my own memory. As the scene returns, Castor's face is ashen, his breathing panicked. "And that's not to mention what I'll do to you, mortal prince. Now, do we have a deal?"

In that moment, Castor's gaze somehow meets mine as he looks out into the void, beyond the throne room. I see the pain, the hurt, the regret. I feel the anger and the helplessness. His gaze finally lowers and, without turning back toward Zeus, he nods.

· · · · ● · ● · · · ·

"*Dýnami, dóse mou dýnami,*" I intone, my fingers playing with the necklace at my throat. The strength augmentation spell takes effect on Castor. He continues to press, the life-force leaving the Hora's body. Castor lifts her aloft until she slackens, and then sinks to the floor, her lifeless body discarded, her esophagus crushed beneath my soldier's hands. Behind me, Zeus roars as he sees her body sprawled on the ground, unmoving.

I turn, my hands raised as the tingling begins to burn. "*Na spásoun pollá,*" I hiss, the chains falling away from my ankles. I carefully kick them to the side, the adamantine burning briefly, as Zeus's murderous gaze follows. Nobody else in the room moves, their terror a testament to my unleashed powers. I can smell their uncertainty, their fear. It reeks of desperation and curiosity.

Zeus raises his arms and summons his golden weapon, the Thunderbolt. My body goes cold, terror shooting through my veins, as it appears from above as though an extension of his giant muscular arm. I've never seen it up close, and the weapon before me brings dread to the others in the hall. Their fear is seeping from their bodies, scenting the air with a mix of cold sweat and panic, as the air is sucked from the room. The scepter, the most powerful weapon known to the gods, gleams in the candlelight. The crackle of its electrical energy pops as he twirls it between his fingers, the pungent scent of ozone overpowering everything else. This single weapon could take me down with one swipe. I spent years in my tiny Underworld hut, planning for this moment, studying the spells and incantations to bring down the king of gods. What I found was disheartening; no amount of power that I possess could ever beat Zeus. My strength, my ability to cast and wield spells, is nowhere near as strong as his bolt. So I kneel in supplication, my eyes lowered to the ground, knowing that I lose and he wins.

· · · ● · ● · · ·

"You know you will never beat me, Hecate." Zeus stands over my prostrated form, the bolt pointed at the crown of my head. With one jab, he could end my existence. I would be sent to Tartarus, never to return, my life forfeit, but that's still a better option than Hera's dank cell. "Look at me, witch. Meet my eyes. I want to watch as I send you to the deepest, darkest depths of the Underworld."

I raise my eyes and stand, two guards now at my back. Zeus takes a step back, the bolt now pointed to my heart. His eyes narrow. I glance behind me at Castor and smile sadly, knowing this is the end of our time together in the Land of the Living. My husband shakes his head, his eyes imploring me to rethink my decision, but he knows there's no other choice. It's either him or me, and if I've done this once, I can do it again.

I reach my hand toward the necklace at my throat and yank it off while at the same time intoning, *"N aftó to froúrio kratiétai, kaneís den tha perásei."* The necklace whips toward Hera, wrapping around her neck as the containment spell takes effect. She gasps and falls back toward her throne, fingers digging at the golden chain now locked into place around her throat.

Zeus's gaze darkens as he looks from her to me. "What is that? What have you done, Hecate?" He presses the bolt against my skin, the energy burning through the sheer fabric and sizzling against my flesh. I hiss, but the guards hold me steady, and I'm unable to move away. I watch as Hera continues to dig her sharp nails into her throat, the wound dripping blood down her cleavage as she tears through sinew and cartilage.

Turning back to Zeus, my stare is intense, my fingers clawlike as the cords in my own neck stretch against my burning skin. "You took everything from me, and now it's time for me to repay the debt." Zeus's eyes widen as I cast the final spell. "*Teleiose.*"

Hera's screams seem to tear the room into two, cracks forming down the middle of the banquet hall. We gods and goddesses wince, acutely feeling her anguish as her powers seep from her body, absorbed into the chain at her throat, the same thing I'd done hours earlier when I was locked away, tucking my powers into the necklace for safekeeping. Hera's fingers dig into the throne, slicing the gold with her strength, her veins protruding from her arms. She's not dead, but she might as well be without her powers to hold over the Olympians.

My own fingertips blaze brightly without the shackles sapping my magic, and the guards back away as I raise my arms from my sides. Castor races to my side, quickly disarming one of the guards as he ascends the dais. He holds his weapon out, pointed toward Zeus, who laughs uproariously.

"Do you really think that paltry sword is any match for the mightiest weapon, my lightning bolt?" He raises the bolt and slices through the metal in one swoop before advancing slightly. I watch in horror as the bolt slides neatly into Castor's chest, tearing through his clothing and skin so effortlessly. Gasping as he slumps to his knees, I catch him and pull him close, the life ebbing quickly from his body.

"No, no, no," I whisper as I move him to the floor, my hands chasing the blood oozing from his wound.

"What did you think would happen, witch? Did you think you would best me? That this mere mortal could ever truly be worthy of you?" He rages, stalking back and forth on the dais, his jaw working as his biceps flex.

Turning back to Castor, I dig through the folds of his clothing. "Where is it? Where's the spell I gave Pollux? I know he must've given it to you!"

Castor inhales, gathering his strength, and digs into his vest, pulling forth a reddened scroll with my chicken scratch handwriting on it. I unfurl the small slip and hold it aloft for Castor to read. "Read it aloud," I plead. "Quickly!"

His breathing stutters and he looks at me, really looks at me, and my eyes well with tears.

"Read it!" I beg again as he coughs, blood spurting from his mouth. I see Artemis flinch from the corner of my eye, something unreadable passing through her features. She reaches her hand out, taking Apollo's, united in their cousin's—my—pain.

Castor shakes his head and reaches for me, his palm cool against my cheek. Zeus stops his pacing, anger and hatred burning from his eyes as he watches my husband and me.

"I'm so sorry, Hecate. There's so much I want to tell you—" Castor manages between painful breaths.

"I saw it, Castor. I saw you, what he threatened to do to your family, to you. I saw it all. I saw *everything*." I hold his head steady, meeting his eyes, and he understands. I heard him.

He gasps, "I'm so sorry. I didn't know that I would be throwing away the life we were meant to have . . ."

Tears well in my eyes and I shake my head. "Please, Cas, please, just read it . . . For me."

"But Hecate . . . I get it now. I get it." His voice softens. "Living forever means nothing without you by my side."

CASTOR

I blink, trying to clear the fuzz from my vision, but it remains. She's fading, and with her all that we could've been.

"Read the damn scroll!" she screams, shaking me, but this makes me cough more. A wet, warm cough that burns my throat and makes my chest throb.

I shake my head again, knowing that resurrecting myself with the spell she's written out is useless with all these gods present. One snap of their fingers and I'm dead again, sent to the River Lethe, my memories of her wiped clean. So instead, I play them back in my mind while I still can. Her anger, the fire within that feisty mind, when I lied to Hades and Persephone about her magic. Her supple rear pushing against me as we rode together through the streets of Sparta. Training with her on the practice field, her body unwieldy under the heft of my country's armor. Finally tasting her, making her truly mine in the tented field of Calydon. Verbally sparring with her, all the while wanting to take her again and again. And the betrayal, the pain I'd seen in her eyes when she realized I had broken us.

I couldn't bear to forget even one moment, good or bad, but I can't tell her all of this now that I'm fading faster.

Instead, I use the last of my energy to tell her the only thing that ever mattered. "I love you," I whisper as the light grows brighter and the blood rushes to my ears.

The noises in the distance grow quieter, but I'm sure I hear her keening in grief, and something is shaking my body.

It doesn't matter now.

I'm already gone.

HECATE

"Castor! Castor!" I scream, shaking his body. My fingertips tingle again as the anger and sadness course through my body, the shock instantly replaced with fury. I comb my mind, thinking of any spells I can use to bring him back, but there's nothing. A resurrection spell only works if uttered by the deceased before the final breath. I lean down, listening for a breath, but nothing comes. He's—he's gone. My body goes cold, and I swear my heart stops beating.

He's gone.

The one person who saw me for who I was, who made me feel safe, who became my home.

He's gone.

My breathing is ragged and a blinding pain pulses behind my eyes. I never even said *I love you*, I realize, a bloom of despair opening up in my chest. My body feels as though it'll split open, break in two and never be whole again, and as I lean over, bloodred tears drip from my eyes onto Castor's sun-kissed skin.

He's gone.

"Stop!" The voice pulls me back from the abyss. I glance toward its source, a figure standing motionless in the entrance, his outline marred by my tears. I push the hair from my face and wipe my eyes, the bloody tears smearing across my cheeks.

Pollux.

He reaches into his vest and takes out a scroll of his own. He unfurls it quickly, and my eyes widen in disbelief. Pollux is going to read the resurrection spell himself, the same spell that I used to resurrect my soul many moons ago.

"*Agapití kardiá . . . énas ángelos pou koimátai. Sikotheíte apó ta vathiá sto fos, xýpnioi apó ton vathýtero ýpno. Anadýetai apó to neró pou anavlýzei, eínai sto fos tou matioú! Ela piso,*" he recites loudly as his boots stomp over the floor of the hall. The guests move out of his way as he strides toward his brother's body. I stand, shaking my head. Pollux doesn't know what he's doing. As a twin, he's not only resurrecting his brother, he's also giving Castor some of his own immortality, thereby making himself weaker.

"Pol—" I begin, but he holds up his hand, silencing me. "Pollux, listen to me," I demand, grabbing his hand.

"Hecate, I know what I'm doing. I *know.*"

My chin trembles as I lower back to Castor's body, stroking his cheek. Pollux nods at me. He knows that, by giving his brother immortality, he will make himself weaker, kill a part of himself. The ultimate sacrifice.

Pollux reaches for his brother, touching his hand to the gaping wound on Castor's chest, and a spark flares. I watch in amazement as my husband's chest rises once. Twice. Color instantly appears in his cheeks, and he coughs, clearing his lungs of the lingering blood.

Finally, his eyes blink open.

My soldier. I throw myself into his arms, but he winces in pain, so I lean back onto my toes, lifting his head with my palm.

"I'm here," I whisper to him, and the corners of his lips quirk up.

We turn together as the door to the chambers crashes open, and a tall woman enters the room. Her shimmering purple gown cascades down to the floor, hissing as it drags along the sleek marble. Murmurs break out among the gods and goddesses. Amphitrite, Poseidon's wife, climbs the dais, her eyes finding Pollux's. He reaches for her, their hands clasping, and both meet Zeus's murderous gaze.

Her chin tipped forward and her shoulders back, she is the epitome of regal, royal. As I look upon her face, however, I see the burning rage within. "I'm here to bear witness against Zeus's crimes," she announces to the assembled guests, "for they are lengthy and atrocious." Her eyes alight on Apollo and Artemis, and as she floats down the steps toward them, they glance questioningly at each other.

Addressing the twins, she says, "I was with your mother when you were born. She traveled far and wide with her niece, Hecate"—she gestures to me—"before finally finding a safe place to birth you both. Your aunt—Hecate's mother—fled Zeus's advances and was thus turned into the island of Delos by his treacherous hand."

"Delos . . . our birthplace," Artemis whispers, her fingers entwining with her brother's.

Amphitrite nods. "Yes, and your mother painfully labored for nine days and nine nights." Her voice catches. "We knew she wouldn't make it. The midwife never arrived." A single tear threatens to spill from her deep-blue eyes.

Apollo's jaw clenches just as Artemis's gaze flashes with fury.

"Hera had forbidden the midwife from attending your mother. Your mother, who later died from the ordeal." Amphitrite slowly approaches the twins, caressing their cheeks with her palms. "I know you've blamed yourselves these many years, but it was them." She points with an accusatory finger to Zeus and Hera. "They are to be blamed for your mother's suffering, the suffering I watched her go through as she brought you both into this world."

The crowd is silent, rapt with attention as Amphitrite raises her arms. "And they will continue to attack, torture, and rape your mothers, your sisters, your wives unless you band together and stop them. Now." Apollo and Artemis single-mindedly draw their weapons and step toward the dais.

Pollux, his gaze now focused on Zeus, climbs the final step of the dais and pulls his own weapon from its scabbard. Castor and I look at each other, the sword foreign to us.

Zeus, however, is familiar with the weapon. "The blade of Metis," he whispers. Athena, upon hearing her mother's name, gasps and takes a step forward, her eyes darkening.

Pollux swallows and nods to her.

"Wherever did you find it, my clever son?"

"It's a relic from one more woman that you've wronged, *Father*," Pollux sneers. "Forged during her imprisonment, she placed it in the care of a god on our side, a god who knows your true nature." His eyes narrow as Athena comes to his side, her weapon drawn on Zeus.

"You too, daughter?"

"I always wondered if what they said was true, that you killed Mama after she helped you win the throne of Olympus," Athena grits through clenched teeth.

"It was only a matter of time, Zeus, before your children rose against you for what you did to our mothers and to the mortals we're bound to protect," Apollo adds, sidling up next to his half sister.

Athena sneaks a look at Pollux and nods to him, her lips thinning. "The oracles foretold a son would replace you as king of the gods. I may not have been born a son, but I am the child the oracles predicted," Athena roars, turning to her siblings, all offspring of Zeus, and they nod to her, bowing low.

"You all deny me my throne? I am the one who made you, created you from nothing and raised you to greatness!" Zeus howls into the silent room, his children's eyes darkening with hatred and murderous rage.

I smirk, my hand in Castor's, as we both realize what Zeus doesn't. I wasn't the only one who wanted revenge.

• • • • • • • • • •

After breaking the Horae's spell on Helen, I usher her and Castor from the banquet with strict instructions to return to my chamber. "I need you to get him into a hot bath and make sure the wounds are fully healed," I tell Helen. "Do you still have the blade I gave you?"

She nods, a sparkle lighting her eyes. "I didn't get a chance to tell you, I used it to kill—"

Castor cuts her off just as my brows shoot into my hairline in surprise. "Hel, there's time for that later. Help me to the rooms," he breathes, his hand holding his side.

As she turns to go, I grab her wrist, pulling her in for a hug. "Please take care of him," I beg. She gives me an odd look before turning and supporting Castor's weight as they slowly make their way to the safety of my chamber.

"Are you ready?" Pollux's question breaks my reverie, and I nod.

We re-enter the banquet, cleared of the various non-Olympian guests. I approach the dais where Athena now holds her mother's blade pointed directly at her father, the poisonous tip glowing slightly blue in the candlelight. Poison strong enough to fell a Titan, specifically Cronus. Metis, Zeus's first wife, used her knowledge of poisons to help free his siblings, only to be imprisoned and then killed when her purpose no longer served him.

Athena, not breaking eye contact with her father, asks, "How does this work, Hecate? How do we send him to Tartarus?"

Hera, the choker still sealed around her neck, wails from her throne.

I ignore her hysterics as, looking between Athena, Pollux, and the twins, I offer my suggestion. "Persephone once said that Zeus is a better ally than enemy." Apollo starts to protest, but I hold my hand up. "Hear me out, cousin."

I explain how, if Zeus were imprisoned in Elysium, my home, I could act as his warden, his jail keeper. "I know the perfect place," I add, thinking of the burnt oak tree on the edge of my cottage's property.

I don't mention what I saw on the Plain, what I know is coming someday in the future: another war. Imprisoning Zeus in Tartarus won't help us when the time comes, when we need him as an ally.

I look between Athena and the twins, and their subtle nods give me the answer I need. Athena takes a small step back, allowing me to come face-to-face with Zeus. For the first time, I stare down at him. Even on his knees, he's nearly as tall as I, but knowing I hold the power, that I have finally stopped his abuses, leaves me feeling ecstatic.

He narrows his eyes at me, goading me to say something, but I've wasted enough of my energy on him already. These final spells I cast will be the last pieces of me he'll have.

I inhale, focusing my mind on the two spells needed to imprison the mighty king of gods.

"*N aftó to froúrio kratiétai*," I intone.

"You'll always need me. I made you great, Hecate," Zeus growls as the spell begins to take.

"*Kaneís den tha perásei*," I continue.

The spell takes hold and he grits his teeth, the barrier wrapping tightly around his body. "You don't know what you're doing. I am the king, I created you—I created all of you!" He rages, thrashing against the hold.

Next to me, Athena's body stiffens and she starts to inch forward, the blade trembling slightly in her hand. I shake my head, motioning for her to return to my side.

The barrier spell complete, I focus now on the metamorphosis spell. Taking one more deep breath in, I bring to mind the ravaged tree, its branches charred and ashy.

"*Gíne mia ómor—*"

"You better hope this spell holds, witch, and that I don't come find you in the middle of the night, all alone in that cottage—"

"*Gíne mia ómorfi petaloúda*," I finish through gritted teeth, my hands burning as the powerful spell hits him square in the chest. Falling back, he groans as his body disintegrates, the particles trembling as they burst into white smoke and fade into the ether.

For the safety of us all, I must immediately return to the Underworld to ensure the spell worked. Apollo nods his thanks, while Artemis and Athena wrap me in a hug. "We'll communicate," we assure one another. Finally, I turn toward Pollux.

He toes the tiled floor, his hands clasped behind his back. I finally take this time to truly look at him, to appreciate all he's done for me on our journey. While he's Castor's twin, I see now how different they are. Before I start to get too emotional, he grabs me, twirling me around and setting me on the ground so quickly I nearly fall over.

"Thank you," I whisper as I lean into his large frame, my face pressed into his chest.

"For what?" He snorts into my hair, and I chuckle, tears blurring my vision.

"For believing in me, and being my friend."

He sniffs and then pushes away, holding me at arm's length. "Make sure that fucker is well and truly imprisoned."

I nod, swiping at my eyes.

"And come visit anytime."

I turn, moving away from the group to cast a traveling spell, when Pollux grabs my arm. "Are you really going to leave him here, Hecate? After all you've been through together?" His face is innocent, free of judgment, but I know deep down he's weighing my actions against his own moral compass.

I lower my eyes and bite my lip, unsure how to answer. Instead, I close my eyes, inhale, and release the words that will take me home. Back to the only place I've ever belonged.

EPILOGUE

I arrive in the Underworld and, after checking that the binding and meta-morphosis spells took, that Zeus is truly imprisoned within the oak, make my way to the palace. It's time I met with Hades and Persephone, not necessarily my mother and father, but more than simply my king and queen.

I'm freshly bathed and scrubbed clean after my impromptu bath with Castor. I spirited myself into the washroom and found my husband in a hot tub of water surrounded by oils and bubbles.

"Bubbles?" I asked, quirking my eyebrow as a smirk edged my lips.

"I was hoping you'd join me, my love. The bubbles are for you. Your favorite scent."

As I inhaled, the calming fragrance of almond and rose, the perfume of Queen Persephone, mixed with the manna aroma of the Spartan hillsides. Walking to the edge of the tub, I was immediately pulled in—bloodied outfit and all—the water spilling onto the floor. Wrapped in my husband's wet embrace, I swept the froth aside, assessing Helen's work. She had sufficiently bandaged his wound, ensured it was healing, before discreetly excusing herself.

"Immortality suits you." Rising from the tub, his naked desire on full display, he swept me into his arms and, dripping wet, carried me to the bed.

It didn't take long before we were wrapped in each other's arms, letting our emotions take over and our bodies simply feel. As we lay atop the furs, sated and gasping for air, I finally shared my feelings, something I'd hidden far too long.

"I love you, Castor," I said, raising to my forearms and looking at his beautiful face. "I've loved you since Calydon, maybe before . . . I don't know. But I know that I love you, and I'm sorry I didn't tell you sooner," I admitted.

He took my cheek in his palm and pulled me in for a kiss. "I love you so much, Hecate. If I'd known what this would be, I never—" I stopped him, crushing his mouth with my own.

"Don't," I said, pulling away. "I would never ask you to choose. It was an impossible situation, and it's over now."

I lowered my eyes, knowing that it's not truly over, not yet. But I kept that information to myself. Instead, I stood and dressed in my Spartan leathers, the diaphanous gown left bloodied and wet in the tub. "I have to return to the Underworld, to make sure that Zeus is truly imprisoned, and to warn Hades and Persephone." I pulled up short, realizing there's so much more to discuss with the people I once thought of as my parents.

Castor stood, dressing slowly, and I offered him a quizzical look. "Are you home to Sparta already? Shouldn't you rest a bit longer?"

He frowned. "Of course not. I'm coming with you."

"Y-You're coming to the Underworld?"

"Why wouldn't I? You're my wife, Hecate. I go where you go."

I laughed, joy coursing through my veins for the first time in days. "What about Sparta?"

He raised an eyebrow. "What about it? It'll keep. There are more important things—mainly you—that need taken care of."

I launched myself at him from across the room and he winced in pain, clutching his abdomen.

"Oh! I'm sorry, I just—"

But he stopped me with a heart-melting kiss as he hoisted me up, grabbing my ass and grinding into me.

Now, as we make our way into the castle, I glance at my husband, walking beside me, and a smile lifts my lips.

· · · ● · ● · ● · ● · · ·

"You knew all along?" I inquire, my eyes boring into Persephone's from across the dinner table.

She shakes her head, taking a dainty sip of wine. "I wasn't completely sure, but the evidence was there. You disappeared. Then, the markings on the back of the baby's neck, the erratic magic of the infant." She smiles sadly.

I reach across the table and place my hand on hers, grabbing her fingers and squeezing. "Persephone, I'm still your daughter, in a way. But I'm also Hecate, your friend. I'll always be here for you. My place—"

Castor clears his throat next to me.

"*Our* place," I amend, "is here, in the Underworld."

Unshed tears well in her eyes, and she nods stiffly. Hades, his arm thrown casually over the back of her chair, rubs her bare shoulder in comfort. He meets my gaze and smiles, a tinge of pride in his eyes.

"I always knew you were special, *daughter*," he says. "Even without the magic, I knew you'd become a wonderful leader. I saw it in the way you interacted with our people, the care and kindness you showed them."

I lower my gaze, unused to accepting compliments. Castor, ever the perfect dinner partner, begins to fill in details of our journey. Hades loves the part about the Calydonian boar hunt, while Persephone is eager to one day meet Amphitrite.

As I sip my wine and take in the company at the table, I realize how lucky I am to be a daughter, Titan, and witch of the Underworld.

I'm frazzled, searching through my bottles and baskets for the right ingredients. I dump the additives into my mortar, ready to combine everything into a soothing salve. Thyme, belladonna, pig fat, and honey complete the recipe, and as I dig the pestle into the mortar, I use all my strength. Tearing a few strips of linen cloth, I add those to the basket as well.

Finally, I cap the tincture I've just finished creating, a poultice for Cerberus's paws. According to Selene, the three-headed beast torched his foot pads when he jumped into the River Phlegethon, the river of fire, as he chased a screech owl.

Heading out into the red dawn of morning with the basket on my arm, I close the door of my restored hut and, looking toward the horizon, slowly saunter toward the oak tree. I pass it each day on my way to Hades's palace, the hollowed trunk still singed.

According to the missives I receive from Artemis, Athena has continued to rule Mount Olympus with a righteous hand these past years. Hera, too, Artemis adds, continues to work diligently as a chambermaid, cleaning the hearths and assisting in the repainting of the palace's murals.

Stopping at the oak, I finally feel ready to restore the tree to its former glory.

Setting down the basket, I kneel in the lush grass and press my palms to the roots, digging my fingers into the dusty earth. "*Aftó to déntro tha fytrósei, ta fýlla tou tha fytrósoun, oi rízes tou tha pioun,*" I intone. I exhale, expending my energy into the soil, emptying the last remnants of the hatred I used to feel for Zeus. Standing back, I watch in awe as the tree blossoms from the ground up, the trunk turning from black to a deep brown, the limbs stretching and creaking with life, leaf buds forming on their tips.

"What made you decide to resurrect Zeus's tree?" I stand still, keeping my gaze on the transforming giant, as the deep voice coils up my spine, sending shivers to the base of my neck. Castor's warm hand lands on my lower back, his thumb finding the skin beneath my top, and I turn to meet his smile.

"I feel it, that we'll need him again." My mouth turns down and my serious tone wipes the smile from his face. "There's a battle coming, and the gods and goddesses will need to unite as one. I felt it on the Plain of Thessaly, in the bones of the Titans. We'll need everyone, even him," I add as I flick my gaze to the now-thriving tree.

Castor looks down, finding my hand and bringing it to his lips. "Until then, we need to get Cerberus his salve. The old grump nearly chewed my hand off during training this morning."

I snort, not surprised that Castor has taken it upon himself to attempt to train the hellhound, what with his love of horses and other large beasts.

Pulling a scroll from the pouch at my waist, I hand it to my husband. "This arrived for us, from Sparta." He unfurls it, a frown pulling at his lips.

"My father cannot be serious," he growls.

I shake my head, the skin around my eyes tightening with a fury that matches my husband's.

"He means to hold a competition for Helen's hand? This is barbaric!" He throws the scroll to the ground in frustration. I take his hand in mine, pulling him closer.

"We must return to the Land of the Living." My eyes convey the unease I feel gnawing in my gut. "For Helen, and also to prepare for the war, to warn the others."

He tightens his hold on me, nodding slightly, his faraway gaze looking beyond Zeus's oak.

I hand Castor the basket, and our hands still entwined, we make our way toward Hades's palace, our home, to say goodbye once more.

THANK YOU!

If you enjoyed reading *Daughter of the Underworld*, please consider leaving a review or recommending it to a friend. Your support, through reviews, word of mouth, and social media shares, helps readers find my story.

Follow Jenn Lynn Adams on social media:

Instagram @jennlynnadams

TikTok @authorjennlynnadams

On the web www.jennlynnadams.com

ACKNOLWEDGEMENTS

This book has been a long time coming, and there are many to thank in its creation. First and foremost, my loving husband Adam, who for years has been encouraging me by yelling, "Write your book!" He's even taught our oldest son, Logan, to join. Without their constant sweet nagging, this dream would've stayed buried— just something I would have hoped to accomplish in the nonexistent "someday" of my life. They pushed me to make that "someday" a reality!

My youngest, Noah Lee, is the inspiration behind Melinoe. As a true Sour Patch kid (sometimes sour, sometimes sweet), she doesn't quite understand what her "Mimi" has done, but I hope I've made her proud.

To my #1 alpha reader, Sarah, thank you for loving my story. You've read each and every version, and without your positivity and friendship, I probably would've spiraled into a depression of imposter syndrome much more often. I have the best "sister" and work wifey ever!

My beta readers, Tiffany and Camille, your time and attention to details is so appreciated. My story wouldn't be even half as amazing without your advice. I hope you're on board for beta reading book two (hint hint).

Anna Corbeaux, my editor (@corbeauxeditorialservices) is an amazingly talented human being. Your kind words, spot-on critique, and professionalism is what made me choose you to edit my book baby. I couldn't be happier with your suggestions; you made my story so much stronger and I can't wait to work with you again... and again... and again!

Franziska, the talented @coverdungeonrabbit, your book designs are to die for. Before my story was even finished, I knew I wanted to work with you. Thank you for being patient with my ideas and helping to design the gorgeous cover. I hope you're still willing to work with me again!

Lastly, thank you to the readers who took a chance on an unknown indie author, picked up this book, and shared it with others.

COMING SOON

It is my pleasure to share with you a teaser of the next novel in the *Daughter of the Underworld* series.

PROLOGUE

In terms of life's journey, my time is measured in "before Melinoe" and "after Melinoe." Standing in the small hut I call home, I stare outside at the giant oak, now grown to its penultimate height, and miss her. I miss her innocence. The simplicity of the life she had. I miss that her problems were small and always black and white, never gray.

My problems, inevitably in varying shades of ash, have been left untended. They have festered and become aggravated, spreading like a rot from this vibrant oak tree. I take a sip of the warm liquid in my mug, a potion concocted to drive away the migraines that have plagued me for the last several months. But nothing can calm my mind, my visions, which have seen what's on the horizon.

"O goddess, O queen of those below, I beseech you to banish the soul's frenzy

to the ends of the earth..."

-hymn to Melinoe

POLLUX

"**H**arder, harder!" the brown-haired woman screams as she rides my cock. Her heavy breasts bounce and I reach for them, but she smacks my hand away and, instead, interlaces our fingers and rolls us over as one.

With me on top, I drive into her, my legs and lungs burning from the exertion. Unwilling to stop and the desire to finish just beyond reach, I grit my teeth and pump faster.

Her squeaks of pleasure intensify, and I join her with a roar of passion just as a loud and unwelcome knock at the door interrupts us.

"Prince Pollux?" the voice on the other side of the barrier questions with a deep baritone.

"In a moment!" I shout as I continue the battle atop the bedding. Even if I haven't seen a real battle in an age, at least I can continue to pillage the willing women of Sparta.

"The Queen demands an audience. Now."

"I said in a moment!" I'm so close my toes start to curl and my vision goes hazy. Just a few more thrusts and—

"Open the door, sir." While my sister addresses the servant, to me her voice is like submerging myself in an ice bath after a hard day of training, and my cock instantly shrivels.

"Fuck," I hiss, covering my bare ass with a blanket while my companion grabs a pillow.

I turn, my face on fire with embarrassment as my sister enters and her eyes assess the situation before her.

"You would make your queen wait while you fornicate with a washer-woman?" Her clipped tone leaves no room for a lovingly snide comment or sarcastic retort, so instead I lower my eyes and offer a contrite head bob. Behind me, my bedfellow scurries to the adjoining bathing area, her pin-straight hair discreetly covering her reddened face.

I edge backward on the bed, wrapping the throw around my waist, and run my hands through my silvery white locks. Without the requisite wars and life of soldiering, there's been no need to keep my hair clipped short. I grab a leather cord from the side table and tie the length back before pulling on a linen tunic.

Moving to the small table near the hearth, I pull out a chair for my sister. She lowers her heavy form with a weary sigh, her palm coming to rest on the bump beneath her chiton.

"Bring the special tea from Hecate and a plate of biscuits." She flicks her wrist at the servant, dismissing him. Once we're alone, her eyes wander over my face, a small crinkle forming between her eyebrows. "You look like kaká."

"I do not look like manure," I retort through gritted teeth.

"You've done nothing except train and fuck since Father's death. It's unbecoming of the queen's brother to behave thusly." The refreshments arrive and she nibbles a biscuit before taking a dainty sip of the acrid liquid.

Ignoring her insults, I nod at the cup and sniff. "What's in that stuff anyway?"

She shrugs and swallows another mouthful. "I have no clue, but I trust Hecate with my life, and if she says it's healthy for the babe, then I'll drink a thousand cupfuls."

I pour myself a pint of ale and greedily drink the entire contents at once.

Helen eyes me from across the table, her lips thinning.

"What?" I ask innocently.

"This is exactly what I'm worried about. Enough is enough. I'm sending you to the Underworld. Let Castor deal with you and your lackadaisical lifestyle for once. Menelaus and I have enough to worry about without you moping around."

"I'm not moping," I grumble as I shove a biscuit in my mouth. "And I don't believe this is your decision, Helen. You'd never rid yourself of your favorite brother." I smile sweetly at her and then widen my eyes and cock my head.

"This is my decision," she responds with a confidence that doesn't reach her eyes. "And Menelaus's, too."

"Ah, the new King of Sparta is tired of his brother-in-law already." I huff in annoyance and rub my jaw. Whether it's sore from the tension I hold there or the tongue-fucking I gave my paramour last night, I'm not sure.

"We both agreed this is for the best. You've been doing nothing but fornicating with anything that walks, unceasingly training for hours a day with no war on, and refusing to sleep or nourish your body with anything beyond wine and ale is not healthy, and I won't have your death on my conscience. Are you even listening to me?"

"No," I answer honestly. Maybe Helen's right. Maybe a change of scenery is just what I need. Plus, I haven't seen Hecate or Castor since Tyndareus's funeral.

"Castor will meet you at the Cape of Taenarum in two days' time. Say your goodbyes to Hilaeira."

"Who?"

Helen stands and shakes her head in frustration. "The woman you were fucking. Her name is Hilaeira, Pollux."

HECATE

"Cerberus, heel!" Castor shouts as we walk the narrow path to the castle proper. With his tongue hanging from his mouth, the giant dog obediently lops to Castor's side.

"I can't believe how much he's improved since you first began working with him." I link my arm with Castor's and nestle into his side as a chilly breeze blows through the pomegranate trees.

"He's gotten tame in his old age."

I sigh, the anxious feeling of unease creeping into my thoughts once again.

"Another headache?" Castor slows his pace and pulls away, looking at me with a worried frown.

"No, not today. I find that dinner with Hades is very refreshing, but with Persephone returning from the Land of the Living in two days' time, I wonder how our weekly feasts will change with her presence."

"You two have made such great progress in the years we've been here. I'm sure she'll be delighted to see you, and you can speak about Demeter and the other Olympians."

"Perhaps," I say, presenting a confidence I don't necessarily feel. We continue our peaceful walk, Cerberus emitting various grunts and snorts as he trots by our side, until the castle comes into view.

My eyes lingers on the window of my childhood bedroom before Castor nudges me and directs my gaze to the unnaturally long line of souls waiting outside the gates.

"I've never seen this many souls waiting before, Castor." I stop in my tracks and shift from foot to foot, my scalp prickling in time with my steps.

"Maybe it's nothing—,"

"Or maybe it's something. The something that we've been waiting for," I clarify as I meet his eyes. The worry and uncertainty in them matches the feeling in my gut.

Castor releases me and I hurry over to the line, searching for someone— anyone— who can tell me their story. How they came to be in the Underworld. What happened in the Land of the Living? But as I follow the crowd closer to the palace gates, I'm met with soul after soul, corpse after corpse, too debilitated to speak or even acknowledge my presence. Necks are slashed. Skulls are crushed. Limbs are missing. Entrails hang from gaping stomach wounds. I cover my mouth in horror until I come upon a young girl and her mother. They seem out of place in this group of gore.

I approach slowly, squat down to the little girl's level, and speak softly. "Please, tell me what has happened."

The girl looks up with shiny green eyes slick with unshed tears and reaches for my hand. I tentatively take it. "How did you come to be here?"

"You did this," she answers me just as clotted blood begins to seep from her nose.

I recoil in horror, but her grip on my hand grows tighter.

"You did this, Hecate, Titan of Witchcraft. It was you who brought this curse upon the Land of the Living."

I'm too stunned to speak, to comprehend what the child is saying, so I shake my head in dismay instead.

"It was *you.*"

• • • ● • ● • • • •

We arrive at the Cape of Taenarum two days later, Castor and I on horseback and Selene riding in a carriage to attend Persephone. This is the first time Hades has been unable to accompany me on the trip to collect his bride. Having stepped in to serve as a fourth judge, his face was gaunt and tired as we bade him farewell this morning. Even now the line of souls remains as long as ever, with more added by the hour.

"What in the Land of the Living is going on out there?" Hades roared when Castor brought me, shaking and nearly catatonic, into the castle. I couldn't get the little girl's words out of my mind.

"You need to send for Rhadamanthus. Hurry," Castor added as he handed me over to Selene. In my mother's absence she frequently joined our weekly dinners, and I was grateful for her presence now.

"He's out there judging the souls," Hades responded, just as Rhadamanthus himself stalked into the chamber. His face was ashen and his fists were clenched. "Ho! General, what news?"

"My king. My princess." Rhadamanthus's gaze flicked warily to mine as he arose from his genuflection, and my breath caught in my throat. Even after all these years, Rhadamanthus continued to address me by my old title and treat me like the stubborn daughter of his liege.

"What's causing the influx of souls?" Castor ran his fingers through his hair, a habit I had learned throughout our years together meant that he was frustrated, worried, or even scared.

Rhadamanthus cleared his throat and clasped his hands together. "Ah, it's hard to say, Your Highness." He avoided meeting my eyes.

I stiffened at the affront. In all the time I'd known Rhadamanthus, from training to protect myself with weapons to learning the methods the Under-world judges imposed to protect our kingdom, he'd never lied to me. Until now.

"There's something you're not telling us, General." As though she can read my thoughts, Selene voices what I was unable to.

He sighed heavily and eyed the exit. Hades, his patience worn thin, bellowed, "Enough, Rhadamanthus! Tell us the cause of this deluge of souls!"

The general's gaze finally landed on mine and I flinched inwardly. "Hecate has caused this by imprisoning Zeus, Your Highness."

That night, back in our warm cabin, Castor paced back and forth, his footsteps shaking the small abode. "I don't understand how overthrowing a rapist led to thousands of souls on our doorstep."

I quietly rolled and unrolled a scroll as I sat by the fire, my mind in chaos as I watched the flames for a sign, a message, anything to help me understand the path forward.

Pulled from my thoughts, I found Castor watching me intently. "What are you thinking, my love?"

I brought my hand to my temple and rubbed at the throbbing that had grown painful.

"You have another migraine? How many is that this week?" He scrunches his brow as the concern transforms his face.

"Three," I respond breathlessly as I continue to massage the painful region. A bright white light had flashed before my eyes as the ache intensified into an explosion. A shriek ripped from my throat as I fell to the floor. Castor rushed to my side.

"Hecate! Hecate!" I heard him yelling as he shook my rigid body, but my mind was lost in a vision. The pain swept from my temple through my body, and I watched from outside my body as the oak tree in the distance ignited with a burst of flames.

www.ingramcontent.com/pod-product-compliance
Lightning Source LLC
Chambersburg PA
CBHW021208310726
48971CB00006B/1491